THE RED DAHLIA

THE RED DAHLIA

Lynda La Plante

SIMON &
SCHUSTER

London • Sydney • New York • Toronto

First published in Great Britain by Simon & Schuster UK Ltd, 2006
A CBS COMPANY

Copyright © Lynda La Plante, 2006

1 3 5 7 9 10 8 6 4 2

Simon & Schuster UK Ltd
1st floor
222 Gray's Inn Road
London WC1X 8HB

www.simonandschuster.co.uk

Simon & Schuster Australia
Sydney

A CIP catalogue record for this book is available from the British Library

978-0-8572-0512-4

Typeset by Palimpsest Book Production Limited
Grangemouth, Stirlingshire

Printed and bound in Great Britain by
CPI Mackays, Chatham ME5 8TD

I dedicate this book to Jason McCreight

Acknowledgements

My gratitude to all those who gave their valuable time to help me with research on *The Red Dahlia*, in particular Lucy & Raffaele D'Orsi, Dr Ian Hill, Dr Liz Wilson, and Callum Sutherland for all their valuable police and forensic advice.

Thank you to my committed team at La Plante Productions: Liz Thorburn, Richard Dobbs, Pamela Wilson, Noel Farragher and Danielle Jenkin. Thanks also go to Jason McCreight, Kara Manley, Catherine Milne, Stephen Ross and Andrew Bennet-Smith.

To my wonderful agent Gill Coleridge and all at Rogers, Coleridge and White, I give great thanks. Special thanks also go to Suzanne Baboneau, Ian Chapman, Nigel Stoneman and all at Simon & Schuster, who I am very happy to be working with on this book.

Chapter One

DAY ONE

It was the kind of crisp, bright January morning that made the residents of Richmond, Surrey, glad to be living out of London's congested West End. The Thames glistened in the early-morning sun. The shops and high street were quiet: it was just before six a.m. Danny Fowler pedalled past the Richmond Hotel, eager to reach the sloping road and freewheel down the hill. He had only three newspapers left to deliver. With his usual finesse, he zigzagged across the street and mounted the pavement, pausing as he folded a *Times* and a *Daily Mail* before propping his bike against the wall and hurrying over to the houses that faced the river. Just a *Daily Telegraph* to go, and then his round was finished; he couldn't wait to get back home for his breakfast. As he returned to his bicycle, stomach rumbling, a white shape caught his eye. Unsure what it was exactly, he swung his leg back over the crossbar and scooted across the road to look down the sloping bank.

It looked like a mannequin or a blow-up doll. Its arms were raised above its head, as if waving for attention, and its legs were spread-eagled. There was something strange about the way it was positioned that Danny couldn't make out from this distance, so he pedalled down the narrow lane that led to the river for a closer look.

What Danny found would stay with him for the rest of his life. He ran screaming, leaving his bike where it had fallen. The woman's naked body had been severed in two at the waist. Her dark auburn hair spread out behind her; her skin so white, it looked completely bloodless. Her face was bloated and the corners of her mouth had been slashed, giving her a clown's grimacing smile.

Detective Inspector Anna Travis arrived at the Richmond Hotel to join the murder team which had taken over the car park. She hurried over to Detective Chief Inspector Glen Morgan who was standing by the police catering truck, 'Teapot One', with a cup of tea in his hand.

'Get yourself a hot drink and then we'll be going over to the tent. And brace yourself: it's not a pretty sight.'

Anna ordered a coffee as the rest of the team huddled in a group around Morgan.

'Paperboy found her this morning. Came in with his mother; he's given us a statement. I let him go as he was very shook up; he's only fourteen.'

Morgan looked across at the second forensic white van drawing up, and then back to the faces of his team. 'I've never seen anything like it,' he said flatly.

'Is she fresh?' someone asked. Morgan shook his head.

'Hard to tell. I'd say maybe a couple of days, but don't quote me. The lab will give us a more specific time.'

Morgan was a good-looking man with cropped dark hair and a leathery complexion. A golf fanatic, he spent most weekends out on his local course. He squashed his empty cup and tossed it into a bin. 'Okay let's get over there, and be prepared.'

'High as a kite, is it?' asked a young detective.

'There's no stench, but what you see will turn your stomach.'

They made their way down the same narrow lane that Danny had taken to get to the river bank. There a white forensic tent was already erected, paper-suited scientists milling in and around it. There was a large box of paper suits outside, along with the usual masks, over-shoes and rubber gloves.

Bill Smart, a forensic expert, came out of the tent and looked at Morgan, shaking his head. 'It's bloody unbelievable.' He removed his rubber gloves. 'I won't be eating breakfast this morning, and that's a first. She wasn't killed on site. Someone brought her here and set up a sick tableau that's had us all stunned. At first glance I'd say we don't have much forensic evidence; maybe come up with more when we get the body over to the lab.'

As the murder team donned their paper suits, Bill Smart removed his, rolling it into a ball and dumping it into the waste bin provided. As he bent down to remove his protective shoes, he had to pause and take a deep breath. In his thirty years as a forensic expert, he had never come across anything so grotesque. It was the hideous gaping smile that had got to him. It would get to them all.

Anna adjusted her mask as she followed Morgan into the tent. This was now her fourth murder enquiry and she had come a long way since that first cadaver that had

3

made her instantly sick. She had not seen DCI Langton, who she had worked with on the Alan Daniels case, since then, but she had often heard about his exploits. She doubted if he had paid any attention to hers, or the fact she had upped her rank from Detective Sergeant. Her subsequent cases had been domestic; to have cut her teeth on a serial killer like Daniels was something a good few junior detectives envied.

The detectives stood in silence outside the police tape encircling the body.

'She's been severed at the waist. The two sections of her body are about ten inches apart,' Morgan said quietly. He gestured with his gloved hand. 'Mouth slit each side. Hard to tell what she looked like before this was done to her. She's got abrasions all over her body.'

Anna inched further forward, staring down at the dead woman. Out of the corner of her eye, she noticed a young rookie detective turn away and hurry out of the tent. Anna didn't look up. She knew exactly how he felt, but remained calm as she took in the awful sight.

'We won't have anything from any clothes, obviously. First priority is to identify her.' Morgan blinked as flash-bulbs went off; photographs were being taken from every angle. He looked over to the doctor, a rotund man with thick glasses, who squinted back.

'Neat job. Whoever did the dissection knew what they were doing. Her blood's been drained: reason her skin is so white. I'd put the approx time of death at two or three days ago.' He headed out of the tent, side-stepping two scientists in his haste. Morgan followed.

'Doc, can you just give me a few minutes?'

'Outside. Can't talk in there.' The doctor and Morgan

moved further away from the tent. 'Jesus God, what animal did that to her?'

'Is there anything else you can tell me?'

'No, I was just called out to determine your victim was dead. I've got to get back to surgery.'

'You said it looked professional,' Morgan said.

'Well it looks like it to me, but the pathologist will give you more details. It's a very neat cut, not jagged, and a thin-bladed knife was used on her mouth. How thin, how long, though, I couldn't tell you. There are further cuts to her face, neck, shoulders and legs.'

Morgan sighed, wanting more details. He turned back to stare at the flapping tent opening. One by one his team came out, subdued and shocked. They removed their paper suits and overshoes. Anna was last out and by the time she'd discarded her suit, the others were heading back towards the car park. She looked up the bank to see that a group of spectators had already gathered on the road. The sightlines between them were clear: the killer obviously wanted the victim found quickly. Whoever it was might even be watching them at work. The thought chilled her.

Richmond police station was only ten minutes' drive from the murder site, so the Incident Room had been set up there. They regrouped at eleven-thirty as a large whiteboard was being erected. Desks and tables with computers were brought in for the team to work at. They busied themselves, selecting their areas, as Morgan stood in front of them.

'Okay let's get started,' Morgan said, and burped; he excused himself and took an antacid tablet. 'We need to know who the victim is. We'll be getting photographs in, but until we get her identified and the lab reports back, there's not a lot we have to go on. According to the doctor, the work on her body looked professional, so we could be after a suspect with medical or surgical experience.'

Anna put up her hand. 'By the way the body was displayed, knowing it would be visible from the road and therefore would be found quickly, do you think the killer could be local?'

'Possibly,' Morgan said, as he crunched his tablet. He stared ahead, as if trying to think of what he should say next, and then shrugged. 'Let's start with missing persons in this area.'

The victim was eased into a thick plastic body bag and removed from the site at one-fifteen. A team of uniformed officers had already been assigned a fingertip search of the area. Due to the good weather and early-morning frost, the ground was hard, so any footprints were few and far between.

Morgan had also asked for a house-to-house to be started on the properties overlooking the river. He knew this murder had been carefully planned, but they still might get lucky if someone had seen a car in or around the area during either the night or early morning.

Photographs of the victim were pinned up in the Incident Room to an uneasy silence from the team. In the past few years, such photographs had been kept in files rather than displayed: it was felt that the investigating detectives were not helped in their work by the emotional impact of constantly seeing death staring down at them. There was also the possibility that a relative or someone being questioned might see them and become distressed; however, Morgan insisted the photographs should be on view. He felt it was necessary for each and every one of his team to understand the gravity of the case. The murder was going to create a media frenzy. Until the killer was arrested, there would be no weekend leave.

By six o'clock that evening, their 'Jane Doe' was still unidentified.

DAY TWO

The lists of missing persons in the Richmond area yielded nothing, so the net was spread wider. None of the residents of the riverside houses had seen anything suspicious, not even a parked car. The area was not well lit, so their killer would have been able to come and go undetected at night. What they were able to ascertain, however, was that a resident walking his dog at two in the morning passed the murder site and saw nothing. Therefore their killer had deposited the body between the hours of two and six.

DAY THREE

Day three and they were ready at the mortuary. Morgan asked Anna and another detective to join him for the preliminary report. Time of death was now estimated at three days prior to discovery. They had not as yet been able to take a rectal temperature as there seemed to be some kind of blockage, but they would have more details after the full post-mortem. The pathologist also confirmed what the doctor had suspected: the incision was professionally done, using a surgical saw, and the blood had been drained before the dissection. There were four lesions where drainage tubes might have been inserted; the amount of blood would have been considerable. He suggested their killer would have needed a place to perform the 'operation'.

'She has severe bruising to her back, buttocks, arms and thighs. It would appear she suffered numerous blows from some kind of blunt instrument. The cuts to either side of her mouth could very well have been done with a sharp scalpel. They are deep, clean and precise.'

Anna looked to where the pathologist indicated. The victim's cheeks now gaped open, exposing her teeth.

'I will need a lot more time, but I understand the need to give you as much as possible at this stage. In all my years, I have never seen such horrific injuries. The pubic area and the skin around the vagina have been sliced numerous times. You can see the slash marks like crosses, up to five inches in length.'

His lengthy report continued as Anna made copious notes, not allowing herself any emotional connection. The constant crunching sound of Morgan chewing his tablets was becoming annoying. The pathologist then removed his mask and rubbed his eyes.

'She must have suffered an awfully slow death and she must have been in excruciating pain as these injuries were forced on her. She has marks to her wrists which I would say were from some kind of wire, so she would have been held down for the brutality to occur. The wire has cut the skin quite badly on her right wrist.'

He slipped his mask up again as he moved around the body, and then gently brushed back her thick auburn hair. His hand still resting on her head, he paused before speaking softly.

'There's more,' he said.

As he continued, Morgan stopped chewing. Anna couldn't write a note. What was described next was so horrific that she felt her own blood draining. It was beyond all their comprehension that someone could have subjected the victim to such atrocities whilst she was still alive.

Anna sat in the rear passenger seat, Morgan up front. He had not said a word for the past ten minutes. Anna turned the pages of her notes and began adding more.

'Back to the station sir?' their driver asked.

Morgan nodded.

'You all right back there?' Morgan asked, as they slowly pulled out of the mortuary car park.

Anna nodded, closing her notebook. 'I won't sleep well tonight,' she murmured.

Back at the Incident Room, Morgan repeated what they had been told at the mortuary. Again Anna noted that strange uneasy silence. The team looked at the dead woman's photograph and then back to Morgan as he took a deep breath.

'And that's not all. Our victim was tortured and humiliated and forced to endure a sickening, perverted sexual assault. We have not as yet had all the details, as they are still working on her.'

Anna glanced furtively around the room; the

detectives' expressions said it all. Two female officers were in obvious distress.

DAY FOUR

Day four and they still had not identified their victim. No witness had come forward. The fingertip search had found nothing incriminating in the immediate vicinity, so the search area was now being widened. Moreover, the forensic report had brought disappointing news: their girl had been thoroughly cleaned up. They had no fibres or hairs; her nails had been scrubbed so vigorously, the tips of her fingers were raw. They had been able to determine that her hair was dyed auburn and her natural colour was dirty blonde, but the make of the dye would take time to identify, as they had so many brands to test. Fingerprints yielded no clue to her identity, as there was nothing on any police record. However, it seemed that she had recently had some dental work done: there was a certain amount of decay to her teeth and two caps were missing, but her fillings were intact. It was possible, therefore, that they might get a result from her dental records. The team also now knew she had been dead for seven days: three days before the body was discovered and the four days they had been investigating her murder.

The team had been waiting for a photograph that was being worked on to remove the clown cuts before being issued alongside the press release. They gathered round as a computer printout was posted up on the board. Her face had been re-created with no imperfections.

'She was beautiful,' Anna said.

Morgan sucked on another tablet. He shrugged. 'Let's hope to God this gets us a result, because we've been going fucking nowhere fast!'

The *Evening Standard*'s late issue carried the picture and a request for anyone with information to ring the Incident Room. The article did not give any mention of the body being dismembered, or any details of the way it had been discovered: just the location.

The phones soon started ringing nonstop, all the team busy fending off the crank calls and listening to the possibles. It was at seven minutes past eight in the evening that Anna received a call from a Sharon Bilkin. Hesitantly, she gave her name and address before saying she was sure that the photograph was of her flatmate, Louise Pennel. The last time Sharon had seen Louise was three days prior to the murder.

DAY FIVE

Sharon Bilkin came to the station at nine o'clock. She was twenty-six years old, a baby-faced blonde wearing too much make-up. She had brought numerous photographs of Louise with her. The team knew immediately Louise was their victim. Sharon was able to tell them that she had last seen Louise at Stringfellow's nightclub; Louise had stayed on after Sharon left, which was just after midnight on 9 January. Louise had not returned home. When asked why she hadn't reported this, Sharon said that Louise often stayed away for two or three nights at a time.

Sharon told them that Louise worked as a dental

receptionist. When the surgery was contacted, they said that they also had not seen her since the 9th. They had not raised the alarm either: Louise's frequent absences from work meant they were not surprised or suspicious when she didn't turn up. Moreover, they had given her notice to quit the week before.

Louise, they also discovered from Sharon, was an orphan; her parents had died when she was a young teenager. There were no close relatives, so Sharon was asked if she would be prepared to formally identify Louise.

Sharon was shaking with nerves; when the green cover was drawn back, she let out a gasp. 'What's the matter with her face? Her mouth?'

'Is this Louise Pennel?' Anna asked.

'Yes, but what's happened to her mouth?'

'It has been cut,' Anna said, giving the nod to the mortuary assistant to re-cover Louise's face.

Sharon spent two hours with Anna and Morgan answering their questions. She gave them a few names, but was sure Louise had no steady boyfriend. She also said that Louise wanted to get into modelling like her, which was why she had so many photographs. One in particular that Sharon showed them was heartbreaking. Louise was wearing a red, glitter-sequinned minidress, a glass of champagne in one hand and a red rose caught in her hair. She had the sweetest of smiles, her lipstick a dark plum. Her large, dark brown eyes were heavily made up and she had a small uptilted nose. She had been a very pretty young woman.

The Incident Room was buzzing with the news that

they had an identification, giving the whole team an adrenalin rush. They had been so frustrated, waiting for their first break. Now she was identified, they could kick-start their hunt for her killer.

DAY SIX

Morgan was back at his desk the following morning at seven-fifteen. A priority was to interview the dental surgeon Louise had worked for. Morgan was busy listing everyone he wanted to see that morning when Anna walked into his office with a copy of the *Mirror*.

'Excuse me, sir; have you seen this?'

'What?'

'Second page.'

Morgan reached across to take the paper. He sat down heavily. 'Fuck. How did they get this?'

'Must have got it from Sharon; she had enough photographs. We put out so many requests for help in identifying Louise, no one would have thought to ask Sharon not to go to the press.'

Morgan sucked in his breath in a fury. The article said little: just that the victim the police were trying to name was Louise Pennel. There were a few sentences about how Sharon, her flatmate, had identified Louise. There was a picture of a scantily dressed Sharon, but the main photograph was of Louise with the red rose in her hair.

Roses are red, violets are blue, who killed
Louise and slit her mouth in two?

Jack Douglas, the *Mirror* journalist who had printed Sharon's story, looked at the single sheet of typed writing that had been sent anonymously to the crime desk.

'Sick fuckers,' he muttered. He screwed it up and tossed it into the waste bin.

DCI Morgan held up the newspaper to the team in the Incident Room. 'We're gonna get a lot of crap aimed at us over—' Before he could finish his sentence, he buckled over in agony, clutching his stomach. There was a flurry of activity around him. He was helped into his office in excruciating pain, unable to stand upright. An ambulance took him to Richmond hospital at ten-fifteen. The team hovered around, discussing what could be wrong with their Gov. By mid-morning they knew it was serious. DCI Morgan had bleeding ulcers and would be out of action for some considerable time. This meant that a new DCI would have to take over the case, and fast.

By early afternoon, they were informed that DCI James Langton was stepping in, and bringing two officers with him.

Chapter Two

Anna watched from the Incident Room window as Langton arrived. It was just after ten. He parked erratically and then slammed the car door shut. He was still driving his beat-up Rover, but was looking far smarter than poor old Gov Morgan had ever managed, in a navy-blue striped suit, a pale blue shirt with a white collar, and a maroon tie.

Langton was joined in the car park by D.S. John Barolli and D.I. Mike Lewis, the other two officers Anna had worked alongside on the Daniels case. They carried a mound of files between them. They chatted together for a few moments before heading into the station.

Anna was sitting at her desk making herself look busy when Langton strode into the room, flanked by Lewis and Barolli. He went straight to the Incident board and looked over it before facing the team. He introduced his sidekicks and, giving a curt nod to Anna, expressed his regret that their Gov had been taken into hospital. Then he moved on to the case.

'I will need to assimilate all the data you have, but meanwhile, you can't waste any time. It seems you have little or nothing to go on, bar the fact you have your

15

victim identified. I want forensics over to the girls' flat as it has not as yet been eliminated as the scene of the murder. I want you to start listing all Louise Pennel's friends and associates and start taking statements fast. She was missing for three days; where was she? Who was the last person to see her alive? Give me until tomorrow morning for my briefing; until then, let's get moving!'

A murmur erupted as he gathered up a row of files and looked around for Morgan's office. A young female DC led him through the Incident Room past Anna's desk. Langton paused for a second and looked at her.

'Hello, Anna. Nice to be working with you again.' Then he was gone.

Anna flushed, turning back to her computer screen. Barolli and Lewis came over to stand by her desk. Barolli made a joke about it becoming a habit. Anna looked confused.

'Well, you were brought onto Langton's team for the Alan Daniels case when Detective Hudson got sick. Now we're together again, but this time it was your Guv'nor who got ill. Putting something into the coffee, are you?'

Anna smiled, but was not amused.

'I suppose that case must have helped to get you a promotion. Congratulations,' Lewis said.

She couldn't help noticing an undercurrent of sarcasm in his tone; it had obviously not helped him. The duo then followed Langton into his office.

The young DC came out from Langton's office which faced the Incident Room and so had blinds for privacy. Anna watched as the DC filled three mugs with black coffee and a plate with doughnuts.

'Good-looking, isn't he? Nice suit,' she said.

Anna smiled. 'He hates his coffee cold. If that's stewed, I'd get the canteen to make a fresh pot.'

'So you've worked with the DCI before?'

'Yes, a while back.'

'Is he married?'

Anna turned away. 'Not as far as I know. That coffee will be cold if it wasn't before.'

As the young DC moved off, Anna looked over to the officer working at the next desk. 'What's her name? I keep forgetting?'

He didn't even look up. 'Bridget; like the diaries.'

Anna smiled. The young DC was slightly overweight but very pretty, with silky blonde hair, unlike Anna's own spiky red. Anna had tried to grow hers longer but it didn't look right, so she had gone back to her usual cropped cut which held in check the curls that liked to spring up.

There was a strange atmosphere in the Incident Room. Langton's remark about their lack of results had hit home and the team were feeling out of sorts. Nevertheless, Anna worked at gathering names and addresses of Louise's known associates and, along with the rest of the team, began arranging interviews. Her first priority was to go to Louise's flat to re-interview Sharon herself.

Louise had lived in the top-floor flat of a narrow four-storey house off Balcombe Street, close to Baker Street tube station. Anna paused to catch her breath; the stairs were steep. The staircase narrowed as she approached flat nine. She knocked and waited.

'Come in,' Sharon called out. Anna pushed the unlocked door open. The small hallway was as narrow as the stairs and was crammed with photographs of Sharon, some of her modelling teenage clothes and others in which she was rather more scantily dressed. There were none of Louise.

'I'm in here,' Sharon called from the kitchen, interrupting Anna's scrutiny. 'I've put the kettle on; do you want tea or coffee?'

'Coffee, please. Black, no sugar,' Anna said as she entered.

'It's only instant,' Sharon said, busily wiping down a sink that was stacked with dirty crockery.

'That's fine.'

Anna sat at the small folding plastic table; the rest of the space in the tiny kitchen was taken up with cheap cabinets, a fridge and a washing machine.

'I don't think there is anything I can tell you that I haven't said already,' Sharon said as she poured boiling water into two mugs.

'I just want to go over a few things to find out what type of person Louise was.' Anna took her notebook and a tape recorder from her briefcase. 'Do you mind if I tape us? It's in case I don't write something down I'll need to check out.'

Sharon hesitated and then nodded, drawing out the other chair.

Anna checked her tape was running. 'You gave us a list of Louise's friends and we'll be talking to them, but can you think of anyone else?'

'I went through my address book again last night and there's no one that I can think of.'

'Did Louise have a diary?'

'I don't know.'

'Maybe we could have a look around later? If you would like to see the Section Eight warrant?'

Sharon shrugged as she munched a chocolate chip biscuit, not even glancing at the document that Anna showed her.

'You mentioned to DCI Morgan that Louise was seeing someone.'

'I don't know his name and I never met him. I only saw him the once, when he rang downstairs for her. He didn't come in. I was just going out, so I saw him go to his car and wait for her; well, I presume that's what he was doing.'

'What type of car?'

'I was asked that. I don't know. It was black and shiny, but I don't know what make.'

'Can you describe this man?'

'I already have.'

'Yes I know, but just for me.'

Sharon finished her biscuit and wiped the corners of her mouth with one finger. 'Tall, maybe six foot. He was wearing a long dark coat, very smart, and he had short dark hair. I only really saw the back of him. Oh yeah, slight hook-nose, I remember that.'

'What age, do you think?'

'Hard to tell; thirty-five to forty-five? He wasn't young and he wasn't her usual type.'

'How long had Louise been seeing this man?'

Sharon shrugged. 'I dunno; I think she knew him before she moved in here. She didn't see him that regular, but she was very keen on him.'

19

'What makes you say that?'

'Well, when she did have a date with him, she spent hours getting dressed, changing her clothes; she even borrowed some of mine. She said she wanted to look smart for him, sophisticated, and she bought some new shoes: very high, spike-heeled ones.'

'Are they missing?'

'I don't know. I haven't looked.'

'We can do that later. I'll also need you to look through her wardrobe and see if any of her clothes are missing.'

'I can do, but I don't know if I'll be able to tell; you see, we shared the flat but, I mean, we weren't close friends.'

'Really?'

'She answered an ad I put in *Time Out* when my last flatmate left. It's rented and I couldn't afford to live here by myself, so I needed someone fast.'

'When was this?'

'About seven months ago. I dunno where she lived before; she didn't have that much luggage. She didn't have a lot of money either; well, her job paid peanuts.'

'You said she worked for a dentist?'

'Yeah, but they paid her a minimum wage, 'cos she was having some of her teeth fixed. She needed some caps and fillings done, so I guess when that had been finished she would leave. She didn't talk about her work much; just that it was really boring and she had this thing about hearing the dentist's drill.'

'And you work as a model?'

'Yes, mostly catalogue work. I also do part time at a café up the road.'

Anna ploughed on, keeping the questions simple, not wanting to unnerve Sharon before trying to ease her onto more personal topics.

Langton, Barolli and Lewis spent the entire morning sifting through the case history. By two o'clock, having worked through lunch, they closed the files.

'They've got nothing,' Langton said, quietly.

'Yeah, well at least they've identified her.'

'We'll have a briefing at the end of the day; in the meantime, I'll go over to interview this Sharon, her flat-mate.'

'Travis is there,' Barolli said.

'I know.' Langton walked out.

Barolli looked at Lewis quizzically. 'He said anything to you about her?'

'What? Travis?'

'Yeah, he did a double-take when he saw her name listed on the team, but then pretended not to have noticed. They got on, didn't they?'

'I was told a bit more than *got on*! In fact, you remember Jean – that stony-faced DC? – she said they were having a scene.'

'No way! She's not the Gov's type for one, and for two, he wouldn't be so crass as to screw someone on his team. He gets his leg over enough women without shitting on his own doorstep.'

'Well, it's what I was told,' Lewis said, slightly embarrassed.

Barolli flicked open the post–mortem file and stared at it. 'You read through all this? What had been done to her?'

Lewis shook his head. They had been under pressure from Langton to get through the files as fast as possible, so had taken half each.

'Bottom of the page.' Barolli used a pen to indicate where Lewis should read. It took longer than just a glance. He turned over to the next page of the report and continued reading, then slowly closed the file.

'Jesus Christ. I thought the beatings she'd taken were bad enough, along with the slashes to her mouth, but this is sick, fucking sick.'

Barolli nodded; the report had turned his stomach. 'Beggars belief, doesn't it? And they haven't finished the autopsy yet! What kind of animal would do that?'

Lewis took a deep breath. 'One we'd better bloody catch.'

Anna was sitting in Louise's cramped bedroom. The single bed, with its pink candlewick bedspread, had not been made up. She had asked if Louise ever brought any guests back to the flat. Sharon had shaken her head: that was one of the house rules and, to her knowledge, Louise had never broken it.

'The landlady lives on the ground floor and she'd have a fit.'

'But Louise often stayed away for nights?'

'Yes, so did I; neither of us had got a steady bloke though, so it didn't really matter not being able to bring anyone back.'

Anna had to move her knees aside so that Sharon could open the wardrobe doors.

'I don't know what's missing. Like I said, she hadn't lived here too long. Oh, hang on!'

Sharon walked out of the room. Anna got up to look at the clothes herself. They were hung in two sections: what looked like work clothes – white shirts and straight dark skirts, a couple of jackets – and clothes for going out, some very expensive, others just high-street glitter.

Sharon appeared in the doorway. 'Her coat: she had a nice maroon coat with a black velvet collar and matching buttons; that's not in here, or in the cupboard in the hall.'

Anna nodded and looked to the bed. 'Did she usually make her bed?'

'No. She was a bit untidy. I was told not to touch it in case they wanted to take away the sheets and things.'

Anna looked at a dress on a hanger: low cut, tight-waisted, with a layered skirt.

'She wanted to be a model. She was always asking me about agents and what she should do to try and break into it. She had a very good figure, but sometimes she wore too much make-up, which made her look older than she was; then she started wearing the dark red lipstick.'

The doorbell made Sharon jump; for all her chattiness, she was actually quite strung out. She went to answer the door, leaving Anna to carry on looking over the clothes. She checked the labels of two cashmere sweaters in the chest of drawers. They were both very expensive and one had never even been worn: it was still folded in tissue paper.

Anna heard Sharon calling to someone to keep on coming up the stairs. She checked over an underwear drawer. Some of the knickers were expensive lace, others well-worn cotton. Anna flushed and shut the drawer when she heard Langton's voice asking Sharon for directions to the bedroom.

Sharon stood behind him as he appeared in the doorway. 'Not a lot of room,' she said.

Langton gave Anna a brief nod.

'You do your own laundry?' he asked Sharon.

'We've got a washing machine but it doesn't work that well, so we use the local launderette.'

'You still have Louise's dirty washing then?'

'Yes, it's in the corner in that basket.' She pointed. 'I don't know what's in there; I haven't looked.'

Langton's eyes roamed slowly around the room and then back to Anna as she gestured to the wardrobe.

'Sharon thinks Louise's coat is missing.'

Langton nodded. His gaze swept the room once more before he turned to Sharon. 'Is there somewhere we can talk?'

'The kitchen?'

He said quietly to Anna that he would leave her to it, and followed Sharon out of the room.

Anna did a thorough search, noting the hairbrush with dark red strands of hair still caught in it. They would take that. She did not find any personal notes or letters; there were very few knick-knacks and no photographs. Louise's cosmetics and toiletries were a mishmash of cheap products. There were a few bottles of perfume, some expensive, two of which were unopened. Anna took the stopper off the cheap-looking Tudor Rose, which was half empty, and sniffed: it was sharp and synthetic. In a rather grubby old floral silk make-up bag, she discovered several used lipsticks in various shades of pink and orange.

Anna found nothing under the bed apart from dust-balls. She looked into the laundry basket: it was full of white shirts, knickers and bras. She shut the lid and then went back to the chest of drawers. She found two empty handbags: one quite good leather but old-fashioned, the other a small, cheap-looking clutch bag. No handbag had been found. Anna made a note to ask Sharon what kind Louise was likely to have been last seen with. Anna found no chequebooks, no diary and no address book. Leaving the room, she frowned as she heard a sound from the kitchen. She could not hear what was being said, but it sounded as if Sharon was crying. Langton's low soft voice talked on.

Anna went into the narrow bathroom; there was just room for a bath and toilet. A glass cabinet held aspirins and some prescription drugs, but the tablets were in Sharon's name and were only for migraines. Anna moved into the hallway and opened the cupboard by the front door to find raincoats and old shoes. Looking up, she saw two stacked suitcases on a shelf. Standing on tiptoe, she read a label: *Louise Pennel*, and the address of the flat. Anna quietly eased the case down and carried it to the bedroom.

The old suitcase was cheap and plastic, with a mock silk lining. Inside, there were two photo albums and a worn address book with various names and addresses listed in no particular order. Sifting through the photo albums, Anna was able to get a better idea of who Louise was. There were some black-and-white snaps of a couple; the woman looked very like Louise and, in a number of pictures, even had a flower in her hair. The man was very good-looking but with a laconic, almost bored air

25

about him: he rarely smiled. There were a lot of baby pictures, then Louise in school uniform and as a camera-shy teenager. The more recent photographs were in the second album. There were some of Louise at parties and others of her standing by the Regent's Park zoo's chimp enclosure, shading her eyes and laughing into the camera. A few innocent-looking snapshots pictured her with various young men, always smiling and hanging onto their arm. Anna jumped as Langton appeared in the doorway.

'I need to get back. You want a lift?'

'Yes please. I'd like to take these with me.'

He glanced at the albums and then walked out.

They sat in silence in the patrol car, Langton up front, Anna in the back. As they drew away, the white forensic van was just parking up outside Sharon's flat.

'Louise was not a whore, but close,' he said, as if to himself.

'I wondered about that. She had some very expensive clothes; lot of cheap ones as well, but a few designer labels and some very exclusive perfume.'

'Sharon, I'd say, is on the game; not that she would admit it. Total denial, but she started to blubber when I asked her if Louise was. They would pick up men from clubs, sometimes together, sometimes not; on the night Louise went missing, Sharon scored herself a rock singer and spent the night at the Dorchester. Louise was often out every night. Sharon said Louise wouldn't cook or eat anything if she didn't have a date, so I guess the one-nighters were literally meal tickets! She described Louise as being very secretive, sometimes annoyingly so. She would be very coy about where she had been.'

26

Anna chewed her lip. Sharon hadn't told her any of this.

'This tall dark older guy is the one we need to trace.'

'Sharon said she thought he might be married, which was why Louise was so secretive about him,' Anna said quietly.

Langton nodded. 'There was also something a bit kinky going on. Couple of times, she'd come back from being with him with bruises on her face and arms, very withdrawn, often crying in her room. She never said what was bothering her; just that she didn't like doing certain things, whatever that means.'

Anna stared out of the window. Langton had got so much detail and quickly.

'The autopsy said there were no drugs.'

'Yes,' Anna said, lamely.

'But she did take cocaine. Sharon said they had an argument about it. After one of the dates with this older man, Louise brought some back and offered it to Sharon. She was pretty sure that Louise was into some serious sex games with this guy. It'd sometimes be a couple of days before she'd return home, looking really knackered.'

'She had some very expensive underwear.'

Langton swivelled round in his seat to face her. 'I think they went a bit further than sexy knickers!'

'Oh.' Anna tried not to blush.

He gave her one of his lopsided smiles. '*Oh?* We'll know more when they complete the autopsy; certainly taking their time. What we know already is pretty sickening.' He turned to face forwards again. There was a long pause. 'So, how's life been?' he asked without looking at her.

'Fine, thank you.'

'Found yourself a nice chap, have you?'

'I've been working too hard.'

He snorted. 'I wish the case looked as if you had; bloody nothing. To lose that amount of time before you got her identified was not good, not good at all, but then old Morgan was never what I'd call a fast thinker.'

Before Anna could reply, they pulled into the station car park. Langton was out and heading directly into the station ahead of her as if she didn't exist. She hurried after him and almost caught a clip from the door as he banged through. It was a repeat performance of the last time they had worked together.

'I'm right behind you,' she said curtly, but he just ran up the stairs two at a time before slamming into the Incident Room.

Langton stood in front of the team looking at his watch, impatiently waiting for silence. It was just after six-thirty. He held up the two photo albums brought from Sharon's flat.

'I want these gone over with a fine-tooth comb: the boyfriends, the friends, anyone that can give us more clues to our victim's lifestyle. Also, importantly, hit the clubs she used. Talk to anyone that knew her or might have seen her on the last night her flatmate saw her alive. We know she was missing for three days before her body was found. Where did she go? Who with? What we do know is that she was sexually permissive and took cocaine and ecstasy; that we found no trace of drugs is down to the fact her body had been drained of blood. Big clue, because any young lad screwing her isn't likely to be able to not only drain her blood, but also chop her in two. The toxicology results might give us more details, but they're going to need at least three to four weeks. The initial autopsy report gave us a lot of unpleasant details and I suspect there are more to come. Whoever carved this young girl up has to have a house or apartment that could facilitate such carnage. The suspect also has to have a car, as he transported the body to the murder site.'

Lewis interjected. 'Maybe the killer could have borrowed a vehicle, even hired one.'

Langton suggested that he immediately check out hire cars for the relevant time and location.

Lewis grimaced; it would be a very long and boring job, and he muttered to Barolli that he should have kept his mouth shut.

'We have found no clothes or other personal items belonging to the victim, so I am sorry if I am going over old ground, but we need to check out skips, bins, the local tip, household waste collections, and someone will have to ascertain when the bins in that area were emptied.'

He turned to the board and pointed. 'Take a look: the saw used to dissect her body did a very professional job, so it was more than likely used by someone who has medical or surgical experience. This narrows the suspects down, so eliminate eliminate until we get some perspective on the killer. We need to track down a tall dark-haired man, driving a . . .' He gestured in exasperation. 'Black car, expensive looking. This man was known to be dating our victim. This man was very secretive; this man used drugs, this man also encouraged Louise into perverted sexual games. Our suspect is possibly married. To start with, concentrate in this area. Any doctor or surgeon struck off for medical malpractice, any doctor or surgeon with a police record. When we have exhausted that area, we widen the net, but I want this man traced!'

Langton dug his hands into his pockets. 'I want a very closed shop on this one: keep your mouths shut about what was done to her. The press get hold of this horror and we'll have a Fred West scenario which we do not want. As it is, I will have the big boys breathing down my neck for a result, never mind some of the heavy-duty females skiing up the ranks.'

Anna felt this jibe was directed at her own promotion, but if it was, Langton never even glanced in her direction.

'I have asked for more officers to be drafted in to help us out.'

Langton continued his briefing for over an hour. Hardly anyone interrupted, even when he said some very derogatory things about the way they had been handling the case to date. He was determined that no more time would be wasted; they had to get results, and fast. When he finished, Lewis and Barolli handed the lists of duties that Langton had ordered to the Operations Manager. There would be no overtime; if needs be, they would have to work around the clock. Langton returned to his office. It was like a whirlwind had passed through.

Anna went over to find out what Lewis had discovered at Louise's place of work: not much. She was always late, bit of a shoddy worker; a very likeable girl, just lazy.

The dentist confirmed that he had given her notice to quit. He also confirmed that she was paid a low wage, as he had been doing a lot of free dental work on her. The other girls working at the clinic got on quite well with her but she kept very much to herself and rarely, if ever, mixed with any of them socially. The dentist was married with four children, and on the night Louise was at Stringfellow's, he was at a family dinner. He did not socialise with Louise and knew little or nothing about her private life; however, one of the dental nurses recalled that Louise had wanted to leave early one day, about a month before she disappeared. She had said she had an important date. The nurse had seen a black car, possibly a Rover, parked opposite the surgery, but she could not describe the man sitting inside. She said that the following day, Louise was very late for work and had showed them a bottle of perfume and a cashmere sweater she had been given by her 'friend'.

It had stuck in the nurse's mind because, mid-afternoon, Louise became very sick and had to leave the surgery, so she had to cover for her. She said that Louise often came to work very hung over. A couple of times, she had also looked as if she had been in some kind of fight: her face was bruised, and once she had deep scratches on her arms. Louise had claimed she had been tipsy and fallen down the stairs of her flat.

Langton rocked back in his chair, flipping a pen up and down as he listened to Barolli going over the wording of the press statements. Langton was being cagey about what they should release: too much information would result in a slew of sickos calling in. The most important thing to get across was that the police wished to contact the tall dark middle-aged man in order to eliminate him from their enquiries. They also needed to know if anyone had seen Louise during those three days she was missing. Langton okayed the use of that same photograph with the red rose in her hair. He then called it quits for himself and went home.

Anna did not get home until late either. She felt too tired to cook, so had bought a pizza on her way home. She had a bottle of wine already open and poured herself a glass. The pizza was cold now, but she ate it anyway as she opened the copy of tomorrow's *Sun* she'd picked up from the tube station. She knew the press release would be coming out the following morning, so it was a surprise when the now-familiar photograph of Louise stared back at her from page two.

The accompanying headline read POLICE HUNT KILLER OF RED DAHLIA. Anna frowned; it was not a dahlia, but a rose in Louise's hair. The article likened the case to a very brutal murder that had made history in Los Angeles in the mid-forties, that of Elizabeth Short: a beautiful girl who was nicknamed the Black Dahlia because of the flower she wore in her raven hair.

The journalist on the *Sun* crime desk had cobbled the story together, but his editor liked it; the catchphrase of the Black and Red Dahlias looked good in print, as did the two colour photographs of the dead girls. Though they lacked any real detail about the Louise Pennel case, they could hang the article on the fact that the killer of the Black Dahlia was never traced, just as the killer of Louise Pennel, the Red Dahlia, remained at large after ten days.

The journalist kept quiet about the fact that he had received an anonymous letter pointing this out. The second contact from the killer lay crumpled in a ball in his office bin.

Chapter Three

Langton chucked the newspaper into the bin in his kitchen.

He snapped angrily into the phone. 'Yeah I just read it. No! Do nothing about it. I've never heard of this Black Dahlia woman, have you?'

Lewis said that he hadn't either.

'Doesn't really have anything to do with us, seeing as it was in the forties and in the bloody USA!'

Lewis wished he had never made the call. 'Right, just thought if you hadn't seen it.'

'Yeah, yeah; look, I'm tired out, sorry if I bit your head off. See you in the morning.' Langton was about to replace the receiver when he remembered. 'How's your son?'

'He's terrific; got over that bug, and he's got rows of teeth now,' Lewis said, affably.

'Great; goodnight then.'

''Night.'

It was after eleven. Langton retrieved the paper from the bin and pressed it out flat on his kitchen counter.

Elizabeth Short, though aged only twenty-two, had been a jaded beauty with raven-black hair, white face and dark-painted lips. The flower in her hair might have been a dahlia, but it wasn't black. In comparison, Louise Pennel looked younger and fresher, even though they were about the same age. Louise's eyes were dark brown and Elizabeth's green but, eerily, the dead girls had a similar expression. The half-smile on their pretty lips was sexual, teasing, yet the eyes had a solemnity and a sadness, as if they knew what fate had in store.

DAY EIGHT

The next morning, Anna stopped off at a bookshop to buy her daily *Guardian*. Next to the till, there was a book-stand of half-price paperbacks, one of which was *The Black Dahlia*. Blazoned across the cover were the words 'TRUE LIFE CRIME'. She bought it. By the time she got to the Incident Room, the phones were jangling; the press release was in all the papers, as was the photograph of Louise with the red rose. Numerous other tabloids had picked up on the *Sun*'s article and were also now calling Louise the Red Dahlia. A couple of articles referred to the original case in LA but most of them concentrated, as Langton had hoped they would, on the fact that the police were trying to trace the tall dark-haired stranger.

Eight days into the enquiry, for all Langton's snide remarks about Morgan he had got no further in tracing

Louise's killer himself, though at least he did now have more facts to give the press. Although they had not been given all the details, the brutality of the murder, even tempered down, made shocking reading.

All the calls to the Incident Room regarding the Red Dahlia enquiry had to be monitored and checked out, so extra clerical staff had been shipped in. Of the many calls, seventy per cent were from either jokers or perverts; thirty per cent still needed investigating. It was a long day, with half the team interviewing Louise's friends, such as they were, or trying to trace the male companions pictured in her photograph albums. Meanwhile, forensics had removed all the dirty laundry and bed linen from Louise's flat to test for DNA. Langton was covering all areas but still felt like a headless chicken. He decided to go to Stringfellow's with Lewis to make enquiries. Barolli was checking out the other two clubs that Sharon had said Louise often went to, hoping that someone would be able to identify their tall dark stranger, or that someone would have witnessed Louise leaving the club. Taxis also had to be checked out; it was an endless, tedious slog, but it had to be done.

The officers who had been scouring the coffee bars local to Louise's workplace had various sightings of her confirmed; she was often alone, though she would sometimes pick someone up and go to the cinema in Baker Street. No one questioned could give a name or recall ever seeing her with the same person twice, let alone a tall dark stranger. She was always friendly and chatty; no one thought she was on the game, more that she needed company – preferably the sort who would pick up the bill.

Anna had not been asked to join the lads on their club crawl, but she didn't mind. Her head ached from monitoring call after call, still with nothing tangible at the end of the day. During her lunch break, she had begun reading the book about Elizabeth Short's murder. It had been written by a former Los Angeles Police Department officer, who had been attached for many years to the homicide division of LA County. He made some startling deductions and even put forward his own father as the killer. Anna continued reading once she was home. She didn't expect to be up still at two o'clock in the morning, but she had been unable to put the book down. Even when she finished it, sleep didn't come: all she could do was think about its nightmarish contents. Although Elizabeth Short had been murdered in the forties, there was nevertheless a sickening link beyond the similarities between her photograph and Louise's. The murders were virtually identical.

Langton and Lewis looked tired out. They had spent hours at the clubs with little result. Louise was remembered by two waiters at Stringfellow's, but so far as they could recall, she was always with a different man. They could not, from the vague description, identify any specific tall dark stranger who had been with her. Her male friends were often young rock singers who she picked up in the club. The last night she was there had been a big showbiz occasion, with many glitzy guests who had been to a film premiere. They had roped off private sections and the place was jumping. The doormen and bouncers were no help; it seemed Louise came and went without a trace.

Barolli had not fared any better; a few people recalled seeing Louise, but not recently. He had tramped from one rather seedy nightclub to the next, showing her photograph. They had all recognised her; some knew she was dead, others didn't. She was often alone, and would chat to the barmen about waiting for a modelling agent to contact her. It appeared she never drank too much and was always polite and friendly; if she was on the game, it was not obvious. Not one person questioned remembered seeing her with an older man; the clubs were mainly for people her age. She was known, but not known; they all thought of her as being a very attractive girl but something about her was not quite right. One barman said it was as if she was always waiting for someone, often looking to the club's entrance expectantly.

Langton had asked for the cashmere sweaters they had taken from Louise's flat to be traced. They were part of a large special deal for Harrods' January sales the previous year, but none of the assistants could recall any tall dark stranger buying one, either with cash or a credit card. The perfume, although costly, could have been sold to any one of hundreds of customers in a range of department stores. The search for Louise's maroon coat also drew a blank. Sharon had made an attempt at describing Louise's handbag, but 'large black leather with a wide strap' was not much use. She also said that Louise sometimes used smaller clutch bags, but could not describe any in much detail. A search of the area where the body was found also yielded nothing. They were back almost to square one.

DAY NINE

Anna placed a call to the crime desk at both the *Mirror* and the *Sun*. She then went into the ladies to refresh her make-up. Running a comb through her hair, she stared at her reflection and took a deep breath. Langton might laugh her out of his office but, then again, he might not.

'Well, this is another fucking fruitless day,' he muttered as she tapped and entered his office.

'I wanted to have a quick chat.'

'I'm all ears.' He wasn't; he was doodling on a notepad, his face set in anger.

'I just want to run something by you,' she said.

He sighed, impatiently. 'Well, bloody get on with it.'

She put the book on his desk. 'It's about the Black Dahlia murder.'

Langton swore, fed up with the constant references to a girl just because she had a flower in her hair, but Anna continued. 'Elizabeth Short was murdered in 1947 in the United States; her killer was never caught. This book is written by a former police officer who believes that his father was the man who killed her.'

Langton stopped doodling and stared at the cover of the book.

'If you flick through to the middle part, I've put a yellow sticker on the relevant pages. There are also mortuary photographs you should look at.'

He sniffed and began turning over the pages. 'What am I looking at?'

'The body: look how she was found.'

Langton frowned, turning the book this way and that

to look at the black-and-white photographs. 'Jesus Christ.'

'There's a website.'

'What?'

'There's a website; it contains more detailed photographs of the way the victim was discovered.'

'Holy shit. I don't believe this.'

'I read it last night and I couldn't believe it either. If you look at the pages marked with blue stickers, they are also relevant, I think.'

Langton sat back and began reading. He read in silence for about ten minutes, then he slowly lowered the book.

'So what are you suggesting? That the same guy killed Louise? He'd have to be in his nineties, for God's sake!'

'No, no: the police officer's father has been dead more than five years. Another possible suspect died in a fire in the sixties. Look at the next set of stickers.'

'What colour?' He looked up and gave her that smile.

'Green. The man they hunted for Elizabeth's murder was never traced; he is described as a "tall dark stranger". There are also some sketches of him.'

'Fuck me!' Langton said, then snapped the book closed. 'So?'

'So, I think we might have a copycat killer. I called both the *Mirror* and the *Sun* and spoke to their crime reporters. The *Sun* described Louise as the Red Dahlia. We thought it was just due to the flowers in the two victims' hair. But they were both contacted.'

Langton leaned forwards. 'And?'

'In both cases they received an anonymous letter; neither thought anything of it, you know possible crank, murder aficionado . . .'

'Yeah yeah, and?'

'They destroyed them.'

'Fuck!'

'But look at the yellow stickers again. The LA killer sent many letters to the police and the newspapers, always gloating about how clever he was and that they'd never catch him . . .'

'I'm reading, I'm reading!' Langton snapped.

Anna waited until he had finished.

'The anonymous note to the journalist at the *Mirror*, as far as he could remember, said something about Louise's mouth being slit in two. The one sent to the other journalist, Richard Reynolds at the *Sun*, mentioned the Black Dahlia case and called Louise the Red Dahlia. Until then, Reynolds had never even heard of the murder of Elizabeth Short.'

Langton flicked back and forwards over the relevant photographs in the book.

Anna continued. 'The first note was sent to the *Mirror* journalist after his article had been published.'

Langton sprang to his feet and shoved his hands into his pockets. 'This is bloody good, Travis, bloody sick . . . but it's possible. Jesus Christ, can you leave this with me for a while and I'll chew it over? Don't mention it to anyone. Not yet.'

Anna nodded and walked out. Langton didn't come into the Incident Room until two hours later. He bent down to place the book on Anna's desk. He was so close she could smell his aftershave.

'Can you get the website up for me?'

'Sure.'

He stared at the grotesque images of the dismembered Elizabeth and then said, very quietly, 'Sick bastard, he even placed our body ten inches off the centre. It's bloody identical. My God, explain this one, huh?'

'Copycat,' Anna said, without emotion.

Langton ran his fingers through his hair so that it stood up on end. 'You think when this book was published it triggered . . . ?' He used his hand to make a winding motion at the side of his head.

'Who knows? Something had to.'

Langton nodded, then patted her shoulder. 'Get over to the offices at the *Mirror* and the *Sun*, see what they tossed; meanwhile I'll bring this up with the team.'

'Okay,' she said, shutting down the computer, adding, 'It's a very popular website.'

'What does that say to you, Anna?'

She shrugged and again he leaned close to her.

'It says, Anna, that there's a lot of sick fuckers out there, that's what it says to me. Who the hell wants to see those mortuary photographs? It should be wiped off the web.'

'We have to find him,' she murmured.

'You think I don't know that!' he snapped.

'It's just that if he is a copycat murderer, there were two others: the police at the time reckoned they were done by the same killer. If he's copycatted Elizabeth Short, then what may happen is he'll go the whole nine yards and kill again.'

Langton stuffed his hands into his trouser pockets. 'I hope to Christ you're wrong.'

He moved off and she was left feeling slightly depressed, not because he hadn't at any point praised her good work; it was his closeness. She had wanted some personal response from him, but had received none. It was as if their relationship from the last case had never existed. She mentally shook herself and told herself to get it together; after all, it had been her that had not wanted to continue seeing him. The truth was, there had been no one she had even been remotely interested in since Langton, and she chided herself for letting her old emotions seep back to the surface.

Langton stood in front of the team, holding up the Black Dahlia book. Anna was well on her way to the *Mirror's* offices by the time he mentioned that DI Travis had brought it to his attention.

'We have a very sick development,' he said.

He showed the mortuary photographs of Elizabeth Short to the team.

'This victim was killed in Los Angeles nearly sixty years ago, but pass the book around and look at the way her body had been dismembered. Pay close attention to the mortuary photographs: you will see they are virtually identical to the way we found Louise Pennel. In fact, the entire scenario is crossing over. Their main suspect was described as a tall man, thirty-five to forty-five years old, well dressed and dark-haired. Their suspect was known to have been driving a very expensive automobile!'

Langton pointed to the Incident board: under WANTED FOR ELIMINATION was their prime suspect. He had been described by Sharon and the dental nurse as tall, dark-haired and wearing an expensive draped coat. Neither woman was able to give the exact make of the car but they described it as large and black, possibly a BMW or a Rover.

Langton looked into the dregs of his coffee, drained the cup and placed it down. He watched as the officers passed the book around, glancing at his watch. Intermittent gasps punctuated the silence in the room. One detective after another saw the horror they were now investigating mirrored in the black-and-white pictures of the murder that had occurred nearly sixty years ago.

Langton continued. 'There were two further murders; both were suspected to be by the same killer. If we are to consider, which I think we have to, that there is some sicko out there emulating this Black Dahlia killer, then it is also possible that he may have already targeted his second victim. Let's hope to Christ we catch this bastard before he gets the opportunity for his next kill.'

A murmur erupted from the stunned team as Langton walked over to the coffee machine for a fresh cup. He turned back to the room as Lewis pinned up the old black-and-white picture of Elizabeth Short on the Incident board.

'The press have already compared the two victims, more or less due to the fact Louise Pennel had a flower in her hair on the photograph they used; they have not, as yet, discovered that the brutality of these murders is almost identical. I am going to ask for a complete press embargo on any further comparisons between the two cases. I don't want what was done to Elizabeth Short sparking a media frenzy of headlines. By withholding some of the details about the atrocities Louise suffered, we will be able to distinguish between the crackpot calls and a real tip-off, and it's a tip-off I am desperate for.'

Langton's mobile rang and he headed into his office to take the call in private. It was Anna, who was sitting in the canteen at the *Mirror*'s offices. She had taken a statement from the journalist who had published the first photograph of Louise.

'The journalist that received the typed note reckoned it was on schoolbook lined paper; the left-hand side was ripped.' She looked at her notebook and read the lines she had copied. 'Roses are red, violets are blue, who killed Louise and slit her mouth in two?'

'Shit!'

'It had to have come from the killer, because we hadn't given a full press release on the cuts to her mouth. I called Sharon and asked her if she had mentioned the wounds to the journalist and she said she hadn't: now for the twist, she also denies ever sending or being paid for the photograph.'

'Could she be lying?'

'I'm not sure; question is if she didn't get paid for the photograph, who did?'

'Where did it come from?'

'He said he paid a runner for it; you know, they have contacts who hang out, taking photographs at clubs. Sometimes they get lucky.'

'Did you get a name?'

'Yep, Kenneth Dunn; I'm tracking him down.'

'Good, okay; keep in touch.'

Anna had arranged to meet Kenneth Dunn at a Radio Shack where he worked part time. Dunn was very eager to speak to her, and broke off a conversation he was having as Anna showed him her ID. He led her through to the back of the shop into a small storage area. Anna showed him the newspaper.

'Did you sell this picture to the *Mirror*?'

'Yes, they've already paid me for it.'

'How did you come by this photograph?'

'I can't divulge my sources.'

'Why not?'

'Because I have to pay them, and we do a trade-off.'

'You didn't take this photograph, correct?'

'That's right.'

'So please tell me who gave it to you, or who you paid for it, or I will have you arrested for obstructing the police.'

'*What?*'

'It is imperative I know where this photograph came from and how it was passed to you, Mr Dunn. This girl was murdered and it could become a vital piece of evidence; so, where did you get this photograph from?'

He sighed. 'I was given it.'

'Who by?'

'Look, I don't want to get her into trouble; it wasn't her idea for me to sell it: it was mine. I make a few quid at weekends hanging out at clubs; you know, snapping the stars as they go in or out – especially out, they love shots of them boozed up and falling down – and their own photographers get bored hanging around. I mean, some nights, I've been there until four in the morning.'

'Who gave you this photograph, Mr Dunn?'

Again he hesitated, his greasy face shining; his dark hair was smothered in a glue-like gel which made it stick up in spikes.

'Was it Sharon Bilkin?'

Anna returned to her car and bleeped it open. She threw in her briefcase as she dialled Langton's mobile.

'She was lying: he got the picture from Sharon Bilkin on the promise he would try and get her some coverage, which he did, as she was featured in the same article. He didn't take the photograph and he also didn't know anything about the marks to our victim's mouth.'

Langton gave a long sigh, then there was silence.

'Are you still there?' Anna asked.

'Yeah, yeah, just trying to get the timeframe organised in my brain. The journalist is sent the photo, or it's passed to him by this Dunn character, who got it from Sharon, right?'

'Yes, that's what he said.'

'They buy it, release pictures; so when did this note *roses are red, violets are blue* shit come in?'

'Day the article appeared.'

'Go back to that silly little cow Sharon. She lied about this; see if she is lying about anything else.'

Anna was almost out of breath by the time she reached the top of the stairs. Either it really was a long way up or she was getting out of shape.

'It's open,' came Sharon's singsong voice.

Anna found Sharon in the kitchen, wearing yellow Marigolds.

'I couldn't face the dirty dishes any more, so I been doing the housework.'

Anna smiled; the kitchen did look a lot cleaner.

'We need to talk, Sharon.'

'Whatever. They come yesterday and took all her bedding and things from her wardrobe.'

Sharon pointed to the cards left on the table by the forensic team, pinned to a neatly written list of all the items removed. 'I said they could take whatever they wanted; I mean, I don't want her stuff and I don't really know what to do with it. And with no rent from her, I've got to find someone else.'

'Ah, so that's the reason for the house cleaning,' Anna said.

'Yeah, well, want the place to look nice, and no way am I going to say to a prospective tenant that the previous girl that shared with me was murdered. So, I don't want her stuff. They took a lot, even her dirty laundry, but there's still drawers full, and that old suitcase.'

'Is there no one she knew that would want her things?'

'I don't know anyone.'

'But you still have her photographs?'

Sharon blushed and began to wash down the draining board.

'Sharon, you said that you did not give that photograph to the press. It's very important, because if you did . . .'

'I didn't sell it,' she said, rinsing the cloth.

'But you did give it to Kenneth Dunn. Sharon, please stop wasting my time.'

Sharon folded the dishcloth and hung it on the cooker rail, refusing to look at Anna.

'Sharon, this is very important. It may not seem as if you are withholding evidence, but I need to know exactly what happened.'

Sharon sat down. 'All right, I know him. He's done some snaps of me: a couple for a magazine called *Buzz*.

He works up in Kilburn at a Radio Shack part time until he gets his career as a photographer off the ground. I just bumped into him by accident: I didn't arrange it; it was just a coincidence. We got talking and I told him about Louise, you know, what had happened to her, and we came back here for a coffee. I showed him some photographs and . . . I didn't think it would matter.'

Anna said nothing.

'Nobody told me not to do anything with them, and I'd already given you a whole lot. Anyways, Kenneth said he could get me some publicity as well, so I let him have the one of Louise with the flower in her hair and some pictures of me.'

'Did you give him anything else?'

'No, he gave me fifty quid. He said he only got a hundred, so we split it.'

'Did you tell Kenneth Dunn about the marks on Louise's mouth?'

'No, no I didn't, I swear I didn't. I haven't told anybody about them, I swear before God.'

'Did you give anything else to the journalist?'

'No, I never met him.'

'Has anyone called you, wanting to talk about Louise?'

'Only calls I've had are about the advert in *Time Out*; in fact, I've got a girl coming round this afternoon, so could you get Louise's stuff out, because I don't want it? It might sound awful, getting someone to move in, but I got to pay the rent and Louise owed me for a month.' Sharon smoothed her skirt with the back of her hand. 'She was always on the scrounge. She'd say "can I borrow five quid?", and I'd always have to ask for it back. She was always short of money, and she wouldn't buy groceries, she'd just eat my stuff. It wasn't just food: she'd take my Tampax and nail varnish remover. I know it sounds petty, but it really annoyed me.'

Sharon was agitated, her cheeks flushed pink. 'I know I shouldn't be talking about her like this, but it's the truth and she was such a liar. I'd say to her about paying me back, and she'd always plead poverty and that she'd pay me on her next week's wages. One time, I was so fed up that when she went to work, I went into her room. She had two hundred quid in a drawer! I faced her out when she came back and she just said that she'd forgotten about the cash!'

'So she did pay you back?'

'Yes, eventually, but the point is I always had to ask. Like I said, she didn't pay the rent on time, so I'm out four weeks. I often thought about asking her to leave.'

'But you didn't?'

She shook her head, then frowned. Anna could almost see Sharon's brain ticking over.

'What is it?' Anna said, encouragingly. 'Anything you think of might help me.'

'You know, there was something about her: I mean, she made you feel sorry for her. It was always as if she was waiting for something. Every time the phone rang, she'd give this expectant look towards it; never pick it up, though. I can't explain it; it was like she was always hoping for something to happen. We did have a few good times. She could be very funny and the blokes always came on to her; she was a big flirt – well, at first.'

'What do you mean, at first?'

Sharon sighed. 'When she first turned up, I rented

the room to her because she was really sort of excited about her future, but after a couple of months, she was different, sneaking in and out, and she got very secretive. To be honest, I couldn't really make her out at all. If you asked her a question about what she'd done before, where she lived, anything personal at all really, she'd never give you a direct answer. I think, well, it was kind of my in-tu- . . .' She frowned.

'Intuition?' Anna suggested.

'Yeah. I knew something was wrong, but I didn't know what. Well, I'll never know now, will I?'

Anna put Louise's suitcase into the boot of her Mini. She'd helped Sharon pack up the rest of Louise's belongings. There wasn't that much: a few clothes and shoes, and some books. Anna was unsure what she would do with them. It was sad that this was all that was left of Louise's life and no one wanted them.

The forensic team began checking over Louise's garments. They were paying special attention to the dirty underwear, in case they found DNA that might be of use at a later date. The clothes were all tagged and listed and then pinned out on white paper, laid flat on a long trestle table. At the same time, the pathologist was completing his detailed autopsy. It had taken considerable time, due to the fact there were so many injuries; the dismembering and draining of her blood had hampered the usual tests. DCI Langton had called for an update and didn't like what he was told. If it was at all possible, Louise Pennel's murder was even more horrific than they had first thought. The pathologist said that it was without doubt the worst case he had ever had to work on, but that he would be able to give full disclosure within twenty-four hours.

A frustrated Langton sat in his office, brooding darkly. Nine days and they still had no suspect. Even with extra officers working alongside his team, they had not come up with a single witness who had seen Louise Pennel in those days before her body was discovered. He had an uneasy feeling that something was about to explode, and he would be at the receiving end of it.

Anna was kept waiting, as Richard Reynolds was not at his desk. She sat in the reception area of the *Sun*'s offices, reading back issues of the paper, for almost three quarters of an hour. She was just getting impatient when Reynolds strode over to the reception desk. He was tall, with a thatch of sandy hair and the most extraordinary blue eyes.

'Hi, I'm sorry to keep you waiting but I expected you earlier, so when you didn't show, I popped out to see someone. I'm Dick Reynolds.'

Anna stood up and shook his hand. 'Anna Travis.'

'Nice to meet you. Do you want to come through to the news desk?' He bent down to pick up her brief-case and gestured that she should follow him. 'If you'd prefer, we can bag someone's office, more private; crime section's a bit like Piccadilly Circus!' He held open a swing door, standing to one side to allow her to pass in front of him.

'Whatever,' she said, pleasantly. It made a nice change from the usual stride and swinging doors of Langton and his mob.

'Someone's office' turned out to be a cordoned-off corner with a desk cluttered with bright potted plants, stacks of papers and computer.

'Right, have a seat, and I'll get some coffee organised.'

Dick left her for only a moment before returning and giving her a lovely wide smile. 'On its way, Anna. Right, how can I help you?'

'It's about the article you wrote, which showed a photograph of the murder victim Louise Pennel.'

'Right, yes; what about it?'

'I need to know where you got the photograph from.'

'Well, that's easy: from a journalist that worked here.'

'You linked Louise Pennel's murder and another case?'

'Right, the Black Dahlia. To be honest, it was a bit far-fetched; I hadn't even heard of the old case, but as they both had a flower in their hair, it was just something to hook the story onto really. I didn't have much else to go on, as we hadn't had a press release.'

'Have you since read up on the Black Dahlia case?'

'No, I've been on the missing kid from Blackheath.'

'So the only similarity between the two cases, as far as you're concerned, was the flower?'

'Yep.'

'You said you got the photograph from another journalist; did he mention to you the Black Dahlia case?'

'No. I wouldn't have known anything about it, but I got an anonymous letter that likened your girl, Louise Pennel, to . . .' He frowned. 'Elizabeth Short was the other victim, wasn't she? Happened years ago in Los Angeles.'

'Yes; have you checked into any details of her case?'

'Nope; went on the internet to get a bit of info, but to be truthful, it was sort of sidelined by this young boy that's missing; he's only twelve.'

'Do you still have the letter?'

'No. I should maybe have kept it, because you are here and there's obviously something going on, but we get a shedload of crank letters every time we headline a murder story. I spoke to someone investigating the case, Richmond station. I did tell them I'd destroyed it. I'm sorry.'

'Can you recall exactly what it said?'

Dick looked to the door as a young secretary carried in a tray of coffee and a packet of biscuits. By the time he had offered milk and sugar and then leaned back in his chair, Anna was feeling very relaxed in his company.

'It didn't say much; just that the Black Dahlia killer was never caught. It also said that there was now another one, the Red Dahlia. In the photograph we had, the flower in Louise's hair looked like a rose to me, but it made a good header.'

'Was it handwritten?'

'No, it was typed. Not from a computer; well, I don't think it was, because it was quite heavy print. It was on a piece of cheap lined paper.'

'I have to ask you that if you do get any further contacts regarding the Louise Pennel case, you get in touch with me immediately. This is my direct line.' Anna handed him her card. He slipped it into his wallet as she put her coffee cup back into the saucer. 'Thank you very much for your time.'

'My pleasure. Have you had lunch?'

'Pardon?'

'I said, have you had lunch? Only I haven't, and there's a nice pub a few minutes away.'

She flushed and buttoned her coat, unable to look at him. 'I have to get back, but thank you for the invitation.'

By the time Dick Reynolds had led Anna back through the maze of corridors and out to her Mini, she had agreed to have dinner with him the following evening. She was feeling very pleased with herself; it had been a long time since she had been attracted to anyone and she had liked him from the moment she had set eyes on him.

Reynolds was soon back at his desk, logged onto the internet. As they had not had a press release detailing the exact similarities, he still believed it was a case of both victims being very pretty girls who wore flowers in their hair and who were only twenty-two when they were killed. He hadn't realised how much information there was: an entire website for the Elizabeth Short murder which detailed much more appalling similarities; with almost sixty years between the two murders, he decided to concentrate on his missing schoolboy story – for the time being, at any rate.

Chapter Four

Anna sat with a surly Langton in his office. 'I knew that silly girl was lying,' he said.

'They sold the photograph for a hundred pounds; split it fifty-fifty.'

'I can read,' he said, as he flipped through her report detailing her interviews with Sharon, Ken Dunn and Dick Reynolds. 'So if they were notes written by the killer, we've lost them! Maybe they were just as they said – some crank.'

'No!'

Langton looked up.

'The first note mentioned the cuts to Louise Pennel's mouth – that detail had not been released. The second was more like a teaser; the journalist had never heard of the Black Dahlia, so just presumed it was the flower connection. Both letters, I think, came from the killer.'

'Really?'

'Yes.'

'Well this last journalist didn't bite or use it, did he?'

'Because he presumed—'

'Yes, yes! That it was just a crank, like the bloody

phone calls we've had from all the nutters. I'm just surprised that neither kept the notes. Probably wet behind the ears; an old pro wouldn't have tossed it.'

'Well, neither of them are old,' Anna said, and felt a hot flush spreading over her cheeks.

Langton leaned back in his chair and grinned. 'Weren't they now? Well, word of warning: you can never trust them, young or old. I would put money on the fact that, after your visit, they'll be beavering around to see what they can dig up, and that worries me. Yes?'

Lewis had tapped the door and peered in. 'You want all the files to go over to the hotel?'

Langton nodded. Lewis closed the door again.

'Bringing in a profiler. Don't know if we can get Parks, as he's writing some book and doing a freebie on the Cunard.'

'What?'

Langton stood up and yawned. 'Profiler we used for the Alan Daniels case. He's since become quite a high-profile himself, so I dunno who we'll get in to look over the case. But whoever it is, I hope to Christ they can help us, as we've still got fuck all.'

He perched on the corner of his desk. 'I don't suppose Sharon gave us any more details on this tall dark stranger and his shiny fucking car?'

'No.'

'Well we've got nothing from anyone else either. I am loath to do a TV slot: if the facts get out, it'll create a nightmare. You know, they never released the details on exactly how the Yorkshire Ripper killed.'

'He murdered eleven women, so maybe they should have,' Anna said tetchily.

Langton ignored her tone. 'They didn't with Fred West, either. Apparently it puts readers off: too much gore and they won't buy the paper; they need just enough to titillate their appetite. We give anything near the truth with our case and it'll create mayhem. I'm going for a press embargo.'

'But we need help from someone,' Anna said, standing.

'I am aware of that,' he snapped and barged out into the Incident Room. Anna picked up her report and followed, as there was to be a briefing any minute.

Langton paced up and down in front of the Incident Room board. He constantly pulled at his hair so it stood up on end; his tie was loose and his five-o'clock shadow made his face look hollow. Anna wondered how long it would be before the Commander paid a visit; her office must be monitoring the progress on their case, or lack of it.

'Right, we're going nowhere fast, so if anything has come in, speak now or forever hold your peace.'

There seemed to be no breakthrough from any quarter. Checks had unearthed no suspicious doctor or surgeon. They also had no further details as yet from the forensic team.

Langton tugged at his tie. 'We have to trace this suspect, the dark-haired, middle-aged boyfriend; it doesn't make sense that none of Louise's so-called friends knew anything about him. Someone must have seen him or met him; someone knows more than we've uncovered. So tomorrow, go back to square one and reinterview her known associates. We know she only lived at Sharon's flat for six months, so dig further back; where she lived before, anyone found out?'

Barolli held up his pencil. 'I've got a bed-and-breakfast address in Paddington and a flat in Brixton off the DSS. She was also at a hostel in Victoria, but so far we're coming up empty-handed: people are saying she used to keep herself to herself.'

'Get back to all those places and try again. Yes!' Langton pointed to Lewis.

'We've got a previous employer: a dog clipper! She worked there for some time before the dental surgery. It's also a boarding kennels. She was a poor worker, always late; she only lasted four weeks. Owner hired her from the Job Centre; we've been back there trying to trace any other work she may have got through them, but so far, not much luck.'

Langton nodded, and stuffed his hands into his pockets. He sounded tired and ratty. 'Louise was at Stringfellow's and yet no one sees her there, or sees her leave with anyone; that was thirteen days ago. Thirteen! For three days and nights, she was somewhere with somebody and whoever that was mutilated her and tortured her to death. Whoever that was drained her blood and cut her in half! And we do not have a single clue to his identity! All we know is that she was having a relationship with an older man, a tall, dark-haired, middle-aged man. Now from the photographs that Sharon Bilkin sold to the press, someone has to recognise her. It just isn't logical for a girl as attractive as our victim to be able to disappear into fucking thin air!'

Langton told the team about the notes that had been sent to the press and destroyed by the two journalists, who could remember nothing unusual about the postage stamps or franking on the envelopes. If they had held a clue, they no longer had access to it now. By the time he finished the briefing, he was in a foul mood, and the entire team was left feeling depressed. They had only one option: to go back over what little they had, hoping to uncover something they had missed.

Anna did not get back to her flat until nine-fifteen. She hoped her dinner date with Dick Reynolds the following evening would not have to be cancelled. She was on the early-morning shift though, so should be able to leave the station by four in the afternoon to give her time to wash her hair, have a nice long bath and get ready. She brought Louise Pennel's suitcase in from the car and left it by an armchair. She was tired out and so just made some cheese on toast and a big mug of tea, which she took into her lounge to eat in front of the TV. She zapped through a few channels and ended up watching some gameshow in which a team of hysterical women were trying to cook a three-course dinner that cost no more than five pounds. She finished her own meal and decided it was bedtime, using the remote to turn off the set.

Without the TV on, the room was almost in darkness; the cheap suitcase drew Anna's attention as she drank the last of her tea. Even though she was tired out, she dragged it over to the sofa, switched on a lamp and opened it up. The clothes she had taken from Louise's bedroom were neatly folded, as she had packed them herself. She took out each item and laid them on the floor. She then searched the suitcase again for anything they might have missed.

The lining was frayed but there was nothing hidden

inside it. She glanced at the sticker labelling the case with Sharon's address, and then looked at it more closely. It had been pasted over another, so she cut the tag off, took it into the kitchen and put the kettle on. Holding it gingerly in the steam, she was able to pick slowly at the corner until she could peel the top sticker off. Underneath, in old-fashioned, looped writing, *Mrs F. Pennel, Seacroft House, Bognor Regis*, was written in ink.

Anna made a note of this and then placed the two labels in an envelope to take into the station in the morning.

Next, she began to check every single item she had removed; things that neither the forensic team nor Sharon had wanted. They smelt of a strange, musty perfume, which Anna recognised as stale Tudor Rose.

There was a child's hand-knitted sweater with a zigzag design and some of the wool fraying at the cuffs. Anna could make out a smudged name on its label: *Mary Louise P, Harwood House*. Again, she jotted the information down. Next came a threadbare flannelette nightdress, a set of waitress's collar and cuffs and a pair of tired-looking low-heeled court shoes with holes in the soles.

Anna knew that the more expensive garments, like the cashmere sweaters, had been taken to the lab for tests. She also thought it more than likely that, despite her protestations, Sharon had picked over Louise's stuff and taken a number of things. The leftovers were a sad array that even the charity shops would not want. There were three paperback books, well worn, with many pages turned over at the top corner: it was a habit, even when exercised on paperbacks, that Anna loathed. There were also two Barbara Cartland bodice rippers and a small leather-bound dictionary; written on the flyleaf was *Harwood House Library* and an address in Eastbourne. It was dated 1964, but Anna knew that Louise Pennel was twenty-two years old, so she must have taken it from the library. The last book was equally well-thumbed with many passages underlined. It was a pocket book of etiquette, from table manners to serving dinners, circa 1950.

Packing all the items back into the suitcase made Anna feel a great sadness for the girl they had once belonged to. The tawdry remnants of her life gave Anna little idea of what kind of girl Louise had been, other than that she had wanted to better herself; the horrific circumstances of her death were a far cry from the romantic world of Barbara Cartland.

About to place one of the novels back into the case, Anna flicked through it; caught between the pages was a folded note written on lined paper. The handwriting was childish and there were a number of misspellings and crossings-out. It appeared to be a draft of a job application and began *Dear Mr* . . . It went on:

I am enclosing a photograph of myself. I would like to apply for the possition of personal assistant. I am presentlly working for a dental practise but have always wanted to travel and as I have no dependents this would not be a problem. I am able to type but do not have short hand.

That was all; no signature, no name and no address. It felt yet again like a step forwards that abruptly stopped.

Anna lay awake for a while, thinking about Louise

Pennel. Could that job application have been how she met their missing tall dark stranger? Anna snuggled into her pillow and tried to distract herself by thinking about what she would wear for her date tomorrow evening. Dick Reynolds had just said a bite to eat, so she didn't want to overdress. She hadn't made up her mind by the time she fell asleep.

Her sleep was deep but not dreamless: the image of Louise Pennel's ghostlike face, with her slit bleeding clown mouth open wide, kept on floating before Anna, as if she was calling out to her. Louise was naked, her skin white as porcelain, as it had been when they had first seen her severed body. She was wearing only the white waitress's collar and cuffs and moved closer and closer as if to touch Anna. That was when she woke and sat bolt upright. It was four o'clock and the alarm would be ringing at six. She flopped down and closed her eyes; so much for a good night's sleep.

Chapter Five

DAY ELEVEN

Everyone had been instructed to gather in the Incident Room for a briefing. Anna had already passed over her report with the findings from Louise Pennel's belongings. As the team waited for Langton, she began checking out the Mrs F. Pennel in Bognor Regis. She had discovered that the Harwood House address had been a children's home that had closed down over five years ago. A Joyce Hughes, Mrs Pennel's carer, answered the phone and told Anna that she was very elderly and bedridden; she was unable to say whether or not she was any relation to Louise. Anna asked if it would be convenient to call again to speak to Mrs Pennel personally, and Mrs Hughes suggested she try again between four and five that afternoon.

Langton came out of his office looking smart in a grey suit with a pink shirt and grey tie. He had obviously made an effort; he had shaved, and even his hair looked neat.

'Right, we all here?'

Everyone looked attentively towards him as the late-comers scurried in.

'We will have the full autopsy report first thing in the morning. We are also being joined by a profiler who has been working on the statements taken to date.'

The double doors to the Incident Room opened, and Lewis held one wide to allow an elegant blonde woman to walk through. She was wearing a tight-fitting check jacket that Anna thought might be Chanel, with a tight black pencil skirt and patent spike-heeled shoes; she carried a bulging black briefcase. She was tall and slender with perfect legs, and although hers was not exactly a pretty face – it was too angular, her nose too sharp – her wide-apart eyes made her appear exceptionally attractive. A comb caught up her hair in a chignon and she wore no lipstick, just a hint of gloss. Her appearance silenced the room.

Langton introduced Professor Aisling Marshe and then gave the names of all those gathered. She gave a small smile and polite nod, then started to remove files from her briefcase. Coffee was served, Bridget wheeling the trolley around the desks, as Professor Marshe talked quietly to Langton and studied the Incident board. About fifteen minutes later, she removed her jacket and placed it on the back of her chair. She had on a white silk blouse, but no jewellery other than a pair of large gilt earrings. She asked Langton to draw the table closer to her chair, which he did very quickly.

Anna had never seen him be so helpful and charming. He was smiling at the Professor all the time; he served her coffee and asked if she wanted sugar; it looked as if he would even drink it for her if she asked him to. Anna realised that when he had mentioned calling in a profiler he must have already arranged to have the Professor on board; he was keeping things as close to his chest as when they had last worked together.

At last the Professor seemed ready to talk to them. The room fell silent.

'Firstly, I'd like to express my thanks to DCI Langton – James – for giving me this opportunity. I am actually in England on a sabbatical.' She turned to flash a knowing smile at Langton.

Anna was stunned; it was very obvious that Langton and this American knew each other extremely well. If they weren't already sleeping together, Anna was certain that they would be soon. She was so taken aback that she missed what was said next. She wasn't alone; some of the other officers had been shooting glances at each other.

'I want you to have a look at my previous work, so I've had a few sheets typed up for you.' She handed them to Langton, who began passing them around. 'Just so that you know more about me, and hopefully trust in my judgement over the Louise Pennel case.'

She was nervous; she kept turning a pencil in her manicured hands. As the team started reading, the Professor flipped open her own file and waited patiently.

Professor Marshe had been working for Court TV in America for the past eighteen months, participating in live discussions on the cases broadcast. They all appeared to be high-profile murder trials. Her previous work had been in connection with the NYPD homicide unit as a freelance adviser. She had been educated at Vassar and had an impressive list of degrees. She had also spent eight months interviewing serial killers in various prisons across America for her latest book and had guested on two high-profile television documentaries. She was single, aged thirty-eight.

Anna folded the CV and, along with the rest of the room, looked towards Professor Marshe, eager to hear what she had to say.

'I would really have liked more time to digest the case history to date, so I will very likely need to get back to you with further details on how I think you should progress.'

She turned to indicate the photographs of Louise Pennel. 'The killer obviously had a lengthy period of time to commit this crime. She was missing for three days. It is quite possible she took that length of time to die. Your killer has to have a place where the dismembering and blood draining could be done. I do think the perpetrator is someone with medical training and I do think you are looking for a male. He will live somewhere in this area, quite possibly close to the murder site itself. This kill is premeditated. Your killer will have taken many months choosing his victim and planning the torture as part of his *modus operandi*; he must therefore have known the victim very well. He would have known that she would not be missed for some considerable time. I am aware that you are hoping to trace a suspect. This description of a tall, well-dressed, perhaps middle-aged man would fit the profile I have begun on your killer. This man, I doubt I have to tell you, is extremely dangerous. I do not think that Louise was his first victim; I also do not think she will be his last. Perhaps it would be advisable to go back into any unsolved cases and look for murders with an exceptional sadistic sexual motive.'

Professor Marshe paused and looked at her notes; she then tapped the page. 'It's quite possible that this killer will have been married; he may even still be married and with a family; grown-up children, I think. He has a hatred of women. So look for someone whose previous marriages have failed, someone who has been humiliated and someone with an immense ego; it is his ego we need to concentrate on, because that's what will lead you to him.'

Anna stifled a yawn. The truth was Professor Marshe had not really told them anything they had not already discussed. Langton, on the other hand, appeared so enamoured with what the Professor was saying that Anna wanted to slap him. She watched, irritated, as Professor Marshe held up the book on the Black Dahlia that she herself had brought to Langton's attention.

'The last book written on the Black Dahlia constantly refers to how clever the killer of Elizabeth Short was: clever enough that, after numerous contacts by him to the police, they were still unable to catch him. It is quite likely that he went on to kill two more women, as if to prove himself above suspicion. Even after these murders he remained undetected. Your killer will have enjoyed reading as much information about Elizabeth Short as possible, because he identifies himself with her killer. If you read the description of Elizabeth Short, she is very similar to Louise Pennel: Elizabeth was twenty-two years old, five feet six inches. She had black hair whereas Louise Pennel was dark blonde, dyed red. Both women's fingernails were bitten down to the quick. I am certain your killer chose Louise Pennel very care-fully and I am certain he will have the same overblown ego as Elizabeth Short's killer. His psychological sick-ness will mean he wants as much attention given to the Louise Pennel case as to the Black Dahlia. For starters, he has alerted the press to the Elizabeth Short case and encouraged them to give your victim the nickname of the Red Dahlia. I am certain that the two letters received by the journalists were sent by him. Now he will become desperate to hear about the enquiry: he will want to read about his exploits; to hear that you have no leads will fuel his ego and provoke him to make further contact. To date, you have not released the full extent of Louise's horrific injuries. I suggest you maintain a very low profile to draw him out. The more he is drawn out to make contact, the more likely he is to make a mistake.'

Anna watched as Professor Marshe closed her file,

indicating that the meeting was over. The team began to talk amongst themselves. Langton and Professor Marshe spent some time looking over the board then went into Langton's office. Barolli wandered over to Anna's desk.

'What do you think?' he asked.

'She's not exactly said anything we haven't discussed. I mean, we are all certain he's a freak, and quite possibly the tall dark stranger that Louise was dating, but the reality is we are no closer to discovering who he is. To be honest, I am not sure if we have the time to play his games.'

'What do you mean?'

'Trying to draw him out and putting a press embargo on exactly what we release might just be a big time-waster. Someone out there knows who he is; someone saw him with Louise, and without a big press push, we might not get anything until he kills again. Which I agree with her, he is going to do.'

'So you didn't rate her?'

'I didn't say that.'

Barolli smiled. 'The bit about the suspect being married with grown-up kids will give us more to work on.'

Anna shrugged. 'I don't see how; we've not even got a possible suspect yet.'

'But she said that Louise had to have been with this guy. You said it yourself: somebody has to bloody know him.'

'Not if he made sure he was never seen with Louise; from what I gathered from Sharon, he never even went into the flat. He waited outside in the car.'

'Yeah, the shiny black one!' Barolli sighed, exasperated, and wandered off.

Anna crossed her legs beneath the desk and swore as she felt her tights snag. She bent down and hitched up her skirt; the ladder was spreading upwards from a large hole on her knee.

'You want to see if this woman in Bognor Regis can give us anything?'

Anna looked up; Langton was leaning on her desk. 'Sure.'

He leaned closer, looking down. 'What are you doing?'

'Oh, nothing; just snagged my tights.'

'Off you go then.'

'Now?'

'Yes, Travis, now; unless you have something else pressing? No need to take anyone with you.' He paused for a moment. 'What did you think of her?'

She knew who he was referring to, of course, but acted as if she didn't. 'Think of who?'

'Professor Marshe?'

'Interesting; not as informative as Michael Parks.'

'Well, he didn't give us much to start off with, if you remember; in fact, I didn't rate him at all when he first talked to the team, but he came up with the goods on how to handle Alan Daniels. Aisling seems to think we are hunting down another sociopath.'

Anna busied herself packing her briefcase. 'Bit obvious; I mean what sane person would commit such a horrific murder? Every time I think about it I feel sick.'

'Let's hope your outing to Bognor Regis proves to be worthwhile.'

'Will it be okay if I go straight home after, as I'm off at four?'

'Why not?' he said, walking away; he then turned back, stuffing his hands into his pockets.

'Eager to get off home? That's not like you; unless you've got a date?'

'No,' she lied, then added that she had been up late working on the report.

'Ah yes; well, enjoy your trip.'

'Thank you.' Anna snapped her briefcase closed. She didn't know how he managed to get under her skin so easily. 'I'll call in if I do get anything,' she said, but he was already moving across the room to speak to Lewis and Barolli.

Mrs Pennel's was a large Victorian double-fronted house with big bay windows, set well back from the road leading down to the beach. All the other properties had gardens that were well kept, if slightly strewn with sand, but this one was very overgrown. Anna rang the intercom at the gate and waited, the wind whipping her coat. At last, a disembodied voice asked who she was, and then buzzed it open. The path and front steps were gritty with sand and the doormat was threadbare; it looked as if it hadn't been swept or moved in years.

Anna rang the bell and stepped back. The front door had stained-glass panels, two with tape over the cracks. It was a few minutes before the door clicked open and a reincarnation of Mrs Danvers peered out. She was dressed in a black crêpe skirt and woollen sweater, with a housekeeper's faded floral smock over it, dark stockings and lace-up shoes. It was her iron-grey hair that made Anna think instantly of Daphne du Maurier's *Rebecca*, as it was worn in an old-fashioned forties style with a roll either side of her head. She had thin, drawn lips and small, button-cold eyes.

'Are you the policewoman?'

'Yes, I am Detective Inspector Anna Travis. Are you Mrs Hughes?' She showed her warrant card.

'Yes; you had better come in.' She opened the door wider.

Anna stepped into a cold and unwelcoming hallway. It was as if the house was suspended in a time warp. The walls were lined with dark prints and old brown photographs, and the glass of the heavy chandeliers was tinted mustard yellow and green. There was a distinct smell of mothballs.

'Follow me. Mrs Pennel is expecting you, but she may be sleeping.'

Mrs Hughes led the way up the stairs past a sick-looking plant on a plinth in front of dark-green velvet draped curtains.

'Have you worked for Mrs Pennel a long time?' Anna asked.

'Yes, twelve years. There used to be other staff but they've not been here for years; nowadays, we just have a cleaner.'

Mrs Hughes stopped on a sparse landing, next to a commode chair and a walking frame, and held up her hand. 'Give me a minute.'

Anna watched as Mrs Hughes entered a room at the far end of the landing.

'Florence, the lady is here to see you. Florence!'

Anna could not hear a reply.

'Do you need me to stay with you?' Mrs Hughes asked, standing to one side.

'No, I don't want to put you to any trouble.'

'There's a bell push at the side of her door; just pull it when you leave. I'll wait downstairs.'

'Thank you.'

'That's all right; I'll be in the kitchen.'

Anna closed the door behind her as she could sense Mrs Hughes hovering. She wasn't really like Mrs Danvers; actually, she'd been quite helpful so far.

'Mrs Pennel?' Anna asked, taking in the room.

It was not as drab as the rest of the house. The walls were apple green, the carpet a darker green and the curtains floral. There was a massive carved wardrobe, a matching dresser with a bow-fronted mirror on top and a four-poster bed with drapes that matched the walls. There were also large potted plants in the corners; Anna presumed they were fake, as the heat in the room was overpowering. A marble fireplace had a large electric fire in the grate with all four bars on. Old-fashioned central heating pipes ran around almost the entire room and, judging by the heat, they were all turned on as well. There were stacks of magazines and fashion books on stools and small tables, and bottles of water, medicine and perfume jostled for space with silver photograph frames on the mantel shelf and dressing table.

Placed close to the electric fire was a floral printed sofa, piled high with cushions. Reclining on it was an incredibly pretty elderly lady with snow-white hair worn in a braid around her head. She wore a nylon nightdress and pink knitted bedjacket; her eyes were heavy with mascara, her cheeks rouged and her lips outlined in pink.

'Mrs Pennel?' Anna asked, moving closer.

'Hello, dear.' Mrs Pennel's nail polish matched her lipstick; her puffy arthritic fingers bore a number of diamond rings and her wrist a large bracelet. She patted a velvet chair near her and smiled.

'Sit down, dear; have you been offered a drink?'

Anna could feel the sweat under her armpits; the temperature in the room was about 80 degrees. 'No thank you. Do you mind if I take my coat off?'

'I have some gin and tonic in the cabinet.'

'I'm fine, thank you.'

'If you want a coffee or tea, you'll have to ring for Mrs Hughes. I did have a kettle in here but I don't know where it is, and some tea cups, but they were taken down to the kitchen and never brought back up again. Would you like a drink?'

Mrs Pennel was evidently hard of hearing. Anna leaned forwards and spoke up. 'No, thank you.'

Mrs Pennel blinked and fussed with her bedjacket. 'Are you from the Social Services?'

It took Anna quite a while to communicate to Mrs Pennel that she was there to ask about a girl called Louise. She seemed not to know the name and showed no reaction when Anna told her that she had found her address on a label attached to a suitcase. It was hard going. Mrs Pennel leaned back and closed her eyes; whether she was listening or not, Anna couldn't tell.

'Mrs Pennel, Louise was murdered.'

No reaction.

'Are you related to her?'

No reaction.

Anna tapped the ringed hand. 'Mrs Pennel, can you hear me?'

The mascara-ed eyes fluttered.

'It has been in all the papers. Could you look at this photograph and tell me if you know this girl?'

Anna held the photograph out. 'This is Louise Pennel.' Mrs Pennel sat up, searched for some glasses, and then stared at the photograph.

'Who is this?' she asked.

'Louise Pennel,' Anna said again, loudly.

'Is it Raymond's daughter?'

'Who is Raymond?'

'My son; that's him over there.'

Mrs Pennel pointed to a row of photographs. There were various pictures of Florence in theatrical costumes and two of a young dark-haired man in military uniform who Anna recognised from Louise's album.

'Is this your son?'

'He married a terrible woman, a hairdresser; he died of a burst appendix and if she had got a brain she would have called an ambulance, but she let him die. I would have helped out if I'd known they were in financial trouble, but she wouldn't even speak to me. Heather, her name was; Heather.'

Anna sat down and showed the photograph to Mrs Pennel again. 'Did Louise ever come to see you?'

Mrs Pennel plucked at her jacket and turned away. 'My son was a foolish boy, but if he'd asked for help, I'd have forgiven him.'

Anna was becoming impatient. She leaned forwards

and spoke loudly. 'Mrs Pennel, I am here because I am investigating the murder of Louise Pennel. I need to know if she came here and if so, whether someone was with her.'

'Yes!' the old lady snapped.

'I'm sorry?'

'I said yes. Yes, yes, yes. My son I would have helped, but not that woman, with her bleached hair and her common voice and cheap perfume. She was to blame; it was her fault he died.'

Anna stood up. 'Mrs Pennel, your granddaughter is dead. I am not here about your son or your daughter-in-law, but about Louise Pennel. I just want to know if she came here and if anyone accompanied her.'

Mrs Pennel closed her eyes; her hands were drawn into fists, her lips tight. 'I said if he married her I would disinherit him, cut him off without a penny, and he spat at me. My own son; he spat at me. If his father had been alive, he wouldn't have dared do that; he would not have dared marry that whore. I nearly died carrying him; I had a terrible time. I was in hospital for weeks after his birth. I only ever wanted what was best for him; I spoilt him, gave him anything he wanted but he just walked out. He chose that terrible woman over me.'

Anna stood up; there was no way she could break into the stream of vitriol that spewed out of the old lady's painted lips. She didn't even appear to have noticed that Anna was picking up her coat, ready to leave. She stared straight ahead into the electric fire, her hands clenched.

Anna headed down the stairs, and she could still hear

Mrs Pennel as she continued to berate her dead son, her voice echoing down.

'Twenty-six years old, his whole life ahead of him and she came and destroyed everything. I loved my son; I would have given him everything I have. He knew that; he knew I adored him, but he chose that bitch!'

Mrs Hughes appeared at the kitchen door. She looked up the stairs, then back to Anna. 'She can keep going for hours until she's exhausted, then she just sleeps. Did you want to know about Raymond? I should have warned you not to bring up his name if you didn't. She's like a broken record!'

'Could I just have a few words with you?' Anna asked.

The kitchen was as tired and old-fashioned as the rest of the house. Mrs Hughes put the kettle on and turned to Anna. 'She's ninety-four; she's been dying for the last twenty years, but hangs on as if she's afraid to let go. I think it's the fury that keeps her alive. She doesn't even want to watch TV, or listen to the radio. She just lies up there in her own world. She sometimes looks through her photograph albums, her days when she was an actress, before she married the Major. He died twenty-odd years ago; everyone she knew is dead.'

'Did you know her son?'

'Not really. By the time I came, he'd left; they had this fight about the girl he wanted to marry. Mrs Pennel cut him off, and he never came back.'

Anna nodded. 'I am here because a girl called Louise Pennel has been murdered; she had a suitcase with this address.'

'That might be her granddaughter; I think one of her names was Louise. Mary Louise?'

Anna took a deep breath; at last she was able to ask the questions she needed answering. She took out Louise's photograph. 'Is this her?'

Mrs Hughes looked at the photograph.

'Yes. I only met her once. She's murdered?'

'She came here? To Harwood House?'

'Yes, about eight or nine months ago. She's been murdered?'

'Yes; it has had extensive news coverage.'

'We don't get the newspapers; she likes the glossy magazines.'

'Is there any way you could recall the exact date Louise came here?'

Mrs Hughes pursed her lips, then went to a cabinet and opened a drawer. She took out a large calendar, evidently a freebie from an estate agent. She began flicking through it, licking her fingertips as she turned over month by month of elegant houses.

'It was last May, the sixteenth; nearly nine months ago now.'

'Thank you, that's terrific. Is Mrs Pennel very wealthy?'

'Yes; well, worth a few hundred thousand, then there's this house and she has some nice jewellery. She has a solicitor who comes round a lot to check on the running of the house. My wages and the bills are paid direct. I think he suggested she move into a home, but she won't have it. She just lives up there; never comes down here, hasn't for years.' She sighed, shaking her head. 'Murdered; that's terrible.'

Anna did not want to get into the details of the murder. She concentrated on her notebook. 'Do you live in?'

'Yes, I've got a room next to hers, in case she needs me at night.'

Mrs Hughes set down the tea tray and poured from a small dented teapot. 'Place is going to rack and ruin, but she won't spend a penny on doing anything; well, I suppose at ninety-four, why bother?'

'Did Mrs Pennel talk to Louise when she was here?'

'No, the old girl was very poorly with the flu; I never thought she'd get over it, but she did. Louise just turned up on the doorstep.'

'So you had never met her before?'

'I knew there was a granddaughter, but the old lady would have nothing to do with her; I didn't even know her name. I said for her to come back and I told Florence she'd called round, but she said if she came again, not to let her in.'

'Did she say why she had turned up?'

Mrs Hughes dipped a biscuit into her tea. 'She needed some money. She said she had a good job opportunity and wanted to buy a new coat. It was strange, you know, never having seen her before; to be honest, I did think she was a bit desperate. She said this job was very important.'

'Did she tell you anything about it?'

'Not really; she said it was going to take her abroad and she would have to get a passport; sounded too good to be true to me. I think she answered an advert in the paper for a PA to someone wealthy. She'd sent a letter and got a reply asking to meet her, so she wanted some new clothes. She needed shoes as well: she had these worn old things on, very down at heel they were.'

'Was anyone with her?'

'No, she'd come on the train from London. She said she was renting a room in a hostel; where, she didn't say, but she looked very shabby and pale, and her hair needed washing. I felt sorry for her, but there was nothing I could do.'

Mrs Hughes cupped her hand to draw the biscuit crumbs from the table then stood, listening, her head tilted to the ceiling.

'She's quiet; probably fallen asleep.'

Mrs Hughes crossed to the old-fashioned big square sink and brushed the crumbs from her hands. She turned on the tap, swilling around the sink and draining board.

'Are you sure Louise Pennel never came here before?'

Mrs Hughes returned to the table and picked up Anna's cup. 'I lost my husband; he committed suicide fourteen years ago.'

'I'm sorry.'

'He was a bankrupt; couldn't live with it. I have a daughter but she emigrated to Canada. I'll go over there one day and see her; she's got three children. I doubt if the old lady will last much longer. Her solicitors asked me to stay on caring for her, so that's why I'm here; I'm supposed to have Sundays off, but I never take them. I'm always here so if the girl had come by, I would have known about it. We hardly ever have any visitors, just her solicitor and sometimes Social Services to check on her health.' Mrs Hughes gave an embarrassed smile. 'Not a very exciting life, is it? But the old lady's solicitors said I'm mentioned in her will; she keeps telling me that after she's gone I'll be looked after, so here I am.'

'But she wouldn't see her granddaughter?'

Mrs Hughes shrugged and began washing the teacups.

'Did you give Louise a suitcase?'

Mrs Hughes kept her back to Anna and made no answer.

'The reason I contacted Mrs Pennel was because there was a label on a suitcase with this address; it was in Louise's flat.'

Mrs Hughes dried the cups, still with her back to Anna. 'It was mine.'

'I'm sorry?'

'I said it was my case, one I used when I moved in here.'

Anna kept her voice very calm and steady. 'You gave it to Louise?'

'Yes.' Mrs Hughes seemed preoccupied as she put the crockery into a cabinet.

Anna persisted. 'Why did you give her your suitcase?'

Mrs Hughes closed the cabinet door. She had two pink spots high on her cheeks. 'I felt sorry for her; when the old lady wouldn't see her, she looked desolate. She kept on chewing her nails, saying she just needed a couple of hundred pounds and that she would pay it back as soon as she got this job. Well, I didn't have the money to give her and I knew if I asked Mrs Pennel for it, she'd go ballistic; her solicitors count every penny – God forbid if I overspend on the groceries. I didn't have any cash to give her.'

Anna smiled warmly. Mrs Hughes was obviously upset, constantly touching the roll of curl at the side of her head.

'So you gave her your suitcase?'

'Yes; there are wardrobes full of clothes that Mrs

Pennel will never wear. I've taken armfuls to the local charity shop.'

'So you gave her some clothes?'

'Just a few dresses and coats and things, I mean they weren't suitable for a young girl but they were very good quality.' The pink spots on Mrs Hughes's cheeks deepened and she seemed flustered.

'Anything else?' Anna asked innocently, wondering why she seemed so nervous.

Mrs Hughes sat down and rested her head in her hands. She then explained how she had gone up the stairs to fetch the suitcase and clothes. When Louise had turned up, she had been polishing some silver in the kitchen. It was not until Louise had left that Mrs Hughes realised that two snuff boxes and a solid silver candle-stick were missing.

Anna calmed Mrs Hughes by asking her to describe the clothing and shoes. The poor woman was so afraid she would lose her job or her place in Mrs Pennel's will that she had never mentioned it to anyone. Anna doubted if the items could have been worth more than a few hundred pounds and she saw no reason to contact Mrs Pennel's solicitors. She would nevertheless have to mention it in her report, so that the items could be traced in case Louise had sold them.

Checking her watch, Anna remembered she had asked the taxi to wait. She knew she'd get a ticking-off at the extra cost, but she had gained some worthwhile infor-mation. She had three quarters of an hour before her train was due and so decided to call in at the local station.

Bognor Regis police station was not exactly a hive of activity. The duty sergeant suggested she talk to a DS

Len White, who had been at the station for thirty years and was now there on a semi-retired basis, giving talks to the local schools.

Anna outlined the reason for her visit to Mrs Pennel. DS White, a grey-haired thick-set officer, listened intently. He had a habit of breathing heavily through his nose, leaning his elbows on the desk.

'I know the old lady, quite a character. I was very wet behind the ears when I was called out to the place: big garden party going on, and the cars had blocked the through road down to the beach. She used to be quite the social queen. To be honest, I amazed she's still going strong; she must be, what?'

Anna smiled. 'She is ninety-four.'

'I reckon she must be, cos she was no spring chicken then. After the Major died, she took to her bed. He was a character: we'd picked him up a couple of times the worse for drink. He had an old Rolls-Royce and we'd find him sitting sleeping over the wheel; he'd wag his finger: 'Not drivin' officer, just sleeping it off.' So we'd take him home and often have a drink together. I was fond of the old boy, but he was an old soak really.'

Anna took out the photograph of Louise Pennel. 'Did you ever see the granddaughter, Louise Pennel?'

'No, never met her. I knew the son, Raymond; he was a sad case. Florence doted on him. We gave him a slap on the wrist when he was caught down by the sea front, cottaging by the gents' toilets. He was warned not to be seen there again; he was, quite a few times, but his mother always pulled strings. She worshipped the ground he walked on.'

'He was gay?'

'Yes; he knew from a very early age.'

'But he married a local girl, didn't he?'

DS White smiled. 'He did. I can't recall her name, but I knew she'd got a bit of a reputation for putting it about. Mrs Pennel called us in once: there was all hell let loose. She was screaming and smashing things up; she wanted us to help her talk sense into her son, wailing and throwing her arms around. Nothing we could do but try and calm her down. I'd got fond of the family, so would help out when I could. A few nights later, I got called out again: she claimed some of her jewellery had been stolen and a silver tea service had gone missing. Turned out Raymond had packed it into a suitcase and gone off with this girl.'

'Did she press charges?'

'No. I never saw her again until years later when Raymond was buried; died of a burst appendix. Apparently he was broke, living in some rented place, with the same drink problem as his father. Mrs Pennel got his body brought home and as far as I recall, his wife never came to the funeral.'

'Do you know what happened to the wife and to Mrs Pennel's granddaughter?'

He nodded. 'Again, I can't be exactly sure of the dates, but about four or five years later, I was told that Raymond's wife had died of cancer. One of her mother's relatives had contacted Mrs Pennel to see if she could take the little girl but apparently she refused, so she went into a children's home; must have been about eleven years old. Sad, isn't it? All that money and that big house and she wouldn't have anything to do with her, and now: tragic. What a waste.'

'Yes,' Anna said, declining to enlighten DS White as to just how tragic Louise's death had been.

Returning to London on the train, Anna felt depressed. Fitting Louise Pennel's background together had not exactly taken the enquiry a stage further. There was one thing that might bring a result: the advert that Louise had answered: they might get lucky and be able to trace a link to their suspect. It was imperative that they discover which paper or magazine Louise had read the advert in. All Anna knew was that Louise was to have a job interview sometime after 16 May. Was that when Louise had met her killer?

Anna sighed. Despite all their modern technology they were, as with the original Elizabeth Short murder, grasping at straws. Sixty years between, and yet they had so far been unable to use any of their scientific expertise to unlock the pitiful clues they had acquired to date. Anna leaned back and dialled the Incident Room on her mobile. She spoke briefly to Barolli to see if he could start running a check on the newspaper ads that Louise might have answered. She suggested they first try *Time Out*, as she knew that was where Louise had read Sharon's advert. She got quite an earful from the frazzled detective as he had had yet another fruitless day's work trying to find previous employers of Louise but, nevertheless, he said they would get onto it a.s.a.p.

She felt confident that the advert, if it was traced, might just be the clue that would break the case. Reassured that it had not been an entirely wasted journey, Anna gave a small satisfied smile: the dinner that evening might just be the cream.

Chapter Six

It was eight-fifteen. Dick Reynolds had said he would collect Anna at eight, so he was late. Anna had hesitated about giving him her home address: it was not really professional, but then again, nor was her eagerness to see him on a personal level. She was wearing a white cashmere pullover she had bought in the sales, black trousers and boots. She had washed and blow-dried her hair and taken more time and care over her make-up than her usual quick powder and bit of mascara required. She opened a bottle of Chablis and left it in the fridge. She wandered around her small flat, adjusting cushions and fiddling with the stereo. It was almost eight-thirty when her doorbell rang.

'Hi, I'm parked out front, so shall we just go straight out?'

Anna hesitated; the wine, low lighting and softly playing CD were about to go to waste.

'There's a nice Italian round the corner; I popped in and they have a table.'

'Oh that'll be Ricardo's. I don't know if it's any good, I've not eaten there.'

'Well, it's always useful to test out your local restaurants,' Dick said, as he jangled his keys impatiently.

'Do you own this or is it rented?' he asked as she locked the door behind them.

'I own it.'

He crossed the road to a badly parked green Morgan sports car. She had to bend low to get into the passenger seat. He waited before slamming her door and hurrying round to the driver's side.

The engine roared as it kicked into start, and he grinned, shouting, 'Needs a bit of tuning, but I've not had the time. You hungry?'

'Yes, I am. I spent most of the day in Bognor Regis.'

'Nothing like sea air to work up an appetite.'

He drove down the road like a lunatic and without fastening his seat belt; the one on her side was broken. She tried not to appear nervous as they screeched up to the restaurant.

They had a very nice table at a booth, with no other table too close. He immediately buried himself in the menu and then tossed it aside.

'Red or white?'

'Erm . . . red please.'

He swivelled round to signal to a waiter, as Anna took off her coat. 'Bottle of merlot and I'll have cannelloni to start and then veal marsala to follow. Anna?'

She had hardly had time to read the menu, let alone make a choice so, rather flustered, she ordered the specials at the waiter's suggestion.

The waiter brought the bottle of wine, uncorked it and poured out a small amount for Dick to taste; he wafted his hand not to bother. Anna watched as the waiter filled their glasses.

'To us; glad you could make it.'

She took a sip; he drained half his glass and then leaned back. 'I'll chill out in a minute. I was late because we had a sudden breakthrough on this missing kid story we've been headlining.'

He picked up his glass and stared into it, then drank again. 'They found his body in Highgate cemetery.'

'I'm sorry.'

'Yep. Stuffed into a half-dug grave.'

Anna winced. 'It's always hard to keep your distance emotionally when it's a child.'

'It's the peripheral things that go on that take it out of you. His poor mother was just in total shock. She couldn't speak, just sat there with these big wide eyes and tears streaming down her face. *Get her to talk about how she feels!* – my editor on the mobile – and I am looking at these tragic people. You don't need to get them to explain how they feel, you can see it.'

He broke some bread and slathered butter over it, then took such a huge mouthful he couldn't speak for a few moments.

'So, how's your case going?'

'Slowly. I actually wanted to ask your advice about something. How would I go about tracing an advert, placed about nine months ago?'

'Advert for what?'

'A job: a PA, with travel.'

Dick ruffled his hair. 'Which paper?'

'I don't know.'

'Well, it won't be easy; there must be thousands of jobs advertised: *Times, Time Out, Evening Standard.* They're all computerised, but if that's all you've got to go on, it'll take someone a lot of . . .' He mimed

87

holding a telephone to his ear. 'Unless you know more?'

'I think it's put in by a male.'

He grinned. 'Do you have the exact date?'

'It would have been around the sixteenth of May last year.'

Dick looked around for the waiter. 'Be like looking for a needle in a haystack. What's so important about it?'

Anna hesitated and then shrugged. 'Maybe a link, maybe not.'

'Link to what?'

Again she hesitated, not wanting to say too much. In fact, she shouldn't have been talking about it all. 'Oh, something that was said. It'll probably mean nothing.'

He finished his glass of wine. 'You mean you won't tell me,' he said, not unkindly.

'Yes,' she smiled.

'Look, Anna, we're having a friendly dinner. I've not come here with you to pump you for any information. I know it wouldn't be ethical, okay? But you have no need to worry about anything you might be telling me being used against you. M'Lud.'

Anna grinned as the waiter topped up their glasses; again, Dick drank half the glass in one go.

'I don't suppose you have had any more anonymous letters?' she said.

'Nope, and your boss man – Langton, is it? – gave us stern warnings that if we did, we go straight to him first. Do you think my note was from the killer?'

'Possibly.'

'God, there are some sick people around. Let's change the subject: tell me about you.'

Anna sipped her wine. 'I'm a detective inspector, so I can be attached to any murder team that requires an officer of my capabilities! That's a joke. I'm still very raw around the edges.'

'Really?' He had the most amazing, penetrating blue eyes. 'So, are you married?'

'Good heavens, no! Otherwise I wouldn't have agreed to have dinner with you.'

'What about a partner?'

'No, there's no one. What about you?' She leaned forwards.

'Me? Unmarried these days; we broke up about a year ago. She's living in Spain with a karate instructor; actually, one I introduced her to.'

'Do you have children?'

'She had a parrot, but her mother took it.'

At that moment, the waiter appeared with their starters. Dick had become much less hyper, and she was starting to enjoy his company. He was very open and witty, and had her laughing over a story about when he first started as a journalist. By the time their main course had been served, they were chatting about all and sundry; in fact, they ended up talking about their different relationships with their fathers. Dick had been very much a black sheep: his father a doctor and man of letters, his mother a very educated linguist. They had wanted him to follow in his father's footsteps, but instead he had left university and gone into journalism; however, his elder sister was now a qualified doctor. It was not until he was talking about her that he referred back to the Louise Pennel case.

'Do you think your killer would have had medical

training? I know we've been asked to put a press embargo on the grisly details, not that we've been given much, but I looked up the Elizabeth Short murder on the internet. Mind-blowing; shocking to think they never caught the guy.'

Anna tensed up, suddenly nervous. She didn't reply, giving just a small shrug of her shoulders.

He twisted the stem of his glass between his fingers. 'So if this Louise Pennel case is similar, it kind of makes the hair stand on end. Dismembering her like that had to have been done by someone with surgical experience or, at the very least, someone with medical training. It's not easy to cut someone in two and drain their blood; well, it isn't according to my sister.'

Anna was just about to reiterate the fact that she could not discuss the case when DCI Langton walked into the restaurant, accompanied by Professor Marshe. It was not that much of a coincidence as Langton didn't live too far away, but seeing him made her blush. She watched him talking intently to Professor Marshe as the maitre d' led them to the table virtually opposite theirs.

Dick turned to see where she was looking and then looked back. 'What's up?'

'It's my boss; he's with a profiler that has been brought in from the States.'

Langton was waiting for Professor Marshe to sit down when he noticed Anna. He hesitated and then approached. 'Hi, surprise; not really I suppose, as this is your local. I've not been here before,' he said, quite affably.

'Nor me. This is Richard Reynolds.'

Dick turned, half-rising. 'Dick Reynolds, nice to meet you.'

Langton gave a tight nod; he recognised the name, but said nothing. 'Enjoy your dinner.' He gave a cold smile and headed back to his table.

Though Langton sat with his back to Anna, she still felt very self-conscious. Dick leaned across the table. 'Why don't we have coffee back at your place?'

Anna was still feeling uneasy when they walked up to her flat. Dick looked at his watch. 'Listen, I have to be up at the crack of dawn; maybe leave coffee until another time?'

'Whatever,' she said, opening her front door.

'Okay, well, I'll call you,' he said, hovering.

'I'd like that. Thank you for dinner.'

'My pleasure.' He leaned forwards and kissed her cheek. He stepped back and looked at her with his head cocked to one side. 'Are you okay?'

'I'd just have preferred not to have been clocked by my boss.'

'Why?'

'Well, he's very . . . I don't know, forget it.'

'If you need any help trying to track down that advert, just give me a ring; maybe I can call in a few favours for you.'

'Thank you, I will. Goodnight.'

Dick gave her a lovely smile and then was gone. She shut the door and leaned against it. Why had it rattled her so, seeing Langton? Was it just seeing him, or was it the way he was behaving with Professor Marshe? And exactly how was he behaving? she asked herself sharply;

well, truth was that he was being courteous. He had looked very smart; handsome, if she was being honest. There had been no one else since she had ended their affair until Dick Reynolds, but she was unsure how that would work out. She wasn't even sure if he felt anything towards her. It hadn't appeared as if he had fancied her; moreover, did she fancy him? Though Langton had wanted to continue seeing her after the Alan Daniels case, she had not wanted to jeopardise her career; she felt that, as a very junior officer, it would have become common gossip. She was now wondering, however, if she should have let the relationship run its course . . .

DAY TWELVE

Langton leaned back in his chair. 'Let me get this straight; you want to check every advert for a PA from nine months ago, but you don't know which newspaper or magazine she might have seen it in? And just how many people do you think I can free up to do this?'

'It's a long shot, I know,' she said, sheepishly.

'*Long?* It's the bloody M1 motorway, Travis! For Chrissakes, see if you can at the very least narrow it down to a couple of possible papers; go back to the dentist, back to that silly cow Sharon – we can't get stuck tracking down every fucking advert for a PA!'

'Yes sir.'

'That journalist you were with last night?'

'Yes?'

'I hope he wasn't pumping you for information.'

'No, he's just an old friend,' she lied.

'Really. Well, keep your mouth shut around him; when

we want the press involved, we will rope them in. Don't
go spilling any beans they are not supposed to be privy
to.'

'I wouldn't do that.'

'Good, I hope not. So how old a friend is he?'

'Oh, we've known each other for quite a while.' The
fib made her blush and she was unable to meet his eyes.

He looked at her, then gave a tight, unfriendly smile.
'They're all the same as far as I'm concerned: I hate
them; they're like leeches, sucking on blood. You watch
what you say to him.'

'I will; thank you for the advice.'

'And don't you be shirty with me, Travis!'

'I wasn't aware that I was!'

He laughed and wafted his hand for her to leave his
office. He flicked open her lengthy report on her day
at Bognor Regis.

There had been no further press reports about the
case; if, as Professor Marshe had suggested, their killer
would be eager to read about their lack of progress, he
would not have been getting any satisfaction. He was
not alone: the rest of the team were still not making
any headway. Checking out every doctor in the area past
and present, paying particular attention to any allegations of malpractice, was time-consuming and, to date,
had yielded no result.

Langton slammed out of his office and paused as he
passed Anna's desk.

'Do you make a habit of retaining local taxis to chauffeur you around? The Bognor Regis taxi receipt is ridiculous. Why didn't you get in touch with the local cop
shop and use one of their patrol cars?'

'I'm sorry. I didn't expect to be at Mrs Pennel's for so long.'

'You have to anticipate these kind of things, Travis: we're not a bloody charity!'

He took up his usual position at the front of the room for a briefing. He was surly and had his hands stuffed into his trouser pockets as he paced up and down.

'I had another meet with Professor Marshe; we discussed our mystery man, the tall dark stranger we have so far been unable to trace. His description matches the killer of Elizabeth Short. This is what the LA homicide reckoned their suspect looked like.'

Langton turned over a blank page on the big drawing board to reveal a drawing of the Los Angeles suspect, drawn in 1947.

'The only description we have of our killer is from Sharon, so let's see how we match up. It could, at a pinch, be the same man: long dark coat, collar turned up; tall, about six feet; dark, close-cropped hair, a touch of grey at the temples. Our guy has no moustache, but he might have grown one if he's as obsessed with copy-catting the Elizabeth Short case as we think he is. We can put this drawing out alongside a request for anyone with any information about him to come forward.'

Anna's desk phone rang; it was Dick Reynolds. She was irritated that he had called her at work until he said, 'I've just had a phone call; I think it was your killer.'

Anna sat bolt upright. 'What?'

'I've just got off the phone; he called the crime desk and asked to speak to me.'

'Did you tape it?'

'Of course.'

'Oh my God, can you bring it to us?'

'Can't you come to me?'

'Hold on.'

Anna put up her hand and Langton, who had continued discussing the drawings, looked over to her, visibly displeased at the interruption.

'Yes?'

'The crime desk at the *Sun* just had a call they think is from the killer.'

Langton almost jumped along the desks to snatch the phone. 'Who am I speaking to?'

'Richard Reynolds.'

Langton took a moment to steady himself. 'Mr Reynolds, I would be most grateful if you could bring over the tape of the call immediately.' Langton listened for another few moments, and then nodded. 'Thank you.' He replaced the receiver and looked to Anna. 'He's coming in directly.'

Langton then looked to the team. 'Professor Marshe was right. Our killer just made verbal contact with the press.'

Twenty-five minutes later, Dick Reynolds was ushered into Langton's office. Lewis, Barolli and Anna were there waiting.

Reynolds took a miniature cassette from one pocket and then, from the other, a small tape recorder with an attachment for plugging into a telephone.

'I've not made copies because I don't have another tape this size. It was lucky I'd got this in my desk drawer. I did miss a section as I was plugging it in.'

Langton gestured for Lewis to insert the tape into

the machine. Reynolds was introduced to Lewis and
Barolli.

'You know Anna Travis.'

Reynolds smiled at Anna who smiled back politely.

'So what happened was, I was at the crime desk and
the call was transferred from the switchboard. It came
straight to me as I was the only person there at the time.
That machine's a bit old and dodgy, so some of his
dialogue isn't that clear.'

'Right,' Langton said, pressing Start. There were a few
moments of silence.

The voice was crisp and to the point.

'*Well Mr Reynolds, I congratulate you on what your newspaper has done on the Red Dahlia case.*'

'*Er, thank you.*'

'*But you seem to have gone silent on it; have you run out
of material?*'

'*You could say that.*'

'*Maybe I can be of some assistance.*' *This was muffled, with
a lot of crackling.*

'*Well we need it, or the police do.*'

'*I'll tell you what I'll do. I'll send you some of Louise
Pennel's things that she had with her when she, shall we say,
disappeared.*'

'*When will I get them?*'

'*Oh, within the next day or so. See how far you can get
with them. Now I have to say goodbye. You may be trying to
trace the call.*'

'*Wait a minute—*'

The phone clicked dead. Langton rubbed his head,
and gestured for the call to be replayed. It was, three
times. Everyone listened in silence.

'Thank you for bringing this in to us, Mr Reynolds,' Langton said and ejected the tape. 'You said you had not made a copy.'

'No. But it must be obvious that I'd like one.'

'I have to ask that you do nothing with this. I do not want this call to be made public until I give you permission.'

'Hang on a second—'

'Mr Reynolds, this is very serious. I do not want the contents of this call printed in your paper or used for any other reason. We will need to have it sent over to the lab and see what they make of it. It will be vital evidence if the killer is arrested, as we will be able to do a voice match.'

Anna went over to her desk to double-check the contacts made by the original Black Dahlia killer, and then returned to Langton's office. She passed over her memo, comparing his original call to the one that Reynolds had received. It was almost word for word.

'I know,' Langton said, quietly.

'So what do we do now?' she asked.

'Exactly what I said: we get the lab to test and see what they can give us. The journalist in the LA case didn't tape the call, so at least we are making some fucking progress. Also, if he has her belongings, he will send them to your friend. The original killer did, didn't he?'

'Yes, he sent the contents of her handbag.'

Langton drummed his fingers on his desk. 'Christ Almighty, this is unbelievable, isn't it?'

She said nothing.

'I hope to God he doesn't play silly buggers and go

to print on it, especially after talking with Professor Marshe; she was very sure that if we kept no publicity the killer would make contact. She's been right so far.'

'Yes, you said,' Anna felt irritated. 'I'm sure Mr Reynolds won't do anything that would harm the investigation.'

'We have to make bloody sure he doesn't,' Langton snapped.

The tape was treated and tested. It did not appear that the caller had been trying to disguise his voice. The lab determined that it was a middle-aged man, well spoken and well educated, with a distinct aristocratic tone, exuding confidence. They felt it would be problematic to try to match it because of the muffled and often indistinct sound. There was no distinctive background noise that would help to pinpoint a probable location but, given time, they could strip the tape down to get more information.

Langton sighed with frustration. He had smoked throughout the briefing. 'Right, outcome: despite the portrayals by the media and the entertainment industry, there are serious limitations for the experts. They seriously doubt being able to identify taped voices; it's looking not very positive.'

There was a unanimous moan.

'I know, I know, but we only have a minute's worth and they need more. They kept on saying that this type of phonetic analysis is very time-consuming; it requires painstaking preparation of speech samples and close observation of their acoustic and other characteristics. So, in the meantime, we stick our thumbs up our arses because it could take weeks. To match an unknown taped voice with another — should we be so lucky to bloody get one — is not a matter of simply making voiceprints which can be compared in the same way as fingerprints. They reject this in court as evidence, because it can create an erroneous picture in people's minds: so, in other words, the chaps at the lab are dicking around trying to bring us something, so that if — if! — we do get a friggin' suspect, we might be able to match it. But this would only give us a lead; nothing more conclusive.'

Disappointed, the team had little to do but continue covering old ground. There was nothing new to work on apart from trying to trace the advert Louise Pennel might have answered. They had so far been unsuccessful, despite contacting virtually every newspaper and magazine, not helped by the fact that they did not know the exact wording; all they could do was to check out anyone advertising for a PA on or around 16 May.

That night Anna couldn't sleep; the call to Reynolds kept on replaying in her mind. They all knew that they were clutching at straws, but she couldn't shake the feeling that this latest contact had to be significant.

DAY THIRTEEN

The next morning, Anna called Sharon and asked if she would be available to meet. She was evasive and said she had an appointment at nine-fifteen, but would more than likely be at home beforehand.

Anna was outside her flat by nine but when she rang

the doorbell, she got no reply. Frustrated, she kept her hand on the bell, but Sharon did not appear. She was just turning away when the door opened.

'She's not in.'

The woman was wearing a tweed skirt and pink twinset with a string of pearls. 'She left about five minutes ago.'

Anna showed her ID and asked who she was speaking to.

'I'm Coral Jenkins; I live on the ground floor.'

'Ah yes, you must be the landlady.'

'Yes; I did get a note to say someone from the police wished to talk to me, but I've been away at my sister's; she's been ill.'

'That was from me. I am DI Anna Travis.'

'I know what it's about. Sharon told me what had happened to her flatmate; it was a shock, not that I knew her. Do you want to come in? I can talk to you now: I don't go to work until eleven today.'

Anna was led into the ground-floor flat which was crammed with antique furniture.

Mrs Jenkins noticed Anna looking round. 'I run an antique stall in Alfie's Market over in Paddington.'

Anna smiled. 'I can tell you have some lovely pieces.'

'I had a lot more, but I had a very unpleasant divorce. I used to live over in St John's Wood but I had to sell the house to pay him off. It was a lump settlement, so I bought this place. It was already divided up into flats so I didn't have to do anything to it, and it's close to my work.'

The woman hardly draws breath, Anna thought. 'Mrs Jenkins, you say Sharon told you about Louise Pennel?'

'Oh yes, terrible, just terrible. I wasn't here, you see. My sister was ill so I had to go to Bradford, just after it happened, I think. Of course I read about it in the papers but I didn't recognise her from the photograph. I didn't pay it much attention, so many terrible things happen.'

Anna interrupted. 'Mrs Jenkins, did you ever see anyone with Louise?'

'I didn't really know her. I know she lived in the top flat. I only allow two to share up there: it's very small.'

'I know you don't allow visitors to stay.'

'House rule: they know when they move in. Reason is, these young girls get a steady boyfriend and the next minute, they've moved them in as well! So, I make it very obvious from the start: no overnight boyfriend full stop. If they want to do whatever they do, they can go and stay with them. Sharon has a new girl renting with her, and I told her straight away—'

'Mrs Jenkins!' Anna was now impatient. 'Did you ever see Louise Pennel with a man friend?'

'He rang the wrong bell once; quite a while back when she had just moved in, and so I answered the door.'

'So you did see a man with Louise?'

'No dear, I said I never saw them together. I saw him, just the once. He rang my bell by mistake, so I answered the door.' Mrs Jenkins got up and crossed to the window. 'I have a clear view of the road outside, but you can't see someone if they're standing close to the front door.'

Anna could feel her heart pounding. 'Can you describe this man?'

'I had no more than two words with him. I didn't

think it was a boyfriend, to be honest; he might have been a relative.'

'What did he look like?'

'Oh, now you're asking; well, he was tall, maybe six foot, slim build, very well dressed, very refined voice. He had on a long dark coat, I remember that, but I doubt if I'd recognise him again. He called here for her a couple of times; never rang my bell again though. He used to ring her bell and then go back to his car.'

'What make of car was it?'

'Oh I don't know. It was black, very polished, but I don't know the make of it; nowadays the expensive ones all look alike to me, but it could have been a Mercedes or a BMW.'

Anna opened her briefcase and brought out the sketch of the suspect wanted in the Black Dahlia case. 'Did he look like this?'

Mrs Jenkins stared at the drawing, then frowned. 'I don't think he had a moustache, but yes, sort of thin-faced and with that hooked nose, but still good-looking.'

'When was the last time you saw him?'

'It would have been the day before I left for Bradford, so the eighth of January. He rang their bell. I looked out of the window, saw it was him and then heard her running down the stairs. She slammed the front door, a bit too hard for my liking, and went across the road and got into his car.'

'What time was this?'

'It was about nine-thirty; it was dark. They drove off.'

'Thank you. You have been very helpful. I really appreciate your time. If there is anything else you can recall, I would be most grateful if you would contact me.'

Anna sat in her car and called the Incident Room to relay what Mrs Jenkins had told her. As she finished her call, she saw Sharon hurrying along the road with a carton of milk and got out of her Mini. Sharon could not help but see her.

'Sorry, they cancelled the audition, but we was out of milk so I went to the shop.'

As Anna followed Sharon into the house, she saw the curtains at Mrs Jenkins's ground-floor window flick open and then close.

Sharon sat opposite Anna.

'The night before you went to Stringfellow's with Louise, were you at home?'

'No. I went to see a friend and I bought a dress from her.'

'So you wouldn't know if Louise had a date that night?'

'Not really; she was in when I got back. She was making herself a cup of tea and I showed her my dress. She was upset about something.'

'Do you know what she was upset about?'

'She'd been crying but she didn't say why; just went into her room and shut the door.'

Sharon leaned closer. 'I've got a new flatmate. She's very nice and I've not mentioned anything about Louise or what happened to her; well, she is sleeping in her bed.'

'I understand,' Anna said, without meaning it. 'Can you just run over the night you went to Stringfellow's with Louise?'

'I've told you all about it.'

'Yes, I know. Did you often go out together?'

'No.'

103

'So this night was unusual?'

'Yeah, I suppose so. She asked where I was going, so I told her and she said she'd like to come along, we'd been there a couple of times before, but not on a regular basis. I've been through all this, you know. Me and Louise were not close friends or anything like that; she didn't talk about herself that much.'

'Not even about this man she was seeing?'

'No, you asked me that before.'

'But you mentioned that you thought he was married.'

'Only because of the way she acted, you know, very secretive; she never even told me his name, so I sort of presumed it was because he was older than her.'

'So you saw him?'

'No, but she said he didn't like her wearing short skirts or skimpy tops; she once said he liked her to look very demure.'

'So on the night you went to Stringfellow's, how did she dress?'

Sharon shrugged. 'She had on her maroon coat, a black dress and high-heeled shoes. She looked nice.'

'Not demure?'

'No, she could look very sexy if she wanted to.'

'Did you think she was meeting someone at the club?'

'I don't think so. When we got there, it was heaving. I knew a few people so she hung around with me till I went off dancing. Then I met up with this guy I knew. I went looking for her, to tell her I was going, but I couldn't find her.'

'She didn't mention that she was meeting this older boyfriend there?'

104

'No, but maybe she knew he would be there.' Sharon leaned back and frowned. 'You know, thinking about it, she was sort of angry, like she wanted to have a good time to prove something. She spent ages doing her hair, changed her dress a couple of times, kept on asking me what I thought.'

Sharon frowned again. Anna could, as usual, almost see the wheels turning in her brain; then Sharon clicked her fingers. 'I just remembered something. She was standing in the doorway there, hands on hips, and she laughed. Yes! Yes! I remember now: she said, He won't recognise me!'

Anna said nothing.

Sharon patted the table with the flat of her hand. 'That would mean she was expecting to see him there, don't you think? And if he'd had this fight with her, and if he always wanted her to dress like a virgin and she was dressing in the exact opposite way to piss him off, then she was gonna see him!'

'Thank you, Sharon, that's very helpful; and should you remember anything else, no matter how small or inconsequential, please call me direct.'

Anna headed down the stairs to the front door. Mrs Jenkins came out of her flat.

'I've been waiting for you. I've been sitting thinking about everything you asked me.'

Anna waited.

'When I opened the door to him, the man you asked me about, I didn't see his face that clearly, but I remember that on his left hand, little finger, he had a large signet ring. I think it had a cornelian stone; it was quite large. His hand was up and covering his face, you see: that's why I saw it!'

Lynda La Plante

Anna smiled. 'Thank you, that's very helpful.'

Mrs Jenkins beamed, and then folded her arms. 'And there's something else: you remember I said I couldn't remember what make of car he was driving?'

'Yes?' Anna was eager now.

'Well, you should ask the owner of the dry cleaner's across the road, because I saw him bending down to look into the car as it was in the residents' parking bay, so he might be able to tell you more.'

Anna smiled; this was good.

Anna made it back to the Incident Room in time for Langton's update. She listened as Barolli gave details of the mass of CCTV footage that they were checking over from the nightclub. They usually recorded over the tapes covering the outside of the club, but there was extensive footage from the interior security camera. After much persuasion, they had been sent the tapes for the night in question, when there had been a lot of star guests. Barolli said they had not as yet seen any footage of Louise, but they were hopeful.

DI Lewis was next up. He had the report from the forensic lab. They had finished work on the underwear taken from Louise's laundry basket. They had found two different DNA samples, so they would have to request samples from friends and acquaintances and start running them through the database.

Anna gave details of her morning at Sharon's and her disappointment that the dry cleaning shop owner had been unable to give any further details about the car. He said that most nights, there was someone or other parked illegally; it was an ongoing frustration to

106

the residents that there were never enough parking spaces.

It was a depressing briefing, because no matter how much work they were all doing, they were making no progress. Langton reiterated that all weekend leave was cancelled. He was determined to push the case forward.

DAY FOURTEEN

It was eleven-fifteen on Saturday morning when Dick Reynolds called the Incident Room to speak to Langton directly.

'Travis, with me; your boyfriend's got a delivery.'

A package had arrived; as per his instructions, Reynolds had not opened it but had placed it into a plastic bag. They travelled across London to the news-paper offices at breakneck speed, sirens wailing. Reynolds was loath to part with it and said that it might possibly be something for him personally.

Langton snapped at him, holding his hand out. 'We'll let you know, Mr Reynolds, but I am afraid you will have to wait to hear what the contents are.'

'No way. I am keeping my end of the bargain; if you don't want this released, then you take me with you.'

Langton stared at him, then jerked his head towards the patrol car where Anna sat in the back passenger seat. 'Get in! And, Mr Reynolds, there is no deal, no bargain; I'm doing this to keep you from making an ass of your-self, because this is a murder enquiry, not some fucking reality TV show. You have agreed to a press embargo along with all the other journalists; you break it and I'll have you served with a warrant.'

Reynolds held the plastic bag gingerly on his knee. He gave a sly glance to Anna who didn't respond, knowing full well that they couldn't actually serve a warrant on him; Langton was just putting the frighteners on. No one spoke as they sped across London to the forensic lab.

Langton asked how long would they need to wait; one of the white-coated scientists told them that it would be done as fast as possible.

Anna sat beside Reynolds, Langton in a chair opposite.

'Like a doctor's waiting room.' Dick smiled.

Langton glanced at him, not amused. His mobile rang and he moved away to take the call in private.

'Pleasant bugger, isn't he?' Reynolds said quietly.

'He's okay, just under a lot of strain,' Anna said.

'Aren't we all? My editor went apeshit when I told her what was going down; if she'd had her way, she'd have ripped open the package to see what was inside.'

'Really?' Anna glanced towards Langton who was some distance away with his shoulders hunched, leaning against a wall.

'Well, for Chrissakes, it's a blinding story, for starters; mind you, it could just be something not connected to your case at all.'

'It would be too coincidental. Your caller said he would be sending a package, next minute you get one.'

Anna checked her watch, Dick leaned towards her. 'How long do we have to wait?'

'They'll be checking everything; it might have fingerprints.'

'Interesting; plus the postmark might be useful.'

'I doubt he'll leave anything we can trace, but that's just my opinion.'

He stared at her. 'Are you okay?'

'Yes.'

'Just, you seem a bit distant with me?'

She smiled. Truth was, she felt slightly awkward. 'Working,' she said.

'You free for dinner this week?'

'I'll have to check my schedule; I may be on nights.'

'Ah, I thought you meant your social calendar.'

She laughed. 'No, I'm not doing anything; maybe you'd like me to cook us dinner one night?'

'That would be good; why don't we say this weekend?'

'I might have to work.'

'Well, call me.'

Langton came back and sat down. He, too, checked his watch.

'While we're here, we should check on the work they have been doing on her clothes,' he said, his foot tapping up and down.

'What clothes?' Reynolds asked.

Langton ignored him. Anna hesitated. 'We took items belonging to the victim for analysis.'

'Oh right: DNA, stuff like that,' Reynolds said. He couldn't think of anything to make conversation with so he took out his mobile and began checking his messages.

Langton glared at him, and then at Anna.

They all turned to the double doors as they swung open and Professor Marshe hurried towards them. Anna was taken aback; the woman certainly loved making an entrance.

'James, I'm sorry; I got here as soon as I could. I can't stay too long: I am on my way to give a lecture.'

Langton rose to his feet and greeted her with a kiss on her cheek; he then introduced her to Reynolds, who stood up to shake her hand. Anna remained seated as Professor Marshe smiled at her. 'Nice to see you again, Hannah.'

Anna smiled, not bothering to correct her. Professor Marshe was wearing another tailored suit and high-heeled shoes. Anna would have loved to be able to wear similarly chic and expensive clothes, but she was nowhere near as tall and slender as Professor Marshe. Anna wished she'd worn something less dowdy and folded her legs to disguise her low-heeled scuffed court shoes.

The door to the lab opened, and Liz Hudson, the forensic scientist, gestured to them from the doorway.

'We're by no means through, but you can come in and see what we've got for you.'

Hudson led them to a table at the end of the lab, covered with white paper tacked down at the sides. Spread out, already dusted for prints and neatly numbered, were the contents of the package. There was a black leather clutch bag, with a suede flower motif and a tasselled zip. Laid out beside the bag were a cheap powder compact, two lipsticks, a small mirror, a used tissue with lipstick marks, and a black leather address book.

Anna noticed that Langton lightly touched Professor Marshe's arm as she leaned closer and guessed that she had been the one calling his mobile earlier.

'Can I just say,' said Hudson, 'before we examine the purse etcetera, that everything here would have been carefully chosen by your suspect. If there was anything that could be of use to us, he would have discarded it. This is him playing out how clever he is.'

Anna nodded, although she had already guessed that. She was impatient to get hold of the address book, but none of them touched anything.

Hudson continued. 'The bag is good quality, but old; perhaps bought from a charity shop. It's got a residue of loose powder in one of the pockets. It also smells of an old-fashioned perfume called Chepre. My grand-mother used to wear it; it's no longer in production. Another thing that makes the bag old is that the label inside is Chanel and I doubt if your girl would have bought this new. The lining is very worn, as is the suede inlay.'

They all moved a few inches down the table, staring intently at the items.

'Next the powder compact, Boots Number Seven; there is no powder puff, perhaps because we might have been able to get a skin test. The lipstick is a pink gloss and has been wiped; you can see by the head of the lipstick it has scrape marks. We have no prints off either. The second lipstick is Helena Rubenstein; it is a very deep red, not a common choice for a young girl. Oddly enough, it has not been used. It's also not sold any more, like the perfume.'

Anna made copious notes as she listened, then looked up as Hudson pointed to the address book.

'You will be able to take this as it's been dusted. There are pages torn out, there're numerous different inks and biro and the entries are in no specific order. Also, the pages are torn out in pairs. We had hoped that we might have been able to see an imprint of what had been written if the writer had pressed hard, but this means we will not be able to decipher anything.'

'We'll need that,' Langton said, and Hudson nodded.

'Not a lot, but you do at least have your victim's name printed in the front of the address book, so we are to presume that these items did belong to her.'

They moved further along the table to the brown paper that had been used to wrap the parcel.

'There is a smudged postmark; we are trying to get you something from it, but it is very faint, and we have so far found two sets of prints.'

'They could be mine,' Reynolds said.

'We'll need to take yours so we can eliminate them.'

'Plus there might be prints from the receptionist that brought it up to my desk.'

Hudson nodded. 'I would say whoever wrapped it used gloves, as there are no smudges. The adhesive tape is of a very common variety; we are going to see if, when we lift it off, there may be something beneath, but I doubt it. We have the time it was posted – six-thirty – and we think it was from the main post office at Charing Cross. It's a very busy central office, so I doubt if anyone saw the sender, or could remember him; there is also the possibility he used someone else to post it. Now we get to the note inside the package.'

Like schoolkids at the Natural History Museum, they moved along to the end of the table.

HeRe ArE tHe Red DaHLia's belOnGingS.
LettEr tO fOlloW.

'The note is made up from letters cut from newspapers: no prints, so I am afraid it gives us nothing. The notepaper is very common and sells in bulk.'

While Reynolds was taken to have his fingerprints done, the others moved to another table in a section of the lab where a young scientist with sprouting black hair and thick glasses was waiting. Before him lay Louise's clothes and underwear taken from her wardrobe and laundry basket, divided into two sections: the very expensive lace thongs and matching bras in pale pinks and greens, and the well-worn, cheap underwear, greyish in colour.

'We split them up because it seems to us that the lady wore the more tasteful items on special occasions, so perhaps took better care of them. We have some body fluids on the thongs but no semen. However, the stains on the other selection are menstrual and identified as belonging to your victim, as are the pubic hairs. We have two different semen stains, but we are unable to ascertain when they were deposited. They can still be visible even after washing, but I doubt this section has been washed recently.'

They moved along the table to see a few more items: a white blouse that was stained beneath the armpits and a petticoat and a nightdress. It was as depressing as seeing the tired contents of Louise's handbag. Anna was relieved when Langton suggested they return to the station.

Langton was impatient to get back to the Incident Room to begin checking over Louise's address book. From the patrol car window, Anna watched him thank Professor

Marshe, who had remained silent throughout, kissing her on the cheek and helping her into the chauffeur-driven Mercedes that was waiting for her in the lab's car park. He slammed into the front passenger seat. 'She'll give us an update on what we looked at in the lab, either this evening or in the morning.'

Anna would have liked to say something sarcastic: to date, the glamorous Professor Marshe had given little or no insight into their killer that they hadn't all pieced together themselves; however, she kept quiet. Langton flicked through the small address book in moody silence. Anna stared out of the window, thinking about a girl she had once shared a room with at training college who had always looked very respectable but was, in fact, far from it. Not only was she promiscuous, she had very distasteful habits. Whenever she was out of clean underwear, she just tipped her laundry upside down and wore whatever had been discarded first. Anna knew that for the past six months, when Louise had lived with Sharon, she had appeared to have only the one secret admirer: their one and only suspect so far. According to Sharon, Louise stayed in unless meeting the tall dark stranger. Had Louise led a very different life before? Anna leaned forwards in her seat.

'Gov, was Lewis checking out any previous boyfriends?'

'We've traced one: a student from the bed-and-break-fast hotel. He's in the clear, as he now lives in Scotland; another boy from the hostel was interviewed, but he works at a pub in Putney and had not seen Louise for eighteen months, but we've a shedload of other names we are still checking out, so we'll need another visit to the hostel and the B&B. The hotel is run by a Lebanese woman; she says Louise was hardly ever there. She wasn't very helpful.'

'Do you think the dentist or anyone from where she worked was seeing her?'

'Not as far as I know.'

'If we go on what we saw in the lab, maybe she had been putting it about more than we think.'

Langton shrugged. 'Two semen stains and grubby underwear does not give us much to go on.'

Anna rested back in her seat and got out her notebook. She spent the rest of the journey flicking back and forth. She remembered that, at her visit to Florence Pennel, the housekeeper had described Louise as looking scruffy with lank hair; she made a note to call Mrs Hughes when she got to the station.

Langton marched ahead of her as usual. She was expecting to have the door slammed in her face as usual, but he surprised her by waiting. 'What is ticking in that little head, Travis?'

'I'm sorry?'

'You always chew your lip, and you were buried in your notebook for fifteen minutes. What? Well, spit it out; what's got to you?'

Anna sat opposite Langton in his office, stirring her coffee.

'This suspect, the tall dark man; I think he puts an advert into the paper for a PA, making it a very inviting job to any applicant.'

'Yes yes, we've been through that. You or anyone else had any joy tracing this advert?'

'Not as yet, but we do have Louise, broke, working for a pittance at the dentist's, hating her job; she was always late and, according to one of the nurses there, often hungover.'

'Can you get to the point, Travis?' Langton snapped as he spooned sugar into his coffee. He then opened a drawer and took out a bottle of brandy, pouring a heavy measure into the cup.

'If we have a man wanting to do a copycat kill of the Black Dahlia, he could have used the advert to find the right girl. Louise Pennel, desperate, bored, broke and sexually permissive, wants to make a big impression; she even goes to visit her grandmother, who she's never met, to borrow money for some clothes to go to the appointment.'

'This is just you surmising.'

'I know, but hear me out; the point is—'

'I am, Travis; can you get to it?'

'The French underwear, the good clothes, she kept clean; so maybe this tall dark stranger had become a sort of Svengali. He's found the right victim: my God, she even chewed her nails like Elizabeth Short. He also had months to work on her; during that time she moves out of the hostel into a B&B and then Sharon's rented flat. The cashmere sweaters, the suit, the shoes: all expensive. It's like we have two women: one, the old Louise in her cheap and dirty used knickers, and the new model.'

Langton sighed, impatiently.

'We need to check where that underwear came from; in fact, check every expensive item Louise Pennel had in her wardrobe. Most important, we need to put more energy into tracking down that advert.' He was drumming his fingers on the desktop; however, she continued, defiantly. 'We do have a bit more to go on.'

'You mean that we now know he wore a ring on his pinky finger? That's a very big lead, Travis!'

He was beginning to really annoy her. 'Add it to the drawing, which got the result from the landlady. We have a tall dark-haired man; the ring might help us.'

'To do what exactly? If we put it in print, it might also tip him off to remove it!' Langton leaned back and lit a cigarette; he squinted at her as the smoke trailed from his lips. 'If we are to go with the copycat theory, then the next person our killer will contact will be me! After sending the package to the LA journalist, he then wrote to what they called the Examiner. In our case it will be me as I am heading up the enquiry, and the letter should be here tomorrow.'

Langton always surprised her. She hadn't realised that he was paying that much attention to the Black Dahlia copycat theory. There was a long pause as he inhaled deeply, and then wafted his hand to get rid of the cigarette smoke. She hesitated for a moment; he looked up and stared at her. 'What?'

'Do you think we should put out more press? Keeping silent has not really worked, has it? I mean, I know you are being guided by Professor Marshe, but this is not LA in 1947. We have far more chance of him entrapping himself if we give him enough rope. There's been nothing in the papers for days.'

Langton stubbed out his cigarette. 'You don't rate her, is that it?'

'I didn't say that. I just mean that the risk we are taking is that he might be forced into proving himself by killing again, simply because he has not been able to read about how clever he is.'

117

Lewis tapped and poked his head round the door.

'The address book; you want to come in and give us a rap on what you want us to do? We maybe need some more help if you want every address checked out.'

Lewis left the door open. As Langton left his desk and passed Anna, he swung it open wider. 'After you.'

Anna collected her briefcase and notebook. 'Thank you. Professor Marshe is obviously working on your social skills.'

'What?'

Anna scooted out ahead of him, pretending that she hadn't heard.

Pasted up along a board were the pages blown up from Louise Pennel's address book. The first page had her name in looped writing, like a child's. As they had been told at the lab, different pens had been used – sometimes a Biro, sometimes a felt-tip pen – other names and addresses were written in pencil and some even in a red crayon. They were not in alphabetical order, but jotted haphazardly. Some had been crossed out; others were scribbled over. They had also blown up the jagged edges where pages had been torn out from the back of the book; these would have been the most recent, and more than likely had the killer's name and address.

Questioning all those people listed would mean hours of legwork, tracing them and taking statements. A number of names and addresses would turn out to be obsolete, people having moved on elsewhere. Everyone would have their work cut out; it would be tedious and painstaking. Anna moved along the board, doubtful they would gain anything: she was certain the most relevant pages were the ones missing. After they had discussed who was doing what, a tetchy Langton drew up further instructions on how they should go about tracing the advert they believed their killer had placed. They had asked Sharon what papers Louise had read, but she couldn't recall ever having seen her with one. Langton suggested they check out the waiting room at the dental surgery where Louise had worked.

It felt like the killer was looking over their shoulders and laughing at their lack of results; however, by the end of the day they knew that Louise would often sit in the reception area of the dentist's and read the newspapers. The surgery only had *The Times* delivered, as the dentist read it himself. They had tracked down twenty-five per cent of the people whose names and addresses were in Louise Pennel's book, and the phones were hopping as the detectives prepared to meet every single one of them. Anna had also contacted Mrs Hughes, who agreed without hesitation that the clutch bag with the suede flower motif was the one she had given to Louise Pennel.

DAY FIFTEEN

Anna arrived at her desk the following morning to a flurry of excitement. It was obvious something was going down: the Commander was in with Langton.

He had received a postcard, sent care of the station. It was bagged immediately and sent over to the lab for them to check out. It was a mixture of handwriting and cut-out newspaper letters.

119

```
18 days. I Was haVinG My fuN witH the
MeTroPoliTan PoliCe, but noW GettinG very
Bored. Signed, the Red D AhliA AvEnger.
```

Barolli copied it out on the board in thick red letters; everyone knew there was pressure coming down on Langton. After ten minutes, the 'big noise' departed and Langton came out of his office. His five-o'clock shadow looked as dark as a beard; his tie was hanging loose and he had a cigarette stuck in the side of his mouth.

He didn't have to ask for quiet as he stood in front of the killer's message. He took a deep drag of the cigarette and stubbed it out in an old ashtray on the side of Lewis's desk.

'I have been instructed by the big shots to respond to this message. Professor Marshe also agrees that, as this maniac is attempting to copycat the killer of Elizabeth Short, we should now feed his ego and play his game. The killer of the Black Dahlia sent a virtually identical message to the LA Examiner. Against my own gut feeling, I am to give the following message in a press release.' Langton dug his hands deep into his pockets and recited without emotion, 'If you want to surrender, as indicated by your postcard, I will meet you at any public location at any time; please give details to the Incident Room at Richmond police station.'

Langton nodded to indicate the briefing was over and headed back into his office. He passed Anna and gave her a cold, dismissive look. She stood up.

'What are you looking at me like that for?'

'Talk to your fucking boyfriend.'

Langton slammed into his office. Anna had no idea

what he was talking about. She hurried over to DI Lewis. 'What's going on?'

Lewis shrugged. 'All I know is, the editor of your pal's newspaper has some very heavy-duty friends. The Gov gets the Commander on his back, and even with Professor Marshe batting for him, they've given him the order to go public and he doesn't like it.'

'It's nothing to do with me!'

Lewis turned away. 'Your boyfriend is going to break the story; be headlined this weekend.'

Anna returned to her desk. She sat for a moment and then packed her briefcase. She called Dick Reynolds and asked if she could cook dinner for him that evening. He said he would be there by eight. Neither of them mentioned anything about the Dahlia story. Anna went up to the duty sergeant and asked if it was okay for her to leave as she had a migraine. He looked at her and grinned.

'If you haven't got one, you will have. Is it true your boyfriend's the journalist Dick Reynolds?'

'He is not my boyfriend!'

Anna banged out of the Incident Room and sat in her car to cool down, then drove home, stopping on the way to buy some groceries. She had decided to make spaghetti bolognaise, nothing special; well, she had decided Mr Reynolds didn't warrant her best culinary offering. She would really like to wring his neck; he had now placed her in a very difficult situation, but it was one she was determined she would rectify, otherwise working alongside Langton would be impossible. Truth was, she had hardly ever thought of Langton over the past eighteen months, but when he had walked into the

Incident Room to take over the case, it was as if it was hours ago, not that he had ever acknowledged their history. Anna Travis was not the usual type that DCI James Langton was known to fall for. They were more like the long-legged Professor Marshe. He had a terrible reputation and she had not been prepared to be another notch on his belt, but that didn't mean she didn't still have feelings for him; she did, very strong ones, and it annoyed the hell out of her that she should be thinking of them.

'Christ,' she muttered to herself, as she dumped her shopping down on the draining board. 'I fucking hate him!'

As she chopped up the onions and began to make the spaghetti sauce, she calmed down. If Reynolds had used her to get more details of the case, this could prove embarrassing. She prepared the dinner, and then took a shower. She got into an old sweater and jeans and didn't even bother re-doing her make-up; she was getting ready to tear a strip off Reynolds.

'Thank Christ I didn't sleep with him,' she muttered, as she opened a cheap bottle of plonk. She filled her glass and sat watching the TV.

'Bastard,' she muttered. Then she checked her watch: he was due any minute, so she returned to the kitchen. The sauce was bubbling away. She was ready for Mr Reynolds.

Chapter Seven

The table in the lounge was laid for dinner; she didn't have a dining room. It was no candlelit romantic setting; though she did have candles, she had no intention of making this evening pleasant. She had the TV still on, the plates warming and everything ready to serve at eight-fifteen. At nine-fifteen Reynolds still had not shown. She was about to eat by herself when the intercom went.

He came charging up the stairs with a large bouquet of cheapo supermarket roses and a bottle of red wine.

'Sorry I'm late, but something cropped up. I was going to call but thought you might have blown me out.' He grinned and handed over his gifts.

'I might well have done,' she said, moving away from him as he went to kiss her cheek. 'Go on through into the lounge. I'll dish up straight away. I am starving.'

'Me too,' he said, shrugging out of his suede coat and tossing it onto the floor by the front door. 'Do you want me to open the wine?'

'Bottle open on the table,' she said, banging around the kitchen as she put the garlic bread into the oven.

He did at least wait to start eating before she sat down, though he had consumed a glass of wine and was already pouring another. 'Cheers, and I'm sorry to be so late.'

'That's all right.' They touched their glasses and he then tucked in with relish.

'This is delicious,' he said, with his mouth full.

She responded by serving him some salad on a side plate.

'Do I detect a slight frost in the air?'

'You do, but let's finish eating.'

'I think I know what it's about,' he said, winding the spaghetti round his fork.

'I should think you do. It's made things very difficult for me.'

'How come?'

She put down her fork and sat back. 'You were asked not to go to press on the Red Dahlia note or the package. I was told tonight that, despite being warned that it would be detrimental to our enquiry, you are going to press regardless: so how do you think I feel? Especially as DCI Langton is more than aware that we are friends, from seeing us together in that restaurant. He actually thinks we have some kind of relationship; he had a right go at me.'

'Did he?' Reynolds wiped his plate with a piece of garlic bread.

'Do you have any idea what repercussions this could have? We have maintained a low profile for a bloody good reason.'

'Tell me about it.' He wasn't smiling any more.

'We have a suspect, one we believe is a very dangerous man—'

'Or not,' he interrupted arrogantly.

'I beg your pardon?'

'Well you may have a suspect, but from what I gather, you are nowhere near identifying him.'

'You gather incorrectly!' she snapped.

'Then I apologise. Who is he?'

She pushed her plate aside and wiped her mouth with her napkin. 'You really imagine I'd disclose that kind of information? Our investigation has nothing whatsoever to do with you!'

'Really?'

'Yes, really!' She was beginning to lose her cool.

'So the conversation I had with your possible suspect was no help? And the package that was sent to me, that I could have chosen not to contact you about? I was, if you recall, witness to the contents.'

'Yes you were and, as I recall, you were also requested not to go to press on either. I have told you: this killer is very dangerous.'

'I am aware of that; I have read up on the Black Dahlia.'

She whipped his plate away, picked up her own and stalked into the kitchen. 'DCI Langton warned you. He'll be coming down on you tomorrow like a ton of—' She dropped the top plate and swore.

Reynolds came into the kitchen as she was picking up the pieces of plate. 'So you think this is all down to me, do you?'

She threw the broken china into the bin. 'Of course I do!'

She opened the fridge and took out some pieces of cheese, then dumped them, still in the wrappers, onto a cheeseboard. 'Can you take this through for me?'

He snatched the board and walked out. She turned the coffee percolator on and carried a biscuit tin after him into the lounge. She banged it down on the table. 'Help yourself.'

'Thank you. Entertain often, do you?'

'This is not funny.' Anna drained her glass of wine and poured another.

'Do you want cheese?' he asked, delving around to find a cracker he liked.

'No.'

Anna watched as he munched his cheese. He was a very good-looking man; right now, however, the expression in his intensely blue eyes was icy.

'You calmed down?'

'Yes,' she said, grudgingly.

'Right.' He refilled his glass and took a sip before carefully placing it down. 'I had nothing to do with the article that will be coming out at the weekend. Just as you have a boss, a.k.a. DCI Langton, I also have a boss: the editor of the paper. She's a very strong-willed woman. She was at some big function for all the bigwigs the day we were at the forensic lab: politicians and crimebusters. Their guest speaker was a Professor Marshe.'

Anna stopped sulking and started listening.

'It appears that your esteemed United States profiler had a lengthy conversation with my editor. Apparently, she even mentioned the fact that we had met at the forensic lab; seemed quite taken with me!' He smiled but Anna was not amused. His tone became more serious. 'I never let any cat out of the bag, Anna. I had a furious editor giving me a lengthy ticking off for sitting on what would be a centre-page spread, if not a headliner. I got another tirade for not telling her what was going on.'

'Is this true?'

'For Chrissakes, Anna!' he snapped suddenly, pushing back his chair. 'You jumped to the wrong conclusions and you never even gave me the opportunity to tell you my side of the story before having a go at me.'

Anna took a deep breath. 'So Professor Marshe told your editor about the case?'

'That's what I've just told you, isn't it? She also said that she feels it is our public duty to let the readers know that we have a nightmare killer at large, and one it appears you are nowhere near even identifying at that.'

Anna took her glass and went to sit on the sofa. He followed, sitting in the large and only armchair opposite her.

'I'm sorry,' she said.

'So you should be. As for you getting into hot water about it, you should have a go at your DCI Langton; he brought her into the case, didn't he?'

Anna said nothing. He crossed his legs, dangling the glass from his hand. 'Shall I open the bottle I brought? It is a slightly better vintage than this one.'

She shrugged; he got up and walked into the kitchen. Anna was feeling foolish and wasn't sure what to say. He returned and filled his own glass, then went over and stood in front of her.

'Refill?'

'Yes please, thank you.'

'My pleasure.' He put the bottle onto the table and then sat beside her on the sofa. 'Forgiven?'

'Yes. I am sorry.'

He sipped his wine, and then looked up at the TV; it had remained on throughout dinner with the sound turned off.

'Is that your only means of entertainment?'

She gestured to the stereo and he got up, rifled through her CDs and put one on, then took out a box of matches and lit the candles on the bookcase. He turned the lights down, the TV off, and as the strains of Mozart began to fill the room, he sat back down beside her.

'This is better.'

'So's your wine,' she said, thawing out.

'So now you know why I was late. I am really sorry, but she wasn't going to let me out of there until I got the article out.' He leaned back. 'No wonder you don't want to talk about it. I logged onto the Black Dahlia website and found all the gory details: sickening. To think there is some maniac trying to emulate that is beyond belief. I know there are copycat killers, but this is freaky; why copycat a murder that happened in 1947?'

'Because the killer was never caught.'

'But the pre-planning – to drain Louise's blood before slicing her body in two—'

Anna closed her eyes and tensed.

He turned towards her. 'Do you get to sleep okay?'

'Usually; it depends. You get used to horror – it's the job, you know – but sometimes images creep into your mind and stay there.'

'You know the image that I can't get rid of?'

Anna didn't respond.

'The look in her eyes. I never knew that dead eyes

held an expression; I thought they just blanked out when the heart stopped, but there is so much pain in her eyes. Terrible.'

'Yes.'

'Did Louise Pennel's face have the same expression as Elizabeth Short?'

'Yes.'

'Why would one human being want to inflict such agony on another? What makes them that way?'

'I don't know: a madness is all one can put it down to.'

'How come you are on a murder team?'

'Because I wanted to be.'

'You chose it?'

'Yes, my father was a homicide officer for thirty years.'

'You ever work with him?'

'No, he died almost three years ago.'

'I'm sorry. No doubt he would be very proud you had followed in his footsteps.'

'Yes; yes, I think he would.'

'What about your mother?'

'She died before Dad.'

He leaned closer, his head almost on her shoulder. 'So you are an orphan?'

'I never really thought about it, but I suppose I am.'

'You ever get lonely?'

'Well, I don't have any relatives that I'm close to.'

'What about friends?'

'Not many; mostly work colleagues. Why are you asking me all these questions?'

'To try and get to know you.'

'Well, as you can see, there's not much to know about.'

He smiled. 'From what I can see, you have a great CD collection, a neat little flat, and you are very pretty.'

She laughed. 'Rubbish.'

'You are. Well, I think so; I love that red curly hair. Did you know you have a ring of freckles over your nose?'

Anna's hand went to her face, involuntarily. 'I am always trying to cover them up, but I didn't do my make-up when I got home.'

'You have beautiful skin, and very pretty hands.' He reached out and caught her hand in his.

Anna was at a loss. She found him so attractive but she was so unused to the whole flirting thing. 'Am I supposed to say nice things about you now?' she asked softly.

'You could. I mean, it's been pretty one-sided up until now. You've not given me much indication that you find me interesting; attractive even.'

'You are both.'

'Good.'

He reached down and picked up his wine glass, drained it and got up for a refill.

'You should be careful; are you driving?'

He turned and cocked his head to one side. 'Are you trying to tell me that I should be leaving?'

'It's just that we've already had one bottle, so if you're in the car, you'll need some coffee. I'm a police officer, remember.'

He smiled as he picked up her glass and topped it up.

'So do you want coffee?' she asked.

'No, thanks.' He sat beside her again, and stretched

out his legs in front so he leaned back again very close to her. 'Do you have a pet?'

'No.'

'Well, there is this disgusting moggy that's sort of moved in with me, her name is Blott: she's a sort of tabby cross with what could be a hamster; she has this very odd, uncatlike face that I think may be from someone having kicked her; it's sort of squashed. Can we go to bed?'

DAY SIXTEEN

It was no good making the excuse that she was drunk. She was a little tipsy, but she knew what she was getting into, though the wine had made her a lot less inhibited. She had never actually slept with anyone who had just suggested bed without any physical preamble; her previous experiences had begun with unbuttoning shirts and blouses and escalated from there. Langton had been a very tender and experienced lover, so totally at ease the morning after; it was a night that she knew had been special. She had not been in a sexual relationship since. It was not that she had been unable to consider anyone else as a lover; it was simply there hadn't been anyone who appeared to find her attractive, let alone make a play for her. Now there was Mr Reynolds. The world had not exactly moved when they had made love, but he was sweet and considerate, and made her laugh during and after sex; in the morning, however, when he had woken her with kisses, it had been more passionate.

He brought her a cup of coffee in bed and then went for a shower. Unfortunately, the coffee was dreadful: it was the stewed brew that had been percolating all night. Anna smiled but said nothing when he came back in, pulling on his suede jacket and smelling of her moisturiser and shampoo. She loved it when he knelt on the bed to kiss her again.

'I'll call you later.'

Then he was gone. She stood on tiptoe in the kitchen, watching him speed off in his Morgan.

She scrambled some eggs and made some fresh coffee. She hummed to herself as she showered, feeling as if a weight had been lifted from her shoulders.

Brimming with confidence, she parked her Mini at the station. She saw Langton's beat-up Rover taking up two spaces; typically inconsiderate, she thought.

As she walked into the Incident Room, the hubbub of voices lowered as the officers glanced over.

'Morning,' she said cheerfully, and crossed to her desk.

Lewis propped up the headline – COPYCAT BLACK DAHLIA KILLER.

She said nothing as she took the paper and glanced over it. It was exactly what they had hoped would not happen. The article compared the old case and the new, complete with photographs of the two victims side by side, and gory details of the murder of Louise Pennel.

'Your boyfriend's got the Gov in a white-hot rage.'

Anna slapped the paper down on her desk. 'My relationship has nothing to do with this article. I resent everyone in this station giving me snide glances and implying that this has something to do with me: it hasn't!'

'He certainly knows a hell of a lot about the cases, so if you didn't brief him, who did?' Lewis said nastily.

'He probably checked on the Elizabeth Short website.'

Anna got up and walked past Lewis to get herself a coffee, not that she wanted one; she could sense all the ears wigging at their conversation. She stood by the board and read the press release that the Commander had instructed Langton to issue when he received the postcard; it requested that the killer should make contact at any location of his choice.

'Have we heard anything back from this?' she asked Barolli, who shook his head. 'Anything from her address book?'

'You mean apart from damage to the eardrums? We've arranged meetings with all the ones we've been able to trace so far. There's a list on your desk.'

Anna had been given four addresses and contact numbers: two girls and one man who had lived in the hostel with Louise, and two men who had known her a couple of years ago. They were scattered all over London.

Anna opened her desk drawer and took out her *A to Z* to work out which route would save her the most travelling time.

'Travis!' came the bellow from Langton's office. She'd been waiting for this and she was ready for him. She ran her fingers through her hair, pulled down her sweater and smoothed her skirt as she headed into his office.

'Sit down.'

She perched on the edge of her seat. He tossed the paper over to her. 'You read this fucking garbage?'

'Yes.'

'What did you give your boyfriend, our case file?'

'No.'

'So he just grasped all of this from thin air, did he?'

'He had to have inside information.'

'You bet your sweet arse he has! This has put us in a bloody awkward situation. The phones are hopping with nutters; we've had Yellow, Blue, Pink Dahlias – it's going to take up a lot of valuable time.'

'I know.'

'You know, do you? Well, for Chrissakes, use this as a lesson to keep your yapping mouth shut.'

'I don't like the way you are talking to me.'

'What?'

'I said, I don't like your tone of voice.'

'You don't like my tone of voice? It's the same one I use on everybody, Anna! Do you think I should treat you any differently?'

'No, but I do think you should show me some respect, and not jump automatically to the wrong conclusion.'

'What?'

'I did not discuss the Red Dahlia case with Richard Reynolds.'

'Christ, even his name is like some cartoon character!' he snapped.

'Professor Marshe discussed the case with Mr Reynolds's editor, who returned to the crime desk and hit the roof. She had not been privy to any contacts made, so when she found out what a newsworthy story it was, she insisted they publish an article comparing the old case and ours. As Mr Reynolds simply works for the crime section, he does not have the power to veto a story; even though he was attempting to honour the press embargo you requested, his editor paid short shrift

134

to it and insisted it was in the public interest to release the facts that we have a nightmare murder and a maniac on the loose.'

She had to gasp for breath, she had spoken so quickly.

'That's enough,' he snapped, and glared. 'I get the picture, Travis.'

'An apology would be nice,' she said, tartly.

Langton glowered. 'I'm sorry; sorry I jumped down your throat and to the wrong conclusion.'

Anna stood up, and smiled primly at him. 'Thank you.'

She walked out, closing the door softly behind her.

She had arranged to meet all four people on her list by the time Langton came into the Incident Room. The phones had not stopped ringing and they had two extra clerks working the switchboard. Langton looked dishevelled: hair standing on end, unshaven as usual.

'We have not as yet had any response to my press release. We have got a stream of lunatics from the newspaper article, but we have to hope one might give us something. Using the victim's address book, we'll cover everyone she knew, see if they can throw any light on this suspect.'

Langton gestured to the drawing of the LA suspect, then he dug his hands into his pockets. 'All we can do is keep going. Now that the public are aware of the comparison between the LA case and ours, we will be inundated with calls, so I am giving a press conference later this afternoon. We will be disclosing our drawing, and expressing hope that someone will come forward, etcetera etcetera. What will not be disclosed is that the suspect may have made contact with Louise Pennel via an advert for a PA. We still do not have anything to back this up as yet, but keep going. We will also not disclose the fact that we have some DNA from the victim's underwear that may or may not help us if and when we catch this bastard!'

Langton covered old ground for another ten minutes and then the briefing broke up. The detectives who were to question the known associates of Louise Pennel prepared to leave.

Anna had been gone only five minutes when DS Barolli got a hit. As Anna had requested, *The Times* had made contact with a list of job adverts covering the period that Louise worked at the dental clinic. There were over a hundred and they had been slowly eliminating each one when Barolli came across something suspicious: a novelist, seeking a PA with shorthand and typing and a willingness to travel worldwide at a moment's notice, but requiring no previous experience: just that applicants should be between 24 and 30, attractive and well dressed. There was a box number only.

Barolli showed the advert to Langton. 'This could be the one: ran eight months ago. It was withdrawn five months ago. Payment was by postal order, and we have a box number to trace.'

Langton stared at it. 'If it's our man, he's covered his tracks, but see if they can give us where the postal order came from and check out the box number.' He smiled. 'Little Travis beavering away again. She's good.'

Barolli raised an eyebrow, 'But not that good if she raps to a bloody journalist about the case.'

'She didn't; it came from another source.'

'Like who?

Langton stood up. 'Someone who has a lot to answer for. I'll see you later.'

Anna's first interview was with Graham Dodds, who had lived in the same hostel in Brixton as Louise Pennel. He was waiting for Anna as she walked into a small, rather seedy hostel in Victoria. He was a small, wiry youth with a nervous tic; he wore torn jeans and a thick poloneck sweater. He looked and smelled like he needed a good wash; his hair and nails were filthy.

'Mr Dodds?'

'Yes, ma'am.'

'Thank you for seeing me. Is there anywhere we could talk?'

He gestured towards the TV room. 'We can go in there. It's usually empty at this time of day.'

The room reeked of stale cigarettes. Ashtrays overflowed on the arms of worn foam sofas and armchairs. The threadbare curtains were a dirty orange.

Anna sat down and smiled pleasantly as Mr Dodds twitched and hovered. 'I know what happened to Louise; I read about it in the paper, it was terrible. I've never known anyone that was murdered before. When you called here, it made me nervous, you know, and I didn't tell nobody what it was about, but I did know her.'

'Would you like to sit down, Graham? Do you mind if I call you Graham?'

'No.' He sat down opposite her and leaned forward intently.

'I am here to ask you about the time you lived in the same hostel as Louise Pennel.'

'Yes, I know, you said that on the phone, but I don't know what I can tell you. I mean, I've not seen her for a long time.'

'Can you tell me a little about the time you were there?'

He nodded. 'I was there for nine months. It was in Brixton; my social worker got me in there.'

'Did you know Louise?'

'Not really; I saw her the odd times she was in the recreational room. It was similar to this. She liked to watch the soaps. I wouldn't say that I got to know her; we just had a few chats. She was signing on at the Job Centre so I saw her there, and once we got a bus back to the hostel together. She was very nice. It's a terrible, terrible thing: I mean, she was only twenty, wasn't she?'

'Twenty-two. Did you meet any of her friends?'

'No, I never saw her with anybody outside the hostel.'

'When she left, did you maintain any contact with her?'

'No, like I said, I didn't know her that well. She got work at some clinic, doctor's or dentist's, quite a distance from the hostel, which I suppose is why she left.'

Anna took out a photograph and showed it to him. 'Are you in this photograph?'

He stared at it for a moment, then nodded. 'Yes, the hostel organised a bus trip to the Regent's Park zoo one Bank Holiday. I'd forgotten about that.'

Anna leaned forward. 'Do you know anyone else in this photograph?'

'That's me; the other bloke is Colin someone or other: he was staying at the hostel as well.' He frowned. 'They didn't like each other, Colin and her. They had some kind of argument over something stupid, like who had ordered Coke or orange juice; he said something to her and she got really uptight: they had a bit of a slanging match and then she walked off, didn't come back with us. She got in really late and I think she got told off because the door closed at eleven.'

'Do you know where this Colin is living now?'

'No.'

'Is there anything else you can recall about Louise?'

'She put it about a bit.'

'What do you mean?'

He leaned back, embarrassed. Anna waited.

'I mean, I dunno for sure, but we used to sort of talk about it, because she didn't have a job; this was before she got work at the clinic, right? There was a bar across the street and she used to go in there, and sort of get blokes to pay for meals and other things.'

'Sex?'

'I dunno, but we reckoned she was on the game. Not seriously, though.'

'What do you mean by that?'

'Well, she had to be in the hostel at eleven, so it wasn't as if she was out on the streets all night.'

'But you think she was picking up men?'

'Yeah.' He flushed.

'Did you actually see her doing this?'

He shook his head.

'When was the last time you saw Louise?'

'You mean apart from at the hostel?'

'Yes.'

'I never saw her again; she never even said goodbye to anyone.'

★

139

Anna returned to her car, the smell of nicotine in her nostrils and on her clothes. The hostel had been a forlorn place, almost on a par with the bed-and-breakfast hotel she next went to in Paddington. Louise had stayed here before moving to live at Sharon's flat. The residents were mostly travelling salesmen and she began to feel it was going to be another waste of time. The woman that managed the hotel was Lebanese, and not very friendly: Mrs Ashkar had already been questioned by DS Barolli and resented having to repeat herself to Anna. She glanced at the photographs and said she did not know anyone; the only person she did know was the victim Louise Pennel and she said that she was very sorry for what had happened to her.

'Did she ever bring back anyone to the hotel?'

'No, not that I knew of, but a couple of times she was with some of the guests at the bar.'

Anna listed a few names taken from Louise's address book. Again, there was no one Mrs Ashkar recognised as ever staying at the hotel, though she did at least flick perfunctorily through the hotel register, her red nail varnish chipped, before shaking her head. Anna next showed the drawing of their suspect.

'Did you ever see Louise with this man, or someone similar? He's tall, well dressed, sometimes wears a long draped black or charcoal grey coat.'

Mrs Ashkar shrugged. 'No.' She had a thick, guttural accent.

'Do you have someone at the bar I could talk to?'

'We don't have a full-time barman. Joe works at the bar and in the kitchens; she used to help sometimes.'

'I'm sorry?'

'I said, she worked in the kitchens sometimes, washing up, cleaning; she was always short of money. Sometimes she would help the cleaner in the morning make up the beds.'

'So this helped pay her bills?'

'Yes, she was moved out of one of the bigger rooms to the boxroom at the back. Joe used to get her to wash the glasses at the bar. I told all this to the other man that came round asking.'

'Is Joe here? I'd like to speak to him.'

Mrs Ashkar gave a sigh and then spoke into an intercom phone in Arabic.

'Go through the double doors, he'll come out and see you.'

'Thank you,' Anna said, disliking the woman's attitude. The so-called bar-cum-lounge was dark and dingy with old maroon velvet curtains and an overpowering smell of stale cigarettes and alcohol. There were a couple of easy chairs and a sofa, all threadbare, and a maroon and yellow carpet whose swirls were heavily stained. The bar itself was a glass-fronted, kidney-shaped counter in the corner of the room. Glasses and bottles were stacked on a shelf behind it alongside packets of peanuts and crisps in open boxes.

Anna turned as Joe breezed in. He was broad-shouldered and unshaven in a stained T-shirt and jeans; his pitch-dark hair was oiled back from his swarthy face and he had a jaded, handsome look. He smiled warmly at Anna and shook her hand. His hands were big, square and rough.

Annie went through the photographs and the names from Louise's address book. No result. When he was asked if any of the customers were friendly with her, he shrugged.

'Sure; she was always in here and if they bought her drinks, she'd sometimes stay up until two in the morning.'

'Did she favour anyone special?'

He shook his head, then went behind the nasty little bar and opened a beer. He proffered one to Anna but she refused. He took a swig then placed the bottle on a stained beer mat.

'She would sometimes go out to the station.'

'I'm sorry?'

'I said she went round to the station, picked up men there.'

He gulped more beer, and then burped. 'Excuse me.'

'Did she bring them back here?'

'No way, not allowed: you get one tart and they come round like ants.'

'Did you ever see her with any regular man?'

'No, she was usually on her own; it always took a few drinks before she loosened up, then she'd be laughing and joking with us.'

Joe turned as the sour-faced Mrs Ashkar walked in, stared pointedly at them and walked out again.

'I better get back to work.' He drained his beer and tossed the bottle into a crate beneath the bar. 'I was sad to see her go, she was quite a fixture, but she'd found a flat over near Baker Street. She was excited about some new job prospect that was going to pay her a shedload of money.'

Anna at last felt she might be getting somewhere. 'Did she tell you anything about the job?'

'Not much; to be honest, I wasn't sure if it was true: she could spin some stories, especially after a few drinks.'

'Joe, it is very important that you try and remember anything she told you about this job.'

He shrugged. 'I only know she answered an advert. I think she worked in some dental clinic; she went out every day in the same clothes: white shirt and black skirt. I know she hated her job, they paid her peanuts, but she said she didn't have any qualifications. I think she was a receptionist, but she often didn't bother going; hung out here and helped change the sheets and stuff like that.'

'I know she worked for a dentist. This other job, can you remember anything she said about it?'

Mrs Ashkar walked in again; this time she said something to Joe and he looked at Anna.

'I got to go back to work.'

Anna whipped round and glared at Mrs Ashkar. 'A young girl that stayed here was murdered. I would appreciate it if you did not interrupt my conversation. I would hate to have to return here in a patrol car, with uniformed officers.'

It had the desired effect: Mrs Ashkar turned on her heel, the door swung open and shut behind her. Joe took a cloth, sprayed it with glass cleaner and began to wipe down the glass on top of the bar.

'Go on please, Joe.'

'Well, like I said, I knew she wanted to find other work; she even asked if we needed anyone here, you know, on a permanent basis, but we didn't. She was always skint and late paying her bill. One night, when she'd had a few too many, she started crying. She said she'd been to see some relative to borrow some money

– she had a job interview and wanted to look good – but they'd refused to help her out. She'd called in sick at her work; she'd taken the day off to go somewhere.'

'Bognor Regis.'

He looked surprised. 'Yeah, right. I knew she'd been somewhere, because she had this big suitcase. In fact, I helped her take it up to her room. She had a couple of things she wanted me to buy.'

'Exactly what did she offer you?'

'Couple of little silver boxes and a candlestick.'

Anna asked how much he had given to Louise for the items. Joe hesitated.

'How much?'

'Twenty quid,' he said at last, somewhat embarrassed. Anna was certain the candlestick alone would have been worth a lot more, but did not pursue it.

'Was it after she came back with the suitcase that she told you about her new job?'

He nodded. 'She never said much about the job, just that she wanted to make an impression and needed money to get some new clothes. The next night she went out, probably to the station; I say that, because she had to have got money from somewhere: a few days later, she passed me in the reception and I hardly recognised her, she was so smart – a reddish coat, high-heeled shoes – when I said how good she looked, she laughed. She told me to keep my fingers crossed as she was going for the interview. I reckoned she must have got the job, because she moved out to this place she said she'd found in Baker Street a week or so later.'

Anna took a deep breath. 'Can you remember the exact date this job interview happened?'

Joe nodded and walked out. Anna heard a gabble of Arabic: Mrs Ashkar was obviously having another go at him. He returned with the hotel registry book and began to flick through it to find the date four days before Louise had left – it was 10 June.

Anna jotted the date down and smiled. 'Thank you. I really appreciate your help.'

'That's okay. I'm sorry about what happened to her.'

'Did you like her?'

He shrugged. 'She was very pretty, but there was something odd about her that sort of put you off.'

'Like what?'

'I dunno, like she was frightened of something, nervous, always biting her nails; sometimes she really needed a wash.'

'But she helped you around the bar and in the kitchens?'

'Yeah that's right; it's just me running the show. We serve full breakfast, no other meals, and then open the bar at night.'

'So who else works here?'

Joe gave a deep sigh. 'A cleaner and an old guy that helps me with the crates and stuff; we pay him in beer.'

'So you would have got to know Louise.'

Joe straightened up and smoothed back his hair. 'I am engaged to my girlfriend!'

'Really? Does that mean you and Louise were never . . .' She wafted her hand.

'Look, I don't want any trouble,' he said, and she could see the sweat on his forehead.

'Did you have sex with Louise?'

He gave a sigh. 'Yeah, kind of; I'd sometimes give her

a few quid for a blow job, but it meant nothing. Like I said, I'm engaged; it was just that it was there and she was needy, you know what I mean?'

Anna said nothing; he looked at his watch.

'I got to go back to work.'

'If there is anything that you think of that might help my enquiry, this is my card and contact number.' She passed over her card. He took it and ran his thumb over the edge.

'I'm sorry. She was kind of sad, but she could be fun sometimes.'

Anna gave a prim smile. She disliked him intensely. 'Thank you for your help. Oh, there is just one thing — could I see her room?'

'What?'

'The room Louise Pennel stayed in while she was here, could I see it?'

Joe hesitated, and then shrugged. 'Sure; it's being used by the cleaner. It's not a regular hotel room.' They headed up three flights of stairs; the carpet was threadbare and the air reeked of stale cooking fat.

'It's from the Chinese restaurant next door,' Joe said as they passed a fire door and a bathroom before stopping at the end of the corridor. He opened the door and stepped back.

It was hardly large enough to be described as a room; a single bed and a dresser fought for space in the dank air. A torn net curtain covered the tiny window. The lino on the floor was filthy, as was what had once been a fluffy yellow bath mat. A picture of Christ on the Cross hung crooked, the frame chipped.

★

146

Anna drove back to the station, desperate for a shower, but there was no way she would have the time to take one until she went home that evening. She distracted herself with the thought that they now had the date when Louise went for her job interview, which would narrow down when the advert could have been placed. That Louise was selling herself to buy new clothes for the interview showed that she was desperate to make a good impression; Joe had described what sounded like Louise's missing maroon coat. Louise had moved into Sharon's flat after the job interview, but had continued working for the dental practice. She sighed, hating that all this might turn out to be a wild goose chase.

Anna joined Barolli at his desk. 'We have any luck with the advert Louise may have answered?'

'We're checking out a postal box; the number listed for applicants to call, we've drawn a blank on. It was a pay-as-you-go mobile number, so we can't trace any contract details.'

'Where was the postal box?'

Barolli passed over his report. The postal box and the mobile phone number had both been paid for with postal orders, purchased at different post offices: one in Slough and the other in Charing Cross. 'If it is our man, he covered his tracks. BT are checking out the line, but he could have used it for incoming calls only. Thousands of those phones are sold; using a very busy post office means there's little hope that anyone would remember who bought a cash order over eight months ago.'

Anna scanned through Barolli's report and then passed it back. 'One step forwards, two steps back. To be honest,

I was beginning to wonder if it was a red herring, but we know Louise went for a job interview sometime in June.'

Anna told Barolli what she had learned that morning.

'Terrific; what do we do? Hang out at Paddington station and question every possible punter using the station!'

Anna pursed her lips; she got the feeling that Barolli felt he had wasted hours of his time. 'No, but if BT can trace calls made to that mobile number, we might find someone else who answered the advert.'

Barolli grinned and pointed. 'Good thinking. I'll crack on.'

Anna typed up her report of the morning's interviews. She then returned to Barolli's desk. 'We found no chequebook or bank account in Louise Pennel's name, right?'

'Yep. But she might have had one under a different name; we've found nothing to indicate that she had an account or credit card.'

'Do we know how her salary was paid?'

Barolli pulled at his pug nose and then checked his file. 'They paid her in cash. She was on thirteen thousand a year! By the time tax, National Insurance, etcetera had been deducted, she was taking home hardly enough to live on.'

Anna frowned and leaned closer. 'If she paid tax on a cash wage! What was the rent at Sharon's?'

Barolli shrugged. 'I don't know. No one asked me to check.'

'Don't worry, I'll find out. Thanks.'

Anna returned to her desk and rang Sharon; she left

a message. Next, she called Mrs Hughes at Florence Pennel's house, trying to ascertain the exact dates of Louise's movements before she moved in at Sharon's.

Mrs Hughes was evasive to begin with, saying that she had done nothing wrong.

'Mrs Hughes, I am sure there will be no repercussions for you, but I need to know exactly what you gave to Louise.'

'Well, they were just some things that her grandmother had given me. I never needed them, and I felt sorry for the poor girl; she looked dreadful.'

'That was very kind of you. Could you tell me what the items were?'

As well as the clutch bag with the suede flower motif, there was a nightdress, a dressing gown and some slippers.

'As I said, they were just things that Mrs Pennel had given to me. They were not worth anything, and I didn't want them.'

'Did you give her any make-up?'

'No.'

'Did you give her any money at all?'

'No, I didn't!'

'Thank you very much.'

Anna put the phone down. She'd hoped for more items that might have been traceable. The date of Louise's visit to her grandmother coincided with her returning to the B&B with the suitcase. Anna tried Sharon again but there was still no answer so, impatient to find out what rent was being charged, she called the landlady direct.

Mrs Jenkins was very guarded, saying that she paid income tax on her rentals. Anna gave her the same

149

reassuring treatment as Mrs Hughes and eventually discovered that the rental for the top-floor flat in Balcombe Street was one hundred and fifty pounds a week, with a deposit of a thousand pounds.

Astonished, Anna returned to Barolli's desk. He was hanging on the line for information from BT. He looked to Anna and gestured that it was all right for her to talk.

'Louise Pennel was paying half of a hundred and fifty quid a week rent, so that's seventy-five pounds a week on her wages. It would have been impossible to even buy a cup of coffee.' Barolli nodded. 'So where did she get the cash?'

Barolli covered the mouthpiece. 'Turning tricks?'

Anna shook her head. 'If Louise had been working as a prostitute, Sharon would have known; so would Mrs Jenkins.'

'She had to have been getting money from somewhere; she moved out of the B&B after the job interview so the two must be linked.'

Just then, Lewis came steaming into the Incident Room. He held up a plastic bag. 'Two more, we've got two more.'

Anna turned to face him. 'Two more what?'

Lewis's face was flushed. 'Sent to the Incident Room, been downstairs since they arrived this morning. You won't bloody believe what they say. Where's the Gov?'

In front of everyone, Langton put on rubber gloves and unzipped the protective forensic bag.

The first note read:

Dahlia's Killer CraCkin. Wants terms?

The second:

```
To DCI James Langton. I will give up in Red
Dahlia killing if I get ten years. DON'T TRY
TO FIND ME.
```

Both notes were written in letters cut from news-papers. The constant ringing of telephones was the only sound in the room as Langton carefully replaced the notes, not wanting to contaminate them. He then crossed to the noticeboard.

'He's a day out on the Black Dahlia timeframe. The LA Examiner received almost identical letters to these on January the twenty-seventh.'

'So he is copycatting,' Anna said.

'That's pretty obvious,' snapped Langton. He looked to Barolli. 'Let's get over to the lab and see if these have anything. Like a fucking fingerprint would be useful!'

Langton and Barolli left the station. Anna was pouring a coffee for herself when Lewis joined her.

'If this nutter is copycatting the original Black Dahlia case, you know what comes next?'

'Yes, we get sent a photograph of a white male with a stocking pulled so tight over his face, he's unrecognis-able.'

'Called him the Werewolf Killer,' Lewis said, pointing to the listings of the contacts made by the Black Dahlia killer in 1947.

Anna sipped her coffee; it was stale, and she pulled a face.

'This is getting hairy, isn't it?' Lewis remarked.

Anna nodded. 'On the old enquiry, they reckoned

their killer was obsessed with Jack the Ripper; ours is obsessed with the Black Dahlia killer. Either way, they are both playing sick games. I doubt we'll get anything from the notes.'

Lewis nodded and returned to his desk. Anna was passing Barolli's when Bridget raised her hand.

'Excuse me, Anna, but I've got someone from BT on the line for Detective Sergeant Barolli; do you want to talk to him?'

Anna nodded and picked up Barolli's phone. She identified herself and then listened as an engineer gave her details of two calls answering the advert. They were made on land lines and so had been traceable; any call made using a mobile, however, they had no record of.

Anna could feel her heart pumping. If those two callers had responded to the same advert as Louise Pennel, this might be the first major step forward in tracing the tall dark-haired man.

Langton sat in a hard-backed chair at the lab at Lambeth. Around his feet were cigarette ends, above his head the NO SMOKING sign. He looked at his watch impatiently. Barolli came out of the gents' toilet.

'Still waiting?'

'What does it look like? I've never sat around like this on any other case. But I *want* these lab reports.'

Langton took out a rolled-up *Evening Standard* from his pocket, and started to read.

'Do you think he's going to go all the way with this copycat scenario?'

'Maybe,' Langton muttered.

'So you think this sick bastard's going to grab some

152

innocent kid, truss him up, put a stocking over his head and send in his photograph?'

'I don't think all that crap with the boy and stocking mask was from the killer; just some other sick fuck wanting publicity.'

'You think those notes are from him, though?' Barolli asked.

'I don't know; if they are, let's hope we get something off them.'

'Think we should we go to LA, Gov?'

Langton folded his paper and stuffed it back into his pocket. 'No, I fucking don't! This guy is *here*, not in LA. He's in London somewhere and we will find him. I am getting sick to death of this Black or Red Dahlia shit. We have a twisted killer with a sadistic mind, and someone somewhere knows who he is.'

At that moment, the swing doors opened. The technicians had finished their tests on the latest notes.

Chapter Eight

Now that she and Lewis had two names to check out, Anna felt really energised. The women lived on different sides of London: one in Hampstead, the other in Putney. They had no luck in contacting Nicola Formby but they left an urgent message on her answerphone; however, Valerie Davis was at home and agreed rather nervously to see them. She asked if it was to do with a parking offence. Lewis said it was nothing for her to worry about; they simply needed to question her about something they would prefer to discuss personally.

Valerie lived in a basement flat close to Hampstead Heath. She was attractive, with shoulder–length blonde hair and the aristocratic tones of a debutante. She was wearing a wide baggy sweater over a very small miniskirt and big furry boots.

'Hi, do come in,' she said. Her cheeks were flushed pink.

It looked as if each of the untidy rooms in the flat was let out to someone or other.

'Sorry about the mess; we've got some friends staying, over from Australia.'

'How many of you live here?' Anna asked pleasantly.

'Four girls and one boy. Tea or coffee?'

They both refused either and sat in the equally untidy kitchen.

'Did you answer this advert?' Lewis went straight in. Anna would have taken more time.

Valerie glanced at the wording of the advert which had been typed out onto a sheet of paper. 'Yes; well, I think it was the same one, about eight months ago.'

Anna's stomach clenched. 'Could you tell us exactly what happened?'

'How do you mean?' Valerie crossed her endless legs. Such a short skirt didn't leave much to the imagination.

'Well, did you write a letter in response?'

'Yes, I sent in my CV, for what it's worth. I don't actually have shorthand, but it sounded like a great opportunity.'

'You sent in a photograph?'

'Yes, though not a very good one: I had to cut off people either side of me, because I didn't really have one that wasn't me fooling about. I was going to go to one of those passport thingies, but I didn't get a chance.'

'When was this?'

Valerie screwed up her face, and then rubbed her nose with the cuff of her sweater. 'Oh gosh, let me think. Be about . . . early June?'

'Did you get a reply?'

'Not a letter; I got a phone call.'

Anna leaned forwards. 'To here?'

'No, I gave my mobile number and this man asked if I would come for an interview. He wanted to see me straight away. But it was granny's birthday, so I told him I was going to the country and he asked something like when would I be available. I wasn't sure, so I said I'd call him when I got back to London, which I did.'

Anna was itching to direct the conversation, but Lewis was the more experienced officer.

'And you arranged to meet him?' Lewis continued.

Valerie nodded, as Lewis made a note and then looked back to her. 'Where was this?'

'At Kensington Park Hotel, just next to Hyde Park Gardens'

'What date was this?'

Valerie looked up to the ceiling as she wound a strand of her hair round her finger. 'It was a Tuesday, about the fourteenth of June. I was to be there at two-fifteen.'

Lewis carefully wrote down the information. 'Can you describe the person you went to meet?'

Valerie shook her head. 'No, because he never showed

155

up. There's a large, well, it's a massive long room, with the hotel reception, a coffee bar and lots of seating areas. I was late; not too much, 'bout ten minutes. I went to the reception desk and asked if anyone had left a message for me, but no one had. I sat on a sofa for a while and then went and had a coffee.'

'So you never met up with the man you had made the appointment with?'

'No.'

Lewis leaned back, frustrated.

'Did he give you a name?'

'Yes, he said his name was John Edwards.'

He turned to an equally disappointed Anna, who asked if Valerie had seen anyone that might have been Mr Edwards. Valerie said she didn't know what he looked like. She was shown the drawing of their suspect, but she did not remember seeing anyone that resembled him.

Lewis stood up, but Anna was not ready to go. She asked Valerie if she could describe Mr Edwards's voice.

'Describe the way he spoke, you mean?'

'Yes.'

'Well, he sounded a bit like my father: quite pompous, upper-crust, but nice at the same time.'

'Could you repeat the conversation you had with him?'

'Well we didn't really have much of a conversation; he just asked me what previous work I had been doing, and if I had a CV he could check. He wanted to know if he could contact anyone to check me out, I suppose. He asked me about my shorthand speed and I said it was a bit rusty, but that I'd worked in a film production office as a runner.'

'Did you ask him what the job entailed?'

Valerie nodded. 'He said it would be transcribing his novel. He said that it would also involve a lot of travel, because it was a book set all over the world, and that it was really very much a personal assistant requirement rather than a straight secretary. He asked if I had a passport and if I was married, as he needed someone that could travel at a moment's notice.'

Anna smiled. 'It must have sounded like a really interesting job.'

Valerie nodded, and then swung her foot in the big furry boot. 'There was something odd though, which is I suppose why you are asking me about him.'

'What was odd?' Anna said quickly.

'Well he asked if I had a boyfriend and did I look like my photograph. When I told my Dad about it, he said it all sounded a bit iffy to him.'

'Did you try and make contact with Mr Edwards again?'

Valerie shook her head. 'I couldn't be bothered.'

On their way to Putney, Anna and Lewis stopped off at the Kensington Park Hotel. The vestibule was as Valerie had described it: very large, with many guests passing to and fro.

'He could have been watching from any of these sofas or at the coffee bar. You can see anyone coming in or out of the hotel.'

'She had too many people around her,' Lewis said, flatly.

'She also doesn't look like the Black Dahlia victim,' Anna said, as they headed out of the hotel.

★

Nicola Formby bore no physical resemblance to Elizabeth Short either, bar to her surname: she was not even as tall as Anna, who was only five feet two. Aside from the height issue, she also differed from Valerie in that she was quite highly qualified, having been a PA to a company director for three years; however, when they met Nicola at her flat, she described almost an identical scenario: she had been unable to meet the 'very pleasant, well-spoken man' straight away because of a migraine; she therefore asked if she could contact him when she was recovered. She had sent a photograph and CV care of the box number, and called a few days later to arrange to meet. She was to meet him in the lobby vestibule at two o'clock, this time at the Grosvenor Hotel in Park Lane.

Nicola Formby had been on time, unlike Valerie three days earlier. She had waited over three quarters of an hour sitting in the reception. She had also gone up to the desk to ask if a Mr Edwards had left a message for her, but he had not. Nicola called the number she had taken from the advert but it had been disconnected so, disappointed, she decided to leave. She then realised that there was another entrance at the other side of the hotel and waited there for another ten minutes, but no one approached her. Nicola had neither seen nor spoken to a tall dark-haired man, with or without a long dark draped coat. When shown the drawing of the possible suspect, she was unable to recognise him.

It was as disappointing as Valerie's interview and showed yet again how very carefully their suspect, if he was Mr Edwards, had targeted the hopeful applicants. He must have been able to see them clearly and discard them without ever having shown them his face.

'What has he done?' Nicola asked, looking at the card Anna had given her.

'We're not certain Mr Edwards has done anything,' Lewis said.

'Is he a rapist or something like that?'

Anna hesitated; she knew intuitively that Nicola could give them something more. Even though she and Lewis had agreed that they would not mention Louise's murder, she sat back down and opened her briefcase. 'We are actually investigating a murder. This is the victim; her name was Louise Pennel.'

Lewis shot Anna a look as she handed over a photograph of Louise.

'And you think this man I was supposed to see is connected to it?'

'Possibly.'

There was a sharp intake of breath as Nicola looked at the photograph.

'There was another girl there, at the hotel. I can't be certain, but I think she was waiting for him too.'

Anna could feel her blood rush. 'Do you recognise her?

'I'm not sure, but it could have been her. She arrived at the hotel about twenty minutes after me. She kept on looking around as if she was waiting for someone, and I saw her go up to the desk.'

Anna leaned forwards. 'The Grosvenor is a very big hotel, very exclusive and fashionable. Why do you think she might have been waiting for the same person as you?'

'Because I saw the clerk at the desk point to me, as if to say, she's also waiting. The girl looked over to me then turned away and went further into the lobby. That's when I wondered if I'd got the wrong entrance, because a few years ago I came to a big ball and we came in another way.'

Anna and Lewis almost held their breath. Nicola continued.

'When I got to the back entrance, I saw her heading up the escalator. She turned back and looked at me again and then carried on up to the next floor. That was when I thought maybe I was wrong, you know about her meeting the same person, this Mr Edwards.'

Anna selected two more photographs and passed them to Nicola. 'Have another look, take your time. Do you think this is the girl you saw?'

Nicola sighed apologetically. 'I'm sorry, I can't be certain. It looks like her, but I couldn't be one hundred per cent sure.'

'Do you recall anything else; maybe what she was wearing?'

'Oh yes I do, I remember that, because it was a very hot day and she was wearing a woollen coat. It was a deep maroon and it had a velvet collar. She also had high-heeled shoes on and she was carrying a small clutch bag under her arm.'

Anna was astonished. 'How come you can remember all that so clearly?'

'Part of my job when I worked for an advertising company was buying stuff for commercial shoots. I suppose it really was more like a glorified dresser, but it did teach me a lot about clothes. Maybe that's why I can't remember her face; I was looking at her coat.'

★

It was almost six-thirty by the time Anna and Lewis returned to the station and past seven when they finished briefing Langton as to how the interviews had gone.

'I'd say it was our victim and Anna agrees.' Lewis nodded towards her.

Langton was tapping a pencil on the side of his desk. 'Did you enquire if this Mr Edwards booked a room in either of the hotels?'

'Yep, and there was no one of that name.'

'So, what, after all that schlepping around, do we have?'

Anna flipped her notebook closed. 'That Louise Pennel met this Mr Edwards on 10th June and a couple of days later moved into Sharon's flat. Her wages from the dental clinic would not have covered the rent per week.'

Langton ruffled his hair. 'So you think she was being paid by this Mr Edwards?'

'Maybe; she got new clothes, some very expensive.'

'But if she got the job working for him, why did she stay at the clinic?'

Anna shrugged. 'Maybe this Mr Edwards was just schooling her for his perversions. She was often late, often hung over at work and didn't seem to care even when she was warned she'd be fired. Sharon said at one time she had bad bruises on her arms. And a black eye, which Louise put down to falling at work.'

Langton took a deep breath. 'And we are still no nearer to tracing this sadistic bastard.'

'I think we are getting closer,' Anna said.

'Do you?' Langton said, sarcastically. He stood up and stretched his arms above his head. 'There was nothing helpful from his last contact: no fingerprints, just letters

161

cut out of newspapers stuck to the same notepaper, so we just sit and wait for his next missive. All we have is that the notes were more than likely compiled by the same person, whoever the hell he is, this Mr Edwards. I dunno; it's like we're going around in circles.'

Anna felt slightly irritated as she thought that she had done a good day's work, but she said nothing, sitting with her notebook in hand.

'How much was she paying out at the B&B?'

Anna flicked over a page then looked up at Langton. 'Almost as much as at Sharon's, but she was making money turning tricks then; I am certain she wasn't once she moved.'

'They both slept with guys for money – Sharon admitted it to me,' Langton snapped.

'Occasionally she might have, but it was by no means regular. For six months, she paid rent, went out, dated the tall dark-haired man and kept up her job at the dental clinic.'

Langton interrupted, wafting his hand. 'Yes, yes, we know all this. But I can't for the life of me think what all this gives us, Travis?'

'That she was being paid by her lover. Now, what she was actually paid for, I don't know, I'd say sexual favours. Sharon has stated that Louise offered her drugs a few times – cocaine – and she was often very distressed.'

Langton slapped the table with his hand. 'But what does this *give* us?'

'For Chrissakes, it gives even more on the suspect!' Anna snapped back at him.

Langton grimaced. 'In case you are unaware of it, we do not have, after two weeks, a clue as to who this suspect is. We are saying he might look like the drawing of the Black Dahlia killer, but he could *not* look anything like him. We have had not one positive identification or, even more important, one shred of evidence against this so-called lover of Louise Pennel. We don't even have any proof that he was screwing her, or that it was him that put the advert in *The Times*. We have fuck all, if the truth be known.'

Anna and Lewis were rescued by Barolli, who rapped on the door and put his head round.

'We've got lucky on the CCTV footage from Stringfellow's. It's only taken fifteen-odd hours, but we've got her up on screen now.'

Langton spread out his arms in a gesture of relief. 'Let's go.'

Langton and Anna sat in the centre, with Lewis on the remote. The room went silent as the blinds were drawn. Barolli stood next to the TV with a pencil in his hand; as the footage began, he gestured for Lewis to pause.

'Okay this is the first sighting of her. She's just walking in, edge of frame on the right. The time coder didn't work, but from Sharon's statements we've estimated it to be around ten o'clock; so this is shortly after they arrived.'

Lewis pressed Play and Louise Pennel walked into view: she looked far more beautiful than in any photograph. She was wearing a low-cut sequinned top and a denim miniskirt, both of which looked as if they belonged to Sharon. Louise had long slender legs and she was wearing very high-heeled sandals, making her even taller. She was wearing a flower in her hair; her face was heavily made-up. It was annoying to watch, as people kept passing in front of her and hiding her from the camera; in particular, Sharon seemed constantly to mask Louise.

The CCTV camera was at the entrance into the disco section and watched over the clubbers moving towards the blinking spotlights. As the camera slowly turned to look into the club's main bar and disco, the performing pole dancers were just about visible, but it was very dark. Sharon was all eyes, looking around, but Louise looked shy; she held her clutch bag in one hand and had the other to her mouth as she chewed her nails. Sharon turned to Louise and gestured for her to follow. They disappeared into the darkness.

Barolli leaned towards the TV. 'Next sighting is, we think, an hour later; this is tape ten. Again she comes into frame on your right and she's alone. Sharon is nowhere to be seen.'

Lewis pressed Play and they all watched as Louise, empty glass in hand, edged over to the bar. A stool became vacant and she moved over quickly to grab it; she sat perched with her long legs crossed as she surveyed the room. A few times, she was almost jostled off, as people in the crowd gestured for the barman to serve them. Louise opened her bag and then leaned on the counter. She said something to the barman and he nodded as she turned back, looking over the dancers. She was handed a glass of beer and she paid for it, still perched on the stool, as a young guy with long hair in a ponytail stood next to her. They had a brief conversation, but Louise was obviously not interested, virtually turning her back on him.

It was like watching a ghost. Louise was so very much

alive on the tape, yet they all knew what a terrible death she had suffered three days and nights later.

Louise remained on the bar stool for another half an hour. She had another beer and was approached by a couple more clubbers; she didn't seem at all interested in being picked up, though she was sitting in a very provocative manner. She delved into her clutch bag a few times and took out a mirror, retouched her lipstick and replaced the compact. Anna noted that it was the same handbag that had been sent to the newspaper.

'I'm getting thirsty,' Langton said impatiently, as they watched Louise order her third beer. He checked his watch. They had no sound on the footage, so they all sat watching in silence, broken only by the occasional whisper. Despite the phones constantly ringing and the muffled voices from the Incident Room, everyone's attention remained on the TV. After three quarters of an hour, Louise left her bar stool and walked off. Sharon was seen passing, her young rock musician in tow. If she was looking for Louise, she didn't appear to be concerned. Lewis stopped the film and Barolli looked at his time sheet. There were more tapes.

'We have two more sightings of her; the next is at the entrance, from when she first came in.'

Louise stood looking around, very much alone, presumably searching for Sharon; this time, she had an empty champagne glass in one hand, her handbag in the other. She returned back into the dark recesses of the club and the film was stopped again.

'Okay last and, I'm sorry to say, least, we've got her passing the bar but not sitting down. This time, she's got what we think is her maroon coat over her arm.'

Louise pushed her way past the crowded bar area; she was jostled and yet ignored. The club had begun to fill up; again, she seemed to be looking for someone: whether Sharon or someone else was impossible to tell.

'So she gets her coat and returns to the bar area, say looking for Sharon, who we know has gone off with her rock-and-roll boy, so what time do you reckon this is?' Langton asked, stifling a yawn.

'Quarter to twelve, maybe eleven-thirty. What we've looked at is running on actual time.'

'I am damned sure she either met her killer in the club or outside it; what about that footage?'

'No go; it was recycled.'

Langton pushed back his chair, pointing to the screen. 'Get that barman in to look at the tape; get anyone you can from the club that night to look at it. Someone might have seen something, though at the rate we are bloody going, I doubt it.'

He rubbed his chin. 'I don't understand it; she's gorgeous, sitting propped up at the bar and we don't get anyone that even remembers her. I'd remember her, wouldn't you?'

He looked at Barolli, who shrugged. Lewis said that he probably would. Langton was just moving when Anna spoke.

'She didn't fit in. Yes she's beautiful, but she's constantly biting her nails and looking around as if she is waiting for someone. Men can detect that needy quality she has; they can also detect, in my opinion, that Louise could be on the game. We know she was when she worked at the B&B.'

'Thank you for that insight, Travis,' Langton said, abruptly.

'I also think whoever it was might have been there told her to get her coat and she was looking for Sharon to say she was going.'

'What makes you say that?'

'At the end of the tape, she has an empty champagne glass. When we saw her earlier on, she was drinking beer. Their prices are high, so I doubt she bought the champagne for herself; as Sharon has said often enough, she was very careful with her money. The handbag, by the way, looks like the one which was sent to the newspaper.'

Langton gave a half-smile. 'Thank you, Travis, good; and this time you go back to the club with Barolli, see what you can come up with. Also put out the description of the clothes she was wearing. Sharon Bilkin had said she was wearing a black dress. She's obviously not, so put the new styles out – who knows, we may get a break.'

DAY SEVENTEEN

Anna was feeling ragged when she got to work the following morning at seven-thirty. She had been unable to sleep; something about the footage had niggled at her for most of the night. It had also occurred to her that if Louise had arranged to meet her lover at the club, there might be a record of the call. As she walked into the Incident Room, Bridget looked up, surprised.

'You're not due in until this afternoon. Aren't you going to Stringfellow's?'

'Yes, but I want to have another look over the footage.'

Bridget pointed to Langton's office. 'He's got it.'

Anna tapped on Langton's office door and waited. He opened the door in his shirtsleeves. He looked as if he had been there all night: he was in need of a shave, and on his desk was a row of coffee beakers lined up next to an overflowing ashtray. Behind him was a TV set, the footage paused.

'Morning. I wanted to look over the CCTV footage,' she said, as he returned to his desk.

'Be my guest,' he said, gesturing to the TV.

Anna drew a hard-backed chair closer to the TV. She told him she'd been unable to sleep, wondering about the phone call she felt Louise might have made. He shook his head.

'No, Lewis checked all the calls from Sharon's land-line. Sharon said she had never seen Louise with a mobile.'

'That doesn't mean she didn't have one,' Anna said.

Langton gave her a hooded look. 'We checked at the dental clinic and no one recalls her using a mobile phone, so it looks like you had a sleepless night for nothing.'

Anna puffed out her cheeks. 'Ah well; would have been too good.'

'I've not slept either.' He lit a cigarette and pointed to the TV. 'I was wondering if we'd got this in the wrong order.'

'Right, that was something I thought of last night.'

He cocked his head on one side.

'We have numerous tapes and they are not time-coded.'

Langton nodded. 'So what do you think?'

'Well, our last shots of her with her coat over her arm and the empty champagne glass could be much earlier.'

'What does that give us?'

'The way she sits at the bar as if waiting, constantly looking around.'

'Yes, and?' He sighed, stubbing out his cigarette.

'It's the way she's dressed; it's as if she is making some kind of statement.'

Anna took the book from her briefcase and showed him a photograph of Elizabeth Short. 'Look at the way she made up her face: white base, deep red lipstick, dark eyeliner.'

'Yes, and?'

'Well, if she was meeting our mystery man, and we go with the Svengali thing, then she made her face up the way he might have wanted it, but her low-cut top and that tiny skirt . . .'

'Yes, and?' He was impatient, rocking in his chair.

'She knew he would be there.'

Langton nodded, then pushed back his chair and picked up the remote. 'Right, let's look at the footage in the order we think it happened and see if it makes any difference.'

They worked side by side, switching tapes, scrolling through until they saw their victim sitting at the bar, ordering drinks, etcetera. At the end of it, they stared in silence at the frozen image of Louise on the screen.

'So having dicked around for half an hour, what do you think?'

Anna hesitated. 'I think our killer was at the club, and someone must have seen him.'

He nodded, and then checked his watch. 'I'll come to the club with you; now I need a shower, so get some breakfast.'

'I doubt anyone will be there; it's not yet nine.'

Langton opened his office door to be confronted by Lewis who was red in the face.

'We've got another letter.'

```
A certain girl is going to get the same as
LP got if she squeals on me. Catch me if
you can.
```

On the back of the envelope, there was more:

```
L. Pennel got it. Who's next?
```

A speeding patrol car took Langton, Anna and the handwritten note directly to the forensic labs to meet a handwriting expert. As they arrived, they received a call from the Incident Room: Dick Reynolds had called; he too had received another note, not handwritten, but using newspaper cut-out letters.

```
HaVe cHanGed mY mind. YoU wOuld Not
hA Ve giVeN me a sQuare dEal. Dahlia kIlliNg
was JuStiFied.
```

The handwriting expert deduced that their writer had taken great pains to disguise his or her personality by printing the message and endeavouring to appear illiterate; however, the style and formation of the hand-writing betrayed the writer as an educated person. He loathed being put under such pressure but he said that the sender was, in his opinion, an egomaniac and possibly a musician.

Langton tried to contain his impatience. 'Musician? What do you mean? I mean, what gives you that he was a musician from these notes?'

'The highlighting of certain letters is as if he is giving a musical weight to them.'

'Really? How about if he's just trying to disguise his writing?' Langton said edgily.

'That's also quite possible.' The expert added that the letter was feeding the writer's ego and that the writer would be unable to keep a secret; in his estimation, what had been written was the truth.

Langton and Anna went next to the *Sun*'s offices. Barolli confirmed to Anna over the phone that the wording of the letters was almost identical to notes sent by the Black Dahlia killer, the only difference that, unlike the LA killer, their sender had not named his next victim.

Anna could see the pressure coming down on Langton: these contacts said so much but held no clue as to the sender. The team had no fingerprints, just the handwriting and the expert's opinion that all contacts to date had been sent by the same person.

Reynolds was waiting in the reception; as he handed over the note in a plastic bag, his mobile rang. He listened and then looked shocked.

'We've got another one; it's in the mail room.'

It was after two when Langton and Anna returned to the Incident Room. The team were stunned to be told that Reynolds had had a second contact. Langton read the message out loud.

```
Go slow. Mankiller says Red Dahlia Case is
cold.
```

Langton was handed yet another letter by Lewis:

```
I have decided not to surrender. Too much
fun fooling police. Red Dahlia Avenger
```

Langton looked around the team and then shook his head. 'This is bloody unbelievable. Four contacts from the crazy bastard, and we can't keep the fucking journalist Reynolds quiet. He's going to print his letters!'

'What do we get from them?' Lewis asked.

Langton glared at him. 'That he's playing silly buggers with us — with me — and that if we are to believe him he's going to kill again!'

'But he says someone is *squealing*: who does he mean by that?' Barolli asked.

'I don't bloody know!' Langton snapped. 'I think he's just goading me.'

Anna watched as he headed towards his office. Everything about him was crumpled; he still had not had time to take a shower. She felt sorry for him. 'Are you coming to the club?' she asked.

'No, I've got my work cut out here; you get off there. Take Barolli with you.'

He slammed the door behind him. Anna was on her way to Stringfellow's with Barolli fifteen minutes later. They were driven in an unmarked patrol car, both sitting in the back with a driver up front. Anna explained to Barolli about the reordering of the CCTV footage.

'It's possible; do you know how many tapes we had to wade through? It's not my fault if we got it wrong.'

'Nobody is blaming you,' she said, quietly.

'Fifteen hours I had to sit through, fifteen!'

'Yes I know. By the way, did you check if Louise ever had a mobile phone?'

'Yes, and we don't think so. But at the same time, she could have bought one of those ten-quid, pay-as-you-go things which doesn't have to be registered.'

'Did you also check all the calls made from Sharon's land line?'

'Yes, don't you read the reports? Hairdressers, agent, nail extensions, hair extensions, gym classes! I bloody checked them all. No calls to our suspect, unless he runs a salon – that girl spends a fortune! So maybe one of them that did her beauty treatment is a suspect. I don't bloody know!'

Barolli huffed and puffed almost the entire way to the club. They had been under pressure for some time without a breakthrough, and it didn't look as if one was coming.

Anna and Barolli were met by the club's manager, an impatient man eager to get on with his day. He had arranged for both doormen and the two bartenders to come in early to talk to them, but none had arrived. He led them through a maze of Hoover cables past the cleaners who were putting broken glasses, cigarette packs and stubs from the previous evening into large black bin liners. None paid any attention to Anna or Barolli as they waited in a velvet-covered booth. Anna looked across to where Louise Pennel had sat and crossed to the bar. Anna sat on a stool, surveying the vast dance floor. She had a clear view of the entire club via the mirrors behind the bar. If Louise Pennel was, as she suspected, waiting for someone, it was a very good position: she could see the main entrance from reception into the disco area. She swivelled on the stool, then slid off to cross to the ladies' room. It also was in the process of being cleaned: by a group of girls who jabbered away to each other in Portuguese as they swept away the mounds of tissues and toilet paper strewn around the floor.

Barolli was drinking a cup of coffee when she returned to the booth.

'Did anyone question the cloakroom attendant?'

'No.'

'Well, we see Louise with no coat on, then with her coat off and over her arm, so she must have left it there.'

Barolli looked at his watch impatiently. 'I'll ask the manager if he can contact whoever was on duty that night.'

Ten minutes later, a heavy-set man with a crew cut, wearing a bomber jacket and jeans, strolled over. 'You wanted to see me?' he said begrudgingly.

'Yes; you want to sit down?' Anna gestured to her side.

'Okay, but I'm off duty you know. I don't usually come in until just before we open.' He slid into the booth. His chest was so wide that he nudged Anna.

'I really appreciate your time,' she said sweetly, and opened her file to take out the photographs of Louise Pennel.

'I've been shown them before,' he said.

'I know, but I would appreciate it if you looked at them again.'

He sighed. 'Like I said before, I work the doors; we get hundreds of girls every night. I remember the ones that cause trouble or the famous ones, but I don't remember this girl at all.'

Anna laid down the photograph of Louise with the flower in her hair.

'No, no memory of ever having seen her here, sorry.'

Anna next laid on the table the drawing of their suspect.

He looked at it, then shook his head. 'I don't know; I mean, he could be a number of blokes, but I can't say he's someone I remember. If you know he's a member that might help, but no, I don't know him.'

'He's maybe older than most people that come here?'

'Not really; we get them all shapes and sizes and all ages; lot of middle-aged guys come here, for the young girls, to watch the dancers, but I'm outside the club.'

'Well, thank you very much,' Anna said, stacking the photographs.

'I can go then, can I?'

'Yes, thank you.'

He squeezed himself out of the booth and walked back towards the entrance where he met another equally broad-shouldered man, who was at least six feet four; he pointed over to Anna and walked out.

Anna moved further round the booth to give the next doorman space to sit beside her. He reeked of cheap cologne and his hair was greased back.

'I've been asked about this girl before,' he said, as he sat down.

'Yes I know, but we are just hoping that something might jog your memory.'

'Right, I understand. I've been reading about her, but you know, I said before, I don't recall ever seeing her; we get hundreds a night in.'

Anna's patience was being tried. 'Yes I know, but could you just look over the photographs again, please?'

It was virtually the same response as from the previous doorman. Anna was relieved when he left; his cologne was making her feel sick.

Barolli returned and hovered. 'No luck?'

'Nope.'

'Well, like I said, I have questioned them, and all the taxi cabs that work the club.'

'Did you get any joy with the cloakroom attendant?'

'Yeah, she's coming in; should be another half hour.'

Anna sighed; it was feeling like a waste of time.

'This is the barman,' Barolli said, nodding over to the reception, as a tall handsome man headed towards them. He was wearing jeans and a T-shirt with trainers. He smiled.

'Hi, I'm Jim Carter. I'd have been here earlier but I had a problem with my car.' He slid in beside Anna.

Anna introduced herself as Barolli wandered off, looking bored.

She laid out the photographs and drawing. 'Do you recall her at all?'

He shook his head. 'Nope, and this guy isn't familiar.'

Anna pointed across to the bar. 'She sat on that stool for some considerable time. Can we walk over there?'

'Sure, anything to help.'

Anna sat on the stool used by Louise Pennel, and Jim Carter moved behind the bar.

'She was sitting here for a good while on the night she went missing. She had two beers, glasses not bottles.'

Jim nodded. 'If I'm serving, I'm on the go; we do a lot of cocktails, so it's shake and serve, shake and serve.'

'She paid for her drinks in coins, counting them out on the counter.'

Anna swivelled on the stool and leaned on the bar with her elbows. Jim stood with his hands on his hips, still no memory.

'She was constantly looking to the doorway into the reception area, as if she was waiting for someone.'

Yet again he shrugged. Anna described what Louise was wearing, and he still looked vague.

'I'd like to help you, but I'm sorry. I mean, she was very attractive, obviously, but when I'm working, you hardly get time to think, never mind remember anyone specifically.'

Anna thanked him and sat alone as he walked out into the reception area. She saw him chat to the two doormen still hanging around; they looked as if they were discussing the waste of their time as they turned back to look at her.

Barolli passed them with another cup of coffee. Anna watched him via the mirror behind the bar. He crossed to the booth and slumped inside. She watched as he tapped his foot, looked at his watch, and slurped his coffee. He leaned back and caught her eye, shrugged, then pointed to his coffee; she shook her head.

It was another ten minutes before Doreen Sharpe

arrived. She was the cloakroom attendant, a single mother in her early thirties.

'This shouldn't take long.' Anna once again laid out the photographs of Louise Pennel. 'Her coat was maroon with a velvet collar,' she said and described the rest of Louise's outfit.

Doreen took her time; she looked from one photograph to the next and licked her lips. 'I've been reading about the murder,' she said, softly. 'Terrible thing; they call her the Red Dahlia, don't they?'

'Yes, that is correct.'

'She didn't leave me a tip.'

'I'm sorry?' Anna leaned forwards.

'She left her coat. I put it on a hanger for her, gave her the ticket; it's sort of a courtesy thing the club has, you know: they don't charge you for leaving your coats, but you make it up in tips.'

'You remember Louise Pennel?'

'The coat didn't fit what she was wearing underneath it – very low-cut top and short skirt – it was more a coat worn by a rich teenager in the fifties. I used to have a second-hand one but it was green, vented collar and six velvet-covered buttons, but hers was red, dark maroon, and came from Harrods. I saw the label.'

Anna was flabbergasted.

'I put it on a hanger for her and gave her a ticket. It was quite early on. I have a system, you know; the early birds I put on the back rail because as the evening goes on, they are the ones that leave late. Don't ask me why, but they do; we get a big rush between eleven and two, people coming in from shows or dinner, and they usually stay only an hour or so, you have to have a system or you'd be searching through the racks like a demented idiot.'

'So you took her coat?'

'Yes, and hung it on the back rail. She took her ticket and went into the bar area, I think.'

Anna could hardly believe what she was hearing.

'It would be about eleven-thirty, maybe a bit after when she came back. I said to her that she was leaving early and she said that she had to go, so I got her coat. I passed it over and she walked off, without so much as a thank-you, let alone a tip!'

Anna showed her the sketch of their suspect. 'This is just a drawing of the man we think Louise might have been waiting for; did you see him?'

'I've been thinking about him,' Doreen said, tapping the sketch.

Anna could hardly contain herself. 'You saw him?'

'Well I think I might have; I couldn't be one hundred per cent sure.'

'In the club?'

'No, outside.'

'Outside the club?'

'Yes, by the fire escape doors, they lead into an alley; when we need a cigarette break, we nip out there. At the end of the alley is the road that runs behind the club. It's only a few feet away, and the parking attendants have a field day because punters think they can park out there, but they hand out tickets like confetti!'

'You saw this man?'

'Like I said, I am not one hundred per cent sure; it could have been him. I didn't get that much of a good look, what I saw was him sitting inside his car.'

'Do you know what make of car it was?'

'Black, very shiny, caught the lights, maybe the new Rover? I'm not good with cars, but my boss on the other job has one and it was similar to his, which is why I remember it.'

'He was sitting inside the car?'

'Yes, then he got out and walked round to the passenger side as she came up to the car. He opened the door and she sort of hung back; then he pulled her towards him and they looked like they were having some kind of argument, but from where I was standing I couldn't hear what they were saying. She pulled away from him and then he gripped her by the arm and pushed her into the car; he slammed the door so hard, it rocked the car. The reason I remember it was I saw her coat and I wondered if he was maybe her father, because I thought she was very over made-up. I mean she was only twenty-two, wasn't she?'

'Yes,' Anna nodded, glancing at Barolli who stared at Doreen in total silence. 'And he looked like this sketch?' Anna persisted.

'Yes, thin-faced, short hair, and he had this long dark coat on. It could be him; quite tall as well, but not well built.'

'Can you recall anything else?'

'No, I went back in, in fact before they drove off. I can only take a few minutes out there or there would be coats up the ying-yang, and I got to get someone to look after the tickets. I usually get one of the girls from the toilets: they have two on duty because people make such a mess in there.'

Just as Anna was about to thank Doreen for coming

in, she dropped another jewel in their lap. 'She had a friend with her, blonde girl, she's often at the club; she's a naughty one. She didn't stay more than an hour.'

Anna closed her eyes; this had to be Sharon.

'So I had to get her wrap, it was one of those bits of fur; you know, sort of a collar thing that's in fashion at the moment: you can't really hang them up on the hangers, you've got to tie them or they slip off. She was quite a little madam: she said for me not to tie a knot in the ribbon; anyways, she came back and she was with her.'

'I'm sorry, who was with her?'

'Your dead girl, she was with her; they were arguing and then the blonde girl opened her bag and gave her some money.'

Anna opened her file, searched around and brought out the photograph used by the newspapers of Sharon. 'Is this the blonde girl?'

'Yes, that's her. I mean, I don't know her, but I saw her picture in the newspaper as well, I recognised them both. The blonde has quite a mouth on her, and they was really having a row, and then she almost threw this money at her and screeched out something, then sort of pushed her; you know, like a smack, but it was a push.'

As Anna put the photographs back in the file, Barolli beat her to the next question.

'Why haven't you come forward with this information?'

Doreen looked startled. 'Well I didn't think it was anything interesting, you know. I didn't think it meant anything, really; it doesn't, does it?'

'It's a great help to us.' Anna smiled, though she didn't feel happy at all. She was furious that Sharon had not told them the truth about her last night with Louise. Doreen led them to the alleyway and fire exit. The road was not that far from the doorway and, as Doreen pointed out, it was very well lit. As they returned to the club, Doreen, who by now fancied herself as some kind of detective, stopped to show them the cloakroom.

'I think there was some jealousy going on between them. I mean, as I said, I didn't hear exactly what they were saying, *but* it was quite a nasty squabble; the dead girl was very upset afterwards. She went into the ladies', then next minute she's wanting her coat!'

Doreen was about to repeat everything she had told them about her methods of running the cloakroom, but Anna cut her short. 'You have been really very helpful, Doreen, thank you.'

'Is there a reward?'

Barolli glanced at Anna as he headed out.

'No, I'm sorry, there isn't.'

Barolli already had the engine ticking over as Anna joined him.

'Don't bloody believe this,' he muttered.

'What, you think she's lying?' Anna said, slamming her door closed.

'No, just the one person I didn't question, and bingo! Not that we got too much out of it.'

'You want to bet? I think that little cow Sharon has been holding out on us, so I want to get to see her a.s.a.p. I know it would be too much luck, but can you check if a traffic warden saw the car parked up? She said they stick tickets on anything parked in that road.'

Barolli nodded and made a call on his mobile as Anna tried to contact Sharon on hers. There was no reply. By the time they returned to the station, it was after twelve. As Anna was updating Langton, they were interrupted with a message to say that there had been no ticket issued to a black Rover; all the other vehicles parked in the road behind the club would now be checked, in case one of them proved to be their suspect's car. Two steps forward, one back, and by three o'clock, Anna still had not been able to contact Sharon.

The team were all gathered for a briefing; Langton had received yet another contact from their suspect. It read,

```
LP derserved to die, another victimm will
pay the same price
```

Partly in cut-out newspaper letters and partly hand-written in ink, it was signed *The Dahlia Killer*. The forensic experts felt this latest note was from the same person, deliberate spelling mistakes and all.

The press office was becoming agitated, wanting an update on what they could or could not release. Langton, with no suspect, was at his wits' end. It seemed, as the killer said, that the police could not catch him; despite the audacity of actually sending the notes to the Incident Room, the postmarks were from so many different locations that tracing the sender was impossible. The cheap lined notepaper and manila envelopes were both sold in bulk. Whoever had sent them had not licked the envelope, leaving no DNA, nor even a single fingerprint.

Langton maintained a calm front but he was looking worn out. Even with the latest information from the night-club, they still were no closer to identifying the tall, dark-haired man. The sketch had been in the papers over three consecutive days; he could not believe that no one had come forward. The Commander and her team were putting the pressure on and considering bringing in backup; to Langton, this meant he could be removed from the case.

Anna had assumed that after Professor Marshe had tripped up with the newspaper editor, she would not be called on again. Anna was wrong. Professor Marshe, looking her usual sophisticated self, arrived as the briefing ended and went straight into Langton's office.

While everyone waited for them to emerge, Anna yet again called Sharon Bilkin. There was still no reply; this time, her answerphone did not click on but made a whirring sound. Anna called Mrs Jenkins, the landlady, also without success. She felt as disillusioned as the other members of the team. They talked quietly to each other, mulling over statements and the nonstop phone calls coming in to the station. To date, they had had three 'confessors': three men of various ages appearing at the station to admit to the murder. It was a known hazard of any murder enquiry; some were even known to the police because they were persistent 'I done it' time-wasters. The three were all questioned and released.

Langton returned to the Incident Room at almost five forty-five, accompanied by Professor Marshe. He did not seem in any way attentive to her; if anything, he was cold and aloof, gesturing for her to sit. She produced notes and files and laid them out, then sat, straight-backed, in the chair.

'I have been studying the original case history of the Elizabeth Short murder, obviously, as you have all been doing, matching the notes and threats alongside your Red Dahlia.' She held up the two women's photographs. 'If we are to believe our killer has an obsession with the Los Angeles murder, and is now making a sickening mirror of it, then we have to take very seriously the threat to kill again.'

Anna gave a sidelong glance to Lewis to see him rolling his eyes at Barolli.

The Professor continued, laying out details of the LA victims, all purported to have been murdered by the same man. The first had been killed before Elizabeth Short: she had been an heiress, and had been found brutally killed in the bathtub of her own apartment. 'If this was his first kill, although it was messy and brutal, it did not have the same hallmarks as the murder of Elizabeth Short; the third victim, however . . .'

She held up a photograph of a woman called Jeanne Axford French. 'She had been kicked and stomped, which was similar to victim one, but this girl also had almost the identical slash wounds to her mouth as the Black Dahlia. The killer used the victim's own lipstick to write obscenities on her naked body: he printed "fuck you" on her chest. As with your victim, Louise Pennel, and as with the Black Dahlia, her underwear and clothes were missing. The killer struck four weeks after he killed Elizabeth Short, and possibly again another month later. No one was ever charged with these murders and it was surmised the killer either left LA or became dormant.'

Langton coughed and she turned towards him.

185

'I don't mean to sound impatient, Professor Marshe, but this has been in the papers! We are all privy to these cases, we've not exactly got the T-shirt but we've read the case history, the books, etcetera.'

'I'm aware of that,' she said, tetchily. 'I'm sorry if this is something you are aware of already, but I think it is necessary for me to explain the reasons for my grave concerns. You have a very dangerous killer on the loose, and one I believe has killed again. You must not think that the letters written are just threats, a ploy to get into the press. As well as enjoying himself playing games, he has to make sure that you are aware of the pattern of murders in the Black Dahlia case.'

Langton interrupted. 'Professor Marshe, we have taken every contact made very seriously. If he does intend to kill again, what we need is a profile that will help us catch him; so far we have the one suspect.'

'That you have been unable to trace,' she said brusquely.

'Not for want of trying,' Langton said tight-lipped.

'If he is intending to kill again, then it has to be someone that would have known Louise Pennel; his last note said that she deserved to die, that she betrayed him, isn't that correct?'

'Yes,' Langton said quietly.

'Then it is imperative you understand that his intention is to prove himself cleverer than you.'

'Me?' Langton said; it was as if he was mocking her.

'Yes, you. This game, although directed at the police as a whole, is a personal cat-and-mouse with the person heading the hunt for him, which is you, right? His notes have been addressed to you personally, correct?'

'Yes.'

'In the Black Dahlia case, the killer wrote copious notes to the press. When they actually made an arrest, he became enraged, saying that they were a forgery and that he would kill whoever sent them. What I am trying to make clear to you is that right now, your killer is out of control. His rage will manifest itself in another kill and it will be someone either that he knows, or that we know.'

Lewis had raised his hand to speak, but she chose to ignore him.

'It will be someone close to this enquiry, someone who will have information as to who he is.'

'We have not interviewed anyone that even knew him, let alone could give us any clue to his identity.'

'Go back and check. I truly believe his threat is very real and someone who knew Louise holds a clue.'

As Anna watched Langton interact with Professor Marshe her mind ranged over anything that she might have missed. If what Marshe was saying was true, then none of them would get home tonight.

Professor Marshe held court for another half hour, discussing each note in detail, but gave them nothing new to grasp, other than the concern that they might have overlooked some clue.

Anna went over to Lewis's desk; he was chatting to Barolli.

'I think she's a bullshitter. I mean, she started off telling us what we all knew and continued rabbiting on.'

Anna tapped his shoulder. 'Listen, if she is right, and it is someone we have interviewed, what about Sharon Bilkin?'

'What about her?' Lewis said, looking at his watch.

'Well, we got some more details today from the night-club: it looks like Sharon lied about what exactly happened at the club between her and Louise, so maybe she's lied about other things.'

Barolli yawned. 'So we talk to her again?'

'I've been trying to contact her, but I've had no reply. Now her answermachine sounds like it's full. I've also tried to contact her landlady, but no answer.'

'Let's haul her in tomorrow,' Lewis said, yet again looking at his watch.

'But I've not been able to get in touch with her!' Anna persisted. Barolli hesitated.

'You want to go over there?'

Anna nodded.

'Okay, I'll get a car arranged; you okay it with the Gov.'

Anna returned to her desk, packed up her briefcase and then went towards Langton's office. As she approached, she could hear raised voices.

'It is still just your submission; you don't have anything that will help me catch the fucker. We sat there listening to most of what you said, having known it before you even came onto the bloody case! If you think we haven't taken seriously these letters from this lunatic, then . . .'

'I never said you had not taken them seriously; what I did say was you have to take them as a real threat.'

'We have, but without a clue as to this fucker's identity and with no DNA, nothing from the letters, nothing from the package he sent, there's not a lot we can do. Right now, I've got the team sifting through every statement we've taken, because you think we've missed something. Well, it would be a bloody good move if you had something that would help; so far, all you've done is hamper the enquiry by gossiping to that editor.'

The door was flung open and an irate Professor Marshe almost bumped into Anna. She turned back into the room to look at Langton. 'I have apologised for that, but I am not staying here another second for you to swear at me!'

'I am almost begging you to give us something we can work on.'

'I have; I did; and that is as much as I can do,' she said, as she stormed past Anna.

Anna hovered a moment before she edged into the open doorway. 'I want to go and talk to Sharon Bilkin,' she said quietly.

Langton lit a cigarette and tossed the match into the ashtray.

'I have been trying to contact her all afternoon.'

'Fine, if you think she has the clue we have *missed* all the better.' He took out a hip flask and poured a measure, a very large one, into a coffee beaker. Anna closed the door, leaving him to drink alone. She suspected he was doing a lot more of the tippling; he had been, to her mind, very unlike himself during Professor Marshe's presentation. Whatever he might think, he usually was able to keep his temper under control, but he had been rude, and pointedly so. Perhaps he wasn't having an affair with her after all.

In the patrol car, she asked Barolli if there was anything going on between Langton and Marshe.

Barolli shrugged. 'She talked to us as if we were all fresh out of training school, and she's a bloody Yank! I don't know why he brought her to see us in the first place, I think she's been ruddy useless. Maybe he is getting the leg over. I wouldn't, frosty bitch.'

Anna gave a sidelong glance at the plump, sweaty detective; chance would be a fine thing. She gave a sigh as she looked out of the window: that was the difference between men and women; a woman would always have a clear assessment of who she could or couldn't pull, but men! As her father had once said to her, every actor thinks he should play Hamlet. She sighed again.

'You're doing a lot of sighing,' Barolli said.

'Am I? Maybe I'm just tired out; it's been a long day.'

'Yeah, for all of us, and another without a result. We carry on like this and old Langton will be replaced. I heard that the DCI he replaced is out of hospital, so they could bring him back; that'll be a smack in the face.'

'Yes,' she said, and sighed again, more quietly this time.

They pulled up outside Sharon Bilkin's flat and left the driver to wait as they rang the doorbell. No reply. Anna stepped back and looked up; there were no lights on. She rang Mrs Jenkins's bell. After a moment, her voice came through on the intercom.

'Mrs Jenkins, this is DI Anna Travis.'

The door buzzed open before she could say that Detective Sergeant Barolli was also with her. Mrs Jenkins hovered at her front door, wearing a towelling dressing gown.

'I was just going to have a bath; this is very late.'

'I'm sorry, but there is no reply from Sharon's flat.'

'I doubt she's in; I've not seen her for days.'

'Did she say she was going away?'

'No, I hardly ever speak to her; I go out to work every day, so I wouldn't really know what she's doing.'

'But doesn't she have another tenant?'

'No. She did have one, but she moved out; they didn't get along.'

'I see, well thank you very much.'

Anna turned to Barolli, who was checking his watch. It was getting late. 'What do you want to do?' she asked.

'Go home; we'll try again in the morning.'

Anna jotted down a note on her card and left it on a small side table in the narrow hallway. Like Barolli, she was ready to get home. Without a search warrant or any real reason to ask Mrs Jenkins to open Sharon's front door, there was not much more they could do. Mrs Jenkins hovered by her own door watching them leave.

Anna decided not to return to the station to pick up her car but get a tube home. Barolli left her walking along the road towards Baker Street station. Midway, something made her stop and turn back to Sharon's house. She rang Mrs Jenkins's bell again and had to wait for some considerable time before her voice answered on the intercom.

Mrs Jenkins was not best pleased and took some persuading to let Anna into Sharon's flat. 'Is it still about the murder?' Mrs Jenkins asked, gasping for breath, as they climbed the stairs.

'Yes.'

'So nobody's been arrested then?'

'No, not as yet.'

'I would have thought you'd have got him by now; it's been quite a while, hasn't it?'

'Yes, yes, it has.'

Anna looked into one small room after another to the soundtrack of Mrs Jenkins's heavy breathing. Louise

191

Pennel's old room was extremely untidy and smelt stuffy; the bed was unmade, and a bag of laundry had been left in the middle of the floor with dirty sheets dumped beside it. Anna looked into the bathroom. Discarded underwear lay on the floor next to the half-full bath; when Anna tested the water, it was cold. In Sharon's bedroom, too, the bed was unmade; clothes were strewn across the chair and the bed, and the tops were off the make-up bottles on the dressing table. In the kitchen, Anna found half a cup of cold coffee and a slice of toast; a bite had been taken out of the crust.

'Looks like she left in a hurry,' Mrs Jenkins said, peering over Anna's shoulder. 'Mind you, these young girls are so untidy. I don't think she's ever used the Hoover, you know, let alone dusted.'

Last, Anna checked the answerphone; as she had suspected, the message box was full. She took her hand-kerchief and pressed Play to listen to the calls that had been left. There were two calls from herself, a few from friends, and two girls answering the new advert Sharon must have put in to rent Louise Pennel's room.

'Well, my bath will be cold,' Mrs Jenkins said as she locked Sharon's front door. They headed down the stairs, and after thanking Mrs Jenkins again, Anna started to walk back to the tube station.

Relaxed after taking a long hot soak herself, and wrapped in a big bath towel, Anna made some Horlicks. She jumped when her phone rang; it was by now eleven-thirty.

'What did you get from the blonde bimbo?' Langton said.

'Nothing, she wasn't home, but I had a look over her flat and it looked like she had left in a hurry.' Anna added that the landlady hadn't seen her for a few days, but that wasn't unusual.

'Right okay, I want you and Lewis with me at the lab for the full details. Maybe he's got something, maybe not.'

'What?'

His voice was slurring, and she asked if he was still at the station. He said he was working over the statements.

He continued talking without really making any sense and it was Anna who ended the call, having to repeat twice that she was going to bed. Unable to sleep, she lay there with her eyes open. The Professor had said that their killer had made threats and they must take them very seriously because someone they had interviewed might know something that connected to him. She wondered what Sharon had not told her about the night at the club; did she know something? Had someone contacted her? The clothes strewn across her bedroom made Anna think that Sharon had been making up her mind what to wear. If she had run a bath and not got into it, made a coffee and toast but not consumed them, something had to have happened to make her leave. She sighed; thinking about what it might have been gave her a very uneasy feeling.

Chapter Nine

DAY EIGHTEEN

Langton was already at the mortuary the next morning when Anna and Lewis arrived. He looked dreadful. Everything about him was crumpled; he was unshaven, his tie was loose and his coat was even covered in dog hairs.

All three went into the lab. Lewis gave a sidelong glance at his Gov.

'Not got home last night, then?'

Langton ignored him, banging through the double doors and heading directly towards the body, draped in its green cover. Bill Smart was waiting, clipboard in his hand. He bellowed for them all to put on masks and paper suits before he would begin.

'We're not likely to contaminate anything at this stage,' Langton mumbled, irritated. 'It's not as if we haven't been here before!'

'Maybe so, but it's house rules.'

Langton, in his paper overshoes, shuffled closer to the body. Bill Smart, satisfied they were all now appropriately dressed, drew back the green cover to reveal Louise Pennel's face and torso.

'Since my last report we've done a lot of tests, so

194

today I can give you the full monty, so to speak. It's not very pleasant.'

Anna was still taken aback by the gaping slash to Louise's mouth. Even though she had seen the photographs many times, to see the reality of the appalling injury the killer had inflicted was shocking.

'Right. We have multiple lacerations to the forehead and the top of the head. There are also multiple tiny abrasions on the right side of her face and forehead. There are further lacerations, a quarter-inch deep, at the side of her nose. There is another laceration, a deep one, from the right corner of her mouth and the same on the left: these cuts opened the cheeks. There are numerous new caps to the front teeth, but at the back there is quite an advanced state of decay. Multiple fractures of the skull are visible. There is a depressed ridge on both sides and on the anterior portion of the neck. There is no evidence of trauma to the hyoid bone, thyroid or carotid cartilage, or tracheal rings. There is no obstruction in the laryngotracheal passage.'

Smart peered at Langton. 'You asked if she had been suffocated or strangled, so the answer is no. Her upper chest shows an irregular laceration with superficial loss of skin to her right breast. The tissue loss is more or less square and measures three and a half inches transversely. There are further superficial lacerations to the chest and an elliptical opening in the skin near to the left nipple.'

Anna stared at the body as the pathologist's voice droned on. Louise Pennel had been slashed and stabbed; part of her breast had been sliced off. But all Anna could see was that terrible gaping smile.

Next, the pathologist focused on the severing of the

195

body. The trunk had been completely severed by an incision straight through the soft tissues of the abdomen, severing the intestine and the duodenum, passing through the intervertebral disc between the second and third lumbar vertebrae.

'There are multiple lacerations on both sides of the torso and, as you can see, multiple criss-cross lacerations in the suprapubic area which extend through the skin and soft tissue.'

'Jesus Christ, it looks like he was carving out a game of noughts and crosses,' Langton said darkly.

Smart covered up Louise's head and torso before drawing the green cloth back to reveal the lower half of her body.

'The labia maiora are intact; within the vagina, we found a large piece of skin, which was from the upper torso. The anal opening is dilated and with multiple abrasions. Her missing nipple had been forced into her anal passage.'

Langton shook his head in disgust. Anna kept ramrod straight; she noticed that Lewis had quietly moved away.

Langton looked at Anna. 'This must never be released.'

Smart continued. 'There was nothing to suggest what she might have ingested as a meal or when she last ate something, so I have run further tests. Not only did we discover faecal matter in her stomach, but it had been introduced into her mouth. She had ingested it before death.'

Langton drew down the corners of his mouth in distaste. 'Is it her own?' he asked.

'I couldn't tell you: your killer removed a number of organs, including the small intestine.'

'Was she alive when these wounds were inflicted?'

'I'm afraid so. This poor little creature must have gone through untold agony; the causes of death were haemorrhage and shock due to concussion of the brain from massive blows to the head.'

'These small abrasions?' Langton said, nodding towards the lower part of the corpse.

'Could be a penknife, a scalpel: something sharp.'

'But there are so many.'

'This criss-cross cutting around her vagina must have been excruciating: the cuts are deep.'

'Okay, thank you.' Langton shuffled out of the lab in his paper overshoes.

Anna watched the two lab assistants prepare to wheel Louise Pennel's body back to the cold room.

'Have you ever seen anything like this before?' she asked Smart.

'No, thankfully I haven't. I think this is one of the worst cases I have ever had to deal with.'

'And you can't tell if she was raped?'

'The body was scrubbed clean and the internal organs were bleached, but I would say her killer subjected her to a vicious sexual attack: both her rectum and vagina have cuts and abrasions. Whether these were caused by a penis, I couldn't tell you. The parts of her breast were stuffed very high up inside her vagina, so it's likely that he would have used some kind of blunt instrument to force them there.'

'Thank you.'

Anna left the lab, discarding her paper suit in the bin provided. She reached the car park to find an irate Langton arguing with Lewis, whose face was red with anger as Langton jabbed him in the chest with his index finger.

'This is not to be released. We keep the lid on all this, including the fact that human shit had been forced into her mouth before she was killed.'

'All I am saying is, it's so disgusting that if someone was shielding the killer, this might just make them—'

'It will be between us and him: when we get him, and we will get him—'

Now it was Langton's turn to be interrupted.

'You so sure? Right now we have fucking bugger all and we need something to help us. Someone has to know this bastard!'

Anna stepped between them. 'Come on guys, this isn't the place!'

Langton turned angrily to Anna. 'I do not want this released to the press! Full stop!' He turned and walked off towards their waiting patrol car.

Lewis shrugged and sighed. 'All I said was—'

She touched his arm. 'I can guess, but if he doesn't want it to be released then he's the Gov, and we go along with what he says.'

They rode back to the station in silence.

Fifteen minutes after they had returned to the Incident Room, there was a call from the Commander. The naked body of a white female had been discovered dumped in a field off the A3, her beaten and brutalised body covered with a maroon wool coat.

Anna was in the same speeding patrol car as Langton and she noticed he used his hip flask during the drive. Lewis and Barolli were in the car behind. By the time they reached the murder site, it was well after midday. All four grouped together in a lay-by and then walked towards a group of uniformed officers, who as they approached parted to reveal the body. Langton nodded for them to remove the coat.

Anna drew in her breath sharply. Sharon Bilkin's naked body was covered in abrasions, and scrawled in large letters across her belly in red lipstick was 'FUCK YOU'.

'It's Sharon Bilkin,' she said quietly.

'Yeah, I know.' Langton took a deep breath. Sharon's mouth too had been slashed. The wound was not as deep or as violent as Louise Pennel's, but nevertheless it mirrored her hideous clown smile.

The uniformed officers told them that a farmer had discovered the body. They waited for the forensic team and the ambulance before they made their way back to their cars. It was a silent foursome that returned to the Incident Room. It was almost certain the killer was the same man they hunted, but until they had the post-mortem and forensic experts in, they could not be one hundred per cent sure. They had no weapon and no witnesses; the body had to have been dumped near the busy road under cover of night.

They would have to wait for the post-mortem to be completed to obtain a time of death. Anna returned to her desk and began making copious notes. She detailed Louise's autopsy report and the discovery of Sharon's body, then sat with her notebook open, tapping her pen. She had been trying unsuccessfully to contact Sharon for the past twenty-four hours; was she already dead, or did she die during that time? The team were frustrated that they were still no closer to identifying their one and only suspect. All Anna could think of was whether she could have prevented Sharon's death.

It was just after seven when Anna let herself into her flat. Ten minutes later, she received a call from Dick Reynolds, wondering if they could have dinner.

'I'm not that hungry.'

'What if I brought over some Cantonese duck and pancakes, with plum sauce?'

She laughed, and said maybe it would be a good idea.

Reynolds insisted he get everything ready. He had brought two bottles of very good merlot and she sat curled up on the sofa with a glass, watching TV, as he busied himself in the kitchen. They ate sitting side by side at her small breakfast bar. As they pasted on the plum sauce and rolled the shredded meat and crisp green spring onions inside the pancakes, Anna realised that she hadn't eaten all day. It was just a takeaway, but was nevertheless delicious. The food and wine, and Reynolds's easy conversation, made Anna relax, taking her mind off the Red Dahlia case for a while.

They were halfway down the second bottle when he asked her how the case was going. It was like a floodgate had opened: Anna couldn't stop talking, first about the discovery of Sharon's body and then the awful autopsy report. It might have been down to the wine, but in any event, Anna became very upset when she described what had been forced on Louise. She repeated a couple of times that Louise had been alive when it happened and then she knew she had said too much.

'Listen, none of this is going to be released, Dick; I

shouldn't have told you any of it, so promise me this is all off the record.'

'You don't have to make me promise,' he said, drawing her close. His arm around her felt comforting.

He asked about their suspects; Anna told him they had questioned several men who had insisted they had killed Louise Pennel and currently had one young soldier in custody, but it was believed that he was yet another time-waster.

'Why are you holding him then?' Reynolds asked.

'Well he was a medical student, then joined the army and was chucked out a few months ago; he has mental problems. We have to go down every avenue to make sure he isn't our killer before he's released.'

'But you don't think it's him?'

'No, none of us do, but we have to check him out.'

'How do you think the real killer would feel if he read about you having a suspect in custody?'

'He'd hate it; anything that takes the spotlight off him.'

'There doesn't seem to be much of that; there was hardly any press last week.'

'Because we can't trace this monster! We have no weapons, no DNA, nothing. He sends in these notes and we still have nothing; even with all the scientific skills we have these days, we can't get a result. He's ahead of us, playing with us: no saliva on the envelopes, postmarks from all over England, and if anyone saw him posting the letters to my Gov, no one has come forward.'

'How can you make them?'

'I don't know. I've said too much. I'm drunk.'

He tilted her chin up and kissed her. 'Okay if I stay tonight?'

'I'd like that.'

Anna had had too much to drink. If Reynolds had, it didn't show; far from it. He was gentle and caring and very affectionate. Afterwards, she slept in the crook of his arm: a deep, dreamless sleep. He, however, was wide awake. What he had learned had appalled and disgusted him, and made him angry. Anna didn't stir when he gently eased her out of his arms and went into the bathroom. He washed his face and was fully intending to go back to bed, until he saw her notebook in her open briefcase on the lounge table.

DAY NINETEEN

Showered and wrapped in a robe, Anna had made some breakfast while Reynolds took a shower. His hair still wet, he nuzzled her neck as she ate her toast. She offered him more coffee but he needed to get going, as he wanted to go home to get a clean shirt.

'Nope, I'm on my way.' He put his cup and plate neatly into the sink, kissed her, and was heading into the hall as the intercom went.

'It might be the postman!' she called out as he lifted the intercom handset. It was seven-thirty.

Reynolds stood at the front door as Langton headed up the stairs. 'Morning.'

Langton stared at him, then nodded his head. 'Morning. Is she up?'

'Yes, she's in the kitchen.'

'Thanks.'

Langton watched Reynolds head down the stairs before shutting the door behind him.

'Boyfriend's gone,' he said, leaning against the kitchen doorframe, looking smart and clean-shaven in a pinstriped suit.

Anna blushed. 'Is something up?' she asked.

'I put pressure on the lab; they said they would talk to me first thing, so here I am. You can drive us in.'

'Do you want a coffee?'

'You go get dressed. I know where everything is.'

'Give me a few minutes,' she said, as she squeezed past him.

By the time Anna came back, he had made himself some toast and was sitting on a high stool at her small breakfast bar, mug in hand, reading his newspaper: very much at home.

'Ready when you are,' she said, trying to sound light. She ran a glass of water and took two aspirin; she had drunk far too much last night.

'Headache?' Langton asked, folding his paper.

'Yes, bit of one.' Actually, her head felt terrible.

'Reynolds a regular visitor, is he?'

'Yes, you could say that.'

'Pumping you for information, I'll bet.'

'We do have other things on our minds,' she said tetchily. He grinned, slapped his thigh with his rolled-up newspaper, and then they were on their way, their dirty crockery abandoned on the breakfast bar.

They drove over to the mortuary. Langton fiddled with the radio then leaned back against the headrest. Anna's headache had got worse; she drove carefully. He had put the news channel on, but there was nothing about Sharon's murder.

'No press release on Sharon yet?'

'Nope. You still feel guilty about not going round there sooner?'

'Yes, but then I don't know if it would have done any good: we have no time of death as yet.'

She swerved to avoid a cyclist.

'I hate those bastards; that dewdrop hat makes him look like sort of some demented insect!' He turned to see the cyclist giving them a V-sign and laughed.

'You seem to be in a good mood this morning.'

'Yeah, well, I crashed out last night early and had a good eight hours' sleep. You look as if you could do with a bit more.'

'Thank you,' she said, flatly.

'So, this thing with the journalist is serious, is it?'

She hesitated, not wanting to discuss her private life with him.

'Sorry, don't mean to pry,' he said, smiling.

She could feel him watching her and it made her nervous: she shot a set of traffic lights, but he said nothing. In fact, they did not speak until they arrived at the mortuary.

They were gowned up and ready to view the corpse. Anna's head was throbbing; the small vein at the side of her temple felt ready to explode. Seeing Sharon with the hideous slashes to her lips, the bruises to her torso, and the red lipstick scrawled across her belly didn't help.

The pair stood in silence as Smart told them that he

had not had time to perform a full autopsy, but could confirm that Sharon had been dead for approximately forty-eight hours before she was discovered. Anna's guilt was somewhat eased; it meant that when she was trying to contact Sharon, she was already dead.

Two hours later, they were in the Incident Room. Langton told the team that it was almost a hundred per cent certain that Sharon Bilkin had been killed by the same man as Louise Pennel. Even the lipstick lettering matched the handwriting on the numerous cards and notes sent to Langton. The mutilations were not as horrific, but nevertheless Sharon had been subjected to torture and pain before she died.

The fact that she had been dead for forty-eight hours meant that, like Louise, Sharon had to have been killed somewhere else before being dumped in the field where she was found. The team were waiting for an update from forensics on whether they had managed to get anything from the maroon coat or the crime scene. Langton gave orders that, in the meantime, Sharon's flat should be re-examined and her phone calls double-checked: it was imperative to find out where Sharon had been before she was abducted. She might have accompanied her killer of her own free will, so they also needed to trace anyone who had seen her before she disappeared.

Langton broke up the briefing, as he had a meeting with the Commander. He was hoping to retain control of both murder enquiries. So that's what the suit was all about, Anna thought.

It was a Saturday afternoon, and neither Anna nor Barolli wanted to be at Sharon Bilkin's flat; nor did the forensic

205

team that arrived to dust for prints: they had already done a sweep of the flat for the Louise Pennel case and now they had to do everything again. Barolli was in a particularly bad mood as his local football team were playing. He and Anna were forced out of one small room and into the next to make way for the paper-suited scientists. In the kitchen, Anna found Sharon's diary, her childish writing giving details of her auditions and, far more frequently, her appointments for hair extensions, manicures and massages. She had had an appointment at a hair salon earlier that week to check over her hair extensions and replace those that had fallen out. The salon's receptionist told Anna that Sharon had not turned up. Next, Anna called an advertising company that Sharon was meant to be auditioning for; she had not turned up there either, so they had given the commercial to someone else.

Barolli was looking through Sharon's chequebooks and paying-in slips, which he'd found in the cutlery drawer.

'This is interesting: a week ago, she paid two thousand pounds in cash into her account.'

Anna looked up, frowning. The headache that had persisted throughout the day was still lurking.

'Is it rent?'

'I dunno; she has regular payments of two hundred going in that looks like rent.'

'Her tenants paid her, then she paid the landlady. What's the outgoing?'

'Shit!' He crossed to Anna. 'She's got twelve grand in her bank account!'

Anna flicked through the statements. As she had

thought, at the end of each month, there was a regular payment out to the landlady. Two five-thousand-pound lump sums had also been paid in.

'We need to talk to her bank manager, and the land-lady.'

Barolli nodded, slipping the chequebook and bank statements into plastic containers. He went back to searching through the kitchen drawer. As he pulled it further out, cutlery clattered out all over the floor. He swore and bent down to pick up the knives and forks, tossing them back into the drawer.

'I really need this on a Saturday afternoon,' he muttered.

Anna closed her eyes: forced to sit it out in the small kitchen, she felt as if the walls were closing in on her. She rubbed her temples to try to ease the pain, but nothing helped.

'I don't feel so good,' she said quietly.

'What?'

'I said I don't feel good. I think I've got a migraine.'

'You want to go home?' he said, banging the drawer shut. It stuck firmly, so he shook it out again. The clattering noise felt like needles going through her brain. Barolli was on his hands and knees, feeling around inside the unit.

'I'm going to be sick,' she said, and walked unsteadily to the kitchen sink.

'Christ, go into the bathroom; don't chuck up in here!' Barolli squinted into the drawer cavity. 'Something's caught between the drawers.' He reached further inside and then pulled out a brown manila envelope containing a bundle of fifty-pound notes.

'Don't handle the envelope too much,' Anna said and then hurried into the bathroom.

Anna filled a tumbler of water from the kitchen tap and sipped. She had not brought anything up, but her head was throbbing and she felt dizzy. Barolli had counted two and a half thousand pounds in cash into a plastic bag and he was keen to get back to the station to see if they could put a trace on the bank notes. When he suggested Anna go home, she didn't argue; she hadn't had such a bad migraine since she was a teenager.

Back in her bedroom, Anna drew the curtains and went straight to bed, an ice pack on her forehead. She lay with her eyes closed, wondering where Sharon had got all that money, but just thinking about it made her feel worse. She started taking slow deep breaths, trying to empty her mind, but she couldn't ignore the fact that they might have got something that would help their enquiry, perhaps even trace the killer. Eventually she got up and took a shower. She still felt very dizzy, so went to lie down again. This time she slept, a deep dreamless sleep, until early morning.

DAY TWENTY

Anna made some mint tea and had a dry piece of toast. She was feeling a lot better, but the shrill ring of her phone at seven-thirty made her wince.

'Travis,' he snapped.

'Yes?'

'You feeling better?'

'Yes, thank you.'

'Well, soon you won't be.'

'I'm sorry?' She tensed: Langton sounded furious. 'I'm sorry about yesterday; it was a migraine. If you need me to come in today, I can make it.'

'I'm coming to see you.'

'What?'

'Now!' And he slammed the receiver down.

She was left holding the phone in confusion, and feeling almost as angry as he had sounded. She wasn't expecting sympathy, but he could have been a bit more understanding: she hadn't had a day off sick since she had got her promotion.

Fifteen minutes later, Anna buzzed the intercom and opened her front door, waiting for Langton to appear on the stairs. If he had sounded angry on the phone, it was nothing compared to the obvious fury with which he approached her, carrying an armful of newspapers.

'You are in deep shit,' he said coldly.

'For Chrissakes, I had a fucking migraine,' she said angrily, slamming the front door shut after him.

'You'll probably have another. Have you read it?'

'Read what?'

Langton slapped down a rolled-up edition of the *Sun* onto her kitchen counter.

'Your boyfriend's article, yesterday's late edition.' He pointed to the paper. 'And if that isn't bad enough, everyone else has run with it!' He threw down the other papers he was holding. 'Look at the bloody *News of the World, Mail on Sunday, Sunday Times, Observer, Express* . . . Exactly what I didn't want, Travis: a media frenzy.'

Anna could feel her body shaking as she picked up

209

the *Sun*. Opening it, she read the headline on page seven
– RED DAHLIA KILLER SUSPECT HELD.

Richard Reynolds's exclusive detailed virtually their
entire conversation. The article stated that the suspect
was a soldier with medical training and that he had
admitted to the murder of Louise Pennel. It also gave
details of the mutilations she had suffered and the autopsy
results.

'He hasn't missed out a fucking thing, even down to
the fact she was forced to eat her own shit!' Langton
was like a caged animal; fists clenched, he paced up and
down the small kitchen. 'What in Christ's name were
you thinking?'

Anna wanted to burst into tears.

'I warned you! Talk about sleeping with the bloody
enemy! Have you any idea what repercussions this is
going to create for me – for the entire team?'

Anna sat on one of her kitchen stools. She was
shaking.

'It's beyond belief that you could be so unprofessional, even after I warned you. Jesus Christ, Anna, how
could you have been so stupid? Why did you do it?'

She closed her eyes, squeezing them shut tight.

'Well? What have you got to say for yourself?'

She took a deep breath. 'I told him that whatever we
discussed was . . .'

'Was what?' he snapped. 'Headline news?'

'I asked him – no, I told him – that whatever was
said between us was private.'

Langton shook his head in despair. 'Private. Private?
You are investigating a brutal murder; what do you mean,
whatever you said to him had to be private? You are a

detective, you know the law — you've broken the law, for Chrissakes, don't you understand? You have given highly confidential information to a journalist. What happened? You have a few too many drinks and couldn't hold your tongue? Is that why you had to leave the enquiry yesterday? Because you were so hung over?'

'That's ripe, coming from you.'

She regretted saying it instantly, but it was too late. His eyes bore into her with such hostility that she had to look away.

'I'm sorry. I shouldn't have said that.'

He rolled up the newspaper and tapped it on the edge of the counter. 'I don't know what I am going to do about this, Anna.'

She licked her lips; her mouth was bone dry. 'Do you want me off the team?'

'That's a possibility. I think, under the circumstances, at the very least you'll have to come off the case. I need a few days to think about it. This could have severe repercussions for me. As it is, I am hanging onto this investigation by my fingernails. This load of shit that's gone down today won't stop with just the one article: every paper has picked up on it and I am going to have to deal with it.'

'I'm so sorry.'

He nodded, then said very quietly. 'You should be.'

Anna heard the front door close behind him. She sat staring at the kitchen wall and began to sob. Every time she dried her eyes and told herself to get it together, she broke down again. She sat on the toilet and cried. She lay on her bed and wept. It was almost an hour later when she managed to close the floodgates, her eyes puffy and red-rimmed. Now she really thought about the consequences, and she knew her error could end her career. As always, the photograph of Jack Travis, her beloved father, was on her bedside table. She stared at his strong face and his deep-set eyes. She hugged the frame.

'Well Pop, I screwed up and I got screwed. This is what it comes down to: the bastard used me.'

She sat up and put the photo back in its usual place. All the years of training, all her ambitions could be swiped aside if Langton so chose. She made her bed for something to do and then wandered into the kitchen. She brewed some coffee and sat feeling wretched, though at least the tears had dried up. She wondered what her father would have advised her to do. She was certain he would never have found himself in the same boat. Langton was right: she had been stupid.

As if on automatic pilot, she finished her coffee, washed up, cleaned the kitchen then tidied the lounge, until everything in the flat was in order; she even vacuumed the hall. She emptied the kitchen bin, the clank of empty bottles a reminder her of her night with Reynolds. They had drunk two bottles of red wine between them; usually, Anna's quota was no more than a couple of glasses, so it was no wonder she'd felt unwell the next morning. She flung the bag into the bin outside the flats. By the time she returned to slam her front door closed, she was angry. Hands on her hips, she stood in the hall and muttered to herself.

'The bastard, he must have done it on purpose!' She reread Reynolds's article and pursed her lips. She *had* been drinking, but she knew there was stuff in there that she had not discussed with Reynolds. She felt physically sick when she remembered opening her briefcase, but not getting round to looking through her notebook, the night that Reynolds had stayed. Now every crime desk was buzzing with its contents.

Anna went into her bathroom and washed her face with cold water. Her eyes were still red-rimmed; she patted her face dry and put on some make-up. She donned her best coat and shoes and headed for the front door. She drove to the newspaper's main gates. When she was asked if she had a security pass, she showed her ID and said that Mr Reynolds was expecting her. She was waved through and told to park in the visitor bay by the side of the building. She was surprised by how calm she felt as she headed towards the reception area. As it was Sunday, there was only one receptionist on duty; fortunately it was the one she had met previously.

'DI Anna Travis.' She showed her ID. 'Dick Reynolds is expecting me: can I go straight through?'

She watched as the girl wrote down her name, time of arrival and who she was visiting on an identification label which Anna then pinned to her lapel. The receptionist was just about to pick up the phone and call through to the crime desk when two more visitors appeared, requiring her attention.

'It's okay, I know where I'm going,' Anna said. As she pressed for the lift, she was pleased to hear the receptionist attending to the visitors rather than speaking to Reynolds.

The lift stopped at the newsroom floor and Anna made her way along the corridor, pausing a moment to make sure she was going in the right direction, then turning into another corridor that led into the main newsroom. No one paid her any attention as she walked briskly between the rows of desks.

Wearing jeans and a blue sweatshirt, Reynolds was sitting with his back to her. He was perched on the edge of his desk with a coffee, regaling his colleagues with some joke. He threw back his head, chortling with laughter. 'I couldn't bloody believe it! He had his trousers round his ankles—' Reynolds broke off as the others clocked Anna walking purposefully towards them. He did a half-turn and almost slid off the desk. 'Anna!' he said smiling, his arms wide.

She walked right up to him, so that their bodies were almost touching, and he blushed.

'This is a surprise,' he said. He edged away from her a fraction.

She took the newspaper from under her arm and slapped it against his chest. 'Not as much as I had when I read this.'

He gave a shrug. 'Look, I'm a journalist.'

'Don't give me your bullshit; this was highly confidential!'

'Now, wait a minute; a lot of it's public domain.'

'Some of this isn't and you know it. How could you do this to me?'

'Anna, like I said, I'm a journalist. This is a big story.'

'You knew what I told you was confidential! And what I didn't tell you, you got out of my notebook. What did you do? Wait until you'd got me drunk? Until I had fallen asleep, so you could creep out of my bed to filch it?'

'Anna.' He took hold of her arm; their confrontation

was exciting a lot of interest among the other journal-ists at their desks.

She swiped his hand away. 'I have been kicked off the case. I probably have no career left, but that wouldn't interest you, would it? You got your story and to hell with any consequences or trouble you might have got me into – and I am in big trouble. I think you are de-spicable!'

Reynolds pursed his lips, then reached over his desk and picked up the Black Dahlia book. 'There was an LA journalist who broke the news about the Black Dahlia suspect. All I was doing was following what happened in the original murder enquiry.'

'None of what I told you was ever connected to that.'

'Yes it was. What you had not told me was what your victim had been subjected to, and it is the same as the Black Dahlia, so even though you are trying to discon-nect the two . . .'

'I'd like you to eat shit!' she snapped. Reynolds knew she was referring to what Louise Pennel had been forced into doing and it angered him.

'Don't be so crass. What you might not realise is that I work for the *Sun*, and although we are part of the same group that publish the *News of the World*, it's a different bloody newspaper.'

'So what did you do? Sell the information? It had to come from you, so don't try and say you had nothing to do with it!'

'Don't you understand? The *News of the World* filched their article from mine!'

Anna continued, her voice rising. 'We had not allowed

that information to be leaked, because if we did bring in a suspect—'

'You have one. You told me.'

'I also told you that it was highly unlikely he was the killer. Now you've blasted it out.'

Reynolds looked around at the people listening and again tried to draw her away, but she wouldn't budge.

'Let's go and have a coffee, talk in private about it,' he said.

'I don't want to be in your company longer than it takes to say what I have come to tell you. I want nothing more to do with you. If this has hampered the enquiry, then you will have DCI Langton to deal with. This is just for my personal satisfaction. You are a creep and a two-faced bastard.' She picked up the coffee he had left on his desk and threw it in his face. It was a good hit: his hair was soaked and his face dripping.

'That's very childish.'

'Maybe, but it's made me feel better.' She turned and walked away as he tried to mop up the coffee from his face and his sopping shirt.

By the time she got back to her car, she was shaking with nerves. She drove home, hardly able to think straight, and her anger was unabated as she parked and let herself into the flat. She almost broke down in tears again, but refused to allow herself to. She tipped out her briefcase and searched through *The Black Dahlia* for the section that Reynolds had mentioned. She carried it into the kitchen and sat reading it over and over.

The original article had been written by a screen-writer and sent to the *LA Herald Express*. As Reynolds had said, it covered much the same ground as his article, describing the gruesome injuries of the victim and revealing that a suspect was being held in custody. Its publication had prompted the real killer to admit the murder, wanting recognition for his hideous crime and to claim the publicity he had earned.

Anna's mouth was dry as she drove to the station. She walked slowly up the stone steps and approached the Incident Room. She stood for a few moments outside the double doors, listening to jangling phones and muted voices, before mustering the guts to push them open.

The room fell silent as everyone turned to stare at her. She walked to her desk and took off her coat, folding it over the back of her chair. She could see the glances passing back and forth, and knew her cheeks would be pink with embarrassment, but she kept going. Taking from her briefcase her notebook and pencil, she proceeded to the front of the room to stand by the white crime board. There were a lot of copies of the newspaper article lying around. It was Lewis who spoke to her first.

'You've got a lot of bottle, Travis.'

'Not really, but I need to say something to everyone.'

'Floor's yours.' He gestured to the room; everyone was listening.

Anna coughed and then lifted her head to stare at a small spot on the wall directly in front and across from where she was standing.

'I really fouled up, and I am here to apologise to everyone. I had too much to drink and I foolishly trusted Richard Reynolds, the journalist. When I told him that what I was saying was highly confidential and not for publication, he promised me that it would go no further. I have no excuse, bar the fact I had that afternoon been through the hideous autopsy report on Louise Pennel and then seeing Sharon Bilkin's body. I can only apologise and, if what has happened as a result of my stupidity creates problems for this enquiry, I am ashamed and deeply sorry. That's all; again, please accept my apologies for my unprofessional and very naive conduct.'

Anna returned to her desk, leaving everyone unsure how to deal with what she had said. It was almost as if they wanted to give her a round of applause for standing up to them. Anna had been so nervous that she had not seen Langton appear, listen and walk back into his office. She packed up her desk, and was reaching for her raincoat when Barolli came over and handed her a coffee.

'I'd just let him brood a few more hours, I'm sure this won't—'

'Travis!' came the bellow before he could finish.

Anna turned to see Langton holding the blinds of his office window open; he gestured for her to join him and then let them flip closed again. She tapped on his door and waited a beat before she went in.

'You've got a lot of nerve,' he said, standing in front of his desk with his thumbs caught in his braces.

'I meant everything I said.'

'I bloody hope you did, but it doesn't alter the facts.'

There was a pause as he glared at her. She felt like a naughty schoolgirl standing in front of her teacher; she had to bite the inside of her mouth hard to stop the tears welling up.

'What do you think your father would have to say?'

'He would be ashamed.'

He nodded, and then checked his watch. 'Go home.'

'I was intending to do that.'

As she walked to the door, she paused a moment. 'Did we get anything from the cash found at Sharon's flat?'

'Not yet; it's Sunday, remember?'

'Oh, I know what day it is, and one I won't forget.'

She walked out and closed the door quietly behind her. Passing through the Incident Room, she got a few glances and smiles, but they didn't make her feel any better. She went up to Lewis, who was printing serial numbers on the board.

'We might get some luck with these. There's over a thousand pounds in new notes; the rest are all odd numbers.'

Anna hovered and then asked if she could speak to him in private. He looked nonplussed and then gestured to the corridor.

Anna gathered her things and went to wait for Lewis. It was a few minutes before he joined her.

'I spoke to Reynolds this morning; his excuse for what he had done was that in the Black Dahlia case, a screenwriter wrote a similar article—'

'Yeah, yeah, I have read the book.'

'Then you know what happened after the article was written: the killer was so angry about this suspect that was held claiming all the credit—'

Lewis interrupted her, impatient. 'We released our suspect this morning; we sent him back to where he walked out from, an institution over in Tooting: it was another time waster.'

'Yes I know that, we suspected it from the moment

he walked in. What I am saying is, the article on the old Black Dahlia case was in actual fact a ruse, made up by the journalist to try and flush out the real killer.'

Lewis sighed, even more impatient. 'Anna, I know: we've all read the book; the time waster we just released had also read the book! You're not telling me anything we haven't discussed this morning. Unless I am hearing you wrong and you are trying to tell me that you gave all the information to this prick at the *Sun* because you were trying to flush out the real killer?'

'No, I am not saying that.'

'Then what exactly are you trying to tell me?'

She hesitated. It was obvious she never intended for it all to happen, but what if it did do some good? 'Listen: what if such a big article, and in all the Sundays, might be enough to dent the real killer's ego? He'll want to make sure we know we are holding the wrong man.'

'The Gov's already reasoned that might happen, so he's been in touch with your boyfriend, seeing if he can repair some of the damage.'

Anna was taken aback. Langton never ceased to surprise her.

'You should thank him, because if he does go down that route, it'll get you off the hook. He'll be saying that the whole nasty episode was a ruse to flush the bastard out. It depends on whether or not we get a result.'

'If you do, does that mean I'm still on the case?'

'Don't ask me, I didn't know you were off it. I suspected you'd be in deep trouble, but you know the Gov – he always protects his team.'

Lewis went back into the Incident Room leaving Anna in the corridor, a lump in her throat.

Chapter Ten

Anna was watching the early-morning news when the phone rang. It was Barolli; he had been instructed to tell her they needed her to help man the phones. She was out of the flat and in the Incident Room in ten minutes. Langton wasn't there; he had been called in for a big pow-wow with the top brass. No one said anything to her; it was just accepted that she was back.

The daily newspapers had all run articles based on the coverage in yesterday's papers, unaware that the suspected Red Dahlia killer was no longer in custody, but correctly saying that the police had received many notes, apparently from the killer, and that each one had been authenticated as being written by the same person. Calls were coming in thick and fast, but by midday, there had been no contact from their killer. Barolli and Lewis were out, trying to trace the bank notes found at Sharon Bilkin's flat; it was the only new development, apart from her tragic murder. Anna worked the phones alongside uniformed and clerical staff. It was Bridget who took the call, and she immediately came over to Anna.

'What is it?'

'It's a woman, and she's very nervous. She's called twice and hung up. I recognised her voice; this is the third time. She says she has information and needs to speak to someone on the enquiry.'

'Put her through to me.'

By the time Bridget returned to her desk, the caller had hung up. They had hundreds of hang-ups along with time wasters, so Anna continued contending with the incoming calls. At three-fifteen, Bridget signalled to Anna. 'It's her again.'

Anna nodded, and Bridget said told the caller she was transferring her to a senior officer.

'Good afternoon, this is DI Anna Travis speaking. Who is this?'

'Are you on the murder?' The woman's voice was very faint. 'The Red Dahlia murder investigation?'

'Yes I am. Who is this?'

Silence. Anna waited a moment. 'Can you give me your name? All calls are treated as highly confidential.'

There was another pause. She could hear the woman breathing.

'Hello? Are you still there?'

'Yes, but I have to be anonymous.'

'But you are calling about Louise Pennel?'

'The Red Dahlia. She is the Red Dahlia, isn't she?'

'That is what the press call her.'

Anna sighed, impatient; she had had so many calls like this. 'Could you please give me your name and address?'

'No, no I can't, but I think I know who he is. She stayed at his house.'

'I'm sorry, but could you repeat that?'

Anna signalled that she wanted a trace put on her call. The tracer team were set up in the Incident Room, ready and waiting, in case the killer himself made contact.

'Oh God, this is terrible.'

'I am sure it must be, but if you do have something that you think could be connected, it would really be appreciated. Could you give me your name?'

'No, no I can't.'

'That's all right, just tell me what information you have. Hello?'

Anna looked over to see if the call was being traced. They signalled for her to keep the caller on the line. Anna kept her voice low, trying to encourage the caller to give more details.

'It is often very distressing, especially if you have suspicions regarding someone you know. Do you know this person?'

'Yes.' Her voice was hardly audible.

'And you say that the girl, Louise Pennel, was . . .'

'The Red Dahlia,' the woman interjected. There was another pause, then an intake of breath, like a gasp. 'I think she was at his house.'

'Could you tell me his name?' Anna looked over again; the officer gestured for her to keep talking: they had not had enough time to trace it. 'You know, anything you tell me will be in the strictest confidence.'

'Oh God, this is awful, and I might be wrong, I don't know what to do.'

Anna again glanced over but the officer still shook his head.

'I think it might really help you if you did tell me what you know.'

Anna listened as the woman gave a dry sob.

'You sound as if this is really distressing you. You said you may be wrong; if so, we could check it out for you and put your mind at rest.'

The line went dead. Anna closed her eyes in frustration. They were only able to determine that the call was from a mobile phone; as yet they could not pinpoint the location.

Bridget joined Anna. 'What do you think?'

'Well, she sounded distressed enough that it could be real; on the other hand, how many of these have we had?'

'A lot. But no one else keeps calling back.'

Anna shrugged; they would just have to wait to see if she called again.

The mail to the Incident Room was being checked over for further anonymous notes. They had been sent several. By mid-afternoon, three had been singled out by their expert as written by the same hand as the ones previously sent to DCI Langton. Again, an attempt had been made to alter the writing, and some words were crudely misspelled.

IF HE CONFESSES, YOU WON'T NEED ME

THE PERSON SENDING THOSE OTER NOTES OUGHT TO BE ARESTED FOR FORGERY HA HA!

ASK THE NEWSPAPER JOURNALIST FOR A CLUE, WHY NOT LET THAT NUT GO, YOU HAVE THE WRONG MAN.

Anna stood in front of the board with the rest of the team.

'They are almost identical to the notes received in the Black Dahlia murder,' Anna said to Bridget. As she spoke, copies were being pinned up alongside the other contacts by the killer. 'Maybe the article has pushed him into sending them, but he's still left no finger-prints and we can't trace the paper. Anything on the postmarks?'

'No, from all over London: Kilburn, Hampstead and Richmond. They were all sent on the same day as well. We've got people out there, hoping someone saw whoever posted them, but it's a long shot.' Bridget gave an open-handed gesture. 'It's crazy, isn't it?'

Justin Collins was not expecting the two officers who turned up to speak to him at the Chelsea antique market. He was very nervous when Lewis and Barolli showed him their ID. He was a tall, thin-faced man with a flam-boyant necktie and tweed jacket with leather elbow patches. Mr Collins specialised in Art Deco figures, paint-ings and crockery. He thought at first that they had come about the handling of hot items, but when told it was about money, he looked confused. He admitted he had withdrawn a thousand pounds in fifty-pound notes from Coutts in the Strand. He opened his ledger to check when he had paid out the money. He had bought numerous items, but none for a round sum of a thou-sand. Lewis asked if he could check out any items costing more. He was sweating as he looked from page to page, saying that he often bought on an *ad hoc* basis from dealers and customers who walked into the shop with goods for sale. He also went to many antique fairs up and down the country.

Lewis showed him the drawing of their suspect. He glanced at it and shrugged.

'To be honest, that could be any one of a few customers I have dealt with over the years. Is he in the business?'

'He is a suspect.'

'Ah well, I wish I could be of more assistance.'

'We hope so too, Mr Collins. You see, that money we have traced to you was found in a victim's flat; this is a murder enquiry.'

'Oh Christ. Let me get my other glasses and check my sales books.'

They waited silently as he sat thumbing through one book after another. Lewis sighed; he was pretty sure what he was witnessing was one set of accounts for the taxman and another that never saw the light of day.

'This could be it.' Collins tapped a page. 'It was at the Kensington Town Hall antique fair; over three months ago, I had a stall there. Yes, this could be it, but I paid more than a thousand: it was actually two and a half thousand.'

'Do you have the address of the person who sold you the item?'

'No no, I'm afraid I don't. I'm also afraid I don't have the brooch. I sold it.'

He flicked through another book and then pointed. 'Yes, I sold it to an American dealer; it was an Art Deco diamond-and-emerald brooch, a very nice piece, in good condition. I have the address of the buyer here.'

Lewis chewed his lip and waited as Collins jotted

down the name and address of a woman in Chicago. Terrific!

Barolli was becoming impatient and leaned forwards. 'Okay Mr Collins, what's important to us is who sold you the brooch.'

'A young woman; she said she had inherited it from her grandmother.'

'Do you have her name?'

Collins became more flustered. 'No, as I said, it was brought to the fair. I looked at it, then went over to a friend of mine who deals in jewellery and he said it was a very good price; in fact, an exceptionally good price.'

'Can you describe the woman who sold it?'

'Yes, yes: young, blonde, quite attractive.'

Lewis took out the photograph of Sharon Bilkin. 'This woman?'

'Yes, yes that's her. I'm certain of it.'

Langton sat at his desk as Lewis explained what they had discovered from the antique dealer.

'What might have happened is that someone gave Sharon the brooch, she then takes it to the antique fair to sell. I think the dealer was telling us the truth. We can double-check with the guy who said the brooch was a good buy; maybe also verify it was Sharon Bilkin selling it.'

'Go back and question any of Sharon's associates; see if they know anything about how she got this brooch.'

'Do you want us to try and find the woman that bought it?'

'In Chicago? Do me a favour!'

'Someone might recognise it,' Lewis said, flatly.

'Yeah, yeah, maybe try and give her a call. Do you have a number?'

'No.'

'Fucking brilliant! Did you get a description of it?'

Lewis shifted his weight. 'Yeah, it was a diamond-and-emerald cluster, like a flower, Art Deco, platinum clasp and safety pin.'

Langton gave an open-handed gesture. 'Get on to it.'

Lewis nodded and walked out, leaving Langton moodily checking over copies of the notes sent in by their suspected killer.

Anna was sifting through her notes and making a list of the people she had talked to about Sharon. She was about to print off a page of names and addresses when Bridget signalled to her from across the room.

'It's her again!' she mouthed.

Anna reached for the phone. 'Hello, this is DI Anna Travis. I am part of the Red Dahlia murder enquiry team. We really appreciate anyone calling who can give us any help.'

Anna listened; the woman was crying.

'If whatever you have to say to us is worrying you, then just stay calm, take deep breaths. Your call will be treated with . . .'

'This is the Red Dahlia murder, isn't it?' The caller's voice was high-pitched and frightened.

'Yes, that is correct. Would you like to give me your name and then I could come round and see you? It might be easier than talking on the phone.'

'No, no, I can't, I can't do that. I don't want you to know who I am.'

Anna kept her voice calm and steady. They were trying to get another trace on the call. 'But you do have something you want to tell me?'

'Yes.' Her voice was fainter, as if she was standing away from the phone.

'And this is connected to the Red Dahlia murder?'

'Yes, yes!' She was close again now and her voice had become shrill.

'So let's just stay calm. My name is Anna, so if you would like to tell me, then I will deal with whatever it is.'

Pause.

Anna looked at Bridget, frustrated: it sounded like the caller was going to hang up again. 'You have been very brave so far; it must have taken a lot of guts to call. If you have some information about someone you know — is that right?'

'Oh, Christ. I can't do this!'

'Just tell me what it is; you'll feel a lot calmer once it's over and done with and . . . hello? Hello?'

Anna was furious; she'd lost her. But then the caller started to mutter something inaudible: she was still on the line.

'I can't hear what you're saying.'

'I think it's him.'

'I'm sorry, I didn't quite hear what you said.'

'I think I know who it is. Oh Christ, this is terrible, this is awful, and he'll know it was me, he'll find out and he'll kill me, he'll hurt me!'

Again Anna thought she was about to hang up, but she was still there, breathing erratically as she tried not to cry.

'Who are you talking about? And if you are afraid of this person, then we can help you.'

'No you can't!'

'We can protect you.'

'No you can't.'

'Why don't you just tell me what you know and then I will be able to help you. If you don't want me to know who you are, then that's all right; it's just that if you do have information that can help us . . .'

It was like pulling teeth. The woman sounded stoned or drunk; her voice had grown more slurred during the call.

'Hello? Are you still there?' Anna listened.

She looked over to the guys tracing the call. They put their thumbs down and gave the signal for Anna to keep her talking.

There was a long pause and then the caller said very clearly: 'His name is Charles Henry Wickenham; Doctor Charles Henry Wickenham.'

The phone went dead. Anna stared at the receiver.

Chapter Eleven

DAY TWENTY-TWO

The team tried not to get their hopes up over this new development: the caller could be a wife or a mistress with a grievance, wanting to create as much trouble as possible. Nevertheless, there was a real buzz in the Incident Room the next morning. Before they could even think of questioning Doctor Charles Henry Wickenham, they needed to find out who he was.

The woman's last call to the Incident Room was traced to a call box in Guildford, but the address listed for Dr Wickenham was for a very substantial property in a village ten miles outside Petworth. Mayerling Hall was a Grade II listed house with quite a history: King Henry VIII was said to have used it at one time as a hunting lodge. The team had been able to secure plans of the property from the council, as there had been many extensions built onto the original house over the years. The estate included stables, outhouses, a staff cottage, outdoor swimming pool, and a barn that had been converted into a fully equipped gymnasium.

Wickenham had no police record but was a doctor. A retired army surgeon, he had travelled the world and was a well-respected member of the community, playing a substantial part in village life in terms of local politics and environmental issues; he was a member of a local hunt, and his stables contained three hunters. He had been married twice, widowed once, and had paid substantial alimony in his second wife's divorce. He had had children with both of his wives: two daughters and a son and heir, thirty-year-old Edward Charles Wickenham. The son lived in a cottage on the estate and had also been widowed, but has now living with a Gail Harrington. Edward had no children; his ex-wife had committed suicide four years ago.

Although the team had discovered so much about the

man they now earmarked as a suspect, they still had not yet heard back from immigration or passport control with further details or photographs of either father or son.

Langton, dressed smartly in a grey suit, pale blue shirt and dark tie, paced around the Incident Room like a caged panther. He was eager not to waste any more time and he felt it was imperative they move as fast as possible, either to eliminate Wickenham or to bring him in for questioning. By midday, it was agreed that they would visit Wickenham rather than request he come into the station. Langton called Mayerling Hall, and ascertained from the housekeeper that their suspect was at home. Langton made no mention of who he was or the reason he was calling. To Anna's surprise, Langton requested that Anna and Lewis accompany him, saying that she needed to come as she might meet the caller and recognise her voice. She was well pleased; it meant her indiscretions had been forgiven.

An unmarked squad car was waiting when the three left the Incident Room at one-thirty. Anna sat in the back with Lewis, Langton up front with a uniformed driver. They headed out of London in silence, towards the A3; only another hour and they would be there.

'We tread very softly softly,' Langton said, twisting an elastic band round his fingers, twanging it, and then winding it round again. They could all feel how wired he was.

They drove past the field where Sharon Bilkin's body had been discovered. Langton stared at the yellow crime scene ribbons still there; the others followed his gaze.

'Could have dropped her body on his way home?' Lewis asked.

There was a moment's silence, then Langton spoke again. 'We know what car he drives?'

Lewis leaned forward. 'We've got a Range Rover, a Land Rover Jeep and two other vehicles: one is a Jaguar, the other's a Mini.'

'What colour is the Jag?'

'Black.'

Langton gave a soft laugh. 'I don't know about you two, but I've got a gut feeling about this guy.'

'Yeah, right,' Lewis said and sat back.

Anna could feel her stomach churning.

'We know how much he's worth?'

Lewis leaned forward again. 'Few million: his property must be up in the three or four millions and he's got an estate in France. You don't get all that from being a surgeon attached to the army.'

It was Anna's turn to pipe up. 'He was left a bundle by his father; the family have lived at Mayerling Hall for three generations, but they were originally farmers. They bought up a load of land after the war for peanuts and sold it for property development in the fifties and sixties, made a fortune.'

Langton shrugged. 'All right for some, eh? My old man left me with a load of unpaid bills and a council house. I got sent the eviction order two weeks after we'd buried him!'

He checked the map and gave the driver directions. 'Not long now before we find out whether this is a waste of time or not,' he said.

The silence fell again; Langton still twisted the elastic band round and round. 'Left now!' he snapped, even though the driver already had his indicator on.

233

They travelled for another twenty minutes, bypassing Petworth and pressing on through a quaint picturesque village. There were a few shops, two olde worlde pubs, a restaurant and, further along, a Chinese takeaway. Langton laughed and said you had to hand it to the Chinese, then hit the dashboard with the flat of his hand.

'Up ahead, left. Left!'

The driver said nothing; again, he had already been indicating. It was a narrow lane; two cars would have been unable to pass, were it not for the many verges. They drove for almost a mile and a half, passing farm gates leading into fields, but few houses. Twice they bumped over cattle grids, and they passed numerous signs that said SLOW – HORSES CROSSING.

At last, they came to a manicured hedge, over six feet high, with few gaps to see what was beyond it. The hedge went on for at least two more miles of the narrow lane, then joined up with a wall: six-feet-high old red brick. As they turned a blind corner in the road, they saw the pillared entrance to Mayerling Hall.

They turned left through the massive open gates, but still could see no property. Thick hedges fringed the drive which led into a much wider, fine gravel pathway, edged with white-painted bricks. As the pathway curved round, it became shaded with massive oak trees that overhung on either side, forming an arch as their branches entwined.

'This is some drive,' Lewis said, looking around, but Langton and Anna stared ahead in silence at the Hall itself.

It was a massive sprawling monster of a house, with griffins high up on the edges of the many roofs. It was originally Tudor, with low hanging roofs and at least eight tall chimneys. The velvet lawns swept down to a lake; statues were dotted around, and a small maze of neat one-foot hedgerows surrounded a fountain where Neptune held up a mermaid, watched by other strange stone creatures. The water spurted high and cascaded down onto the water lilies floating on the large circular pool. On either side were ornate gardens with manicured roses and rhododendrons.

'Wow, this is some place; you would never know from that lane what was here, would you?' Lewis's jaw was open at the opulence: it was like a *House & Garden* glossy centrefold. 'Need plenty of gardeners,' he continued. There was no one in sight; the silence was only broken by the fountain's gush, punctuated by birdsong.

They pulled up outside the Hall's wide front steps. Planters potted with ivy and blooms were placed on each shallow stone step, and the double front door was studded, with an old iron knocker and large handle.

They stood for a moment, looking up at the ornate building with its myriad stained glass-and-lead windows, many featuring knights in armour. Langton looked to Lewis and Anna, gave a brief nod and walked up the steps. There was an old iron bell pull, but neatly hidden was a modern doorbell; he pressed and waited. It was almost a minute before they heard footsteps, and then one of the studded doors swung open.

The housekeeper was about seventy, rotund, with flushed cheeks and an apron. Langton showed her his ID and asked if he could speak to Dr Charles Wickenham.

'Is he expecting you?' she asked, pleasantly.

'No, but I believe he is at home.'

She nodded, and then stepped back to open the door wider. 'I'll tell him you are here; this way, please.'

They trooped after her into a rather dark, oak-panelled hall, festooned with paintings. The honey-combed ceiling was yellowish in colour; and there was a suit of armour whose right hand rested on a vast umbrella stand containing many big black umbrellas and some bright golfing ones. Above them hung a huge iron chandelier, and on the oak table were stacks of books and a big wide bowl of fresh flowers.

They were led into a drawing room; it had a low ceiling and wide polished wood floorboards. Precious Persian silk throw carpets were placed around the vast room. The dark red velvet sofas and chairs were positioned comfortably around a brick fireplace, its stacked logs ready to be lit. Again, there was a profusion of oil paintings and, on a large grand piano, many silver-framed photographs. Langton was heading over for a glimpse of them but turned as he heard footsteps.

All three listened to the housekeeper speaking to someone outside the room.

'It was not the housekeeper calling in, by the way,' Anna said quietly. 'The woman sounded much younger; well spoken.'

She stopped abruptly as Edward Wickenham walked in. Over six feet tall, he looked very fit in jodhpurs, boots and a bottle-green sweater. His hair was dark like his eyes, but his cheeks were flushed very pink.

'I'm Edward Wickenham. Did you want to see me?'

He had a deep, aristocratic tone. He looked to Langton and then to Lewis.

'Actually we wanted to see your father. Is he home?'

'Yes, somewhere. It's not about this ruddy congestion charge, is it? I can't believe it! I mean, I have said I would pay the fine, and yet every day I seem to get another letter telling me it's doubled.'

'It's not about any congestion charge. I am Detective Chief Inspector James Langton.' Langton went on to introduce Travis and Lewis.

'Why do you want to see my father?'

'It's a personal matter, sir. If you could just get him to come and see us.'

'To be honest, I am not sure where he is; he could be over at the stables.' After a moment's hesitation, he turned abruptly and walked out.

Langton turned to Anna, his voice low. 'Well, he's dark-haired, and he's got quite a nose on him. What do you think? Could it be him?'

Anna shrugged; she was looking at the family line-up on the piano top. Countless silver-framed photographs of young children, some on horses or ponies, and various women, but she couldn't see any of the man they had come to talk to.

Langton came to her side. 'Any tall, dark, handsome, hook-nosed middle-aged . . .' He stopped as he heard a door open and close in the hall. They waited, but whoever it was walked away. It was another five minutes before Edward Wickenham returned.

'I've paged him, but he might have gone out with one of the horses. Can I get you some coffee?'

'No thank you. Maybe you could walk us over to the stables?'

He hesitated, looking at his watch. 'I suppose I could do, but as I said, I am not sure he is over there.'

'Why don't we go and see?' Langton said firmly.

★

237

Edward Wickenham opened a studded oak door leading to the kitchens and gave a rather apologetic smile.

'It's a bit of a maze, but this is the quickest route; we'll go through the kitchen to the back door.'

The kitchen was huge, with two Agas and a vast pine table with matching chairs. The stainless steel equipment was immaculate and the glass-fronted dressers were filled with china. The housekeeper was peeling potatoes at the sink; she smiled as they trooped past. They entered a small narrow corridor with a laundry room off to their left, then came to another studded door with an array of Wellington boots lined up beneath a set of old rain-coats, hanging on hooks.

The back yard was surrounded by a very high wall and still retained the sixteenth-century cobblestones. The gate at the end was painted green. Edward Wickenham pulled back the heavy bolts to open it.

'We could have walked around the house; this way's far shorter but it might be a bit muddy on the other side. We've had such bad weather lately.' He gestured for them to follow.

There was a vast barn with ivy covering the roof, old carts and rusted machinery resting against it. Edward Wickenham paused.

'Let me check he's not in here; one moment.'

Wickenham walked in, leaving the door open behind him. They could see an indoor pool with an electric cover; beyond the pool were steps leading to a gymnasium, with ultra-modern equipment and floor-to-ceiling mirrors, showers and changing rooms, all empty.

'No; let's hope he's at the stables,' he said, as he shut the door behind him and checked his pager again.

They followed him around the barn through another gate which led into a large stable with stalls for at least ten horses. Only three were occupied. Two men were mucking out, using hoses to swill down the yard.

'Is my father around?' Wickenham called out. They shook their heads.

'I'm sorry I have no idea where he could be. Unless . . .' He turned back to one of the men. 'Is he out on Bermarsh?'

"Yes sir, he was over in the paddock, maybe gone up to the woods.'

Wickenham waved his thanks and looked at his watch. 'Was he expecting you?'

'No, he wasn't.' Langton was beginning to get tetchy.

'I'm afraid I have to go out; in fact, I am going to be late, so I suggest we go back to the house.'

'Let's just try the paddock,' Langton said.

The ground was muddy and they all had to sidestep deep puddles as they followed Edward Wickenham who strode ahead, obviously annoyed.

Almost on cue, a rider emerged from the wood that ringed the paddock, taking the fences on a seventeen-hand chestnut gelding. If he saw them waiting, he gave no indication, but continued to wheel the horse further away to take the jumps.

Edward Wickenham waved and the rider pulled in the reins. They could not see his face as he was wearing a riding hat, the collar of his tweed jacket turned up. He wore cream jodhpurs and black boots. He leaned down to talk to Edward then sat bolt upright as he stared across to them. He nodded and heeled the horse forwards.

They stood together in a line as the horse slowly approached. Charles Wickenham looked down at them. 'My son says you wished to see me.'

Langton showed his ID and looked up into the man's face. Dark, dark eyes, a hooked nose and a thin, cruel mouth. He slid from the horse and handed the reins to his son.

Langton introduced Anna and Lewis, but Charles Wickenham paid them hardly any attention, turning to his son. 'Get Walter to check him out: he's got a slight limp to his right foreleg; it may be just a shoe troubling him.' He patted the horse's rump. 'Getting on, but he was very slow this morning.'

'Will do.' His son swung up into the saddle and kicked the horse forward.

Wickenham eased one of his leather gloves loose as he stood in front of them, looking from one to the other. 'What's this about?'

'Could we please return to the house?' Langton said, quite pleasantly.

'Of course, but I would like a shower first, if you don't mind.'

'It won't take a moment.'

'Whatever; follow me then.'

Charles Wickenham did not lead them back through the kitchen gardens but round the entire house and back to the front of the Hall. He eased off his riding boots using a grille by the front door. He glanced down at their muddy shoes but said nothing as he opened the door and walked inside.

'Please go through. I'll just take my jacket and hat off.'

He walked off towards the kitchen, removing his riding hat.

They stood in the drawing room waiting; after about five minutes, Charles Wickenham returned. He had combed his hair and his riding hat had left a red rim across his forehead. He was wearing a checked shirt beneath a pale yellow cashmere sweater, and monogrammed velvet slippers.

His cheekbones were high and his hooded eyes were unfathomable, but his white, even smile made him more attractive. His hair was greying at the temples. He bore a close resemblance to their drawings of the tall dark stranger.

'I don't know about you, but I need a drink. Can I offer you something?'

'No, thank you,' Langton said.

Wickenham ambled over to a heavy oak chest on top of which stood a high top cupboard, and swung open the doors to reveal that it had been made into a drinks cabinet. He picked up a cut-glass decanter and poured a measure of whisky into a tumbler, then turned casually towards them and raised his glass.

'So what's all this about? Please, please do sit down.' He settled himself in a chair.

Anna could see on the little finger of his left hand a large gold and cornelian signet ring. She went and sat down on one of the velvet chairs, opened her briefcase and took out her notebook to jot this down. She showed her pad to Langton, who had sat on the arm of her chair, but he made no acknowledgement.

'I am leading an enquiry into the murder of a young girl called Louise Pennel.'

Wickenham didn't seem to be listening; he was frowning at a cushion cover which he flicked at with his fingernails and then tossed aside.

'The newspapers have given her the nickname of the Red Dahlia,' Langton continued.

Wickenham nodded and sipped his drink.

'We are also investigating the murder of another girl, Sharon Bilkin, possibly killed by the same person.'

Wickenham suddenly stood up, placed his glass down on a side table and walked over to the door; he called down the hallway to the kitchen. 'Hylda, I won't want a big lunch, just something light!'

Anna looked at Langton who gave a half-smile, shaking his head. Wickenham strolled back in and sat down again, picking up his scotch.

'Sorry, but if I don't warn her, it's a meat and potatoes job.'

Langton held up the photograph of Louise Pennel. 'Do you know this girl?'

Wickenham leaned forward and stared at the photograph. 'No.'

'What about this girl?' Langton held up a photograph of Sharon Bilkin.

Wickenham stared, cocked his head to one side and then smiled. 'Sorry, no, I do not.'

Langton didn't appear to be in any way put out; next, he selected the drawing that had been made of their suspect. 'Would you say this is a good likeness?'

Wickenham leaned even closer. 'Of me?'

'Yes, of you, Mr Wickenham.'

'Could you explain to me why you are showing me these photographs and that . . . drawing, is it?'

'We have made many requests via the press and television for this man to come forward. He does look very similar to you.'

'I do apologise. If I had seen it, quite frankly I would not have thought that it was me, so I would have had no reason to make contact.'

'Did you ever visit Louise Pennel? The girl in the photograph I first showed you?' Again Langton held up the photograph.

Wickenham drained his glass and shook his head. 'As I have said, I do not know her, so it would not really be logical for me to have visited her.'

Langton persisted, returning to Sharon Bilkin's photograph. 'Did you ever visit this girl?'

Wickenham sighed. 'No.'

Langton shuffled his photographs and sketch like a pack of cards. 'Do you have any idea how we came to have this drawing of a person who does, even if you do not agree, bear a very strong resemblance to yourself?'

'None whatsoever.'

'A witness, two witnesses in fact, working with a police artist and a Photofit expert, and without conferring with each other, produced this profile: tall, hook-nosed, dark eyes, dark-haired, with slight greying at the temples. Contrary to what you say, I think it is an exceptional likeness; perhaps the best solution is if you agree to take part in an identity parade.'

'Me?'

'Yes, Doctor Wickenham, you. Would you agree to assist our enquiry? This way, it will eliminate you or, conversely, prove that you did, on numerous occasions, visit the victim, Louise Pennel.'

'When am I supposed to have been calling on this woman?'

Before Anna could refer to her notebook for the exact dates given by Louise Pennel's landlady, without any hesitation Langton replied, 'The ninth of January.'

'The ninth of January? Would that be this year?'

Langton nodded. Wickenham got up.

'Let me get my diary; it's in my study.'

He walked out. Lewis watched for a moment as Langton put the photographs back in the file.

'What do you think?'

Langton's reply was hardly audible. 'He's wearing the signet ring described. Right, Anna?'

She nodded.

'Well, he's a bloody cool customer,' Lewis muttered.

Langton crossed to the piano and looked at the photographs. He turned as Wickenham walked back in with a large leather desk diary.

'The ninth of January, you say? I had meetings with my solicitors in Cavendish Square. It was quite a lengthy meeting, as my ex-wife has started to become even greedier than she was when we were married. I had lunch at my club, the St James, and then I returned home. I had guests for dinner that evening.' He closed the book. 'What time of day am I supposed to have met this girl?'

'Can these meetings be verified?' Langton asked, keeping his voice steady.

'Of course; if you wish, I can contact everyone and they will get in touch with you.'

'Thank you. You were a surgeon; is that correct?'

'Yes I was, almost in a past life. I retired ten years

ago; I had grown tired of travelling, tired of army life, really.' He gestured expansively to the room. 'I did not need the salary and I decided that I would prefer to spend more time here, and with my children. To be honest, it was never a career I enjoyed, but then peer pressure is not something you do ever enjoy. My father's death sort of coincided; I inherited the Hall and wanted to get it back into more of a habitable place. It required a lot of work, not to mention money.'

Langton smiled. 'Thank you very much. You have been very helpful. I am sorry to have taken up so much of your time.'

Anna was astonished but got to her feet, as did Lewis.

'I'll show you out.' Wickenham smiled and gestured for them to go ahead of him.

As they walked down the front steps, Langton turned, smiling pleasantly. 'I will arrange a line-up and, if necessary, I can send a car to collect you.'

For the first time, Wickenham's eyes flickered slightly; he covered up fast. 'By all means, but I doubt when my diary has been verified it will be necessary.'

'I'll be in touch.'

Langton headed over to the waiting car and yanked open the passenger door. They hurried after him and got into the back seat. Wickenham even had the audacity to give them a slight wave of his hand before he went back inside.

'Fuck me, he's a piece of work,' Lewis said.

Langton nudged the driver. 'Go left, down the drive beside the house, would you?'

Around the side of the house were garages. A Range Rover was having thick mud hosed off its wheels. Parked beside it was a gleaming new Jaguar saloon. Langton stared at the car and then at Lewis and Anna.

'We get that line-up organised; let's hope to Christ that landlady can identify him.'

'I have my doubts, you know,' Anna said, uneasily. 'She did say that he kept his face hidden.'

'She described his fucking ring, didn't she? His hook nose? If needs be, he can keep his hand over part of his face. I need him to be identified, because we have fuck all else on the bastard.'

The driver asked if he should turn around, but Langton pointed to the lane running beside the garage. 'See if we can get out that way, take a look at his estate!'

They drove onto a gravel lane that led them past a small thatched cottage. It was immaculate, with lead windows and an abundance of flowers around the quaint former stable door, the top half of which was open.

'Staff quarters, do you think?' ventured Lewis.

'No, too nice by far. They'll be stuck somewhere out of sight,' Langton replied, just as Edward Wicken-ham appeared at the stable door. He looked at them and then disappeared inside, closing the door behind him.

'Must be the son 'n' heir's place,' Lewis said, as they drove past.

'You remember what Professor Marshe said?' Anna leaned towards Langton. 'Killer might be having some friction with his wife? Well, he told us she was trying for more money, reason he was at his solicitors.'

'Mmm.' Langton nodded. He looked down into the footwell and picked up the elastic band.

246

'You know, something we've not really delved into is what if it's two of them: father and son?' Lewis asked.

Langton pinged his elastic band. 'What I think is we just met the killer. He might use his son, probably has some hold over him, but I think Charles Henry Wickenham is the sick bastard we've been looking for.'

Anna licked her lips, uncertain, and said nothing.

They drove back into the village and Langton suggested they have a drink and some lunch at the pub.

They all ordered beer and sandwiches. Anna and Lewis sat at a table close to a window overlooking the village's main road. Langton sat on a bar stool and began a lengthy conversation with the young barman.

Lewis and Anna didn't say much as they ate, but watched Langton hardly touch his sandwich as he talked. He did order a scotch though, and it looked like a large one. Anna and Lewis waited impatiently, but he seemed in no hurry to leave.

Langton eventually joined them, looking as if he had knocked back a few more large ones. He was ebullient, grinning as they got back into the car. They stopped at the local village grocery shop as Langton said he wanted cigarettes; he disappeared inside for over half an hour and was grinning again when he came out. He slammed the door so hard the car rocked and then pushed his seat back so far, it was against Anna's legs, then lowered the headrest and slept for the rest of the journey.

Langton went straight into his office, then emerged, rolling up his shirt sleeves, to take the briefing. He was about to start when the double doors opened and the Commander and her DI walked in. Langton hurried

across and had a brief conversation with them; then they
drew up chairs and sat down. Bridget went over to offer
coffee, raising her eyebrows at Anna on her way past. It
felt like they were back at school and the head teacher
had appeared in the classroom unannounced.

Langton clapped his hands and the room grew quiet.
The top brass looked on expectantly as he pointed to
the sketch of the tall dark stranger.

'Charles Henry Wickenham could have sat for that;
he's got everything, including the gold signet ring.'

He wanted a line-up arranged fast: the next day if
possible. Someone joked that he could stand in line.

'Sorry, but I've got blue eyes,' he grinned, sharing
the joke; his humour did not last for long. 'Right, I had
a long chat to the barman at the St George pub; he
was a mine of information. His father had worked at
the Hall as a gardener for thirty-odd years. He said that
our suspect's father was a nasty old sod that went after
everything in a skirt; it got so bad that the local girls
wouldn't go near the Hall. He was also a Doctor, not
medical as we first thought, but of philosophy; he never
actually held down any kind of a job. He ran the Hall.
At one time, most of the land around it belonged to
the Wickenhams; it was our suspect's father who made
a mint selling it off to housing projects, etcetera. He
was loathed by the locals as he destroyed a lot of the
woods and sold up pastures for houses that none could
afford. Anyway, he was, to all intents and purposes, a
mean and vicious man and his only son, our suspect,
was terrified of him. His mother, Annabelle Wickenham,
died in childbirth, leaving Charles as the only heir. The
old boy never married again but was known to bring

in prostitutes: he was well known for sending his Rolls to Soho so his chauffeur could load up the girls and bring them back.

'When he died ten years ago, his son, Charles Wickenham, had not been living at the Hall, but travelling around the world as an army surgeon. The old boy had spent a lot of money on poor investments and he had let the place go to rot. Charles Wickenham began by infuriating the local community by doing exactly what his father had done before him, i.e. selling up their grazing land. His first wife died of cancer; his son, Edward, is their only child. Charles's second wife, Dominique, is French and she had two daughters. Dominique Wickenham got a heavy settlement and lives off the alimony; Wickenham said himself she was after more money. We need to trace her and see what she can give us.'

Langton hardly paused for breath. Anna sat in awe: all this he had gathered in front of their noses, in the pub, and yet he had not said a word to them. She was even more amazed when he began to relate the conversation he had had while buying cigarettes.

'The son is possibly involved. Edward Wickenham's wife committed suicide: her body was found in the barn. This was before it was converted into a spa, swimming pool and gymnasium. There was a police enquiry; nothing came of it, but the rumours from the locals were that she may have had some assistance tying the knot! But nothing could be proved. She had a high level of alcohol and traces of cocaine in her bloodstream, and statements from staff had said she was of a very nervous disposition.'

Langton pushed his chair back. 'The lady in the shop implied that there was a lot of sexual activity at the hall, a lot of all-night, all-week parties and drugs, though no one has ever been arrested. Wickenham used to bring in local girls, but the gossip festered, so he now hires in from different companies. I want them checked out. Okay, now we come to Edward Wickenham's girl-friend. She is the daughter of the late Sir Arthur Harrington, northern industrialist; mother was Constance, also deceased. That's about all we know, apart from that she's not been seen for weeks. Check her out, she's maybe the caller – she's apparently at a health spa right now.'

Anna sat back in her chair as Langton paused, frowning, his hands stuffed into his pockets.

'Okay, you can say none of this adds up to any evidence against Charles Wickenham, or even against his son – because they may be in this together; there again, they might not be. However, my gut feeling is that we have at long last found our killer. Now we have to draw him in and tread very carefully. Even if it transpires that he lied and did know Louise Pennel and Sharon Bilkin, it is still not enough to arrest him. I don't want to scare this creature off before we have that search warrant granted and we check out that sumptuous place he lives in. I need the names of people that went to parties at the Hall. If our caller is telling the truth, Louise Pennel was a guest at that ancestral pile; he might also have cut her body up there. I want to interview the local uniforms at the village. I want to know what this son of a bitch eats for breakfast. I want to talk to Edward Wickenham's girlfriend, track back to Wickenham senior's army days;

in fact, we need to talk to anyone that knows him now, who knew him then. We leave no stone unturned. So let's get moving.'

Langton went into his office, accompanied by the Commander and her DI, leaving everyone breathless.

As Anna sat writing copious notes, Lewis came and sat on the edge of her desk. 'He never ceases to screw me up! I mean, why not let us in on this when we were in the patrol car?'

'He keeps things close to his chest,' Anna said, though she felt the same way.

'I mean, he's damned sure it's Wickenham, but we can't prove it, so all that big speech was for what? To impress the Commander?'

'Hang onto this case, more like it,' said Barolli, joining them.

Anna was surprised: she had never heard either of them deride their Governor before. She kept her mouth shut.

Lewis yawned. 'Well we've got our work cut out schlepping around, but if he's right, then we should crack on.'

'What did you think?' Barolli asked Anna.

'I didn't like him; like the Gov said, he was wearing the signet ring, so he was maybe lying about not knowing Louise Pennel; if he knew her, then he would also have known Sharon Bilkin.'

Anna was grateful when the case manager interrupted their gossip, calling them over to break down Langton's requests. Whatever anyone felt, there was now a renewed energy in the Incident Room. They at long last had a suspect, and with the Commander being privy to the briefing, it was pretty certain that Langton would not be replaced.

Chapter Twelve

DAY TWENTY-THREE

Anna arrived at the station early the next morning. She was about to head up to the canteen for breakfast when she saw Professor Marshe arrive by taxi. Anna gave a small nod of acknowledgement and continued into the station.

She was midway up the stairs when Professor Marshe called out. 'Excuse me; it's Detective Travis, isn't it?'

'Yes.'

'Is DCI Langton in?'

'I think so; his car's outside.'

'Good, I need to speak to him.'

Anna hesitated. 'I'll tell him you are here if you'd like to wait.'

'It's all right, I know the way.'

'I'm sorry, but the Incident Room is only for officers connected to the case.'

Professor Marshe gave her a cold, arrogant glance. 'In case you have forgotten, I was brought in on the case by DCI Langton. Excuse me.'

Anna stood patiently on the stairs, watching her pass.

Today, she was not wearing her hair in a chignon but loose, held back with a velvet alice band. It made her look a lot younger and prettier, if rather old-fashioned. She was wearing a chic, tailored suit in pink and black tweed.

Anna changed her mind about going up another floor to the canteen and instead followed Professor Marshe into the Incident Room, eager to see the reactions.

Professor Marshe headed straight into Langton's office, leaving a waft of perfume behind her.

Lewis looked over to Anna and raised an eyebrow. 'She's a pushy piece, isn't she?'

Anna watched Bridget put two coffees on a tray and head towards Langton's office.

'I'll take that in, Bridget; I need a quick word with the Gov.'

'Oh, thanks.'

Anna balanced the tray on her forearm and was about to knock on Langton's door when she heard his familiar bark. 'It's none of your business!'

'Of course it is. You brought me onto the case and you haven't even got the decency to call me and give me an update. I wouldn't even have known that you had a suspect, but I saw the Commander last night and she told me. I felt like a total idiot.'

'After what happened with you and the press, I presumed you would have been too embarrassed to discuss it, let alone with the Commander.'

'I am not embarrassed in the slightest; if you want my input then I am prepared to give it. The Commander felt that I would be invaluable: that's why I am here.'

'Why? Do you need another chapter in your book

of exploits, capturing serial killers that no one could have arrested without your help?'

'Don't be crass.'

'I wasn't aware I was being crass, sweetheart.'

'Don't call me sweetheart! Just tell me straight: do you want my advice or not?'

'As you are here, why not? But don't let's waste time: if you have anything to say about our suspect, do it in front of the team.'

'I need time to read the update on who he is.'

Anna nearly dropped the tray as Langton opened the door. 'Ah, Travis; can you sit with Professor Marshe and give her an update on Wickenham? You might as well have my coffee. I'll be in the Incident Room.'

He passed Anna, leaving his office door ajar. Anna carried the tray in and placed it down on his desk. Professor Marshe was sitting cross-legged in the straight-backed chair, one leg swinging back and forth in irritation. 'Christ, he's a chauvinistic bastard,' she muttered.

Anna smiled sweetly and proffered the coffee. Professor Marshe reached for the cup and looked into it. 'Do you have any cream?'

'No, but I can get you milk if you want.'

'Forget it.' Professor Marshe took a bottle of water out of her briefcase. 'So tell me about this Winchester character.'

'Wickenham,' Anna corrected, and hesitated before sitting in the chair behind Langton's desk. Professor Marshe opened her notebook, clicked on her pen, and tapped the page.

'Right, first give me his personal details: age, etcetera etcetera, marital status, children?'

Anna excused herself to get her own notebook. Langton was sitting with Barolli and Lewis in the Incident Room.

'Keep her out of my hair, Travis: be aware she's very pally with the Commander, so anything you do say to her will be repeated.'

'Yes, will do.'

Langton weaved through the desks to come to her side. 'We're still getting the line-up organised for this afternoon but don't tell her that; just see if she can bring anything to the table.'

'Okay.' Anna hesitated; she could smell alcohol on his breath.

'What?' he said, glaring at her.

'There's a packet of mints in my drawer if you want one.'

He frowned, and then walked back to join Lewis and Barolli. Anna returned to his office. He was beginning to really concern her; it was still only nine o'clock.

It was after eleven when, accompanied by Professor Marshe, she went back into the Incident Room. Anna had felt at times that she was being interrogated, but by the end she was impressed. She watched Marshe go up to Langton and talk quietly with him for a while before he called for everyone to pay attention. They did not exactly jump to it, but the room eventually fell quiet.

'Charles Wickenham, I believe, is now your prime suspect. When I was first brought in, I mentioned that your killer's marital status would be an important factor. I think it is imperative that you interview his ex-wife: the profile I have been compiling for you underlines that your killer has a hatred of women. This is very deep-rooted and would have begun in his early child-hood.'

She continued, repeating virtually all that Langton had discovered from the locals about Wickenham and his father; although it was still only hearsay, it appeared to be the focus of her profile. As she talked, some of the officers continued to double-check Wickenham's alibis for 9 January. Langton paid little attention, constantly sending and receiving text messages. The rest of the team were also becoming impatient: they were already privy to so much of what she was saying. Then there was a pause. She twisted a lock of her blonde hair round and round her manicured index finger before she eventually spoke. Her voice had changed; she spoke quietly and calmly.

'I have discussed a sociopathic tendency; it is quite rare for them to become violent.'

Anna glanced at Langton, who was looking at his watch impatiently.

'However, in this case I think you are dealing with a very, very dangerous specimen. I do not doubt that you have the right man. Everything I have discussed is a profile of someone with a compulsion to create terrible pain. His own self-loathing is so deep that he can go to horrendous lengths and feel no remorse whatsoever. This man enjoys the act of torture, of mutilation, and of watching his victims die. I would say he was addicted to drugs, probably amphetamines to get high and, I think, something to iron his hyperactive side down: it could be grass, even morphine. He will have access to these drugs due to his background, and this is where you have to tread carefully, as he is also quite likely to commit suicide: not due to any kind of remorse, but one, to escape from incarceration, and two, fuelled by his fury at being caught.

'His ego is such that he believes he is above suspicion. He thinks his intellect is above that of any of the officers leading the enquiry. I would say he will have arranged his alibis and be very confident that he is safe from prosecution. You have no witnesses. You have no weapons. His tools of torture will, I am certain, be close to him; he will enjoy cleaning and inspecting them. He will also enjoy the fact he is under suspicion, because he is certain he can outwit you. The key will be to allow him to think that is the case; the more you give this man rope, the more he will move towards placing the noose around his neck and hanging himself. But tread carefully, because he will even enjoy hanging!'

Langton was still texting, but the rest of the team were now listening very attentively. He did look up when she started on how they should proceed.

'I have spent some time with the pathologist that completed the autopsies on both of your victims. I also had a close friend, a police surgeon, discuss the mutilations. He told me that surgeons make very bold, clean incisions through each layer of tissue with the correct amount of pressure to divide only the tissues. An amateur cutting would more than likely underestimate the amount of pressure it takes to divide the skin, let alone cut the intervertebral disc. The surgeon's procedure often results in cuts that are serrated at the ends from going over the tissues repeatedly. This is known as "staging laparoscopies" – going through the skin in stages – but with an amateur wielding the knife, the wound would

257

look as if it had been skived. The professional cuts through the skin at an angle to the horizontal plane, so that one edge is feathered, the other peeled. He suggested that our killer was educated enough not to attempt to cut through the bones of the lumbar spine and was professional enough to locate and divide at the disc space. It takes tremendous skill and a very sharp instrument to divide the spinous ligaments and the thick paravertabral muscles. An amateur would no doubt leave hacking wounds.'

She closed her notebook. 'My associate said he believed without doubt it had to be a professional surgeon to have been able to prolong the torture without killing his victim prematurely. Your suspect is a qualified surgeon, therefore very much to my mind the killer. He will no doubt be as abusive to his son, Edward, as his own father was to him. Anyone around him, close to him, as I said before – his ex-wife, his daughters – go to them first. It will infuriate him because he is unable to control these interviews; not being privy to what is said might easily push him into your laps, but again I must impress upon you that you must tread very carefully with this man. He has spent many hours planning how to kill the Red Dahlia, even giving her that name to the press. No one was ever arrested for the murder of the Black Dahlia, so he will have been very diligent in covering his tracks, just as the original killer was. His obsession with the Elizabeth Short murder will be a sort of guide for him. He will believe he can never be arrested or charged, because he associates himself with her killer. I would advise you to let him think that he is getting away with his crime as you manoeuvre behind his back.

I know you do not have enough evidence to make a formal arrest. However, do not let this man out of your sight because I think he is preparing to kill again.'

The team remained silent. Professor Marshe asked if anyone had any questions. Langton told her that they were preparing a line-up and asked what she felt about it. She nodded over to the details on the board.

'Well, if he is identified by the landlady, it will mean he has been caught out in a lie, but she never saw his face clearly.'

'She described his signet ring.' Langton said.

'I know, but so many men of his class wear them.' She shrugged.

The meeting broke up, and Professor Marshe went into Langton's office. The team were fazed by her speech. She obviously believed Charles Wickenham was their killer; any doubts they may have had were not even mentioned. It yet again gave the team an added energy, as the hunt that had taken so long to get under way was now closing in on the man they all now suspected was their killer.

A car was sent for the landlady to be at the station for two p.m. At the same time, Wickenham himself was called and he agreed to be present. A car was also sent to collect him, even though he offered to drive himself. He did not ask for a solicitor to be present. He had been asked to wear a long dark coat; he was told that if he did not possess one, then one would be provided.

At one forty-five, Langton, accompanied by Anna and Lewis, drove to the purpose-built identity suite, with its two-way glass for officers to watch the interaction and the one-way window for witnesses to walk alongside as they viewed the nine men. An officer unconnected to the case would brief the landlady on what she should do. Langton and his team would not be allowed to discuss anything with her.

When Wickenham arrived, he was relaxed, and appeared to be as helpful as possible. He had brought in a long, dark navy, cashmere draped coat and asked if it was suitable. He was asked to draw the collar up, as were all the other men. He chose position number five. Anna and Langton watched the way he smiled at the other men. He was told to hold the numbered card up with both hands.

Mrs Jenkins was very nervous. She kept on saying that it had been a long time ago, and that she doubted she would be able to pick anyone out. She was calmed down and given a cup of tea by the officer who explained that she should take her time; if she wanted, she could ask him to ask the men to turn right or left or look full face towards her. He repeated numerous times that the line-up of men could not see her through the one-way glass.

Langton and Anna waited patiently as the viewing began. Mrs Jenkins did take her time; she walked back and forth and then paused in the centre exactly opposite Wickenham. She asked if they could all turn to their left, then right. She asked if they could place their left hand up across the lower part of their faces. This they did, and she walked the length of the window again. She paused for a second time opposite Wickenham.

'Do you recognise the man that called at your house on the ninth of January this year?' asked the officer.

Mrs Jenkins licked her lips. Langton took a deep breath.

'He is not wearing the signet ring,' Anna said, quietly.

'I know; hang on.'

Langton turned up the sound. She had now asked if the men could say something. When asked what she wanted them to say, she said something like, 'I'm sorry to disturb you.'

The men repeated the line one after another; again, she stood in front of Wickenham.

'Come on, come on,' Langton hissed, under his breath.

They both watched as Mrs Jenkins hesitated and then turned to the officer.

'I think it's number five, but he had a ring on his little finger when I saw him; he sounds like him, I just can't be one hundred per cent sure.'

Langton looked at Anna. 'Shit; not good enough.'

'Close though. She picked him out.'

'Yeah I know, but it's not one hundred per cent. I'm going to let him go.'

Anna nodded and they went out into the interview room allocated for suspects. Wickenham was staring out of the window, his back to them, as they entered.

'Thank you very much for your time, Mr Wickenham. We really appreciate you coming in to see us. The car will drive you back to your home.'

Wickenham slowly turned to face them. 'I knew it would be a waste of time. I do apologise for not getting back to you with all the contact numbers for you to check out, but I no longer have a secretary. Will later this afternoon be acceptable?'

'Yes sir, thank you very much.'

Langton forced himself to be cordial through gritted teeth as Wickenham shook his hand and then gave Anna a smile. 'Nice to see you again. It was really rather inconvenient, but I suppose you have to do what you have to do.'

'Yes,' she said, pasting on a smile like Langton.

Langton then asked if Wickenham could provide contact addresses for his ex-wife and children as they needed to interview them. Anna was looking directly at Wickenham and saw his eyes narrow and his jaw tighten.

'My family? What on earth for?'

'Just procedure, sir. If you would like to accompany us to the Incident Room, we can make it as fast and as convenient for you as possible.'

Wickenham gave a sigh and sat down, taking from his jacket pocket an electronic personal organiser. 'I'll do it now, so as not to waste any more of my time.'

'Thank you very much.'

Anna copied down the addresses and phone numbers of his son, his daughters and his ex-wife. She didn't react when it transpired that one of his daughters lived in Richmond.

'Dominique is in Milan, but she does come back and forth to London to see the girls. They spend most of their holidays with her. Emily is a student and Justine runs a stables. My son, as you know, lives on the estate with his partner, Gail Harrington.'

Throughout he was affable and helpful, even joking that they might find it difficult to interview his ex-wife as she was constantly travelling.

'Or shopping! Milan is the Mecca for shoes.' He laughed.

It was coming up to five o'clock when Langton returned to the Incident Room to update the team. The surveillance guys were already up and running. They would check out Wickenham's alibis and begin the interviews the following morning. Of the family contacts to follow up, earmarked first was Justine Wickenham as she lived in Richmond, not far from where Louise Pennel's body had been discovered. They now had a direct link to the murder site.

'He might not have been a one hundred per cent ID, but it's good enough for me, and we've done as Professor Marshe suggested: given him a lot of rope! So good work today; let's keep it up. We go at eight tomorrow morning.'

By now all the relatives had been contacted and agreed to meet the detectives. They were told simply that they needed to be questioned regarding an ongoing enquiry. Dominique Wickenham was in Paris, due to return to Milan the following day. Langton would be going over there to conduct the interview; by the time they broke up for the evening, everyone was still wondering who would be accompanying him.

Chapter Thirteen

Anna didn't realise until she got home how much the tension of the day had exhausted her. She had a shower and a quick snack before she went to bed and crashed out. The next day, she and Barolli were to interview the younger daughter, Emily Wickenham, a student at the London School of Economics, living in a small flat close to Portobello Road. Langton and Lewis were to meet with Justine Wickenham; they would reconvene at the station and then go to interview Edward Wickenham at the Hall. The only person they had been unable to contact was Gail Harrington: they were told she was still away at a health farm. The alibi given by Wickenham for 9 January was still being verified, but so far those contacted had agreed that he had been with them as he had stated.

DAY TWENTY-FOUR

Barolli and Anna met up at the station the following morning so they could leave together for their meeting with Emily at eight-thirty. She had said she had lectures at ten, so it would only be convenient that early in the morning. Her flat was above a shop at the less well-heeled end of Portobello Road; the street was hopping with stalls, even on a weekday.

They buzzed the intercom; two other girls were listed, presumably flatmates. The aristocratic, high-pitched voice asked them to keep walking up the stairs.

The front door buzzed open. The staircase had thread-bare carpet in an oak brown, the stair rods were loose. Barolli led the way as they got to the second floor.

Emily Wickenham leaned against the open doorway. 'Come on in. I'm eager to know what this is about; is it the break-in?'

'No.' Barolli showed his ID, as did Anna, and they followed Emily into the rather scruffy rented flat. It was full of rock-and-roll posters; the seedy kitchen looked disgusting.

'We don't have a lounge, but we can use my bedroom. Do you want tea or anything?'

'No, thank you.'

'It's the second time in six months we've been broken into! This time they took all the CDs; it's a real pain.'

She gestured for them to sit on her unmade bed and curled up in an old wicker armchair.

'It's not about the break-in,' Barolli said, sitting gingerly on top of a bright orange duvet.

Anna took a good look at the girl: she was very tall, at least five feet nine, with a skeletal frame. She was actually very pretty, but looked as if her hair needed washing; she wore no make-up and had badly bitten fingernails. She had her father's dark colouring and the same deep-set eyes. Anna wondered if she had an eating disorder, she was so thin.

Anna knew she must be very bright as she was only

seventeen, so she must have taken her A-levels a year early to be at university already.

'Have you ever seen this girl?' Barolli brought out the photograph of Louise Pennel. Emily glanced at it and then shook her head. Next he showed her Sharon Bilkin's picture; again she shook her head.

'Were you here on the ninth of January this year?'

'Yes, I mean, I don't remember if I was here, *here* if you understand, but I was in London.'

'Do you go home frequently?'

'What is this about?' she asked, chewing her fingers.

'We are leading a murder enquiry; both the girls we have just shown you were murdered.'

'Were they students?' she asked, without much emotion.

'No. Do you go back to your family home at week-ends?' Anna asked, smiling pleasantly.

'No, I go home as little as I possibly can. Why do you want to know?'

'It is connected to our enquiry. Do you have a good relationship with your father?'

'No. Why do you want to know about my father?'

'Just for elimination purposes.' Barolli shifted his weight; sitting on the low bed was uncomfortable.

'Do you have a good relationship with your brother?'

'Not really; I hardly ever see him; he's my half-brother, actually.'

'When was the last time you were at home?'

'Oh God, I don't know. I mostly spend any free time with my mother. Why are you asking me these questions? I don't understand what you want to know about my family for.'

'Do you know if your father or your brother entertains young girls, maybe like the ones we have shown you?'

'I wouldn't know. I mean, Daddy is always having weekend parties but I don't go; we don't really get along. Has he said something to you?'

'About what?'

'Well, that we don't see a lot of each other. Mother says it's because I am too like him, but it's not that at all – we just don't particularly like each other.'

Barolli looked at Anna, unsure which way they should direct the conversation.

'Any particular reason?' Anna asked innocently.

'We just don't get along. I don't understand why you need to know about my relationship with my father. Is he – I mean, has he done something wrong?'

'These weekend parties; could you tell us a bit more about them?'

Emily fidgeted in the creaky wicker seat. 'I don't go to them, I just told you that.'

'Yes I know, but maybe before you lived here; when you lived at home?'

'I didn't really live at home. I was at boarding school and then when they divorced, I lived with Mother.'

'Why did they divorce?'

Emily was becoming agitated. 'Ask them! It was years ago. They weren't happy.'

'Did your mother entertain at these parties?'

'I don't know! I keep on telling you, I never went to them: we were not allowed to join in when we were kids. It's pretty obvious, isn't it?'

'But you must have been privy to some action when you were older?'

267

'No! Why do you keep asking me? I wasn't! Daddy was very strict with us; well, with me more than Justine; he wanted me to be a doctor, you know, go to medical school, but I wasn't interested. I couldn't wait to leave home. I think that's why I used to work so hard, you know, to get out and live by myself. Daddy was into his own thing.'

'Which was what?'

Emily bit at what was left of her thumbnail. 'Drinking and things.'

Anna took out the photographs again. 'Will you have another look at these photographs, Emily, and see if perhaps you recall seeing one or other of these girls at your family home?'

'No! I have already looked at them and I don't remember ever seeing either of them.'

'They were both brutally murdered, Emily. One of them, this girl, was called Louise Pennel: the press call her the Red Dahlia.'

Emily was getting tearful; she looked at the photographs again and shook her head.

'These weekend parties; did your father entertain young girls like these?'

'Sometimes, but I don't really know. I think you should leave, because I think you are trying to make me say something about stuff that I don't know about, and you are frightening me.'

'I'm sorry, Emily, that is not our intention. We are simply trying to ascertain if either of these poor girls ever visited your father at Mayerling Hall; if not your father, perhaps your brother?'

Emily now began twisting her hair round her fingers.

'I have told you that I don't go home very often. If Daddy knows these girls, why don't you ask him about them? I don't know anything and I don't want to get into trouble.'

'Trouble with your father?"

'Yes, he's very strict. I don't know how many more times I have to tell you that I have never met those girls; you just keep on asking me the same thing.'

'Did your father have many girlfriends?'

Emily sprang up from the chair, near to tears. 'I think you should go, please. I am not going to talk to you any more; this is very upsetting.'

Barolli and Anna had heard nothing to indicate that either Wickenham or his son knew the victims, so, reluctantly, they did as Emily asked.

Justine Wickenham was wearing jodhpurs, black riding boots and a thick, cable-knit sweater. She had been mucking out at the stables. When Langton and Lewis turned up, she carried on, saying she had to get it done before the morning rides. Like her sister, she thought they were there to question her about a minor incident. She had driven into the back of someone on the high street and there had been an altercation. Lewis said they were here about a personal matter and needed to talk to her privately.

They ended up in the tack room. Justine was as tall as Emily, but broader and with thick blonde hair. Whereas Emily had his deep-set eyes, Justine had her father's hook-nose. When asked about him, she was far more forthcoming than her sister.

'I hate him. We don't speak. Whatever he's got up to

is his business. I don't want to get involved.' Her tone was strident.

Justine was unable to recognise either Louise or Sharon but did say that they looked the type that were often at the Hall. 'Daddy likes them young!' she said, turning down the corners of her mouth with disgust. She was told the girls had been murdered. 'That's awful, but I don't know them.'

Langton held up the photograph of Louise Pennel. 'This girl's body was found here in Richmond, on the river bank.'

Justine gasped as it sank in. 'Oh my God, I know about that. It was in all the papers; I ride past that bit of the river most mornings. I almost had heart failure, it was terrible. I wasn't here at the time; I was staying at my mother's apartment in Milan.'

Langton asked if she lived close to the river and she said that she did, in a rented flat owned by the stables. When asked if her father ever used her flat, she shook her head.

'You must be joking. I mean, he pays for it, but he's never been inside it. I never see him.'

'Were you in London on the ninth of January this year?'

Justine glanced at a wall calendar and said that she had been at her mother's for the weekend.

'Does your father have a key to your flat?'

She shrieked and said that she wouldn't let him near the place.

'What about your brother?'

'Edward?'

'Yes, does he have a key?'

'To my flat?'

'Yes.'

'Gosh, I doubt it, no; he's not been to see me for months.'

Langton detected a sudden change in her demeanour; she wouldn't meet his eyes, looking down at the toes of her boots.

'Do you have a good relationship with your brother?'

'He's my half-brother,' she said, quietly.

'Do you get along well?'

'No, we don't; I have no idea what he's said to you, but we just find it better to keep apart.'

'Why?'

She shrugged, still staring at her boots. 'We just do; I'm not into all that stuff.'

'What stuff?'

She sighed, and began to chew at her lips. 'Just stuff that goes on. Edward gets a lot of stick from my father because he's not that bright. I mean, he's not stupid or anything, he's just not very intelligent; for a while, he took too many drugs.'

'Your brother?'

'Yes, he got kicked out of Marlborough for smoking dope. Daddy wouldn't have minded the dope, it was being caught out that really got to him. Poor Edward was really in a terrible state. Daddy put him into rehab, but he wasn't a real addict. Anyway, it was horrible and now he works for Daddy at the Hall; you know, it's a big place to run.'

'His wife committed suicide, didn't she?'

Justine nodded, becoming very tense. 'Why do you want to know about Edward?'

271

Langton said it was for elimination purposes, but she was suddenly very guarded. 'I don't like this. I mean, shouldn't I have someone with me? Why are you asking me all these questions about my brother and my father? You can't seriously think they have done anything wrong or are involved in those awful murders. I mean, you can't think that.' She rubbed her head and sighed. 'Oh my God, I know why: it's Emily, isn't it? What has she been saying? You can't really take anything she says seriously; she's got a lot of problems. You know she's bulimic? She almost died a couple of years ago, got down to five stone.'

'I have not talked to your sister,' Langton said.

Justine cocked her head to one side. 'I don't think I am going to talk to you any more.'

Back at the station, Anna and Langton compared their interview notes. Langton wanted to get a warrant issued for Justine Wickenham's flat so the forensic team could get in there and search for bloodstains. It was possible that Wickenham had used her flat the night of the murder: it was literally a stone's throw from where they had found Louise Pennel.

'Question is, which Wickenham?' Anna said.

'Yeah I know; the brother's shaping up as a possible suspect.'

'Unless they are in it together?'

Langton nodded and then changed the subject, asking if her passport was up to date. She said it was.

'Good: we go to Milan tomorrow.'

Anna grinned; she had not thought she would stand a chance of being selected.

'I want a woman with me when I interview the ex-wife; sometimes old Lewis is like a block of wood.'

She smiled and said Barolli was a bit on the wooden side as well. Langton laughed. She had not heard him laugh for a long time. His lovely warm chuckle altered his whole being, making him boyish.

'We'll just stay overnight, back next afternoon, so get off and arrange it,' he said.

'Will do.' She was about to open the door to leave when Langton took a call and he signalled for her to wait.

'Listen, Mike, I don't give a fuck, I want his phone tapped. What? Put her through then! Yes! Christ.'

Anna waited as he listened and then spoke quietly into the phone. 'Commander, thank you for getting back so promptly. I cannot express too strongly how much we really need this man monitored. As you know, Professor Marshe . . .' He winked at Anna. 'Yes, yes she did, and it really is more or less on her advice.'

He grinned at Anna as he smoothtalked the Commander, his eyes raised to heaven. 'Thank you, and again I appreciate you getting back to me, thank you.'

He hung up and shook his head. 'Wanker. Anyway, we've got the go-ahead for the phone tap. They all pussy-foot around but she's a decent girl, just has to go by the rule book. She's also given us some extra officers to back us up.'

Dominique Wickenham had agreed to meet with them on the Saturday, the morning after their flight. On Langton's instructions, they had booked into the Hyatt Hilton hotel. There were a few raised eyebrows, as it was a very luxurious and expensive hotel. The fact that he was travelling with Anna had also created quite an undercurrent. Barolli and Lewis had both expected to be with Langton. Together they had a quiet moan, though neither spoke up or queried it in front of the team, as Langton wanted them at base to monitor the phone taps and report to him if anything came in.

DAY TWENTY-FIVE

Langton was wearing a suit and freshly ironed shirt. They had both been driven from the station to the airport. Langton had only a small folding carrier and his brief-case. He had glanced at Anna's pull-along suitcase with some amusement.

'It's almost empty,' she said.

'You won't have much time to shop if that is your intention, Travis. We meet the ex-wife at ten tomorrow morning and get the next flight back to London in the afternoon.'

Anna made no reply; she had hoped for a half-hour blitz on the shops. She hoped that she could at least have a quick whiz round the duty-free.

They had cut the time short, so no sooner had they checked in and gone through security and passport control, than Langton insisted they go straight to their gate to wait for boarding. They were sitting together, his head buried in the early edition of the *Evening Standard*, when she saw Professor Marshe heading towards them. Anna was astonished. She had not really allowed herself to think that the time alone with Langton meant so much. It did, and she suddenly felt foolish; he must have arranged for the Professor to join them.

'James!' The Professor was wearing another of her chic little suits and high-heeled shoes, her hair once more in a chignon.

Langton looked up and folded his paper. 'Good God, what are you doing here?'

Anna pursed her lips, irritated; the act was all rather unnecessary.

Professor Marshe sat next to Langton. 'Are you going to Milan?'

'Yes, we are, are you?'

'Yes, I've got a lecture and talks with a publisher there to bring out my latest book in Italian.' She gave a cool nod to Anna.

'Well, what a coincidence,' Langton said.

Anna clenched her hands. He was a dreadful actor. She felt like the proverbial spare part as he made conversation about her book. Professor Marshe asked what seat numbers they were in; he looked at Anna to check their tickets.

'Maybe we can switch so I can sit next to you?'

'Fine, yes; we're going to meet up with Wickenham's ex-wife.'

'Where are you staying?'

'The Hyatt Hilton.'

She laughed, showing her even white teeth.

'As if she didn't know,' Anna thought. No wonder Langton hadn't wanted Lewis or Barolli with him; she felt like the perfect stooge.

They boarded the plane. Langton was all over Professor Marshe, lifting her bag into the locker, checking her safety belt, even folding her spiffy little jacket so as not to crease it. Anna sat almost at the very back of the plane, next to a very large, sweating man whose many magazines and newspapers spilled out onto the floor. Langton and Professor Marshe were in the second row, just behind the curtain separating the economy and business class seats.

Arriving at Milan airport, Anna passed through customs way behind Langton and Professor Marshe. They seemed to be in deep conversation; he was constantly bending down to listen to her, guiding her with one hand at the small of her back. There was a familiarity about them that Anna found upsetting, though she had no right to feel that way. It seemed that the Professor was a regular visitor to Milan, and in the taxi they discussed which restaurant they should dine at that evening. She was staying at the Four Seasons hotel, so they dropped her off before they went on to the Hyatt. Langton waved goodbye as the valet took her bag and waited for her to go into the hotel.

As they drove away, Langton gave a sidelong glance to Anna. 'I don't want this spread around the Incident Room, Travis.'

'What exactly?'

'That she's here; they won't believe it's coincidental and they'll put two and two together and come up with Christ knows what, so let's just keep this between ourselves, okay?'

'Whatever,' she said, petulantly.

'I wouldn't be surprised if the Commander tipped her off, you know, that we were coming here. She even wants to talk to the ex-wife.'

'Will you allow her to do that?'

'I dunno, maybe. I was quite impressed with her yesterday.'

Before they could continue, Langton's mobile rang and he spent the rest of the journey to the hotel listening as Lewis reported the phone tap results. He hardly said a word until he cut off the call.

'Well, our suspect isn't making any calls, but his daughters have phoned each other and talked about their interviews. It seems the skinny one . . .'

'Emily,' Anna interjected.

'Yeah, she's in therapy.'

'I'm not surprised, she was very nervous, but she's also very bright.'

'She kept on asking Justine if she knew what we knew, and if so, who had told us; what do you make of that?'

'I don't know. Maybe their mother will enlighten us; didn't you say Justine was staying with her when we found Louise Pennel's body?'

'Yeah.' Langton looked out of the car as they arrived at the hotel. 'Do you want to have dinner this evening?' he asked, as the porter opened their car door.

'No thanks; best get an early night.'

Anna waited for her case to be removed from the boot before she followed Langton inside. He was standing at the reception desk, checking them both in; it gave Anna a moment to take in the vast foyer of the luxurious hotel. She had never stayed in one as elegant or as costly, and she was impressed at the way Langton appeared to be very much at ease. He dangled her key and told her that she was on the seventh floor. There was a sauna, health spa and swimming pool, if she felt like some exercise.

'I didn't bring my costume.'

'There's a boutique in that corner: you can buy yourself one.'

'I am not really in the swimming mood.'

'So you don't want to eat?'

'No, I'll get some room service sent up.'

'Fine, well, I'm in room 307; if you need me, just call down. Let's have breakfast in the morning.'

They stood side by side as the elevator glided up to the third floor. As the doors opened, Langton was checking his text messages.

'Goodnight, Travis.'

'Goodnight.' The doors closed and she continued up to the seventh floor. The porter was waiting at the door of her room, and gestured for her to go in ahead of him. It was large and very spacious with a double bed and a small balcony. She gave him a tip; as soon as the door closed behind him, she flopped onto the bed. Somewhere in her mind she had been scripting a scenario of her and Langton together, trying to work out how she would react to him making a pass at her. Now she realised he had not the slightest intention of doing so; she felt foolish and angry with herself that she could have so misjudged him.

Langton left the hotel and walked to the Four Seasons where Professor Marshe waited in a pale blue chiffon cocktail dress, carrying a small silver handbag that matched her sandals, looking cool and sophisticated.

'Not brought little Travis with you?'

'No, she's getting an early night.'

'Do we eat here or would you like to go somewhere else?'

They took a taxi to Bebel's on the Via San Marco.

Remote in hand, Anna switched the TV from channel to channel. She decided she'd watch *Titanic* as she hadn't seen it the first time round. She had eaten her dinner and drunk half a bottle of wine from the mini bar; wrapped in her towelling robe, she propped up the pillows and settled back on her bed. After only fifteen minutes, she fell asleep. She woke with a start, just as the *Titanic* was sinking; the room phone was ringing and so was her mobile.

Anna scrambled off the bed, delved in her bag for her mobile and at the same time tried to reach for the phone on the bedside table. She did a perfect pratfall as her mobile cut out and the room phone fell silent. She swore, picking herself up, and checked caller ID on her mobile. She tried to call back, but it would not connect. She was about to call down to the front desk when the phone rang again.

'Travis?'

'Yes.'

'It's Mike Lewis. I've been trying to contact the Gov, his mobile must be turned off and he's not in his room.'

'He may have gone out.'

'Well that's bloody obvious! Can you contact him?'

'I don't know where he's gone; is it important?'

'It might be. I know you are meeting up with Wickenham's ex-wife in the morning, so I wanted to run this by him.'

'You want to run whatever it is by me and I'll pass it on?'

'It was a call from Justine Wickenham to her sister.'

'Let me get my notebook.' She put the receiver on the bedside table and went to her briefcase.

'Ready when you are,' she said, pencil poised.

Lewis coughed and asked if he should play the call or just give her the nitty-gritty.

'Mike, just tell me what you've got.'

'Okay. They first talked about whether or not they had contacted their mother to tell her they had been interviewed; neither had. Justine kept on asking if Emily was okay, and then asked if she had told *them* anything; by *them*, I reckon she means us. Then Justine asked if *they* knew about what had happened. Emily said she didn't say anything and got quite upset and Justine tried to calm her down; she said, and I quote, *no charges ever happened, so they wouldn't be likely to know*, but if they were to ask her anything about it she should refuse to tell them because it would *all blow up again.*'

Anna jotted down the conversation in shorthand in her notebook.

'You still listening?'

'Yes yes, go on.'

'So this is what made me want to tell the Gov: Emily became very distressed and Justine kept on trying to calm her down, but she got really uptight. She said that she wished she had gone through with it and made him pay for what he had done to her, but it was family pressure that had persuaded her.'

'Just slow down a second. Okay, then what?'

'The next part was inaudible as she was crying: she

said that it was all right for Justine, because it hadn't happened to her. Justine then said that she had tried to protect her because it had: he had constantly tried to *do it* to her.'

'*Do it*?' Anna asked.

'Yes, that's what she said. Emily, in a real state, then said that even if he had done it with you, it was her that had to have the abortion, not Justine; she then went on to say how much she hated *him*.'

'*Him* meant who?' Anna injected.

'Well, we take it to be her father that molested her, or performed an abortion on his own daughter. It could have been her brother that had sex with her, but as the father is a surgeon, I'd say he would have done the abortion.'

Anna wrote it all down; Lewis said they had cut the call short as Justine said someone had arrived at her flat.

'Okay I'll relay this to the Gov; thanks for calling.'

Anna put the phone down and studied her notes, then put in a call to Langton's room but was rerouted to the hotel's answer service. She tried his mobile, but it was dead. She then called Professor Marshe at the Four Seasons and left a message for Langton to call her urgently. It was by now eleven-thirty; she presumed, correctly, that he was still at dinner.

Anna pottered around her suite for another three-quarters of an hour and then went to bed. She almost hurtled off the bed in shock when her door was rapped. She hurried to open it.

'What's so urgent?' he asked, leaning against the door frame. She could tell by looking at him he had had quite a bit to drink.

281

'Lewis was trying to contact you, but your mobile was turned off.'

Langton swore and fished in his pocket, muttering that he'd turned it off when he went to dinner. He sat on her bed as he checked his text messages, frowning.

'What did he want?'

'They recorded a phone call between Justine and Emily Wickenham that they thought you should know about before we interview his ex-wife.'

'What's so important?'

Langton flopped back on her bed as Anna repeated what Lewis had told her. 'The girls might have put two and two together and come up with a lot more. I mean, they did not at any time mention that it was her father or who had done the abortion.'

Langton yawned, staring at the ceiling, then leaned up on one elbow. 'Tomorrow, before we leave, get back to them; if charges were started, even if they were withdrawn, someone somewhere has to have a record of them.'

'My God.'

He looked at Anna. 'My God what?'

'In the Black Dahlia case, there was a court case involving their suspect: his own daughter accused him of molestation and attempted rape.'

Langton sat up. 'Yeah, if I remember rightly, when they questioned his wife, she stood by him. How old was the daughter?'

'Twelve when the accusations of rape and sexual harassment happened, but the trial didn't begin until she was fifteen.'

Langton rubbed his hair. 'What was the outcome? I've forgotten.'

'The allegations were proved unfounded; they claimed his daughter was suffering from delusions and the case was dropped.'

Langton gave her a sidelong glance and yawned again. 'What a mine of information you are, Travis.'

'Do you want a coffee or tea or something?'

'Nope. Get off to my bed. Did you eat?'

'Yes, thank you.'

'Did I wake you?'

'You did, actually.'

'Sorry.'

'I thought you might want to call the Incident Room; they were concerned that they couldn't contact you.'

'You tell them who I was with?'

'I just said you might have gone out for dinner.'

'Very thoughtful. Thank you, Travis.'

She hesitated. 'Do you mind if I say something?'

'I haven't before, what is it?'

'I think you are drinking too much.'

'What?'

'I said, I think you are drinking too much.'

'I've just been out for dinner, for God's sake!'

'I don't mean tonight; sometimes I can smell it on your breath in the mornings. If you need help, you should get some.'

'Drinking too much,' he said thickly.

'Maybe it is not my place to say anything, but I am working with you and I can tell when you have been on the sauce and when you have not.'

'It's none of your business.'

'Listen, I know you must really be irritated by me

even bringing this up but I'm only doing so because I really care about you and I am concerned.'

'I really appreciate your concern, Travis!' he snapped sarcastically as he walked towards the door.

'Do you want to talk about the taped call?'

'No, I'm tired. Goodnight.' He closed the door behind him, unusually for him, very quietly.

Anna sighed and went back to bed. Maybe she shouldn't have said anything to him, but they had been quite close; obviously not close enough.

DAY TWENTY-SIX

The following morning, Anna ordered room service again. She wondered if she should give Langton a wakeup call, but it turned out not to be necessary, as he called her himself to say he would be in the lobby at nine o'clock. Though he made no reference to what she had said the previous night, he sounded very cold and aloof. She dressed in one of her good suits and a cream silk shirt, and went downstairs to find he was already waiting for her.

'I've already called her and she is expecting us; said it would only take a ten-minute drive.'

He was wearing a linen suit and a white, open-collared shirt. He caught her glancing at him. 'What?'

'Nothing. You look as if you slept well.'

'I did, thank you. Did you?'

'Took me a while to get off. I was worried that what I had said to you might get me into trouble.'

'Travis, your concern was appreciated; maybe I have been imbibing a little too much lately. Let's just forget it, all right?'

She nodded. 'Have you had breakfast?' she asked.

'Nope. Let's get a coffee: the cappuccino here is good.'

They went to one of the cafés inside the hotel. He ate a croissant and drank his coffee, hardly speaking as he constantly checked his messages, making no mention of their contents. Then it was time to leave.

Dominique Wickenham's apartment block on the Via Spiga was very exclusive and modern. The reception area was like a greenhouse, all glass with an abundance of plants. The doorman led them over to the gleaming gilt elevators that would take them up to the penthouse apartment. At floor four, the doors glided open to reveal a thickly carpeted corridor with yet more plants. Apartment C4 appeared to be the only one on the floor, with a large white front door with brass studs but no number. They rang a discreet bell and waited. After a few moments, the door was opened by an elderly maid in a black dress and small white apron. Langton showed her his ID and she smiled and nodded, gesturing for them to enter the hallway behind her.

The hallway was empty apart from a massive display of orchids on a glass-topped table. They were led to a set of white double doors, which were opened by Dominique Wickenham. She was a well-preserved woman in her mid-forties, with an amazing figure, wearing grey slacks with a cashmere scarf knotted over her shoulders; her white silk blouse was set off by a luminous set of pearls. She was very tanned, her blonde hair was streaked and she wore large pearl and diamond earrings.

'Please come in; would you like a tea or coffee?'

'No thank you,' Langton said, then introduced Anna.

Dominique wore a large diamond ring on her wedding finger. She also had a gold charm bracelet that shimmered and twinkled with gold and diamond charms.

'Please sit down; there's iced water if you need it.'

'Thank you,' Langton said, as he glanced around the vast, sun-drenched room. The windows were floor to ceiling, affording them a clear view across the city. The thick carpet was pale pink, the sofas and chairs a slightly darker shade with matching cushions. Anna sank into the sofa; it was so large that if she sat back, her feet would be off the ground. Langton rested back in one of the armchairs; being so tall, he didn't have the same problem.

'You have a very beautiful apartment.'

'Thank you.' Dominique Wickenham sat on the arm of one of the chairs opposite him. Her grey high heels matched her slacks and, though she smiled with glossy lips that Anna was certain had been enhanced by cosmetic surgery, she was tapping one foot.

'So, here we are,' she said. She had a deep throaty voice and a distinctly French accent.

Langton began quietly, asking her about her husband, and saying briefly that they were there as they were heading a murder enquiry. He took out the photographs of Louise Pennel and Sharon Bilkin. She did not recognise either.

'Perhaps you have had a wasted journey.' She gave an apologetic smile.

Langton smiled back and showed her the sketch. She laughed softly, and passed it back.

'It is a very good likeness.'

'This man is a suspect in the murder of these two girls.'

'Oh, I thought it was my husband.'

'He does resemble him very closely; it was compiled using statements from witnesses that saw this man with both the victims.'

'Good heavens; you suspect Charles is involved?'

Langton replaced the photographs and sketch without answering. 'Your husband is a surgeon.'

'Yes; well, he was, he has retired now – and I am his ex-wife: we divorced some time ago.'

'But you still retain your married name?'

'For convenience and for my daughters.'

'They would be Justine and Emily.'

'Yes, that is correct.'

'Can you tell me if on the ninth of January this year, your daughter Justine stayed here with you?'

She tried to wrinkle her lineless brow and crossed to an ornate desk. She flicked through a small white leather diary, then smiled.

'Yes, it was for a weekend; my girls come and stay as often as possible.'

'But they don't stay at the Hall very often.'

'No, they do not; they do not get along too well with their father. He can be very strict and you know, girls will be girls.'

'What about your stepson?'

'Edward?'

'Yes; do the girls get along with their half-brother?'

'Of course, he is a sweet boy; very much under his father's domination, but he's working very hard.'

'Can you tell me about his wife?'

Dominique looked slightly fazed, then shrugged.

'She committed suicide, didn't she?'

'Yes, it was very sad; she was a very highly strung girl. Although she had been in treatment for depression, she took her own life.'

'She was addicted to drugs, wasn't she?'

Dominique stiffened, seeming to dislike the direction the conversation was going in. 'I believe so, but what she did in the privacy of her own home I was not aware of. It was just very sad.'

'There was a police enquiry, wasn't there?'

'Yes, isn't there always in a suicide? They found nothing untoward; she hanged herself in the barn. This was before it was converted into a gymnasium and play-room.'

'Were you questioned about a police enquiry regarding your youngest daughter?'

'I'm sorry?' Again, she tried to frown.

'Emily tried to bring a complaint against her father, your ex-husband, for sexual harassment and attempted rape.'

'No, no, no; that was all very wretched and not true. Emily is very highly strung and with an over-vivid imag-ination. There were no charges, and Emily went into therapy afterwards, which helped her. She is very very emotionally insecure and only now I think making headway since she became a student. She is exception-ally clever and considering all her health problems, she always did very well at school. She suffers from bulimia and at times has been very ill. But she is also recovering from that problem, in fact, I think she really has over-come her nervous disorder and is much better; possibly being in her own little flat and doing well in her studies helps.'

'Did she have any boyfriends?'

'Emily?'

'Yes.'

'Well she is only just seventeen, so I doubt she has had serious relationships. To be honest, I am not aware of any boyfriends she might have now, as I am mostly abroad.'

'So the operation?'

'What operation?' The foot twitched again.

'Was Emily ever pregnant?'

'Emily?'

'Yes, your youngest daughter; was Emily ever pregnant and did she have an abortion?'

'No, no I would have known! This is preposterous, unless you have talked to Emily and she has started making up stories again. She made up so many lies and it really did create a terrible situation.'

Anna felt as if she was at a tennis match, constantly looking over to Langton and back at Dominique. He really and truly never ceased to amaze her. He had only been given the information the previous night when he had been well and truly pissed; yet here he was, not missing a trick. Yet again, she found herself staring at him in awe.

Langton was looking down at the carpet, his foot inching forward into the thick pile and then back a fraction. He suddenly looked up. 'So you are unaware of any termination?'

'Yes! I have just said so! I would have known; I do have a very close relationship with my daughters.'

Langton leaned forward slightly, his fingers playing with the fringing on the arm of his chair.

'So what operation do you think your daughter could have been referring to?'

'I am nonplussed. I don't know and I really don't quite understand why you are asking me these questions.'

'Your husband was a surgeon?'

'Yes, that is correct.'

'Did he perform the operation? Let me rephrase that: could he have terminated the pregnancy of your daughter without you being privy to it?'

'No: as I said, I have a good relationship with my two girls.'

'What about with your stepson?'

'As I said before, he is a very dear, hard-working boy. I don't have quite as close a relationship with him as my daughters, but then he is my stepson: his mother was my husband's first wife.'

'He also had a drug problem, didn't he?'

'No, he was just a very young and foolish boy at school. He was found smoking a joint and they expelled him, but it was just some grass, he was never addicted to any hard drugs.'

'Unlike his wife: the autopsy found cocaine and . . .'

'I really cannot tell you anything about my daughter-in-law, it was a very sad thing that happened, and affected us all.'

'Does your husband use drugs?'

She took a deep breath and shook her head. 'Not that I am aware of, but we have been divorced for a number of years, so what he may do now, I am not privy to.'

'Can you tell me about the parties at the Hall?'

She shrugged and then got up and crossed to her desk. She opened a silver cigarette box, and took one out. 'What exactly do you want to know about them?'

'Well, could you describe some of these events?'

She lit the cigarette and then carried a cut-glass ashtray to the table beside her chair. Langton asked if she would mind if he smoked as well and she apologised for not offering him one. This relaxed her; she even offered Langton her lighter. The gold charm bracelet tinkled as she flicked away the ash.

'Charles was always very fond of entertaining and we had a very good chef. We used the converted barn, as it has such a large space for dining and there is also a snooker table.' She inhaled and let the smoke drift from her mouth. 'There is also a swimming pool, a gymnasium with a sauna and whirlpool.' She laughed, tilting her head back slightly. 'Some dinner parties did go on for a long time; in the summer, the south wall would slide back so we could dine al fresco, and in the winter we'd have a massive log fire: all really rather pleasant.'

'Did your husband ship in prostitutes for these dinners?'

'I beg your pardon!' She gave an almost theatrical impression of being shocked.

'Your father-in-law was well known for sending his chauffeur to Soho in London and bringing back numerous girls.'

'I never knew my father-in-law or his chauffeur!'

'I just wondered if his son, your ex-husband, carried on this enjoyable tradition of wining and dining these girls.'

'No, he did not!'

'Could you tell me why you got divorced?'

'I don't think it is any of your business!'

'Yes, it is. You see, Mrs Wickenham, although our witnesses described the man last seen with the victim so clearly that our artist could produce this likeness, that was not the reason we made contact with your ex-husband. We received a phone call naming him as the killer of Louise Pennel.'

She got up and went to get another cigarette, this time lighting it from the butt of her previous one.

'This call could have been from your daughter Emily.'

Anna watched Langton closely as he upped the pressure a notch. She knew as well as he did that Emily Wickenham was not the caller, nor was her sister Justine.

'Why would Emily do such a terrible thing?' She stubbed out her cigarette, leaving the fresh one in her mouth. Anna began to see that although Dominique Wickenham had the appearance of a very obviously wealthy, pampered woman, she lacked class.

'That brings me to the possibility of her own father performing an abortion on her.'

'No! I have already told you that did not happen! I think perhaps you should really speak to me through my solicitor. Your questions are of a very personal nature and I do not feel inclined to answer any more.'

'I do apologise,' Langton said, stubbing out his cigarette, but making no sign of leaving. He leaned back in his chair. 'I am leading an enquiry into a really horrific murder. Louise Pennel, known as the Red Dahlia, was sliced in two. We are certain that the torture and humiliation forced upon her before she died was more than likely committed by a qualified surgeon.'

Dominique wafted her hand and said she was certain that there would be many other ex-surgeons, or even practising ones, that could fall under suspicion. She was adamant that her ex-husband could have had no part in these murders, just as she was certain that he had never made sexual advances to her daughter. She was tight-lipped with anger as she insisted that he would not have performed any kind of illegal operation. She went on to say that, although they were divorced, they still respected each other and maintained a loving friendship which helped both their daughters.

Langton was becoming frustrated. His foot began to shake, a sign of a gathering storm. He leaned forward and clasped his hands.

'Mrs Wickenham, I really am trying to make sense of everything you say. You had an amicable divorce and you have maintained a loving friendship for the benefit of your daughters. Correct?'

'Yes, that is exactly what I have said.'

'So, I am confused as to why you would have two dysfunctional girls: one suffering from bulimia and in therapy, the other openly antagonistic towards her father. In fact, she stated that she hated him! And they neither spoke well of your stepson.'

'I can't speak for them,' she said, looking at her watch.

'Surely you can? You are their mother: they spend most of their free time with you.'

'Yes, yes they do.'

'Does your ex-husband also spend time here with you?'

'No, he does not.'

'But you remain very fond of him?'

'Yes, that is correct.'

'And fond of his son and heir, Edward.'

'Yes. Really, why are you asking me these ridiculous questions? I do not know these poor girls you say were murdered, I cannot help you in any way. You are making me feel very uncomfortable, as if you are trying to make me say slanderous things about my ex-husband that would be completely untrue.'

'I apologise if it seems that way.'

Anna coughed and they both turned towards her as if they had forgotten her existence. 'May I use your bathroom?'

Dominique got up and crossed to the double doors. She opened one and her charm bracelet tinkled as she pointed down the corridor.

'First on your left.'

'Thank you.'

Anna closed the door behind her. She didn't need to use the bathroom, but was hoping to have a private conversation with the maid, Danielle, who she was certain had been listening outside the door. She stood in the expansive hall, trying to work out where the kitchen was, when she heard the clink of dishes from behind a door at the far end of the hallway. She gave a very light tap and opened it. The maid was unloading the dishwasher; she turned, startled.

'I wondered if I could talk to you for a moment?'

Danielle crossed to a cabinet to put away some glasses. She closed the cabinet and returned to the dishwasher.

'Do you speak English?'

Danielle gathered up some dinner plates, stacking them neatly. She wouldn't look at Anna, but continued moving back and forth to the dishwasher. Anna wondered if she was deaf. She asked again if she understood English and, at last, got a response.

'I cannot talk to you, please excuse me. Thank you.'

'It is very important: we need to ask you some questions.'

'No, please.'

'It's about Emily and Justine; they stay here a lot, don't they?'

Danielle nodded and then sat down. 'I love them like my own children. I love them.' She bowed her head as she started to cry, taking a handkerchief from her apron pocket. 'I know why you are here. Is Emily all right?'

Langton lit another cigarette and stared at Dominique with slanted eyes. The smoke drifted up towards the air-conditioning vents. He slowly appraised the room and then fixed his gaze on her once more. She was standing in front of the fake log fire, with one elbow resting on the white marble mantelpiece.

'He doesn't speak very highly of you.'

'I beg your pardon?'

'Your ex-husband referred to you as money-grabbing; he implied that you were putting pressure on him to pay you more alimony.'

She arched one eyebrow and did not reply, but looked pointedly at her watch.

'Has he agreed to pay you a substantial amount more?'

She pursed her lips. 'You have no right to ask me personal questions. I would like you to leave please.'

'I can very easily check it out, Mrs Wickenham. Have you recently been paid more money by your ex-husband?'

'No.'

'Are you expecting to be paid for being such an admirable and caring ex-wife?'

'That is enough!'

Dominique stalked over to the double closed doors; she was just reaching for the handle when Anna walked in.

'I'm sorry.'

'You are just leaving,' she said icily, looking at Langton with distaste as he stubbed out his cigarette and stood up.

'Yes, thank you for your time, Mrs Wickenham. Oh, just one more thing; before your marriage, what did you do?'

She blinked and then shrugged, smiling. 'What on earth do you want to know that for?'

Langton laughed; he leaned over and took her hand. 'I just wanted to hear what you would say. I obviously know, but you lie so beautifully, madame.'

She snatched back her hand and slapped the door closed. She went so red, her eyes bulged.

'You dare to come here, asking me questions and insinuating things about my family! Then you accuse me of lying!'

'You were an exotic dancer.'

Anna thought Dominique was going to slap Langton's face but she controlled her temper, clenching her hands into fists.

'Who have you been asking about me?' she spat.

'It wasn't too difficult; you have a police record, madame. You are still on record in Marseilles. Now I don't know if your husband is, or was, aware of your rather colourful past.'

'My husband knew everything about me.'

'Did he hire you; is that how you met? I know he has a predilection for very young prostitutes. I also suspect that he couldn't keep his hands off his own daughter.'

Her face was now white with fury. 'Get out. Get out!' She gasped, yanking the door open so hard it banged against the pristine white wall.

Langton nodded to Anna to move into the hall ahead of him. He passed the shaken Dominique, close enough to be almost touching her.

'He must be paying you a lot of money,' he said, very quietly.

She shouted for her maid, but there was no sign of the elderly woman. She pointed to the front door. 'Please go, please go.'

Anna could see that Langton was not finished; he had that glint in his eyes. He reached the front door and was about to turn the handle and walk out when he paused, instead snapping open his briefcase. He took a moment to select the exact picture he wanted: the mortuary shot of the mutilated Louise Pennel.

'Take a look, Mrs Wickenham: this is the Red Dahlia.'

Dominique averted her eyes.

'Look at it.'

'Why are you doing this to me?'

'You should know what this monster did to this young woman. I came to see you specifically to—'

'You came here because you wanted me to implicate my ex-husband in this horror. Well, I do not believe for a second he is involved. I have never seen either of those two girls you showed me; you seem to be intent on shocking me into—'

'I just want the truth, Mrs Wickenham; but you seem to be incapable of being honest,' Langton interrupted, clicking his briefcase closed. 'You cited in your divorce hearing abusive and threatening behaviour, your husband's sexual demands and constant infidelities. You also gained custody of both your daughters, because you stated that living with their father was not a healthy environment for young girls.'

'I never saw either of those women you showed me, and what one states in a divorce hearing is not necessarily . . .'

'The whole truth and nothing but the truth?' Langton interjected.

'I wasn't going to say that; at the time, I had to protect myself and my future. We have now made very amicable arrangements. It's quite common, you know, to be unable to live with someone and yet still care for them after separation.'

She seemed to be back in control. Danielle appeared and Dominique asked her to show the 'guests' to the elevator. Langton snapped that it would not be necessary.

Reflected in the elevator's gilt edging, he could see Mrs Dominique Wickenham still staring after them, composed and elegant; she slowly closed her front door.

Langton was in a foul mood on the way back to their

hotel. They had really gained very little from the trip. His extensive knowledge of Mrs Wickenham's past had fazed Anna but had not brought any results.

'She was a whore,' Langton said, as they went into the hotel lobby.

'Must have been quite young,' Anna said.

'She was. I traced two arrests for soliciting in Paris. No way is she going to give us anything on Wickenham, because he pays out a fortune to her in alimony. That apartment must cost a bomb and like he said himself, the lady likes to shop.'

'So what's the next move?'

'We do as Professor Marshe suggested: weed out any known associates of Wickenham's and see if they can enlighten us.'

'If they were involved in any of these parties, then they are unlikely to be that helpful. I think we concentrate on the old housekeeper, the son and track down the girlfriend at her health farm.'

'Is that what you think, Travis?'

'Yes.'

'I detect a slight frisson; what's the matter?'

'It would be helpful if you had enlightened me with what you know, as maybe I could have had some input. I had to sit there just watching as you came out with the fact she was an exotic dancer, details of her divorce and her record for prostitution.' She asked for her key at the reception desk, warming up to have a row with him. 'I know you like to play things close to your chest, it's the way you work, but sometimes you should share information. I couldn't give you very much help.'

'Do you think you could have?'

'Yes! Well, I say yes; obviously, I'm not sure. I would have maybe taken it a bit calmer, teased it out of her.'

'Teased what out of her?' Langton asked.

Anna sighed; they had by now crossed to the elevators and were heading up to the third floor.

'Well, if she was what, eighteen, nineteen, years of age when she married Wickenham?'

'Not that young; she was twenty-five.'

'Okay, about my age. She's been arrested and she gets this rich-as-Croesus Englishman who must have brought her over from Paris; it's not a brain surgeon you need to tell you that it was the sex. So she hooks him, marries him, has two children . . .'

The elevator stopped, but Langton didn't get out; instead, he pressed to go to her floor.

'I think Dominique was not saying anything untoward about her ex-husband,' Anna continued, 'because she must have played quite a part in these soirées, and here's something else that's quite freaky: when the Black Dahlia suspect was arrested, his wife made him out to be a loving and caring man, when he'd been accused of molesting his daughter.' She headed towards her room, Langton following. The bed had not been made as she was checking out; her case was packed and ready for her to leave.

'If our suspect is Wickenham,' Langton responded, 'he has an obsession with the Black Dahlia case. It would therefore stand to reason that he would have primed his ex-hooker wife to stand by him and instructed her to give no indication that there was anything dubious connected to his younger daughter. I would say the incentive is money. The Black Dahlia ex-wife was broke and couldn't pay her rent; I don't think Dominique is hurting for money, but she is greedy: Wickenham said so himself.' He sat in a chair by the window; he had one leg crossed over the other, his foot tapping.

'Whichever source you used to get the details you had on Dominique Wickenham, were they able to tell you how large her bank balance was?'

Langton said nothing, glaring at his shoe. He then swung his leg down and took a beer from her mini bar. 'I had some help from Professor Marshe; she has a lot of contacts.'

Anna shook her head. 'How was she able to get this information?'

Langton opened the bottle. 'She worked in Paris, she's able to pull some strings, and she is also very well respected.'

'That doesn't mean a thing. She was privy to a police record and to divorce statements.'

'I checked out the divorce. Just don't ask too many questions, Travis. I'm sorry if I was like a bear with a sore arse, but I really hoped I'd be able to get that bitch to open up. Do you think I was too heavy-handed?'

'Slightly.'

'It was that bloody jangling charm bracelet, got on my nerves. She was lying to us from the moment we walked through the front door.' He swigged his beer from the bottle.

Anna sat opposite him. 'How can a woman know that her ex-husband had made advances to their daughter and that, as a result, an abortion had been performed, possibly even by him, and not want him stripped naked and whipped?'

'My gut feeling is that Dominique Wickenham would sell her own daughters if the price was right. You know the old saying don't you, a whore is a whore . . .' He frowned. 'I've forgotten the rest,' he said. He looked depressed. 'Well, pretty wasted journey. Might as well get to the airport and catch an earlier flight.'

Langton half rose out of his chair as the phone rang. He plonked himself back down again as Anna answered. She listened, then said thank you before replacing the receiver.

'Package has just been delivered. Were you expecting one?'

Langton shook his head.

'Well, it's on its way up.'

Anna opened the door and waited. A porter came out of the elevator carrying a brown manila envelope, addressed to them both but with their names misspelled. Anna tipped the porter, took the envelope and handed it to Langton. The envelope had been used before and the flap had been taped down. He opened it and tipped the contents out onto the glass table. There were seven photographs.

'What have we got here?' he murmured.

As he arranged the photographs so that they faced upwards on the table, Anna checked the envelope. A square white label had been stuck over the original address. Anna carefully eased as much away as possible without tearing it, to see that it had been mailed to Dominique Wickenham. There was a smudged date: it was March 2002. She called reception to ask if they could give a description of the person who had delivered the package.

Langton was staring at one photograph after another. 'You think Dominique sent these over?'

'I think from what they said downstairs it was her maid. Apparently it was an elderly woman in a black coat.'

Langton handed her one of the photographs. 'See what you make of that.'

Anna looked: it was a group of men and women lazing in a hot tub with glasses of champagne. 'That's Charles Wickenham centre, his son Edward, and I think that's Dominique half-turned towards camera. Is that Justine, the girl across from her?'

Langton nodded and looked at another photograph. 'Same crowd; hot tubs seem to excite them. Let's see if we can get an ID on the hairy-chested chaps. There's three women in this one, but none look like family.'

Anna glanced at the group of sweating, laughing people, toasting the camera with raised glasses and smiles. The men had their arms wrapped around the naked girls. Anna found the seediness of the photograph repellent, the two middle-aged men leering at what looked like teenagers.

'It's getting pornographic now: same men but different girls, blowjob time, and getting into costumes and bits of leather. Christ!'

Anna looked up.

'Jesus Christ, look at this! Just on the edge of the picture, on the right-hand side. Is that who I think it is?'

Anna got up and stood, looking over his shoulder. 'Where are you looking?'

Langton pointed. 'Girl in the leather boots and G-string.'

Anna leaned further over. 'It's Justine Wickenham.'

Langton picked up another photo, and shook his head. 'Christ Almighty, they're all screwing her.'

'His daughter?'

'No, Dominique Wickenham. When do you think this was taken?'

He turned over the photographs but nothing was written on the back of any of them.

'Well, the envelope has 2002 on it, but these could have been taken years ago, so it's not much use to us. If it is her, what does that give us?'

Langton looked up; they were almost touching. 'Well, she's bonking her stepson as well as everyone else, so it's not that old is it? How old would you say he looks?'

'Hard to tell from what I can see of him. But Justine looks about thirteen or fourteen to me.'

Langton sifted through the photographs and then frowned. 'This looks like some kind of cellar. There's two girls tied up. Look at all the equipment: the sicko's got a private dungeon! There's chains and some weird machines.'

'Looks like old farm equipment to me,' Anna said, sitting back down.

'No way; this is state-of-the-art masochistic gear.' Langton got up and started to pace to and fro, then took another beer from the mini bar.

Anna carried on looking at the photographs. 'Why did she bring these to us? There's got to be something we're not seeing. I mean, we have a pretty good idea of what Wickenham gets up to, but in the privacy of his home, there's not a lot we can do about it.'

'Well, there's the one photo of his daughter.'

'I know, but it still doesn't give us any connection to Louise Pennel or Sharon Bilkin. So Wickenham has sex parties: it's not against the law.'

'What if the girls are all underage?'

'Well, one, we have to trace them; two, we could find that they're not unwilling participants. We also have no dates, so we don't know when these were taken, and they're not all from the same time.' Anna pointed out that in one photo, Wickenham had a moustache, in another longish hair, and in another short hair: there could be years between when they were taken.

'Well, there is one person that can give us a clue, and that's Dominique.'

'You suggesting we go back?'

'Thinking about it.'

'You'll get the maid into big trouble.'

Langton nodded as he opened a packet of peanuts. 'How about talking to just the maid?'

Anna shrugged. 'We could do, but we are scheduled to fly back this afternoon. It's up to you.'

Langton tossed a peanut up into the air and caught it in his mouth. 'I think we should return as scheduled. We need to talk to Justine and the son.'

Chapter Fourteen

DAY TWENTY-SEVEN

Anna slept through her alarm and was annoyed at herself for being late for work. She grabbed yesterday's suit, but put on a clean shirt. She arrived at the Incident Room to be told that Langton was in the boardroom, being given a briefing by the key team. Lewis, Barolli, Bridget and two other officers were sitting around the huge table listening to the taped calls from the phone taps. Langton was looking very smart in a pale blue shirt and dark navy tie, his suit immaculate. He glanced up with irritation as Anna entered.

'Sorry, my alarm didn't go off,' she said rather lamely as she took the nearest chair. She put down her brief-case, taking out her notebook and pencils. No one spoke; they all seemed to be waiting for her to settle. 'Sorry,' she repeated, embarrassed, and busied herself turning over the pages of her notebook until she found a blank one.

'We've been discussing the phone taps on the Wickenham family. Lewis thinks that Charles knows we're monitoring his calls: he's very cagey and abrupt, unless it's something innocuous.'

He turned to Lewis and gestured to the tape recorder.

Each call had been numbered. Langton asked him to play a specific one for Anna's benefit: it was a recording of Edward and Charles Wickenham talking. Wickenham senior's voice was harsh and angry.

'*I fucking said there was something wrong with him when I last had him out. Why you can't do a simple thing like get the fucking vet to see to him? He's lame now, a lot worse than he was, and that's down to your stupidity; why can't you just do what I tell you, when I tell you to do it?*'

'*I'm sorry. I had to go and collect Gail.*'

'*Why couldn't she get a car and get herself home? She's a bloody liability. What she needs is therapy, not a few weeks in a health spa.*'

'*She's fine now.*'

'*I hope to Christ she is. You keep her in line: you give her too much rope — mind you, if you gave her more, she'd probably hang herself, the stupid bitch.*'

'*It's her nerves.*'

'*Well, that doesn't interest me; what does is that the horse won't be able to hunt for at least a month, so get him sorted out, never mind your bloody girlfriend.*'

'*She wants to get married.*'

'*What?*'

'*I said, she wants me to marry her.*'

'*I would say after your last disastrous marriage, it's the last thing you want to do.*'

'*Maybe I should.*'

'*Maybe you should? Why, exactly? She lives with you; she gets whatever she wants.*'

'*She's very nervous.*'

'*Well, for Chrissakes, shut the stupid bitch up.*'

'*That's why I should marry her.*'

There was a long pause; then Wickenham sighed. 'You do whatever you need to do, Edward. She has to be controlled, and if the way to do it is by marrying her, then go ahead.'

'I don't know what to do, Pa.'

'Have you ever? Let me think about it.'

Charles slammed the phone down, leaving Edward still on the line; he sighed before hanging up too.

Langton twisted his pen round and round. 'We need to talk to Edward's proposed bride. Pop sounds like a real tetchy son of a bitch, doesn't he, Travis?'

Anna looked up from her note-taking. 'Yes; maybe the horse he was referring to was the one we saw him on the day we were at the Hall?'

Langton glared at her.

'If it is, we have a timeframe,' she continued.

Langton ignored her, resting his elbows on the table. 'Reading between the lines about the proposed daughter-in-law's problems, keeping her under control, etcetera, I wonder if she is the anonymous caller that tipped us off.' He nodded to Lewis, asking for call sixteen to be played.

This was the most recent call they had on tape: it was from Dominique. It was very brief and she sounded tense and angry, especially when Wickenham said he couldn't talk to her.

'Well, I need to talk to you, Charles, so don't ring off, because if you do I will simply keep calling you back until you do talk to me. The police were at my apartment today and they were asking me a lot of questions about . . .'

'Shut up!'

'What?'

'I said shut up! If you wait a few minutes, I'll be able to call you back, not on your land phone.'

'What does that mean?'

'I'll call you on your mobile, your cell phone, Dominique; I can't talk to you at the house.'

'They were asking me all these questions, first about Emily . . .'

'Not now: later.'

The phone went dead.

Langton spread out his fingers flat on the tabletop. 'It's obvious he knows we're taping him.' He looked at Anna. 'This was as far as we'd got before your late arrival, so now we can concentrate on the other calls: one in particular.'

He nodded to Lewis again. It was Edward Wickenham talking to his girlfriend Gail.

'I'll be there to collect you. You might have to wait, as father wants me to do some errands, but it shouldn't be too long.'

'Like how long? You knew I was leaving here today.'

Bridget put up her hand. Lewis stopped the tape.

'That's her: that's the woman that called the station. I'm sure of it.'

Langton looked at Anna who shook her head. 'Could I hear a bit more? It does sound like her.'

The tape continued.

'Can't you ask your father to do whatever needs doing later? He just makes you run around after him all the time.'

'He pays the bills, Gail.'

'I know; I know that.'

'So just wait: I'll be there!'

The call ended and Anna nodded. 'Yes, I'd say it's her. Have we done a voice match on the calls that came in to be one hundred per cent sure?'

Barolli looked at his watch. 'We only got this in last night, so they might not have got it together yet. Want me to check?'

Langton wafted his hand. 'Later. Let's hear the rest and then get up to speed all round on what we came up with in Milan.'

They all listened to calls between Emily and Justine Wickenham. There was nothing suspicious and nothing that linked to their enquiry; they just talked about a party for some friend and the dinner menu, with Justine giving Emily a cooking class over the telephone. The sisters were quite at ease with one another; Emily appeared to be very much calmer than when they had interviewed her.

The team listened to call after call for over fifty minutes, then Lewis stopped the tape. 'This one is interesting, though a bit indistinct, so we are having it cleaned up. It's a call from Emily's mobile to Justine's land line.'

'Do you know what time it is?' Justine was asking.

'Yes.' This was very blurred and slurred.

'Where are you?'

'I'm at a party.' Again, this was hardly audible.

'Are you drunk? Ems, are you drunk or something? Hello, are you there? Emily, where are you?'

'I want to kill him!' came the high-pitched scream.

'For Chrissakes, Emily, where are you? I can come and get you.'

'No! I don't want you to see me, I just need some

. . .' It was then a totally incoherent ramble of slurred words with long pauses in between.

'Em, are you with someone?'

'Yes.'

'Are they a nice person? Are they looking after you?'

Emily laughed, a strange and hollow sound, devoid of any humour. 'Are they nice?'

'You know what I mean, Em. You're not being taken advantage of, are you?'

'Would it matter? I've been taken advantage of since I was fucking ten years old, so what the fuck does it matter where I am? I am going to pay him back, Justine: one day, I'll pay him back.'

'By getting drunk and acting dumb?'

'Shut up!'

'You bloody called me, Em, so don't tell me to shut up. I am trying to help you. If you tell me where you are, I'll come and get you.'

'You'll see. I'll get him. I'll make him pay. Danielle will help me.'

Anna looked across at Langton on hearing this.

Justine's voice became lower, almost threatening. 'You be very careful what you tell her. I mean it, Em: you have no idea what Daddy can do.'

'Yes I have. I bloody know!'

'Then listen to me: keep your mouth shut. I've already had Mother on the phone: the police were asking questions about you. That woman detective was in Milan. I warned you about saying anything to the police.'

'I didn't tell them anything!' Emily was crying.

'Then from now on, refuse to speak to them unless

I am with you. Just do what you are told to do, otherwise terrible things will happen!'

Emily was sobbing, her voice hardly audible. 'They
already have happened. There's nothing anyone could
do to me that would be worse.'

And then she hung up. The team sat in silence.

'Bit like father like daughter,' said Langton. 'She's a
piece of work, Justine Wickenham; from what we were
able to discover in Milan, she is not an innocent: far
from it.' He showed the team the photographs.

Although it was Anna who had talked to Danielle,
Langton talked them through the details of their conversation. 'We are certain that Danielle has no idea about
the murder enquiry. She thought we were there regarding
Wickenham's sexual antics with Emily. Though we've got
photographs of him and Justine rather than Emily, the
maid was very concerned about her and with good
bloody reason. She wants him punished! I think that goes
for all of us; the question is how we go about drawing
the net over his sickening head. We have it raised, but
we still need more concrete evidence: a lot of what we
have is hearsay and won't hold up in court. We need
confirmation that Louise Pennel was at that house and
that he has lied about not knowing her; someone there
must have seen her and I think that someone could be
the son's girlfriend. We now need to question Edward
Wickenham and Gail Harrington, but we have to be
very careful as the son could also be implicated; he may
be a partner in his father's perversions.'

Lewis tapped the photograph of Edward and
Dominique Wickenham. 'I'd say he's very much a part
of it: he's screwing his stepmother!'

Langton nodded and tapped the other photographs. 'Let's see if we can identify these other guys.'

They went on to discuss getting a search warrant for the Hall; Langton said they could get one any time, but he wanted to hold off until he had some firm evidence. The meeting broke up and the team regrouped in the Incident Room. Langton asked Anna to join him in his office; she asked if she could first finish typing up her report. He shrugged and walked off with Lewis. When she headed over a short while later, the door was ajar: she could hear their conversation clearly.

'She was at the airport! Ruddy woman gets everywhere; anyway, it proved to be worthwhile, as she filled in some details about Mrs Wickenham the exotic dancer. I have to hand it to her, she's a really devious woman. She could get blood out of a stone; well, I know she can – she got me to take her to dinner. She wanted to go to this place called Bebel's on the Via San Marco. It cost a fortune. Good job it was worthwhile: my expenses went through the roof.'

So Anna had been wrong about Langton and Professor Marshe after all: it had been a coincidence. She tapped on the open door and Lewis turned.

'See you later then.' He passed Anna.

'Shut the door, Travis,' Langton said, loosening his tie. Anna hovered by his desk.

'I want you to have another go at Emily Wickenham. It's pretty obvious she's flying close to the edge, but she might just know something that will help us. I'm getting copies of the photographs done, so she might help us identify the men in the hot tub.'

'Okay.' She nodded.

'Are you?'

'I'm sorry?'

'Are you okay?'

She frowned, confused. 'Yes, why? Don't I look it?'

He shrugged. 'You're wearing the same clothes as you travelled in last night, your hair needs something doing to it, and you've got a ladder in your tights.'

She flushed.

'So, is there anything you feel you want to tell me?'

'I overslept.'

'That was pretty obvious, you were late. It's just unusual – well, I think it is – when a woman wears the same clothes two days in a row.'

'I just didn't have time to find another suit.'

'Don't get stroppy! It's just not like you, that's all: you always look fresh as a daisy. This morning, you look beat.'

'Thank you. I'll have an early night.'

He nodded, and loosened his tie even lower down his shirt front. 'This journalist still seeing you?'

'No.'

There was a pause as he checked his watch. He looked up at her and smiled. 'See you later.'

She walked back to her desk, feeling like she'd been hit over the head with a mallet. She was rifling around in her briefcase for a spare pair of tights when Barolli breezed over, grinning.

'We got a hit: the anonymous caller has been identified.'

Anna looked up. 'Is it Edward Wickenham's girlfriend?'

'Got it in one! Well, let's say we're pretty sure it's her.'

'You going to interview her?' she asked.

'Dunno; be down to the Gov. But good news, huh?'

'Yes.'

' You okay?'

She sighed. 'I am fine!'

'Just you look a bit under the weather. Mind you, this case is getting to all of us. Poor old Lewis is knackered: his son is teething, keeping him up all night.'

Langton appeared. 'Can you cut the bloody chitchat? Did we get a result?'

Barolli grinned. 'We certainly did: voice match!'

Anna watched as they went into Langton's office together. She picked up her tights and hurried off to the ladies'.

Straightening her skirt, Anna noticed a stain down one side and scratched at it with her finger. She dampened some toilet tissue and tried unsuccessfully to clean it off. She took a good hard look at herself in the mirror and was taken aback. Her hair needed washing, she had no make-up on and the white shirt that she'd seized was looking very drab.

'Christ, I do look a mess,' she muttered, embarrassed: she was even wearing awful old sports knickers. 'What are you doing to yourself?' She glanced down at her shoes: they were comfortable, but old and scuffed; unsurprising, as she'd had them since college.

Letting yourself go, that's what, she thought. She returned to her desk with grim determination: at lunchtime, she'd book an appointment for a cut and blow-dry, then when she got home, she was going to weed out all her old clothes and send them off to the Red Cross.

★

315

'You going with the Gov?' Barolli asked as he shrugged into his raincoat.

'What?'

'Interview Wickenham's girlfriend?'

'No, I'm on the daughter.'

'Oh; well, he was bellowing for you a few minutes ago.' Barolli headed out.

Lewis hurried past. 'Gov is looking for you.'

'Christ! I just went to the toilet,' she snapped and was about to head towards Langton's office when he appeared.

'Where've you been?'

Anna gestured, exasperated. 'The ladies'!'

'Well, I want you with me: you did the phone-in with her, so maybe it's good you're along.'

'But what about Emily Wickenham?'

'What about her? You can see her when we get back.'

Langton strode off. The hairdresser would have to wait.

It was pouring with rain, as though someone up there was turning on taps. Anna had held her briefcase over her head as she ran across the car park, but by the time she got in beside Lewis, she was drenched.

'Christ Almighty, this is like a monsoon!' he moaned, as he rubbed his soaking wet hair.

Langton was sitting in the front next to the driver, wearing a brown raincoat with a shoulder-wide cape. He looked bone dry; Lewis, wiping his face with a hand-kerchief, leaned forward.

'Didn't you get caught in it then?'

'Yep, but there are such things as umbrellas, pal!'

'Right, thanks, brilliant. I'm effing soaked and so is Anna.'

Langton turned to grin at them both; he gestured to his raincoat. 'You should get one of these: down to the ankles, shoulders double up with this cape thing. I got it in Camden Market, it's worn by bushmen in Australia.'

'Rains there, does it?' Lewis said, as he pulled at his soaking wet shirt collar.

Anna could feel her hair curling up beneath her fingers. She knew it would dry into a frizzy mop, and make her look like a Cabbage Patch doll. That was what her father used to say to tease her when she was a child.

'Okay let's get this show on the road,' Langton said, as they pulled out of the station car park.

He had not contacted Gail Harrington directly but, as before, established that she was home from speaking to the housekeeper. He doubted with the downpour that she would be riding or out anywhere.

'This is something else, isn't it?' Lewis said, as he watched the rain streaming down the windscreen.

'It's the global crap,' Langton said, swivelling round to face Anna. 'Right, Travis, let's just go through the interaction you had with Miss Harrington when she called the station.'

Anna repeated the conversation, thumbing through her notebook to find the shorthand notes she'd taken at the time. Langton watched as she turned over page after page of her small square book, covered in cramped neat writing. He leaned on his elbow as she described how she had tried to persuade the woman they now knew to be Miss Harrington to give them her name and, most important, the name of the man she suspected

317

of being involved in the Red Dahlia murder. 'She wouldn't give her own name, but then just blurted out his: Doctor Charles Henry Wickenham.'

They drove in silence for a while; then Langton said, softly, 'We focus so much on Louise Pennel and hardly ever mention Sharon Bilkin, but I think about her a lot.'

There was another silence and then Anna said quietly, 'She lied to us.'

'She was young and greedy and silly,' Lewis said.

Langton turned to him, his face set. 'That doesn't make it any better. She died spread-eagled out in a bloody field, lipstick scrawled across her body: "fuck you"!' He turned back and smacked the dashboard with the flat of his hand. 'Fuck *him*! Christ, I want this guy.'

'We all do,' Anna said.

'Right now we don't have a thing on him, no DNA, not a single piece of evidence to prove he's a sick pervert that screwed his own daughter.'

Lewis leaned forward. 'If we get someone to corroborate the statement of the maid in Milan, that Louise Pennel had been at the house . . .'

'Hang on,' Anna said. 'When I talked to the maid alone, she was very distressed and afraid that Mrs Wickenham would walk in on us. She said she might have seen Louise, but she couldn't be certain. Her concerns were about Emily. I was only with her for about ten minutes.'

Langton shrugged. 'So maybe she was there. We still don't have evidence to prove he is the killer. From the sound of it, he had girls staying over whenever he felt like getting his rocks off.'

'Well maybe we'll get an ID off the photographs you brought back.'

Langton sighed. 'Yeah, but those guys might not have been around to see Louise Pennel. He's a cagey son of a bitch; I doubt he would have paraded her in front of his cronies if he was intent on killing her.'

'Unless they were party to his plan,' Anna said, and then wished she hadn't, as Langton gave a bad-tempered grunt.

'With the press we've had, you'd never get witnesses to talk. Anyone else in those orgies ain't gonna come forward; they'll keep their mouths tight shut.'

'You think we should up the ante and put out more press?' Lewis asked.

Langton turned to Anna. 'That's what her boyfriend thinks, or wants . . .'

'He's not my boyfriend!' Anna snapped.

'Excuse me,' Langton said, with mock sarcasm. 'If we need him he'll play, but until we get more . . . Believe me, we need a hell of a lot more than we've got.'

'Going round in circles, aren't we?' Anna said.

'Yeah yeah, I hear you but, hell, it whiles away the time. We're almost there.'

They turned off the A3 towards Petworth, churning over in silence everything that had been discussed, until they headed down the long lane towards Mayerling Hall.

Langton instructed the driver to take the slip road down to the cottage. The rain had not let up and the car bounced into foot-deep puddles. Smoke twirled from the chimney.

'Looks like they're home,' Lewis said.

They pulled up next to a mud-covered Land Rover and an equally muddy Mercedes sports car. Langton sat for a moment before reaching for the door handle.

'Okay, softly softly approach. Anna, you give us the nod that we haven't screwed up and the girlfriend is our anonymous lady.'

'It was checked out,' Lewis said, opening his door.

'Yeah I know, but we need a face-to-face. Edward Wickenham might have more than one woman, if his father's anything to go by.'

Langton stopped speaking as Edward Wickenham appeared at the door. 'Hello,' he said, affably. 'If you want to see my father, he's over at the blacksmith's.'

'No, no we came to see you and . . .'

A tall, slender woman with thick, waist-length chestnut hair in a single plait, a black velvet ribbon wound round its base, appeared behind him for a fraction of a moment, then disappeared from sight.

Langton pulled up his collar. The rain was still coming down heavily. 'You mind if we come in?' he smiled.

'Sorry, yes of course. Ghastly weather: would you mind using the rake by the door? The mud trails everywhere.'

They were shown into a low-ceilinged room, with dark beams and panelling and wide polished floorboards. There was a large brick open fire in which masses of logs were burning. More logs were stacked either side of the iron basket. Langton had scraped his shoes; Lewis had taken his off as he'd trodden in a puddle as he stepped from the car. Anna had been nimble-footed and just wiped her shoes on the mat, glad she was wearing her old ones.

'Well, what can I do for you all?'

'We would like to talk to you and your girlfriend. Just a few questions.'

'What about?'

'Could you ask her to join us?'

Wickenham held out his hand for their coats. 'I'll hang these up for you. I'm not sure where Gail is; if you would just wait a moment.'

He was so tall that he had to bend his head as he went through the low doorway. Langton sank into a large worn velvet armchair.

'How do we want to work this?' Lewis asked, sitting opposite. It might be a bit daunting for all three of them to talk to her.

Langton nodded, looking around the room, which was filled with an antique dresser, side tables and large bowls of potted plants.

'We take Wickenham; Anna . . .' He stopped as Wickenham returned.

'She's not here.'

'Yes she is. We saw her as we arrived, so please let's not waste time.'

Wickenham hesitated and moved closer, lowering his voice. 'I would prefer it if you arranged another time, Gail has not been well and she's very frail. In fact, she has only just returned from staying at a health farm.'

Langton smiled. 'Well, why don't you let DI Travis just have a few words with her and us gentlemen can talk in here.'

'But what's it about? Why do you want to talk to her?'

'We are making enquiries—' Langton was interrupted.

'But you were here before. My father talked to you.'

'Yes he did. And now we want to talk to you.' There was a slight edge to his voice.

Wickenham hesitated again, then gestured to Anna to follow him. As soon as they were out of the room, Langton got up and walked around, picking up books and china figures from the dresser.

'Bigger inside than you think, isn't it?' Lewis said, still sitting in the low armchair. In his stockinged feet, he didn't give a particularly convincing impression of a hardened detective at work.

'Money,' Langton said softly. He crossed to look at a small oil painting of a hunting scene as Lewis opened his briefcase and took out a file.

Anna followed Edward Wickenham up a thickly carpeted, narrow staircase with only a cord for a handrail. A bowl of flowers stood on a big antique chest on the landing; the ceiling was even lower than downstairs.

'Must be quite hazardous,' Anna said lightly.

Wickenham turned, frowning. 'What?'

'Being so tall.'

'Ah, yes; well, after a few cracks over the head you get used to it. She's in here.' He tapped on a small, dark oak, studded door. 'Sweetheart, the policewoman wants to talk to you.' He turned back to Anna. 'I'm sorry, I've forgotten your name.'

'Anna, Anna Travis.'

He opened the door and stepped back so Anna could enter; he then leaned in and smiled.

'I'll be downstairs, darling. If it gets too much, just call me; I've said you are feeling poorly.'

Anna thanked him and waited for him to close the door. The bedroom was lovely: floral curtains fell in folds to the ground, framing the leaded windows. An old oak wardrobe with carved figures on the doors stood beside an equally old carved chest. There was a kidney-shaped dressing table, its frilled skirt matching the curtains, covered with bottles of perfume. Propped up on white pillows on the four-poster bed was Gail Harrington, her legs curled beneath her. Beside the bed was an old nursing chair. Anna gestured towards it.

'May I sit down?'

'Yes.'

Gail Harrington was very tall and slender; her pale face and dark hair made her seem fragile. There were dark circles beneath her wide-apart hazel eyes. Her cheekbones were like carved marble and her lips, devoid of make-up, were colourless. She was wearing a diamond ring on her engagement finger, a large single teardrop-shaped stone. It seemed too big for her slender fingers, and she constantly twisted it round and round.

'Why do you want to see me?'

'May I call you Gail?'

'Of course.'

Anna placed her briefcase on her knee. 'I think you know why.'

'I really don't.'

Anna looked at her and smiled. 'I recognise your voice, Gail; I was the officer you spoke to when you called the Richmond Incident Room.'

'No, you must be mistaken; I have never spoken to you.'

'We have matched your voice, Gail. It will be far easier if you could just be honest with me. If, on the other hand, you maintain that you did not make any such calls, then I will have to ask you to come with me to the station, so we can do the interview there.'

'No, no I can't.'

'So you do admit you called the station, specifically about the murder of a girl called Louise Pennel?' Anna paused. Gail twisted her ring round and round, coiled up like a frightened child. 'She is sometimes referred to as the Red Dahlia.'

'I read about it.'

'You said that we should talk to Doctor Charles Henry Wickenham.'

'Yes, yes, I know; I did say that.'

'I need to know why you gave us his name.'

'It was a stupid thing to have done, I'm sorry.'

'But you must have had a reason, unless you are saying that you did it for some ulterior motive. We take every call very seriously; if we find out that it was a silly prank, you have wasted valuable police time.'

'I'm sorry.'

'There are repercussions for wasting police time, Gail. Would you like to tell me why you—'

'No reason! There is no reason. I really am very very sorry. I did it because I was not well. If you want, I can get a doctor's certificate to prove it. I have had a sort of nervous breakdown. All I can do is apologise.'

'I will need your doctor's name and contact number.'

Anna watched as Gail uncurled her legs and slid from the bed. She was at least five ten and stick thin, and she was trembling as she went to the dressing table and took out a diary. She sat down and wrote on a page, ripping it out and then passing it to Anna. 'It's Doctor Allard.'

'Thank you.' Anna placed the note into her briefcase.

She held up the photograph of Louise Pennel. 'Have you ever seen this girl here? As a guest, maybe?'

Gail sat on the edge of the bed and stared at the photograph. 'No, no I have not seen her.'

'What about this girl? Her name was Sharon Bilkin.'

Gail swallowed and then shook her head. 'No, I have never seen her.'

Anna put the photographs back into the file and slowly took out one of the hideous mortuary photographs of Louise Pennel. 'Louise Pennel's body was drained of blood and severed in two. She suffered terrible injuries. Her lips were slashed from ear to ear . . .'

'Please don't! I don't want to see. It's terrible, it's awful! I can't look at it.'

'Then look at Sharon Bilkin. She was found—'

'No, I don't want to see. I can't stand it, I won't look.'

Anna put the photographs down on the bed. Gail was really shaking, her hands twisting and the ring turning turning.

'The man we are hunting for in connection with these murders was possibly a trained surgeon or doctor. We have a drawing of him made up from witnesses' descriptions. Will you please look at it for me?'

Gail slipped open a drawer and took out a small bottle of pills. She tipped a few into her hand, picked up a glass of water from her bedside table and gulped them down. Then she turned to stare at the sketch Anna was holding up. Eventually, she shook her head.

'Do you recognise this man?'

'No.'

'Are you certain? Doesn't he remind you of someone?'

'No.'

'Well, I think he does look very similar to the man you named, who is also a doctor. You told us to question Charles Wickenham, didn't you? So you must have had a reason other than being unwell.'

Gail bowed her head. 'I make things up; my doctor will tell you.'

Anna now made a great show of putting the photographs back into her briefcase as if the conversation was over. 'We'll obviously talk to your doctor.'

'He will confirm everything I have told you.'

Anna smiled. 'I'm sorry you have been ill.' She snapped her case closed and placed it beside her chair. 'Were you a model?'

Gail lifted her head and blinked, surprised by the question. 'Yes, yes I was; not very successful, but I did a lot of catalogue work.' She smiled.

'I would have thought with your looks you'd have been on a par with Naomi Campbell; you must be what, five eight?'

'Five ten, but modelling is a very tough career; they want the girls so young. When I worked in Paris, there were girls there as young as sixteen, plucked straight from school; they have such confidence.'

Anna nodded. Now that she had changed the subject, Gail was becoming less tense and nervous. 'But you must be very photogenic with those cheekbones.'

Gail put her hand over her mouth and gave an odd laugh: 'I had them helped a bit.'

'No!'

'Yes, it is very common now, they just put something into the cheek.'

'I would love to see your photographs.'

Gail hesitated and then crossed to open the wardrobe; she bent down and took out a large professional port-folio and some loose photographs. 'I haven't worked for a couple of years now; well, not since I've been living with Edward.'

'How long have you been together?'

'Oh, two years, maybe more.' She was searching through the album.

'Did you know his first wife?'

Gail stared resolutely at the pictures. 'Not well, but yes, I did know her.'

'It was suicide, wasn't it?'

'Yes, it was. I am trying to find you some of my better pictures.'

'Why did she do it? Do you know?'

Gail looked up sharply. 'Who knows what makes people do the things they do? She was depressed, I suppose; we don't talk about it.'

'It must have been very shocking for Edward.'

'Well, more so for his father, as he was the one who found her; Edward was away.'

'Do you get along with Mr Wickenham?'

Gail laughed and turned over a laminated page. 'I don't really have much choice.'

'How does Edward get along with him?'

Gail sighed and plopped the book on the bed. 'He has to get along with him: Charles is his father and Edward's the heir, so I don't know if that answers your question. His sisters don't have a good relationship with him; they very rarely come here any more, but then that's because of Dominique. She's not very pleasant, and

327

that is putting it nicely.' She turned over a page, and then moved the book round for Anna to see clearly. 'These are some of my last pictures. I haven't had a job since I met Edward; he doesn't approve. Well, he wouldn't really mind, it's his father. He's a snob, you know: we are treated like the poor relatives; but then, I suppose we are.' She gave an odd shrill laugh.

Anna leaned forward to look at the photograph. From the transformation taking place before her eyes, she was wondering if the pills she'd seen Gail gulp down were some kind of speed: from being so shaken and nervous, she was now talking quite animatedly and even sat closer to Anna to show her more photographs. She was certainly very photogenic and, although they were not *Vogue* quality, in some shots she looked stunningly beautiful.

'These were taken about two and a half years ago. I started to do some good sessions; before that, as I said, I'd mostly been doing catalogue work. It's actually really tough, as you have to do so many pictures per day with so many changes, but the money is very good. I did a lot of country-styled clothes: me with dogs, me standing by fences in a tweed coat and brogues . . . I didn't really have the figure for doing lingerie.' Flicking through the pictures, Gail seemed to take a childlike pleasure in showing herself off.

'Do you have a family?' asked Anna.

'What, you mean children?'

'No, parents? Sisters?'

Gail gave a rueful smile. 'My parents both died years ago. I have a sister, but we don't really see much of each other; she has a brood of children and a very boring husband.'

'Do you want children?' Anna asked, trying to steer the conversation back to the reason she was there.

'Yes; do you?'

Anna smiled. 'Yes I do, very much. When are you getting married?'

Gail looked at her massive diamond, and then wafted her hand. 'Whenever my prospective father-in-law allows Edward some time off. He works him terribly hard and pays him a pittance.'

'But this estate will all be his one day,' Anna said, glancing at the continuing display of Gail's modelling work.

'Yes, yes it will.'

Anna, who had not really been paying attention to the pictures, had to catch her breath. 'This is a good picture of you,' she said, hoping that she had not given Gail any indication of what she was actually looking at.

'Oh, it's from two years ago, maybe. It's for a big leisurewear catalogue: lots of ghastly velvet tracksuits.' As Gail was about to turn over, Anna placed her hand flat on the page to stop her.

'The blonde girl, the one standing by the saddle.'

'It was supposed to be a stable, but they just put down some fake grass and a bit of fence and stuck the saddle over it.'

The blonde girl was Sharon Bilkin. Anna remembered Sharon saying that she did catalogue modelling. 'Do you know who she is?' Anna asked, quietly.

Gail shrugged and stood up to put the book away.

Anna opened her briefcase and took out the picture of Sharon Bilkin. 'This is the same girl, isn't it?'

Gail blinked rapidly then turned away, kneeling down

329

to put the album away again. Anna moved fast to stand directly behind her.

'I need to take that, Gail. Please just move away from the wardrobe and let me take it.'

Gail sprang to her feet and pushed Anna in the chest so hard that she banged into the corner of the four-poster bed.

'Leave me alone! I won't talk about it; you don't know what will happen. You have to go, I want you to go.'

Gail, for all her skinny frame, was incredibly strong; her bony arms squeezed the breath out of Anna as she hauled her towards the door. She tried to break loose, but Gail wouldn't let go.

'He will kill me, he will make my life hell if he ever found out what I have done!' Gail held Anna in her vice-like grip, their faces so close they were virtually touching.

'Let go of me,' Anna said, forcing herself to be calm.

'I'll end up in a madhouse!'

Anna managed to struggle free. All of a sudden, it was as if all Gail's strength had evaporated. She slowly sank to her knees, then let her body fall forwards and sobbed.

'Oh God, oh God, oh God; what have I done?'

Chapter Fifteen

The bowl of Edward Wickenham's glass rested between his fingers as he swirled his brandy round like liquid honey.

'I don't understand,' he said slowly, his face flushed.

Langton was leaning forward slightly, total concentration on his hawklike face. 'Do you want me to repeat myself? What don't you understand, Mr Wickenham?'

'You suspect my father of . . . ?'

'Murder; yes, that is correct. The Red Dahlia murder, to be exact.'

'But I don't understand. I mean, do you have evidence? These are terrible accusations; to be honest, I can't quite take it in. Have you arrested him?'

'No, not yet; currently, he is just under suspicion of being involved.'

'Involved?'

His aristocratic tone was needling Langton. 'Yes, involved, and the reason we are here is that I would like you to answer some questions that may or may not prove my suspicions incorrect.'

Wickenham drained his glass, then looked across to the drinks cabinet again, but obviously thought better of having more to drink. Instead, he carefully placed the glass down. His hand was shaking and he looked perplexed.

'I am unsure what I should do.'

'Simply answer my questions.' Langton smiled.

Lewis inched further forwards in his seat. Wickenham was not reacting like any other man he had ever seen questioned; he just seemed dazed.

'But you've already questioned my father.'

'That is correct. Now we would like to talk to you.'

'But shouldn't I have a solicitor with me?'

'Why?'

'This is a very serious allegation.'

'We have not accused you of anything.' Langton opened the file and held up Louise Pennel's picture. 'Do you know this girl?'

'No, I don't.'

'How about this girl?' He showed Sharon Bilkin's picture.

Edward Wickenham shook his head. 'Sorry, no.'

Langton looked at Lewis and sighed. 'You have never seen either of these women here at your father's property?'

'No, I have not.'

Langton pursed his lips. 'Could you tell me where you were on the ninth of January this year?'

'Oh God, I can't remember. I'd have to look in my diary.'

Langton suggested that he do so. Wickenham stood up, turning this way and that, then said his diary was in the dining room. Lewis said he would go with him.

They returned a moment later. This time, Wickenham didn't duck and cracked his forehead against the doorframe. Swearing, he stood flicking through a small black diary. His hands were shaking badly.

'I was here with Gail; we were at home.'

'Good, and she will verify that, will she?'

'Yes, because she was ill. She has migraines; she was in bed, so I cooked dinner. Christ, I just can't believe this; it's beyond belief. I am standing here answering questions about . . .'

'Your father?'

'Yes, my father. You have to be mistaken.'

'Quite possibly, but in a murder enquiry, we have to explore every avenue. We have a sketch drawn from the descriptions of two witnesses. Would you like to see it?'

Without waiting for a response, Lewis showed it to Wickenham who stared at it and then shook his head.

'Looks very like your father, wouldn't you say?'

'I suppose it's similar.'

'Similar?'

'Well, yes.'

Langton pursed his lips and then asked if father and son had a good relationship.

'Yes, of course.'

'Would you say you were very close to your father?'

'Yes, I work for him.'

'And you also had a very close relationship with your stepmother, didn't you?'

'Pardon?'

'Dominique Wickenham.'

He had now become extremely nervous: his cheeks were flushed and he was sweating. 'They're divorced.'

'We know that, but before the divorce, you and your stepmother were very close, weren't you?'

'Why are you asking me about my stepmother?'

'Because we have been given some information – well, more than that. We have some explicit photographs.'

'What?'

Langton sighed; he closed his eyes and pinched the bridge of his nose. 'Let's stop playing games, Edward. We know an awful lot about you and your family. I would say you were a lot closer than would be considered normal: you had a sexual relationship with her, didn't you?'

Wickenham stood up. 'I refuse to answer any more of your questions.'

Langton also stood up, facing him. 'What about your half-sisters? Were you as close to them as to your stepmother?'

'I am not answering any more questions. This is not right. I want to talk to someone.'

'Why?'

'You are insinuating things.'

'Bit more than insinuating, Edward; a lot more, in fact. Why don't you sit down and start to explain what exactly . . .'

'I don't have to explain anything to you,' he snapped.

'Fine. If you don't want to do it now, we can always continue this discussion at the station.'

'But this has nothing to do with me!'

'What hasn't?'

'Whatever happens here in the privacy of my own home is my business. You have no right whatsoever to force me to implicate myself.'

'Implicate? What do you mean by that?'

'You know damned well what I mean! If you have

spoken to my stepmother and she has said things, then that will be her word against mine! She is an unscrupulous woman: she is a liar and if you are here because of anything she may have told you, then I suggest you speak directly to my father.'

'Believe you me, we will be talking to him. I just wanted to give you an opportunity to extricate yourself.'

'From what?'

Langton paused. 'Were you also involved in one of these murders? Perhaps as an accomplice?'

Wickenham was really fighting to maintain control but could not stop himself from shaking and sweating. 'I swear before God, I do not know either of those women you showed me in those photos. I have never met them.'

'Do you think your father knew them?'

'I can't answer for him, but I very much doubt it. If you have any evidence, I am damned sure you would not be here talking to me – you would have had him arrested.'

Langton gave a long sigh and looked to Lewis. 'Can you see if DI Travis is ready to leave?' he asked, and Lewis nodded.

Left alone with Wickenham, Langton tapped the Persian carpet with the toe of his shoe.

'This is a very nice piece; silk, isn't it?'

Wickenham said nothing. Langton stared at him for what seemed like a very long time.

'Edward, don't protect him.'

'What?'

'I said, don't protect him. If he killed these two

335

women, he is a monster. Do you know how we found their bodies?'

Langton showed him the horrific mortuary shots of Louise Pennel and Sharon Bilkin, with the red lipstick scrawled over her belly.

'Louise's mouth was slit from ear to ear, her body severed in two, her blood drained. We found her legs and torso on the banks of the Thames near Richmond. Sharon was discovered not that far from here, in a field, Louise's coat covering her naked body. It was a maroon red coat with a velvet collar; ring any bells?'

'Jesus Christ.' Edward Wickenham looked as if he was about to faint; he felt for a chair behind him and sat down.

'Your father was a doctor, a surgeon?'

'No. No, this is terrible. Please, I really think someone should be with me.'

'In case you implicate yourself?'

'No.'

'Implicate your father?'

'No!'

Langton paused, clicking his briefcase closed. 'I know about your stepsister Emily, but whether it was your child or your father's that was aborted . . .'

Edward's face was redder than ever and his fists clenched. 'I refuse to listen to another word. This is just disgusting and not true: it's all lies, my sister is mentally ill. She made these accusations when she was sick, she didn't know what she was saying. It is not true!'

'Your wife committed suicide, didn't she?'

At this, Wickenham caved in; he leaned forward, clutching his head as if it would break open. 'Stop this!'

Langton crossed over and rested his hand on Wickenham's shoulder. 'You stop it, Edward. Tell us what you know.'

With his hands covering his face he wept, gut-wrenching snorts, and repeated over and over, 'I can't, I can't take any more.'

Lewis appeared at the door and gestured for Langton to join him. They eased out of sight.

'If you think his sobbing is bad, you should go upstairs. His girlfriend's folded completely and Anna thinks she may need a doctor.'

'Shit!'

'But she's got something: a photograph of Gail Harrington on some modelling job; she's with Sharon Bilkin.'

'Fuck!'

Langton chewed his lips and then said he wanted to go over to the main house and talk to the housekeeper.

'What about the wailing wall here?'

'Let it howl. Get your shoes on and get Travis down here!'

The rain was still sheeting down, so they drove the short distance from the cottage to the Hall. Their car rocked and splashed through deep ruts and puddles before moving onto the tarmac road leading to the main house. By now, Anna had given Langton a full account of her talk with Gail Harrington, adding that she thought she was on some drug or other, maybe speed or other amphetamines.

'I bet you any money his son wishes he was,' quipped Lewis. 'We left him like a lump of jelly, shaking and crying. He may have had sex games going on with the entire fucking family, but somehow I just don't think he's an accomplice; unless he helped to move the bodies. I dunno; what do you think, Gov?'

Langton shrugged. 'They're all involved, whether as accomplices or not. They know what that bastard is, and they keep their mouths shut because of this place.' He nodded towards the house. 'I need to take a leak; stop the car.'

The driver pulled over on the grass verge. To their amazement, Langton got out, walked across the lawn to a shrubbery and took a piss. Both Lewis and Anna shook their heads in disgust.

'Christ, what does he think he's doing?'

'You tell me,' Anna said.

Lewis turned to face her. 'Well, for one, I think we should have a search warrant; for two, I don't think what went on in the cottage was kosher, even though we got a link to Sharon Bilkin. Haven't we got enough to pull the father in, and the son for that matter?'

'Maybe, but you know Langton.'

'Obviously not as well as you do,' Lewis said, with a snide smile.

Anna decided not to reply. She did not want to discuss Langton, especially not with Lewis, who had a big yapping mouth. Gossip had probably already done the rounds of the Incident Room, but at least no one had mentioned anything to her.

They both looked over to Langton who was having a conversation on his mobile as he strode across the lawn. He stopped a moment to listen and then slapped his phone shut.

'Right, that's better,' he said, getting back in and slamming the door. He leaned his arm along the back of the seat.

'Maybe you should chat with the old housekeeper, Anna; you seem to have a way with the women.'

'Okay.'

'We need further confirmation about whether or not Louise Pennel was a visitor, and Sharon. I want to take another look at the family snapshots on their grand piano. We still have not identified the other sickos off the photographs from Milan, so show her those as well.'

'Will do.'

'Shouldn't we have a search warrant, Gov?' Lewis asked.

'Yeah, but we need more. This way, it looks like we are still floundering around. The fact we think our victims came here is not enough evidence to make an arrest – yet! When we come in to search, I want warrants for all the premises, plus the vehicles: get a bloody army backing us up, because this is a massive place. There are outhouses, the barns, the cottage, the staff cottage and we will need a warrant for each building: that's the law. When they started to suspect Fred West, they only had a warrant to search his garden, did you know that? It was West himself who suggested they were digging in the wrong place.'

Langton stopped speaking as the car pulled into the horseshoe drive. Standing at the studded front door was Charles Wickenham. 'There he is,' Langton said, softly. 'Look at him! There's got to be someplace here that he uses for those sex games: cellar, maybe in the barn somewhere. He maybe had an alibi for the ninth of January when Louise Pennel was last seen, but not for the twelfth when her body was discovered. So check out if the ponce over there was at home.'

'He did give us a pretty thorough alibi for that date, Gov, and it all checked out, his club and his . . .'

'Yeah yeah and that's another reason we don't charge in with the warrant. It's slowly slowly catchee monster!'

They all got out of the car. Anna and Lewis walked behind Langton as he headed over to Wickenham.

'Good morning.' Langton stretched out his hand and shook Wickenham's.

'Not weather-wise: the rain's not stopped. Though I suppose it is good for the crops.' He smiled and nodded to Anna, and then stepped back. 'Well, there must be some reason for this visit, so please come in. I was expecting you.'

'Your son called?'

'Yes, he did. I have to get the doctor to see his poor fiancée: she's exceedingly distressed.' He glanced coldly at Langton. 'All rather unethical, isn't it?'

'What is?'

'Questioning Gail. She has been very ill; surely she should have had someone with her?'

'She could have asked for anyone to be there; it was just a routine visit to ask her a few questions.'

'Routine or not, we should have been given notice.' He strode ahead, leading them back into the sumptuous drawing room.

Wickenham gave no polite offers of tea or coffee, nor did he ask them to sit. He walked to the fireplace and, with his hands in the pockets of his immaculate fawn trousers, turned to face them.

'So what is this all about?'

'Do you mind if we sit down?'

'Not at all, go ahead. Do you mind if I remain standing?'

'Not at all,' Langton replied archly, sitting in a wing-backed chair. He opened his briefcase, as Lewis hovered beside him.

'DI Travis would like to talk to your housekeeper, if that is all right.'

'Why?'

'Just to corroborate a few things. She is here, isn't she?'

'Yes, do you want me to call her in?'

Anna smiled and said she remembered the way to the kitchen.

Wickenham shrugged. 'Go ahead, but remember she is in her seventies. May have all her marbles in the culinary department, but otherwise, she is very vague.'

'Thank you.' Anna again smiled and walked out.

She walked along the stone-flagged corridor, passing the laundry room, and then entered the vast kitchen without knocking. Mrs Hedges was sitting at the pine table with an array of silverware laid out on an old towel.

'Mrs Hedges?'

She paid no attention, but continued to polish away with some rolled-up newspaper. Anna raised her voice and the plump, friendly woman looked up, surprised.

'I'm sorry, I didn't hear you come in. I'm a wee bit deaf in my right ear.' She took off her rubber gloves.

'Please don't let me interrupt you. I just wanted to have a word.' Anna drew out a chair and sat midway down the table.

'Does Mr Wickenham know?'

'Yes, he's in the drawing room with my superior officer.'

'Oh, well, if he said it's all right.'

Anna opened her briefcase and took out her notebook and the thick file of photographs, which was beginning to get slightly dog-eared.

'Do you want a cup of tea?'

'No, thank you.'

'There's one made; I've just had a cup myself.' Mrs Hedges fussed around, taking down a cup and saucer, crossing to the fridge for the milk and then back over to the Aga where a teapot was sitting on the side, a knitted teacosy keeping its contents warm.

'I can't think what you want to talk to me about,' she said as she poured the tea, using a silver tea strainer. She then held up the milk and Anna nodded; next she held up a sugar bowl and Anna smiled.

'No thank you, no sugar.'

Mrs Hedges took a white napkin and placed it down beside Anna with the tea. She sat back down and Anna could see that she was unsure whether or not to carry on polishing.

'Please, don't let me stop you.'

Mrs Hedges nodded and put her rubber gloves back on. 'I used not to wear them, but it's the newsprint, it gets my hands so dirty and it's hard to wash off.' She picked up some scrunched-up newspaper, and dipped it into a bowl. 'Trick of the trade. I never have to use silver polish, just water and a drop of vinegar, it's amazing what a shine you can get.'

Anna smiled, but kept her attention on her notebook,

not wanting to get into any further discussions about polishing. 'Do you recall the ninth of January this year?'

'Oh I couldn't say; what day would that be?'

Anna spent a good five minutes waiting as Mrs Hedges yet again removed her gloves and went to a wall calendar. She huffed and puffed, patting her pockets, then taking out a pair of glasses. 'I was here, as usual.'

'Could you tell me about the day itself, if there were any visitors, if Mr Wickenham was here?'

'Which one? Mr Charles or Edward?'

Anna sipped her tea as Mrs Hedges went through her day's routine: how she planned each menu ahead, when the cleaners came in, when the linen was changed, etcetera etcetera. She could not recall anything out of the ordinary happening on that specific day, or any house guests staying, as it was mid-week. She said she did not cook as Charles Wickenham was dining in London. She could not recall what time she saw him return, as she was usually in bed by nine-thirty.

'Unless we have guests and there's dinner, but we get help in for me, you know, to serve and clear. I mostly just run the house day to day. I have done for fifteen years. Before him I worked for his father, so all in all I've been here for forty years.'

'So Mr Wickenham entertains a lot?'

'Yes he certainly does; well, a lot more so in the past, when Mrs Wickenham was here. It was most weekends then, and we needed extra help most of the time. She liked to have big dinners. They used the barn when it was converted: there's a big entertaining room there now. The dining hall here is not that big and really only seats twelve comfortably.'

'So these dinner parties were a regular weekend occurrence?'

'Oh yes, we've eight bedrooms. The guests would arrive on a Friday afternoon, leave sometimes on Sundays or even Monday morning.'

'And the extra help, did they stay as well?'

'Yes, in a staff flat above the stables.'

'Did you serve the guests?'

'No, well, I'm getting on; like I said, I go to bed early. My room is right at the back of the house. It's very quiet; well, if it wasn't, I'd not get much sleep.'

'Why is that?'

'Well all the comings and goings and the music, and in summer they use the pool and the spa, and then there's the stable boys, they have to exercise the horses, and that's always around seven in the morning when they start arriving.'

'So they don't live in?'

'No no, they're local lads, they do all the mucking out and grooming. Mr Charles is very particular.'

Anna nodded, and then opened her file. 'I am going to show you some photographs to see if you recognise anyone. Would you look at them for me?'

'Yes dear but, you know, I don't get to meet his guests. Like I said, I prepare the food sometimes then I'm off to my bed.'

'But not when Mrs Wickenham was here?'

For the first time there was just a flicker of unease. 'No, well, she was quite a handful; she was very keen on getting in caterers. She didn't like my offerings – said they were "meat and potatoes" – they wanted this *nuvo cuisine*. Well, to be honest, I was happier cooking for the children than running around after the people she had down here.'

'You didn't like them?'

'I never said that; they were just not my type of people. The children were always my priority, and Mr Charles. You see, before I worked for him, I was cook for his father. I've been working at the Hall since I was in my thirties, and I'm seventy-two years old now.'

'That's a long time.'

'It is. My husband died in an accident on one of the farms, so I came to work here. No children of my own, so I really enjoyed . . .' There was a strange unease about her body language: she seemed to twist and turn in her chair as she rubbed at the silver. 'I loved them like they were my own.'

'So you know Danielle, Mrs Wickenham's maid?'

'Yes, yes I do, she was here for years and thank God she was, because I couldn't have run after her ladyship the way she had to. Mrs Wickenham had a right temper on her, she could be a handful to deal with.'

Anna first showed Louise Pennel's picture. Mrs Hedges shook her head; she also didn't recognise Sharon Bilkin. Anna was disappointed. She took out the photographs of the sex games in the sauna, which had been doctored so that only the faces of the men they were trying to identify were visible. Although Mrs Hedges was unable to recall his name, she said she thought that one of them was Spanish, a well-known artist.

'He was not a very nice man; he used to stay many times, always over at the barn. He used to paint there sometimes.'

'Was this before it was converted?'

Mrs Hedges hesitated.

'Edward Wickenham's wife committed suicide in the barn, didn't she?'

Mrs Hedges took a deep breath and then wafted her hand. 'Yes yes, terrible, very sad.'

Anna was not expecting Mrs Hedges to continue, as the mention of the suicide had obviously distressed her very much, but she leaned forward and lowered her voice. 'Things have gone on in the house. I've learned over the years to do my job and go to my room. What the eyes don't see . . .'

'But if you thought these things were bad, why did you stay?'

Mrs Hedges picked up a polishing cloth and started buffing up a silver goblet. 'My husband died young, he left me in some financial trouble and old Mr Wickenham helped me out. This is, I suppose, the only real security I have ever had. I've no family, so the girls and even Edward have been like my own. They look after me, treat me very well.'

'So you must have been very concerned about Emily?'

Bingo. At last Anna had hit a target that Mrs Hedges could not polish away, and she became tearful.

'I made excuses, because of the way he was treated. But not over Emily; that was unforgivable.' Her voice was hardly audible. 'I knew there had to be a reason why you were here. If I tell you what I know, and Mr Charles finds out, then God knows what he'll do to me. But I've saved all my money, I can go somewhere.'

Anna reached out and gently stroked the elderly woman's hand, encouraging her to continue. She clasped

Anna's hand tightly. 'I should have done something when I knew what was going on.'

Charles Wickenham was fending off every question like a master duellist. He parried and queried and never at any time appeared fazed or ashamed when asked about his sexual proclivities; in fact, he seemed to relish discussing his house parties. When Langton brought up the accusation of his relationship with his own daughters, he dismissed it with a waft of his hand.

'Not this again. I have already discussed my daughter's problems and her overactive imagination; we have doctors and therapists who can also verify that Emily is a dreadful little liar. I did not have a sexual relationship with my daughter.'

'What about the pregnancy?'

Langton watched Wickenham closely. There was not so much as a flicker.

'It was all in her mind. Of course, I questioned the staff: you know, the stable boys and gardeners, whether any of them had been having sexual intercourse with her, obviously I did, as she was underage, but there was no truth in it; all in her addled little mind.'

'She claims that she had an abortion.'

He sighed, shaking his head. 'Claims! Well, if you have any evidence of this abortion then I would dearly like to know about it, because it is a total fiction!'

'So you did not operate on your daughter?'

'Me! Good God, what do you take me for? I am her father! This is a very serious allegation. You know, I really do think that I should have someone here to listen to all this.'

'It is just an enquiry at this stage,' Langton said quietly.

'An enquiry into *what*, for God's sake? That I had intercourse with my daughter and operated on her, when I have told you repeatedly that she has mental problems, and you cannot trust a word she says? Next, you ask me for times and dates relating to a murder enquiry, a double murder enquiry: well, this is all rather preposterous, isn't it? I mean, are you scouring all the unsolved crimes to give yourselves an excuse to make a pleasant trip out to the country rather than do the work you are paid to do in London?'

'I do not find any of this pleasant, Mr Wickenham.'

'Nor do I, Detective Chief Inspector Langton, nor do I, and I will consider making a formal complaint to the Commissioner.'

'That is your prerogative.' Langton was finding it difficult to maintain control: he wanted to wrap his hands around the audacious, posturing man's throat. Wickenham stood in front of them, leaning one elbow against the mantelpiece or tucking his hands into his pockets. He kept touching his tie and patting down his collar. He picked off tiny balls of fluff from his pale yellow cashmere sweater, but not one gesture gave any indication that he was unnerved or even worried by the questions.

Langton displayed the headshots of the men taken with Wickenham in his own hot tub. He casually glanced at each face, said he did know them and they were not close friends, more associates that he occasionally entertained.

'For sex parties?'

Wickenham shrugged. 'Here we go again. Yes, we do

have fun here sometimes, but whatever goes on in the privacy of one's home is exactly that: private.'

'Your wife and son also enjoyed these *fun* times.'

'Yes, yes they did; again, they are consenting adults. Our sexual fun may not appeal to you, but again that is a matter of choice.'

'Your daughter Justine?'

Wickenham sighed with irritation. 'She could do whatever she liked. She was eighteen years old; if she chose to join in, that was her prerogative. Nobody ever forced anyone to do anything.'

'We have a witness who said Louise Pennel was here the weekend before her murder.'

Wickenham was some actor; he gave no visible reaction whatsoever, but closed his eyes. 'I'm sorry; say the name again?'

'Louise Pennel.'

'Ah yes, the Red Dahlia, I believe the papers are calling her.'

'Sharon Bilkin knew your son's fiancée; did you know that?'

'Sharon who?'

Langton was getting tired of the game playing and stood up. 'Sharon Bilkin: her body was found just off the A3 in a field.'

'Not one of mine, I hope,' he smirked.

Langton knew that nothing he could throw at this man was going to produce the goods: he had an answer for everything. Wickenham had obviously intuited they were here on a fishing trip, and was determined that they would have to leave without a catch.

'Thank you for your time.'

Lynda La Plante

Langton glanced at Lewis who had remained silent throughout. He stood up to join Langton and asked if he could use the cloakroom.

Wickenham gave a soft laugh. 'The *cloakroom?*' He gestured to the door. 'Straight out and down the hall, second door.'

Lewis hurried out, leaving Langton standing opposite Wickenham. Langton stared hard but he was met with a steady eye contact.

'Bit of a wasted journey?'

'Not at all, it's been very informative. We will be checking on your associates to verify what you have said.'

Wickenham laughed, shaking his head. 'By all means, but you know, they are all very wealthy and well-connected people. I doubt if they would want to go into details about their sexual exploits here at the Hall.'

Langton turned away and looked over the photographs on top of the piano. Wickenham remained standing, watching him; he checked his watch. Neither man said another word until Lewis returned and stood at the open door. 'Sir, DI Travis is still with Mr Wickenham's housekeeper, she said she won't be a moment.'

'I suppose this will mean lunch is going to be delayed.' Wickenham opened a drawer and took out a cigar box; he proffered one to Langton, who shook his head.

'We'll wait for her in the car.'

'Okay, I'll pass that on.' Lewis hovered for a moment and then disappeared.

'Cuban,' Wickenham said, holding one of his cigars up, then taking a silver clipper and snipping off the end. 'Can't beat a hand-rolled.' He bit on the cigar; the action gave him a grimace of a smile.

350

Langton walked past him, and then turned at the door. 'Thank you for your time, Mr Wickenham.'

'I wish I could say it was a pleasure. Let me show you out.'

Wickenham watched from the front door as Langton returned to the car. Lewis was not there.

'Where's Mike?'

'He went to get some air, round to the stables I think, sir,' said the driver.

Langton checked his watch again and then lit a cigarette, leaning against the side of the car. He turned when he heard the crunch of the gravel on the drive. Anna was walking towards him.

'I came out via the kitchen door,' she said.

'I gathered that. Have you seen Lewis?'

'No.'

Anna opened the passenger door and tossed in her briefcase. 'How did it go with Wickenham senior?'

'He knows we've not got enough on him.'

Anna gave a small smile. 'His housekeeper was not that forthcoming to start off with, but once I touched the right button, she didn't stop talking.'

'What was the button?'

'Emily Wickenham.'

There was another crunch of footsteps and they both turned. Lewis, his cheeks flushed, gestured for them to follow him. 'Can you bring the photographs?'

Anna looked to Langton; he bent into the car and took out his briefcase. They followed Lewis round the winding drive towards the stables.

Lewis was standing by an open stable door; inside

was the big chestnut gelding. Langton was irritated.
'What, Lewis? You've brought us back to see the bloody
horse?'

'No, you need to talk to the stable lad; he's just
checking over something with the vet. He reckons he
saw Louise Pennel. He reckons she was here on the
eighth of January.'

Chapter Sixteen

The Incident Room was waiting eagerly for an
update. Langton had ordered a briefing for ten
minutes after their return. He began with a brief
summary of his session with Charles Wickenham. He
had the team laughing when he struck up the same pose
and mimicked his upper-class drawl. Then he went quiet,
shaking his head.

'He maintained that attitude throughout, denying
knowing Louise Pennel or Sharon Bilkin. He was dismissive about any kind of incestuous relationship with his
younger daughter Emily. He said he could provide a
doctor's certificate to clarify his daughter was mentally
unstable. There were no charges and we have not as yet
re-interviewed his daughter.'

Langton lit a cigarette and paused; he then looked to
Anna and gestured for her to step forward. 'Whilst Lewis
and I tried to get a handle on Edward Wickenham, DI

Travis was interviewing Gail Harrington. So, over to you, Anna.'

Anna gave a detailed report, referring to her notes. She described Gail's nervous state and aired her suspicion that Gail was taking some kind of drugs.

'She is very, very nervous, very scared of her future father-in-law and, I would say, close to a breakdown. I think she does know more than I could get out of her. She also sported an oversized diamond engagement ring – maybe to keep her quiet.'

Langton coughed and gave a twist of his hand for her to get on with it; she flipped through her notes.

'When shown the photographs of Sharon Bilkin and Louise Pennel, she denied ever seeing or meeting either of them. You will recall that Sharon Bilkin was a model, doing mostly catalogue work. Gail Harrington was also a model and, in an attempt to get her to be more at ease with me, I asked about her work. The press cuttings and her CV model pictures took some ploughing through, but in one photograph, the other model with Gail Harrington was Sharon Bilkin.'

There was a low murmur. Anna asked for a glass of water, and Langton handed her one.

'My next interview was with Mrs Hedges, the housekeeper.'

Again Anna referred to her notes, explaining that it had taken some considerable time for Mrs Hedges to open up. Langton was looking at his watch, his foot tapping.

'I did not really get to the nitty-gritty until she told me about looking after Charles Wickenham's father. She said he was a really bad-tempered man with a vicious temper. He was, however, very generous to her, which was one of the main reasons she remained with the family. She described how the old man would not just ridicule his only son, but was also very violent towards him. The boy was subjected to terrible punishments; at times, he was unable to go to school due to his beatings. Mrs Hedges said she always tried to protect Charles from his father, but eventually he was sent away to boarding school. During his vacations, the punishments would begin again; as he got older, they would result in even worse physical violence. He would tie him up and leave him in the old barn; this was before it was renovated into the playground it is now. When Charles Wickenham grew old enough to retaliate, the old man introduced him to sexual perversion. Every weekend, there would be a carload of prostitutes shared between father and son. Mrs Hedges never even attempted to do anything about what she knew was going on, and there was no mother around to intervene. She did, however, tell me that there was a punishment room, beneath the barn; it had been an old wine cellar.'

Anna sketched out the main house, barn and stables in big square blocks and indicated on her rather crude drawings where this cellar would have been, pointing out that it might have been demolished as part of the renovations to the barn. Langton was now leaning forward; he stared intently at Anna and then at her drawings.

'Charles Wickenham went to Cambridge and qualified as a doctor. He spent two years working as a houseman in Bridge East Hospital before he joined the army. He rarely, if ever, returned home as he was travelling the world; for a lengthy period he was stationed in the Far East. He married Una Martin. Her father was a major in the same regiment, but Mrs Hedges could not recall which one it was. She was Edward Wickenham's mother.'

Anna now began to draw out the family tree, and although she had everyone's attention, they were beginning to get restless.

'Una Wickenham died of cancer shortly after they returned from abroad; Charles Wickenham had quit the army to take over the running of the estate. His father was dying and had lost a considerable amount of money; he had also sold off vast areas of land. By the time his father died, Charles Wickenham was running the estate full time. Like his father, he angered the locals by selling off vast tracts of land and some of the farms that bordered onto their property. He subsequently married Dominique Dupres: as we know from our time in Milan, the new Mrs Wickenham had quite a past. The parties that had been part of the old man's lifestyle now began again. Like father like son. So much so that by now, Edward Wickenham was being subjected to a similar punishment regime to that his father had suffered. He married a local girl and they lived in the thatched cottage he still occupies.

'The new Mrs Wickenham gave birth to two daughters, Justine and Emily. As soon as Mrs Hedges began to talk about the girls, her manner changed and she became very distressed. She referred to the suicide of Edward's wife as being a tragic cry for help: she had been detested by her father-in-law and scared of what she knew was going on. Mrs Hedges said she was constantly bedridden and became very frail; she could easily have been describing Gail Harrington!'

Anna took a sip of her water. Everyone was focused on her again.

'Mrs Hedges knew that Charles Wickenham was molesting both girls, and from a very early age. She said that Dominique had to be aware of what was going on, but did nothing; to quote Mrs Hedges, "the detestable woman was too busy doing dirty things with all these house guests, even her stepson": the sex sessions were taking place virtually every weekend. I asked about the abuse, and if she had ever witnessed the girls being sexually used by their own father. She was very tearful and shook her head, saying that she did not need to see, it was obvious, especially with the youngest child. I asked if she knew if Emily Wickenham had been pregnant. She refused to answer, and then began to cry. When I persisted, asking her again, she still refused to answer and kept on telling me how much she loved the girls. Just as I was thinking about calling it quits, she said, "Justine was tougher: she could handle him; she was like her mother, but little Emily was too young. He did a terrible thing and when she tried to make him stop, they sectioned her."' Anna closed her notebook. 'That's it.'

She frowned. 'Sorry, not quite. Just as I was leaving, I asked Mrs Hedges if Charles Wickenham had ever had a secretary. This goes back to the advert we think Louise Pennel answered and therefore how she came to meet him. She said there had been a number of girls that came and went; none stayed long. He was a hard taskmaster and they were always too young and inexperienced. But if Wickenham is a serial killer, as Professor

Marshe suggested, he would probably have killed before the Red Dahlia, so perhaps this is something we should follow up.'

The room was quiet as Anna returned to sit down. Lewis got up next and gave them the details from the stable boy. When he told them that he had seen Louise Pennel lying naked in the barn on 8 January, the room erupted – they all knew that was the day before she was murdered.

Langton then stepped back up. First, he moved to Louise Pennel's photograph. 'He lied about Louise.' He moved to Sharon Bilkin. 'We can assume he also lied about Sharon. It is quite possible she came to see him; if we question Gail Harrington further, we can find out if she had been at the house as one of those weekend guests. We have one guest identified but I'd like to press on to get more ID on the other men.'

Langton paused, frowning; then sighed. 'Do we have enough to bring him in? Without doubt, yes we have, but we still do not have any DNA evidence that links him directly to the murders. The fact that they had visited at his property does not mean he killed them: we know he had a truckload of tarts down most weekends, so these two girls could have just been there and left. Our killer could also be one or other of his house guests – it could even be his own son, Edward – but Wickenham is our prime suspect. The fact that this piece of scum had sexual intercourse with his own daughters has already been brought to the attention of the police and the case dismissed. He can prove that Emily is mentally unstable; what we have to prove without doubt is that Charles Wickenham is the Red Dahlia killer.

357

Although it might look as if we have a shedload of damning evidence against him, it's still circumstantial. We have no weapon, no bloodstains, nothing that pinpoints Charles Wickenham as our killer. We do not know if he and his son are in this together. We do not know if the house guests also played a part in the torture and murder of our two victims.'

Langton took a deep breath. 'What we do have are warrants. We now have enough to gain access and search their properties: that's the barn, the main house, the stables, the thatched cottage and the cars. I intend going in with a fucking army. If there is a torture chamber in the old cellar, we'll find it. There may have been other victims, but we can't at this point in time open up more enquiries: we concentrate on our Red Dahlia. We also keep in mind that the original killer of the Black Dahlia was never brought to justice. Wickenham will have covered his tracks, but we'll derail him!'

Barolli wafted his hand and Langton smiled over at him.

'The taped call made to the journalist: can we still use it?'

'We can try, but even if he is the voice on tape, sick thing is, he could claim to be a pervert getting kicks out of wasting police time; we get enough calls every day from the sickos.'

Langton glanced at Lewis, who held up a small tape recorder. 'I taped him today, so we'll get a match or not anyway.'

Langton chuckled and wiped his shirt front. 'No flies on me!'

★

Lewis and Langton were closeted in his office, working on 'the hit', when they would search Wickenham's estate. It had to be carefully orchestrated, and they needed a lot of extra hands to ensure nothing was overlooked.

Anna spent the rest of the afternoon writing up her official report and when it came to just after six, she decided to call it quits for the day. She had just packed up when Barolli called over to ask if she was going to interview Emily Wickenham as per the duty list for that day. Anna sighed.

'I can do it on my way home, I suppose.'

Anna called Emily Wickenham twice and hung up when her answerphone clicked on. She decided to do some grocery shopping and try again afterwards, so she packed up her briefcase and left.

She was driving out of the station car park when the call came in to the Incident Room from the forensic team. They had discovered blood spatterings in the bathroom of Justine Wickenham's flat. They were taking the samples to the lab, but wanted one of the team over at the flat. As soon as Langton was told the update, he was eager to get over there himself; this was possibly the big break they had been waiting for.

Langton and Barolli arrived at Justine Wickenham's flat which was owned by the woman who ran the riding school. Justine paid her a monthly rent for the small, rather scruffy flat on the middle floor of a house that backed onto the stable yard. By the time Langton and Barolli walked in, the forensic team had packed up, apart from Ken Gardner who was sitting on the stairs having a quick cigarette.

'What you got for me?' Langton said.

'Not a lot, but it took a long time to find; the place may look like a tip, but somebody did a big cleaning job. We went through every room with a fine-tooth comb, as they say, and didn't think we'd get a result.'

He stubbed out his cigarette under his shoe and pocketed the stub. They followed him up the creaking narrow staircase, which was carpeted in hemp. Ken nodded to it. 'This is a bugger: it's rough and we had to go inch by inch; leaves a lot of fibres, but all we got was a face full of dust.'

He led them into a small, untidy sitting room and pointed. 'Lot of stale food left around which is unpleasant; the young lady is not very hygienic. The bedroom sheets look as if they've not been changed for months; we've taken them in.'

Langton said nothing as they looked into a dirty kitchen with a stack of pans piled in the sink.

'We had a real stinky time in here; something's wrong with the plumbing so, just in case, we took out the U-pipe – it was clogged with tea leaves and crap, but no body parts.'

Langton checked his watch irritably. Ken liked the sound of his own voice. Langton asked him to get a move on.

'Yeah, yeah; but I wanted you to know how many hours we've been holed up here; after the Dennis Neilson epic – you know they found a thumb in his drainpipe? – so we have to be diligent.'

'How did Justine Wickenham react to you being here?'

'Well, Miss Hoity-Toity made an appearance, said a

few foul words, and then left. She kept on saying that it was all a *fucking* waste of time, as she was in Milan when the girl was murdered; she said that a couple of times. Anyway, she eventually left, slamming the door so hard it almost came off its hinges! Okay, the bathroom: now, we had to do a considerable amount in here, removing floorboards, etcetera. We tried to ease the bath out, but it broke a few tiles.'

Langton sighed; this was all to cover themselves for the damage claim that would no doubt be coming in.

Ken stood in the doorway. The bathroom was actually larger than Langton had expected. The toilet was on one side, the washbasin beside it. The cracked white tiles were dirty and the room had a mouldy smell. 'Water has leaked at some time beneath the bathtub and from the toilet, so it's pretty dank in here.'

Langton looked to the small red arrow stickers on the far side of the bath.

'Between six tiles, we found very, and I mean very, tiny droplets of blood, no seeping; it's like a fine spray hit the back rest. It had, as you can see, been washed down; these tiles were a lot cleaner than any of the others. Tiny spots were on each tile and some of the cement in between also had a faint smear. We have them being tested.'

Langton frowned. Louise Pennel's body had been drained of blood; it seemed to him very unlikely that this was where it could have happened.

'You know the victim's blood had been drained,' he said to Ken.

'Yes, I know; to be honest, I doubt if she could have been cut up here: I mean, that's pints of blood. We'd have found traces in the drains. This was more like a spray, the tiny drops were only the size of a pinhead, and they were at an upward slant.'

Langton was disappointed, but thanked Ken for his diligence, and he and Barolli decided to go over to the nearest pub for a pint and a sandwich.

Anna was parked on Portobello Road opposite Emily Wickenham's flat, trying to call her. The answerphone came on again. Anna looked up at the window. The curtains were drawn and the lights were on.

Anna locked her car and crossed the road. She was about to ring Emily's doorbell when the front door opened and a young girl with her hair in dreadlocks came out.

'Hi, is Emily in?' Anna asked, smiling.

'Dunno; she's the flat above mine, straight up the stairs.'

'Thank you.' Anna smiled again as the girl walked off down the road in thick heavy boots, her red skirt swirling.

Anna headed up the stairs to Emily's flat. She was about to knock when she noticed the door was off the latch; she heard raised voices.

'I am telling you what is happening; they are at my flat, Em, the police. Now, you have said something? Because why else would they be there?'

'I didn't! I swear, I didn't tell them anything!'

'Yeah, well, you can't remember one thing from the next! You must have said something. I can't go to my own flat, for Chrissakes!'

'I didn't say anything!'

'I hope to Christ you didn't, because you know what he'll do: he'll stop my fucking allowance. He won't listen to me. He won't believe that I never said a fucking word and he'll take it out on me! So tell me the truth, what did you tell them?'

Emily's voice screeched. 'I keep on telling you, I didn't say anything; they kept asking me but I never told them! I didn't, I swear I didn't!'

'Well, why are they at my flat then? I mean, why are they searching my flat? They all had white paper suits on: they were forensic cops, they were taking up my fucking carpet, Em!'

'But they won't find anything; you cleaned it all up!'

'I know, but the fact they are there freaks me out. If he cuts off my allowance, he'll do worse to you: he'll make you go back home.'

'I won't go, I won't go!'

Anna was literally the other side of the door; she could hear every word clearly. She was now in a quandary as to how to approach the girls. Should she walk straight in? She decided to go back down the stairs and call up: that way, they could never accuse her of breaking in.

As Anna got to the bottom of the stairs, she heard Justine becoming even more angry, then a door slam. Anna took this as her cue to call out.

'Hello! Hello!'

Justine stood at the top of the stairs with a furious look on her face.

'Hi, I am DI Travis; I was about to ring the bell when your friend from the flat below let me in. Your front door was open.'

Justine moved slowly down the stairs. 'Then you can

363

just turn around and get the hell out of here. This is
private property, so fuck off!'

'I just want to talk to Emily.'

'She doesn't want to see you, and you have no right
to break in here! Get out!'

'If I could just see your sister for a moment?'

'You can't; I just told you. She is not seeing anyone,
so turn around and get the fuck out of her flat!'

Justine was wearing jodhpurs and riding boots, and
brandishing her riding crop. 'Don't make me use this,
because I will. I also know the law; you have no right
to come in without a warrant. This is private property,
so I am giving you warning. Get out!'

Emily's frightened face now appeared at the top of
the stairs. 'What's going on?'

'Go back into the flat, Emily, and shut the door; this
woman wants to talk to you and she can't.'

'Why not let me just speak to her? It will only take
a few moments,' said Anna calmly.

'No. If she talks to you, she wants a solicitor with her.'

'Why don't you stay with her?'

'Because I don't want to! I don't want you here. I
am going to make a formal complaint. Now go away.'
She lifted the riding crop.

Anna hesitated; she looked past Justine to the frightened Emily, and shrugged. 'Okay, you can contact your
solicitor, and he can accompany you to the station. I
was just hoping that this could be less formal.'

'Why do you want to see me?' Emily asked in a high-
pitched voice.

'I am not prepared to discuss this on the stairs,' Anna
said firmly.

'I don't want to go to the police station!'

Justine turned towards her sister. 'Go back and shut the door. Just do what I tell you to do; you will not be taken to any police station.'

'Well, she very likely will be, if she doesn't talk to me now.'

Justine turned her fury back to Anna. 'Piss off! You can't frighten me! She has done nothing wrong and you should just leave her alone.'

'I only want to ask a few questions.'

Anna was caught off guard as Justine suddenly launched an attack. The riding crop in her left hand, she jumped down the stairs, and with her right hand she gripped Anna's shirt front, pushing her backwards and hitting her head against the wall. Justine hauled Anna back to her feet and was about to bring down the crop on her face.

'Stop it, stop it!' Emily ran down the stairs and tried to get between them but Justine turned and grabbed her sister's hair, hauling her away, giving Anna a chance to back off. The doorbell rang; whoever it was kept their hand on the bell so it was a persistent high-pitched wail. Emily ran back up the stairs and into her flat.

'Don't answer it!' Justine shouted, as Anna made her escape. She ran to the front door and opened it.

Langton stood there. 'What the hell is going on? I could hear screams.'

Before Anna could explain, Justine appeared.

'Get out. Do you hear me? Get out!'

Langton stepped between them; he gripped Justine by the throat and pushed her hard against the wall. 'Calm down, you hear me? Calm down or you'll be arrested.'

Justine tried to bite him; she was almost frothing at the mouth with rage, but he held on and forced her to drop the riding crop. She looked crazed; her eyes bulged and spittle formed at the corners of her snarling mouth. 'Arrest me for what? She broke into my sister's flat; I know the law!'

Langton slowly released his hold. His voice was low and threatening. 'You have two seconds to leave, and don't think you've heard the last of this. One . . .'

He never got to say 'two' as Justine shrugged him off and walked out of the house. Emily was nowhere to be seen. Anna looked past him and up the stairs to the flat.

'The door was open; I just came to the stairs and called out . . .'

'How did you get in to this floor?'

'Someone let me in; another tenant, I think.'

He nodded, then frowned as he looked at her face; she had a slash mark on her cheek. 'Did she do this to you?'

Anna rubbed her head. 'Yes, she pushed me against the wall.'

'Do you want to bring charges?'

Anna shrugged. Langton looked at his hand where Justine had tried to bite it. 'Strong as an ox, isn't she?'

He gently held her head and felt where it had cracked against the wall. 'Going to have a god-awful bump on the back of your head. Do you feel dizzy at all?'

'No.'

He ran his thumb along the red weal on her cheek. 'Well, it didn't break the skin.' He sighed. 'Christ, what a fucking family.' Langton looked up at the closed flat door. 'We found some bloodstains at Justine's flat; they're being tested. You think this is a good time to talk to Emily or do you want to leave it?'

'Well, if she lets us in, why not, as we're both here?'

They headed up the stairs and knocked on the door. There was no answer; then Anna noticed water dripping down the wall into the stairwell. They could hear the gush of an overflow pipe.

'Is it from her flat?' Langton asked, staring down.

Anna said it had to be. He put his shoulder against the door. It took a good few tries before the lock gave way and the door burst open.

Emily Wickenham was lying in the bath, the water becoming a deeper red by the second. Langton hauled her out, getting soaked in the process, as Anna called for an ambulance. Emily had not made a very good job of her suicide attempt: only one wrist was cut to the artery. Langton made a tourniquet from a pair of tights drying on a line in the bathroom.

They both travelled with Emily to the emergency ward at Charing Cross Hospital. She was tested for drugs and the doctors pumped the paracetamol out of her stomach. Langton contacted Charles Wickenham and told him about Emily's situation. He said little, just a curt thank you for letting him know. Langton was still wearing his bloodstained clothes, his cuffs and shirt front stained heavily. He went off with a nurse to see if they could find something for him to wear. When he returned, he was wearing a rugby shirt borrowed from a male nurse and carried his own shirt in a plastic bag. He sat beside Anna and checked his watch.

'You want a coffee? There's a machine up the corridor?'

'No thanks.'

Langton walked off. It was another hour before they got news that Emily was in the clear, though very weak and sorry for herself. The doctor doubted that she would be in a fit state to talk to them, but it would be up to them if they wanted to wait.

It was after eleven when, to their surprise, Edward rather than Charles Wickenham arrived. He said little but seemed very agitated, not due to Emily's suicide attempt, but the inconvenience it had created.

'She's tried this before; her wrists are like a patchwork quilt!'

The same young doctor returned and called a nurse to take Edward in to see Emily.

Langton yawned. 'I guess we can go; nice of him to thank us.'

The nurse appeared and gestured to Langton. He joined her and they conferred before he returned to Anna.

'Emily wants to see you.'

'Me?'

'Yes, you. I'll wait here.'

Edward Wickenham was sitting in a chair by Emily's bedside, reading a newspaper. 'I can't wait much longer. Father said you had to come back with me. I've spoken to the nurse and doctor.'

He gave an irritated glance at the interruption as Anna tapped and entered. She was shocked to see how pale Emily was; her eyes were sunken and her skin looked like parchment.

'You wanted to see me?' she asked tentatively.

Emily nodded. Both her wrists were bandaged and she had a glucose drip in her right arm. She gave Anna a pleading look, then glanced back to her brother.

'She can't talk to anyone now, that must be obvious.' Edward Wickenham folded his newspaper. 'I'm arranging to take Emily home; anything that you need to speak to her about can be done from there when she has recovered. My father is, after all, a qualified doctor so there is no need to worry about my sister's care.'

Edward seemed not to notice Emily shrink with fear, but Anna did.

'Perhaps you should talk to my superior; he's still outside in the waiting room.'

Wickenham pursed his lips; he moved close to the bed and whispered to Emily. 'Don't say anything you will regret. I'll be two seconds.' He hesitated, not wanting to leave Anna alone with his sister, but then walked out.

Anna went close to the bed. Emily's voice quavered, frail. 'Please don't let them take me; they'll get me locked up. Please help me.'

'I really can't stop your brother; I have no right to do that.'

'You wanted to talk to me; I will, if you help me.'

Anna looked across to the door and then back at Emily. 'I'll see if they need to keep you in overnight. I would have thought they would automatically want to keep you in for observation.'

'Yes, yes, let me stay here.'

Anna felt uneasy leaving the girl alone, but knew she had to act quickly.

Langton was still sitting in the waiting room; when she walked in, he looked at his watch impatiently. 'There's not a lot either of us can do here. I suggest we leave and see her tomorrow.'

'Did her brother come in to talk to you?'

'No.'

Anna sat beside him. 'She's terrified of being taken home. She said they will section her, put her away. If that happens, you know we will have a hard time taking anything she says as evidence.'

'We can't stop him; they're her family.'

'Isn't there something we can do? Maybe talk to the doctors and suggest they keep her here overnight? Or at least until we've had time to talk to her: because she will talk now, I'm sure of it.'

Langton stood up and stretched his arms. 'Thing is, what do you think she knows? I mean, we know she was not at the house when Louise Pennel was there, so whatever she knows must hark back to the incest situation, which we are pretty sure went on. But it still doesn't give us any evidence connected to the murder.'

'But what if she does know something? You saw her sister was vicious enough and angry enough to try and stop her talking to me. It's worth a try getting them to keep her here and giving me a chance to see what she can give us.'

Langton yawned and looked at his watch again. 'Let me talk to the doctor but I'm not hanging around here any longer; I'm knackered.' He left the waiting room.

Anna sat for a moment before she returned to Emily's room. She was sitting up on the edge of the bed; they had put some thick pink woolly socks on her feet. The girl was skin and bone, and the white hospital-issue nightdress gaped at the back. She was still hooked up to the glucose drip and now seemed even more frail and frightened. Her hair hung in limp strands around her wan face as she stared at the floor.

Anna sat beside her. 'I've asked my superior to talk to the doctor, but there is really little we can do to keep you here if they agree to your release.'

Emily said nothing. She didn't even raise her head when the door opened and a nurse came in to take her blood pressure.

'Surely she should be kept in overnight?' Anna said to the nurse, who wound Emily's left arm in the black Velcro-tipped cloth. She slipped on the gauge and pumped, watching the dial, and then let the air hiss out.

The nurse was packing away her equipment when Edward Wickenham walked in. He gave a cold glance to Anna and said, curtly, 'You have no reason to be here with my sister. I would like you to leave, please.'

Anna wanted to say something to Emily, but she remained impassive, staring at the floor. Anna hesitated and then slowly left the room.

Outside in the corridor, Langton was ending his conversation with the doctor. Anna did not interrupt but leaned against the wall. It was almost midnight, and she was tired out. Langton gestured for her to join him, as the doctor went into Emily's room.

'I have said that we will need to question Miss Wickenham regarding a very serious incident, and quite possibly make an arrest. I do not want her removed from the hospital, blah blah!'

Anna looked to the closed door. 'Thing is, with her father being a doctor, her brother's no doubt given them a load of garbage about caring for her.'

371

'Yeah I know, but the doc's on our side; he thinks she should stay overnight and talk to their resident shrink.'

He shut up fast as the door to Emily's room opened and Edward and the doctor came barrelling out.

'My sister will have the best care possible. This is ridiculous; I can have her home in an hour. I can have her in bed with a private nurse in attendance. Her father is a qualified doctor!'

The young doctor closed the door. 'I am sure you have every good intention, but my patient is not, in my opinion, fit to be released this evening. Added to this, Miss Wickenham does not want to be . . .'

Edward interrupted him, irate. 'She's seventeen years old, for God's sake! She doesn't know what is best for her!'

'Then you must take my opinion very seriously. This is not the first suicide attempt. She has also had her stomach pumped, her blood pressure is frighteningly high and she is desperately underweight. I would say her family to date have not taken care of her health, and I am not prepared to release her into your custody this evening. Tomorrow may prove to be a different matter, subject to her recovery.'

They continued to argue for some time, moving into the small waiting room, leaving Anna and Langton standing in the corridor.

'Well, he's fighting in our corner,' Langton said.

Fifteen minutes later, Langton watched Edward Wickenham walking away, very obviously angry. He didn't even go back into Emily's room. When Langton tried to thank the doctor, he got a cool response.

'Your allegation that my patient is at risk from her family is not the reason I have insisted she remain here. Whatever questions you need answered must wait until tomorrow. Emily Wickenham is a very sick young lady, and, I would say, both mentally and physically she requires treatment.'

Langton put in a call to get a female officer stationed outside Emily Wickenham's room at the hospital. By this time, it was fifteen minutes after one. Anna drove him home; both of them were tired out. As she drew up outside his flat, only ten minutes away from her own, he rested his left hand on the handle of the car door.

'You did good work today, Travis.'

'Thank you.'

He was silent for a moment. 'How's your head feel?'

'Fine; bit of a bump, but nothing to worry about.'

Her heart flipped as with his right hand he gently rubbed the back of her head. 'A right little trooper, aren't you? Well if you want to make a late morning of it, come in at twelve, rest up.'

'Thank you, but I think I should get over to talk to Emily first thing.'

'Ah yes; tell me, why were you at her flat?'

She shrugged. 'Well, I had arranged to interview her. It was on my schedule before we went off to the Hall so I had a word with Barolli – well, he had a word with me – and I said I'd talk to her on my way home.'

'Well, cut the risk-taking from now on; you should have had someone with you. I thought you would have learned that from the last time we worked together.'

'I didn't know Justine would be there.'

'That is no excuse! Emily could have had a fucking gun with her, never mind that mad cow with a riding crop: learn to get backup organised. You are not a one-man band; we work as a team, so start thinking about being a team player.'

'Like you?'

'Exactly.'

Anna raised her eyebrows at the irony but bit her tongue.

'See you in the morning.' He leaned across and kissed her cheek. The smell of him physically hurt. It only happened in movies: the moment the heroine clasps the leading man's face in both hands and instigates a deep, lustful kiss. She hadn't the bottle to do anything so crass, but after he'd slammed the car door, she wished she had.

Anna parked her car, and used the lift though her flat was only two floors up: her legs felt leaden. Letting herself in, she tossed the keys onto the side table in the hall, eased out of her coat, and then toe-heeled each shoe off, leaving a trail of discarded clothes from the hall into the bedroom.

She flopped down on the bed, arms spread wide. She was so tired she didn't even have the energy to get up and clean her teeth.

She took a deep breath and moaned. 'Oh shit.'

James Langton was back, occupying so much of her mind and heart that denying it was pointless.

Chapter Seventeen

DAY TWENTY-EIGHT

Sleeping, Emily looked so young and fragile. The glucose drip was still in place; both her long thin arms were above the tightly drawn sheet and her bony hands rested one on top of the other. Someone had drawn her hair back from her face with an elastic band, accentuating her high, chiselled cheekbones. Her big, wide eyes seemed sunken beneath the closed lids.

A nurse brought Anna into the room. She had been very concerned when she was told that Justine Wickenham had spent a considerable time sitting beside her sister.

'During the night?'

'Yes, apparently; in fact, you only just missed her.'

'Is the doctor going to release Emily?'

'I don't know; I'm just taking her blood pressure.'

'Will you wake her?'

The nurse checked the time and gave a rueful smile. ''Fraid so. It was very high again last night, but it had dropped a wee bit earlier this morning.'

Anna stepped back as the nurse gently lifted Emily's arm and wrapped it in the black pad. The pumping action seemed loud in the silent room. Anna moved round to see Emily more clearly as she had her pulse taken. She was awake, staring ahead with dull expressionless eyes, ignoring the nurse. Anna waited until she had left the room before she went close to the bed.

'Emily, it's Anna Travis.'

'I'm not blind,' she said, in a low, bored voice.

'I don't want to disturb you more than is necessary.'

'Terrific.' She pressed the bed lift to sit up higher.

Anna drew up a chair. 'I need to ask you some questions.'

She didn't respond.

'Have you had breakfast?'

'I'm not hungry.'

At least it was a start. Anna debated how she should continue; Emily was behaving in a totally different manner to the previous night.

'I kept my part of the bargain: you remained here last night.'

No reaction.

'Emily, will you look at me, please?'

She turned her head very slowly towards Anna; her eyes were like saucers, and so full of pain. She reminded Anna of a sick bird; it seemed as if her head was too heavy for such a slender neck to hold up.

'You said you would talk to me and answer my questions. It's very important, Emily.'

'No. Go away.' She didn't say it in anger; her voice was tired and wavery.

Anna hesitated and then reached out to hold her hand. 'You know, if I can, I will help you again. Maybe I can arrange for you to be looked after.'

'Maybe I'll just die and then it will be over.'

'Tell me what happened to you, Emily.'

The thin hand twisted and then clung to Anna's.

'I know about your abortion.'

Her eyes filled with tears, and her hand grasped Anna's even more tightly. 'He used to say how much he loved me; whatever he did to me was because he loved me, and I believed him. But then I began to get sick.'

'Was it your father's child?'

'I've never been with anyone else. I didn't know I was pregnant until Daddy examined me. He said he would make it all better, make it all go away, so no one would know.'

'How many months pregnant were you?'

'I don't know.'

'So when he made it all better for you, where were you?'

'At home.'

'Did your father operate on you?'

Emily released her hand and curled up on her side away from Anna. She picked at the plaster holding the needle to the drip in her right arm.

'Was there a room in the house he used?'

'Yes.'

'Tell me about the room.'

Emily didn't answer.

'Is there medical equipment in this room?'

Anna leaned closer and the girl half-turned towards her. It happened so quickly Anna wasn't fast enough to get clear. Emily vomited and then clung onto Anna as she retched and spewed up again.

★

Langton let the receiver drop back onto its cradle. Lewis was sitting opposite him.

'Travis is at the hospital with Emily Wickenham. Emily just chucked up all over her so she doubts she'll be able to question her for a while, but she admitted her father did the abortion, and inside the house. Travis was trying to ascertain where it took place, if there's medical equipment that could have been used in the Louise Pennel murder. I mean, there's got to be some-place he cut her body in two, for Chrissakes!'

'Well, when we go in, we'll find it,' Lewis said.

Langton pursed his lips. 'Yeah, but he could have got rid of the gear, and it might not necessarily be at Mayerling Hall.'

'So when do we go in?'

Langton stood up and pulled at his tie. 'We should wait until we get a result from the blood spotting at the other daughter's flat; has it come in yet?'

'No, they need twenty-four hours at least. Why the hesitancy?'

'We get one big hit. To get the amount of SOCOs I want there is gonna cost and I don't want to blow it.'

'Your shout,' Lewis said, standing and placing the chair back against the wall.

'Yes, yes it is; let me think about when we make the move.'

Lewis gave a small shrug, and walked out. Langton opened his top drawer and took out a half bottle of brandy, then thought better of it and dropped the bottle back into the drawer. He picked up the phone. If it was possible to arrange for the troops and warrants to be ready in time, they would hit Mayerling Hall at dawn the following morning.

Anna had washed her shirt front, and her face and hands, but the smell persisted. The doctor had examined Emily and sedated her, as she had become hysterical. Anna had a few words with the doctor who was, if anything, even younger than the one who had attended to Emily the previous night; he too, however, was very concerned about her. Emily was very dehydrated and undernourished and her blood pressure was fluctuating. It was a comfort to Anna that they were not about to release the girl.

It was less reassuring that Justine Wickenham had been allowed in with her sister. The officer they had asked to guard Emily was very much on the defensive.

'I couldn't do anything: she's family; she's got a big mouth on her and she was very aggressive. I was outside the door and I didn't hear much dialogue; the patient looked pretty sick and I monitored them every ten minutes or so. Which was all I was told to do.'

'Right yeah, sorry if I sounded off.' Anna was just glad she hadn't had to confront Justine; the previous evening had been enough to last her for a long time. She thanked the officer and released her.

The doctor had Emily's medical records; he glanced down and then looked back to Anna. 'How well do you know Miss Wickenham?'

'I am with a murder team. Miss Wickenham is just someone we need to talk to. I happened to be there when she attempted to kill herself.'

'Well, she has tried a few times.'

He stared at the document, and then back to Anna. 'She should be transferred to a different unit, whether or not we can arrange it . . . She's only seventeen years old, so we would need parental permission. We tried to get some previous medical history but nothing has come in yet.'

Anna asked if it was all right for her to see Emily and he said it was fine, but if she was sleeping, not to waken her. He passed the clipboard with Emily's notes to the same nurse who had taken her blood pressure earlier.

Anna followed the nurse into Emily's room, and waited as she placed the clipboard on the end of the bed.

The nurse bent over Emily, who was lying curled up like a small child. 'Hi, Emily, would you like a cup of tea?'

There was no answer, and after checking the drip and straightening the bedclothes she turned to Anna.

'I think she should be left to rest. She was sedated, and she needs to get some strength back.'

Anna decided she'd go home to shower and change before going into the station. She bleeped the car open and drove away, unaware she had been watched and was now being followed.

In the small car park of her block of flats, Anna grabbed her handbag from the car in a hurry; she didn't bother to close the garage doors, as she would be leaving shortly. As she walked up the first flight of stairs, she heard the door from the garage bang open and shut. She paused for a moment, then continued, turning into the corridor on the first floor and up the stairs to her second–floor landing. She paused as she heard footsteps, but when she stopped, so did the footsteps. She listened. Silence.

'Hello? Is someone there? Hello?'

Silence.

Uneasy, Anna took out her flat keys in readiness. As she stopped at her front door, she sensed that someone was behind her and she whipped round.

Justine Wickenham was just walking out from the stairwell.

'What are you doing here?' Anna asked, keeping her voice steady as she turned the first lock. She wished she didn't have the additional security lock, because she had to use another key. Justine was coming closer and closer. She turned, keeping her voice calm and steady. 'I said, what are you doing here?'

Her hands shook and she couldn't insert the second key. At last, it slotted in the lock and she turned it fast.

'I hope you are fucking satisfied, you cunt!'

Anna pushed open the door ready to get inside before Justine could reach her, but she was too late. Justine gripped Anna's right arm so hard it hurt.

'They'll take her away this time, and that's your fault!'

'Just let go of my arm, Justine.'

'I'd only just got her straightened out and now you've fucking destroyed all that, but you wouldn't listen to me!'

'Let go of me!'

'I'd like to smash your face against the wall!'

Anna jerked her arm up with all her strength, hitting Justine in the face; Justine lost her balance and stepped back, but it still didn't give Anna time to make it inside and to safety.

'Didn't you hear what I just said?' Justine's face was twisted in anger.

'I heard you, Justine. You had better just step back and away from me. Get away from the door!'

Justine slammed her fists against the door and it opened wide. 'How's that? Go on, get in. Get in!'

Anna was desperate to avoid being trapped inside the flat with Justine. 'What do you want?'

Justine pushed her face close, flushed with anger. 'I'd like you to know what you've fucking done to my sister.'

Anna was fast: she gripped hold of Justine's left arm and twisted it up behind her back then, with her other hand, yanked her thumb almost out of its socket. Justine screamed in pain; she crumpled and howled.

'Why did you do that? What did you do that for?'

Anna pushed Justine clear of her, but it wasn't necessary: she leaned against the wall and started to cry.

'That hurt! You hurt me.'

'You had better leave, Justine. I mean it, get out. Go on, go away.'

'No, I won't.'

Anna knew she had the upper hand, and her fear subsided. 'What do you want?'

Justine covered her face with her hands and started to sob. 'You don't know what you've done, you don't know!'

Anna watched as she slid down the wall and sat hunched up on the floor, crying.

'Why don't you tell me what I'm supposed to have done?'

Langton was having a heavy session with the Commander. As it was now twenty-eight days without an arrest, she had been considering bringing in the Murder Review team; Langton argued that since he now had a prime suspect, that was unnecessary. The Commander said it was impossible to arrange everything he requested for the following morning. She felt he should wait out the twenty-four hours to gain the results from the blood tests.

Langton did, however, get the backup he wanted and it was agreed the extra teams would all gather at the Richmond Hotel. They would all be briefed in the Incident Room, and then move in convoy. When he passed on the details to Lewis, he was taken aback.

'Jesus Christ, they've agreed to all this? That's one hell of a manoeuvre!'

'Lot of arm twisting but yes, like I said, we are going to have this one big hit, so let's hope to God we come away with something that will prove it was worth it.' He sighed. 'Truth is, we need the time, so let's get cracking and use every minute. We have to get this so well organised they'll not scream at the cost. Has Travis called in yet?'

Lewis was heading out of his office. 'Nope, lemme call the hospital and check; she might have gone back there.'

'Okay, let me know what she's up to.'

This time, Langton did unscrew the bottle cap. This was indeed one hell of a manoeuvre and he just hoped to God he wasn't going to come up empty-handed.

Justine sat on Anna's bed; she took the glass of water gratefully.

'Thank you.'

Anna checked her watch. She opened her wardrobe and took out a fresh shirt and jacket. There was no way she would take a shower: she was loath to leave Justine by herself for a second. Instead, she left the bathroom door ajar as she washed her face and hands: she could see Justine in her washbasin mirror, sitting with the glass of water cupped in her hands.

Anna began to button up her shirt. Justine drained the glass of water and looked around the bedroom.

'You're as untidy as I am.'

The clothes Anna had taken off the previous evening were still on the floor.

'Well, they run me ragged at work.' She unzipped her skirt and tossed it onto the bed, picking up another.

Justine stood up. Anna watched her warily, but she just placed the empty glass onto the dressing table.

'Can I have a coffee?'

'Sure, I'll make us both one.'

Anna was unsure what was going on; she was no longer scared of Justine but, at the same time, she didn't trust her.

Justine followed her into the kitchen; the sink was full of dirty crockery. 'Don't like washing up either? Nor do I.'

Anna put the kettle on and fetched two mugs and some instant coffee which she spooned out, then opened a tin of biscuits. Justine seemed to have calmed down but when she sat on one of the kitchen stools, her foot twitched.

'You want sugar?'

'Yes please, three; thank you.'

Anna placed the coffee down and sat on the stool next to Justine.

'I got Emily out of this place my father had put her in; it took a lot of persuasion, he didn't think she should be released. I was the only one that visited her. She was desperate: it was hideous, with all these crazies.'

'How long ago?'

'Oh, eight months, maybe more; I can't remember. You may not think it, but Em's really bright. She'd got a place at college so I fixed up that flat for her to stay in. He was furious, but then he sort of relented because Em was really okay; it wasn't as if we were asking him for any money, God forbid!' She sipped her coffee, and then delved into the biscuits. 'He never went to see her; he hardly ever sees me now, but you still always feel he knows whatever move we make. He's promised to get me my own stables, you know, set up a riding school of my own. He says he will, but not until I've had more experience. I do some shows, dressage, stuff like that; I'm pretty good.'

Anna listened as Justine went on about the competitions and how much work they made her do at the stables.

'Did your father come to your flat there?'

'Nope, well maybe I've had the odd visit, but not recently.'

There was a long pause and then Justine whispered, 'I hate him.'

Anna watched as she ate another biscuit. Her foot was tapping so hard, her stool shook.

'How do you get along with your brother?' Anna said tentatively.

'Edward really is a wet prick.'

Anna laughed softly and Justine gave her a smile.

'He's scared of him; scared of doing anything that'll lose the inheritance, for one, but he knows that Daddy would kick him out just like that if he didn't do whatever he wants.' She clicked her fingers.

'Do you do what he wants?'

'No; well, not now.'

'You used to?'

'Yes.'

Anna picked up her mug and took it to the sink. 'I don't know if I should tell you this, Justine, but I've seen some very explicit photographs.'

'Oh yeah?'

'Yes, of a very sexual nature.'

'You should see the videos!' She gave a harsh, brittle laugh.

'Are you serious?'

'About what?'

'That your father videoed these . . .'

'Orgies?'

Anna rinsed her mug, trying to act casual.

'They went on most weekends.'

'And you took part in them?'

'Yes.'

'And your brother?'

'Yes, yes, and his girlfriends and the tarts, and when Mother was at home, she would like swinging from the chandeliers as well. They'd watch porno films, eat and drink themselves into a stupor and then take anything they could get hold of to get them sexed up. I tell you, whoever invented Viagra should be put in the stocks.'

Anna returned to sit next to Justine, whose leg was

now twitching as if she couldn't control it. Her anger was palpable.

'I couldn't wait to go away to school: anything to get out, anything to stop him, but it was hopeless. I couldn't do anything. I knew it was happening but I had no one to turn to, no one to help me, so I just went to school and refused to think about it.'

'Didn't your mother ever stop him molesting you?'

'Me? Oh, he went off me very fast. I was too big. It wasn't me he was after.'

She squeezed her eyes shut tight.

'Emily?' Anna said softly, and Justine nodded.

'I thought he would leave her alone if I did whatever he wanted, but he used to take her out of her bedroom.'

'How old was she?'

'Seven or eight.'

'Your mother knew?'

Justine shrugged. 'She was as bad as Edward; if she knew, she did nothing. She was only interested in how much she could get out of him, and she got a fortune.'

Anna's phone rang.

'Shouldn't you get that?' Justine said.

'No, it'll only be my boss asking me where I am. Let's have another coffee.'

Justine drained her mug and held it out.

'Yes please.'

Having got no answer from Anna's mobile, Langton called her flat. The answermachine clicked on. He called the hospital and they said that Anna had left some time earlier. He was told that Emily Wickenham had been taken from the hospital by her brother.

Langton was worried; why wasn't Travis answering? He went into the Incident Room and asked if anyone had heard from her. No one had.

Lewis was eager to get the overall plan of action from Langton, as the pressure was on for everything to be coordinated for the raid at Wickenham's estate. It had been easy to get copies of the plans of the Hall, the barn and outhouses, plus the thatched cottage, as the conversion of the barn had had to be surveyed and planning permission granted. Looking over the plans, Langton knew he really had one big job on his hands. He and Lewis set to work on the organisation of who would do what, where and when.

'We get any joy on the tape match to Wickenham?'

'Not as yet,' Lewis said. There was also still no contact from forensics regarding the blood splattering at Justine Wickenham's.

'You get someone to take my bloodstained shirt over to the lab? It'll have Emily's DNA for elimination.'

A frazzled Lewis said Bridget had taken it personally as soon as he had brought it in, then he went back to concentrating on dividing the estate into sections for the search.

Justine spooned in heaped teaspoons of sugar and stirred her coffee. 'So I was always guilty, you know, about leaving Em, she was such a sweet little soul. I think our old housekeeper tried to protect her, but with Dad, no one was safe.'

'When did she become pregnant by him?' Anna asked and Justine didn't appear to question how she knew; she just bowed her head.

'Oh God, it was terrible. She was so young, she didn't understand. Her belly was distended and she thought it was something she'd eaten, that's how innocent she was.'

'How old was she?'

'Thirteen. When he found out he was hysterical, like it was her fault; it was terrible.'

'Did he perform the abortion?'

She nodded, tears trickling down her face. 'And worse, as if by doing it, he would never have that problem again.'

'I don't understand.'

'He operated on her, he did a hysterectomy: she can't ever have kids. He did that to her. That's what started her being sick and crazy; then he sent her away for electric shock treatment.'

Anna was sickened and reached out to take Justine's hand, but she wouldn't allow her to hold it.

'I'd like to kill him. I used to plan how I'd do it, but he used to get round me, you know, saying that poor Emily was really mentally sick, like he had nothing to do with it when it was all his fault.'

'When the child abuse investigation happened, who instigated it?'

'Well, me, not that he knew it. I persuaded Em to go to the police station and tell them, but it was a farce. He was the local bigwig doctor, he could pay anyone off; in this case, I don't think he needed to bribe anyone because he'd already had her institutionalised. He said it was all in her mind and that she had this sick, overactive imagination. He made her life hell after that. It was part of the reason Mum left him; she'd had enough, not that she did anything for us. She had a weapon now

389

and could squeeze him for a lot of money; it's all about money with her. It was awful her going away, because we lost Danielle, her maid. She was like the old house-keeper; at least they tried between them to help Em, but she just got sicker and . . .'

Justine took out a handkerchief and blew her nose. 'She started self-mutilating: her arms, her thighs; a couple of times she really dug the knife in deep. Anyway, she was in and out of these awful places until I persuaded Dad that she was okay and I would be responsible for her. He said if I did take care of her, he'd buy me the stables. You see how he works? Promises, dangled prom-ises, because he doesn't care about anything or anyone but himself.'

'Do you know why I first began asking you ques-tions?'

'Yes, yes of course. I don't know anything about those two girls, and to be honest I don't care a shit about them.'

'They died brutal deaths.'

'Yeah, me and Em have had a pretty shitty life, so what are they to me? I never met them, didn't know them, and nor did she.'

'When he operated on your sister, did he have a room or a place he used?'

'You mean his surgery? Well, that's what he calls it. It's full of his drugs and sicko stuff. It's part of the old cellars; well, it was: I've not been there for a long time. You can understand why.'

'Not been to the cellars?'

'No, the fucking house. I can't stand to look at his face. I hate him so much, I hate him!'

The ferocious anger was building. Anna was feeling exhausted from the strain of listening to what she was saying while keeping her calm.

'If he is guilty, though, he would be out of the way for a long time.'

'Ha, you must be joking. I bet he won't get caught. If he did anything, he can always cover it. You don't know him: he will get away with murder. He can get away with anything.'

'Would you be prepared to make a statement about what happened to your sister?'

'It wouldn't do any good. Even if you did a physical examination of Em, you'd never prove that he was involved. That's why I came here to see you: I wanted you to know.'

'Know what?'

'That they were coming for her; that they were going to take her back to that stinking mental hospital. Anything she says will be treated as her delusions. They'll say you cannot believe a word she says. We've been over all that fucking shit before: they'll drug her to keep her quiet, and whatever you try and prove, they'll just put it down to her having too vivid an imagination!'

'But you know it isn't.'

'Yeah I know, my brother knows. His wife topped herself because she was so sickened by him; Dad was even fucking her! And now, by you asking poor Em all about it, she's tried to top herself again. I told you to leave her alone, I told you!'

Anna knew she had to get out of the flat and fast. The rage was coming back.

'Listen, why don't we get back to the hospital and see if we can stop them taking Emily? It's still only . . .' She looked at her watch: it was already twelve o'clock. 'I know the doctors didn't want to release Emily. Shall we get over there? I know we can help her.'

Justine clenched and unclenched her hands. 'Edward said Dad had arranged it.'

'Well, we won't know unless we go back there, will we?'

Justine chewed at her lip, and then nodded. 'Okay, okay.'

Inwardly, Anna sighed with relief. She went and got her jacket as Justine hovered at the front door. 'I'll follow you, my car's parked outside.'

Anna felt her legs shaking as she started up the car. She backed out of the garage and into the road. As she adjusted her rearview mirror, she saw Justine was directly behind her. Anna had no intention of returning to the hospital: she was going to head directly to the station. She called the Incident Room. Lewis answered.

'Where the hell have you been? We've been trying to contact you.'

'I will explain, but not now.'

'The boss was going apeshit, we called the hospital and . . .'

'Is Emily Wickenham still there?'

'No, her family took her out a couple of hours ago.'

'Shit! Can you get a squad car to tail me? I'm on the Edgware Road, and I need some help. There's a dark blue Metro car directly behind me, reg 445 JW: it's Justine Wickenham and I want to lose her.'

★

It was all round the Incident Room, but all they knew was that DI Travis had asked for backup and a squad car had intercepted her as she reached Marble Arch.

When she came into the Incident Room, Lewis said that she had better go and see Langton directly. Anna put down her briefcase, took off her jacket and with a deep breath went into his office.

'Where in Christ's name have you been?'

Anna felt dizzy; she couldn't speak. She pulled out the chair in front of his desk and sat down.

'Anna, what the hell is going on?'

She stared at the floor. 'I am not sure where to begin.'

'Try the beginning.'

Anna licked her lips; she was churning over the entire interaction with Justine. She knew if she was to explain how at risk she had felt when Justine followed her, to then invite her into the flat would look totally un-professional. She didn't want another lecture.

'Well I got the opportunity to have a talk to Justine Wickenham, so that is what I have been doing.'

'At the hospital?'

'No, at my flat.'

'Your flat?'

'Yes, we had coffee.'

He leaned back in his chair and gestured for her to continue.

Lewis received the forensic report at three o'clock. The bloodstains found beside Justine Wickenham's bathtub did not belong to either Sharon Bilkin or Louise Pennel. He went to give Langton the information. Langton gave a curt 'come in', listened, and then nodded for him to leave. When Lewis hesitated, he snapped. 'Get out!'

Lewis backed out fast and shut the door. There was a long pause.

'So you did the right thing, you got a squad car. What happened to Justine?'

'I don't know. She was behind me; I think she turned off when she saw me being pulled over. She might be at the hospital, but I've been told Emily Wickenham has already been released.'

'Yes, they had to let her go, she's not eighteen so parental permission, etcetera etcetera.'

Anna had an overwhelming need to cry. Try as she might, she couldn't control it. She bit her lip as her chest heaved.

'I'm so sorry,' she said softly, but her eyes filled with tears. 'I'll go and make up a report.' She could hardly get the words out. She so didn't want to allow herself to cry in front of him and she half rose out of the chair, but sank back down.

Langton moved round his desk and gently took her in his arms, resting her head against his shoulder. He stroked her hair.

'Shush, shush, it's okay, just take it easy, take a few big breaths. You know, sometimes when you have to listen to raw pain, it buries little shards inside you: best to let them out.'

She nodded mutely. He released his hold. That really made her want to cry: it had been so comforting to have his arms around her.

He opened the drawer, took out his half bottle of brandy and passed it to her. 'Take a good slug. I'm sure you'll have your stock of peppermints handy.'

She took two big gulps, coughed and then passed it back. 'Thank you.'

He slipped the bottle back into his drawer. 'Maybe take the rest of the afternoon off to get back to speed.'

'No, I'd prefer to work.'

'Suit yourself, but today's a short day anyway, as we go into Wickenham's tomorrow morning. Operation Red Dahlia kicks off at dawn and it will be a long day.'

She gave a glum smile. 'I don't care, however long it takes.'

'Feeling is mutual, even more so now after what you've told me. I just hope to Christ I haven't jumped the gun.'

'I'll type up my report.'

'Good girl,' he said softly.

She walked out of his office, wanting him more than ever to wrap his arms around her again.

Lewis looked over to Anna. 'Is he in a good mood?'

'Yes, I think so,' she said.

'They've just confirmed that the blood splattering on the bathtub wall in Justine Wickenham's flat belongs to Emily, not one of the victims.'

Anna thought it was probably one of Emily's attempts to kill or mutilate herself. She looked over to the Incident Room board. Louise Pennel and Sharon Bilkin seemed to be staring directly at her. She ran over in her mind exactly how Justine Wickenham had reacted to the fact that her father might be their killer. Her own pain was too heavy; her sister's heartbreaking torture by their sadistic father was much too consuming

395

for either of them to be able to care about anyone else's.

Anna looked from one victim to the other. She cared, and she knew every single member of the investigation team was energised by the possibility of at long last making an arrest. The killer of the Black Dahlia had escaped arrest: no one was ever charged with her murder. She again thought back to what Justine Wickenham had said: even if her father was guilty, they would never catch him — he could get away with murder.

Anna returned to her desk. She spent a long time writing up her report and then went through the case files, which were now so numerous that they overflowed in stacks beneath the table. She went back to her desk with the details of the attempted child abuse case against Charles Wickenham. She took down the name of every person who had been involved, including the doctors at the mental institution who had given statements about Emily's mental state. There was nothing connected to her physical condition. If Justine had been telling the truth, a hysterectomy at her young age must have been documented somewhere.

Anna knocked on Langton's office door. He looked up at her, frowning. She kept it to the point: she would like to interview everyone she had listed. He sighed.

'Drop it for now, Anna. We are heading up a murder enquiry: hand that over to the Child Protection Unit. After we're through with him, they might dig up more.'

'But there must have been someone who examined her.'

'He got away with it and, as sick and disgusting and tragic as it is, we have to leave it alone for now, unless we screw up and tomorrow is just a waste of money. Now why don't you go home, get some rest: it's a big day.'

She felt like a schoolgirl standing in front of him. She tried to make light of it. 'I could say the same to you.'

He gave a soft laugh. 'Not to the ringmaster, you can't. It all stands on my decisions and I sure as hell don't want to come back empty-handed. I want that bastard. Goodnight.'

Again, she had the impulse to reach over with both hands to hold his face close and kiss him. Instead she gave a small nod, and walked out.

'Goodnight, Gov.'

Chapter Eighteen

DAY TWENTY-NINE

The Richmond Hotel car park was crawling with police vans, fifteen in all: there were the forensic team, the SOCOs – scene-of-crime officers – the murder team, the Territorial Support Group, and another six officers drafted in to assist. They had two sets of tracker dogs and handlers; there was also a caterer's truck, all on standby. The hotel had been very accommodating but had asked that they keep as quiet as possible, so as not to disturb residents; opportunely, the hotel was having a lot of construction work done, so there were very few guests.

Everyone gathered in the hotel's ballroom, where rows of chairs had been set out. Lewis was pinning up detailed diagrams of the entire estate when Langton entered. It was two forty-five a.m. He looked tired and anxious and wore a dark grey suit and white shirt and a tie. He had divided the teams up: one group would focus on the cottage, another on the barn, and the largest group would concentrate on the main house. They knew from the surveillance team that Charles Wickenham was at home; Edward and his fiancée were at their cottage.

Langton pointed to the aerial photographs.

'Going to give you all a quick history lesson. The main house was built around 1540 and was owned by a high-ranking Catholic family. The sixteenth century was the period of the persecution of Catholic priests. There was a piece of anti-priest legislation that created a massive number of English Catholic martyrs: in those days, harbouring any Catholic priest was seen as treason and was punishable by death. The reason I've brought this up is that it's quite possible, therefore, that the house contains a lot of hidden rooms and boltholes. There's a property of similar age in Kidderminster which has over ten hidden priest holes – beside chimneys, beneath stairs, under cellar floors – so we search very thoroughly.'

Langton showed them the plans of the barn. 'This was recently converted from an old maize barn: it's massive in size and there was a large cellar beneath that. According to the council that gave permission for the renovation, it was converted into a gym with a whirlpool bath, hot tub and swimming pool. We have to check out they didn't leave an area for our suspect to use as some kind of torture chamber. It could also have been used to dismember our first victim, Louise Pennel. Our suspect has to have had somewhere to cut and drain her body and I think it is possibly somewhere in this estate.'

Langton continued until he was satisfied that everyone knew their jobs. He checked his watch; it was by now three-fifteen a.m. Operation Red Dahlia was ready to roll.

They travelled in convoy, led by Langton in an unmarked patrol car, accompanied by Lewis and Barolli. Anna followed with three other members of the team in the car behind, then came the vans and people carriers, plus special vehicles to provide lighting for the officers. It was still dark and there was little traffic on the roads. They made the journey to Wickenham's village in three-quarters of an hour. By the time they hit the small winding lane, it was a little lighter, but the sky was still overcast and slate grey. They moved slowly over the cattle grids until the lead car stopped and moved into a lay-by so that one of the big double-fronted trucks could move ahead. Langton did not want any signal to be given that they were there, so he was not wasting time ringing doorbells. He ordered the truck to smash straight through the gates.

By four-thirty, they were moving down the winding pathway with the overhanging trees towards the main horseshoe drive of the house. The vehicles peeled off to the cottage and round to the barn and stables. Everyone had their duty lists. The raid was worked out with such precision that no one needed to ask what was coming once they were inside.

Langton went up to the main front door of the Hall. He used the old iron knocker to rap so hard, it echoed. Lined up behind him were Anna and Barolli and ten SOCO officers, plus the Territorial Support Group ready to secure the area.

At almost exactly the same time, Lewis and five SOCO officers knocked on the door of the thatched cottage.

Three more officers moved to the barn area, and the dogs and handlers were heading to the stables.

Virtually in unison, the officers showed their warrants. First to be read his rights was a shaken Charles Wickenham. Langton told him that he was being arrested under suspicion of the murders of Louise Pennel and Sharon Bilkin. Second was Edward Wickenham and then, screaming with fright, Gail Harrington: both were arrested on suspicion of their involvement in the murders of Louise Pennel and Sharon Bilkin.

The officers waited for the suspects to dress; two females remained with the hysterical Gail Harrington as she changed out of her nightdress. Another officer waited with Edward as he dressed. He kept on saying he wanted to speak to his father, but no one replied; he became so angry that at one point he was warned that, if he did not come quietly, he would be handcuffed. He then changed his tune, demanding a solicitor. He was told he would be allowed to make a call from the station.

Both Edward and his fiancée were driven from the estate fifteen minutes later. Charles Wickenham was refusing to get dressed; he said that, by law, he was to be allowed to remain at his property to oversee any items that were to be removed. Langton conceded, on the understanding that there would be a uniformed officer with him at all times. Now dressed, Wickenham was taken into the drawing room; he even had the audacity to ask if he could be given some breakfast. If anything, he seemed amused by the activity. At some point, he was given a cup of tea but he had only a moment to drink it before he was handcuffed, the two manacles linked by a solid bar. His hands were cuffed in front of his body and he was warned that if he created any kind of trouble, he would be cuffed behind his back.

'I won't be any trouble. I can finish my tea, even with these hideous things attached,' he smirked, as he sat reading *The Times* as if nothing untoward was occurring.

The search began. The officers allocated the cottage went from room to room. They stripped back carpets and emptied cupboards and wardrobes. They went up into the loft and, by torchlight, did an inch-by-inch search of masses of old furniture. They climbed into the old chimney above the open fireplace. They checked walls for recesses and any hidden rooms. They found a stack of family albums, pornographic magazines and videos but, after three and a half hours, they were otherwise coming up empty-handed.

The housekeeper, Mrs Hedges, was frightened and confused. Anna asked that she remain in her room until further notice. The forensic officers began their search of the main house on the ground floor and worked upwards, combing the place for bloodstains or any other incriminating evidence.

By twelve o'clock, the search was still very much in progress. Langton moved from the main house over to the cottage, disappointed that they had had no results so far; however, when he looked into Gail Harrington's bedroom and saw the jewellery boxes, he called Anna to get her over. Sharon Bilkin had sold a diamond-and-emerald brooch to the antique dealer; here were the earrings and necklace to match, which were listed and bagged to be taken in; it was something: not a lot, but something.

The barn was split into two levels. The games room on the upper floor had a full-sized snooker table, and another vast area with a wide, open brick fireplace and two massive cushioned sofas with a long pine coffee table between them. The walls were dominated by racing pictures and photos from horse shows. There were a few knickknacks, a lot of large floral arrangements and a cabinet full of crystal glasses and rows of bottles containing every conceivable brand of liquor. There was also a white wine fridge and a rack stocked with good-quality reds. This entire area was easier to search, as it was reasonably sparse. The lower section had a gym, a sauna and whirlpool bath, plus a hot tub and swimming pool. Cabinets contained creams and oils, and fresh white towels were stacked on wooden shelf units. They examined a large laundry basket, but the towels inside didn't even look used. There was further storage space under the barn roof that had an access ladder by the sauna. The officers searched up there, but found only yet more furniture that was not in use. Two officers also spent a considerable amount of time tapping on the walls to see if there were any hidden compartments, but found none.

They had asked the stable lads to take out all the horses and these were being walked up and down as each stall was checked, but came up clean. They also searched the stable boys' quarters, but found nothing remarkable but the stench of sweaty socks.

A drug-trained spaniel sniffed and trotted about. The trainer took it for walks every half hour so it would be refreshed, but so far it had found nothing in the barn and stable area; the second dog, trained to find weapons, was sleeping beside his handler while they waited to enter the main house.

They broke for lunch at one-thirty. Langton, Lewis and Anna pored over the drawings of the house. Justine had described a cellar, a room her father used; however, the only cellar they had on the drawings would have been where the sauna and whirlpool were now located. They were becoming anxious but tried not to show it.

Throughout, Charles Wickenham had remained in the lounge. He had rested on the sofa after finishing the newspaper and actually had a snooze, he was that relaxed.

Anna knocked on Mrs Hedges's door. She was sitting in an old rocking chair, reading a magazine.

'I've brought you some lunch.'

'That's very kind of you, I appreciate it. Is Mr Wickenham still here?'

'Yes, he's still here.'

Anna watched as Mrs Hedges sipped her tea and carefully unwrapped her sandwich. 'Where's the cellar located, Mrs Hedges?'

'There was a very big one, running the whole length of the barn. We'd keep all the furniture that needed to be repaired in there, but when they converted it, I think they dug down to make space for a gym and pool.'

'Surely this house has to have one?'

'Yes it does, but I've not been down there for years: the stairs are very steep.'

'Where is it?'

'Behind the laundry room.'

Anna thanked her, and went back to Langton. 'There's a cellar here; its access is in the laundry room.'

Langton frowned. 'It's not on the survey.'

'Well, Mrs Hedges has just said it is there; she said it had very steep stairs.'

Langton wiped his mouth with a paper napkin. 'Let's take a look.'

They stood in the small, windowless laundry room. One wall was taken up with all the security boxes for the gates and estate; another had two washing machines and tumbledryers, a very high-powered-looking pressing machine and an ironing board stacked against it; the third had rows and rows of shelves, with sheets and towels in colour-coordinated stacks.

Langton sighed. 'Move the shelves.'

Lewis bent down; they were secured with bolts to the floor.

'We'll have to dismantle them,' he said.

'Do it: get some of the SOCO boys in here to give you a hand.'

'There are four female SOCO officers sir, do you need them as well?'

He turned and glared at her. 'Don't give me this *female* crap now, Travis!'

He stalked out past Anna. She could see he was getting

very tense; it was now after two and they had found nothing incriminating.

Langton paced up and down outside the house, smoking. Barolli joined him.

'We're coming up with fuck all over at the barn.'

'Yeah, so I've been told.'

'You want to release some of the men?'

'No, keep going.'

'Found a hidden room behind the fireplace at the cottage, just a square sort of chamber. You could get up and out of the chimney, if you were an anorexic dwarf.'

'Shit!' Langton muttered. This was worse than he could have anticipated.

'His study was clean as a whistle. We moved out hundreds of books, but some heavy porn videos and magazines is about all we've got so far.'

'Plus the diamond-and-emerald necklace.'

'Oh yeah, right. You think Wickenham bribed Sharon Bilkin with the brooch?'

'Right now, pal, I can't think; this whole thing is looking like a fucking fiasco.'

Just then, Lewis appeared at the front door.

Langton looked over, anxiously. 'We got something?'

'Think so: we started to dismantle the unit, but there's a spring attached – the thing moves and opens like a door.'

Langton could feel the blood rush to his head. He ground his cigarette into the gravel and hurried into the house. The shelving unit was partly dismantled; behind it was painted chipboard. Langton watched in anticipation as it was eased gently back and removed. Langton ducked around it to see what it had hidden.

There was a studded door with an archdeacon arch. It had a heavy bolt across the top and bottom. They were silent as Lewis eased back the top bolt and then bent low to loosen the one at the bottom. He straightened and turned the iron hand ring. It moved easily, as if oiled, with no creaking or groaning sound. The door opened inwards.

'This isn't on any of the plans,' Langton said quietly.

Lewis stepped back to allow Langton to have the first view of what lay beyond the door. There were stone steps, steep ones, and below they could see nothing but inky darkness.

'Is there a light?'

Lewis peered around, but could see no connection. A torch was passed in; a few of the team had gathered outside the laundry room. The torch's beam lit up the stairs but did not reach beyond them. Langton began slowly to descend. There was a rope banister, attached to the wall with iron rings. Behind him, Lewis and Anna followed cautiously.

At the bottom, there was a thick slabbed wall of what looked like York stone. There was hardly enough space to turn, it was so close to the bottom stair. Langton shone the beam of the torch to his right; there was another archway, a door partly ajar. He inched forward, and stopped. There was a strong smell of disinfectant. Two more torches were handed to Anna and she passed one to Lewis as they now slowly made their way through to the next chamber.

The room was larger than they expected, at least twenty-five feet long and fifteen feet wide. The walls and floor were stone. There was an operating table, and a swill table with a big stone washbasin.

'It's like a fucking Victorian mortuary,' Langton said, and put out his arm to stop either Lewis or Anna passing. 'Stay back. I want forensics down here fast; we don't go in any further.'

Anna shone her torch over chains and handcuffs, cabinets filled with bottles of medical supplies. The beam lit up an array of surgeons' saws, all neatly laid out on a table with a white linen cloth.

The three detectives backed out slowly as the forensic team streamed past with their equipment.

'Get me a paper suit, Travis. I want to be down there with them.' He smiled. 'Feeling better now!'

Wickenham obviously knew about the discovery, but had hardly shown any reaction. The uniformed officer who had remained in the lounge with him was relieved by Constable Ed Harris. Seeing that Harris could hardly contain himself, he was slightly peeved that he'd missed all the excitement and scuttled off to get some tea.

Harris looked over to where Charles Wickenham reclined, his manacled hands resting against his thighs.

'Any damage and you'll all pay for it,' he said indolently.

They had discovered the light switches for the cellar, attached to their own small generator. The cellar was flooded with light as the forensic team set to work. Each saw was carefully bagged and tagged. One officer was carefully removing the taps and the drainage system, examining the pipes and taking a lot of samples. Their voices were hardly above a whisper. One after the other was finding blood samples. Langton saw them with-

407

drawing some long hairs from the pipes before deciding to remove the entire waste disposal unit.

Another officer was examining the drugs in the cabinet. There was a considerable amount of morphine and formaldehyde in big canisters, as well as a substantial quantity of cocaine and heroin. It was as if they had opened a twisted version of Aladdin's cave.

Meanwhile, the rest of the officers gathered outside and watched as large plastic bags were carried out; one contained at least a hundred pornographic videos.

Langton came out. He stripped off the paper cover from his shoes and began to rip off his paper suit. Anna went up to him.

'We going to take him in now?'

Langton smiled. He handed to Anna a clipboard listing what had been discovered to date. 'I want him to look over this: we've got heavy-duty bloodstains and hair, and in the incinerator Christ only knows what. It's a makeshift operating theatre, with as much equipment as a hospital emergency room.'

A shout went up from the house; they turned as Lewis hurtled out. He was red-faced and shaking.

'He's fucking gone; did anyone see him come out this way?'

Langton could hardly believe what he was hearing. 'Gone? *Gone?* What the fuck are you talking about?'

'Wickenham: he's gone'

Constable Ed Harris had been hit over the head and was semi-concussed. A chair had been overturned and some cushions were on the floor, but otherwise the room was as they had left it. Langton was beside himself. Somehow, Charles Wickenham, despite being surrounded by officers, had done an amazing disappearing act. The stables, the cottage, the surrounding outhouses, the woods and fields were all searched; it seemed he had vanished into thin air.

Anna went to see Mrs Hedges. She was sleeping, and woke startled.

'Mrs Hedges, has Charles Wickenham been in here?'

'No, no, I've been alone, what's happened?'

Anna hesitated, then sat down. 'We found the cellar, and we have discovered a number of items.'

'I never went down there,' she said defensively.

'If it wasn't for your help, we might not have found it, but I am afraid you will have to remain in your room.'

She nodded and then took out a soiled handkerchief. 'I didn't know what to do. I used to hear things from down there, but I couldn't do anything.'

Anna was through with the pleasantries. 'Of course you could. You must have known! Maybe not about anyone else, but you knew he took his own daughter down there.'

'No, no, I swear before God, I was here, here in my room.'

'Hear no evil, see no evil? You could have gone to the police. You could have done something to protect her.'

Mrs Hedges broke down in tears. Anna showed her disgust by walking out and shutting the door firmly behind her.

It was after seven by the time they had cleared the cellar. The forensic teams departed, leaving the murder team still searching, assisted by the SOCO officers and the

TSG. The dogs were let loose, but by this time they were as tired out as their handlers: they had been given Charles Wickenham's clothes so they could trace his scent, but as he lived at the house and used all the surrounding buildings, their noses kept leading them this way and that, round in circles.

By nine o'clock, Langton released the SOCOs. His own team would continue the search. They were all tired out, but Langton would not stop. By ten-thirty, it was so dark without arc lamps that it was getting impossible to continue the search outside. Their tea wagon had gone and it was almost eleven when an exhausted Langton called everyone together.

'We leave eight officers here; we start an alert to airports, stations, the bastard can't just have . . .' He trailed off and gave a helpless gesture: Wickenham had disappeared into thin air. They had all been diligent; Langton could not apportion blame to anyone other than Constable Ed Harris, who had been taken by ambulance to the local hospital.

The eight officers who would remain at the estate were given orders to pair up and be in radio contact with each other, taking up positions inside and outside the main house. The surveillance officers were certain they had not seen anyone leave the premises, but by midnight, Charles Wickenham had not been found. Langton, with Anna and Lewis, left Mayerling Hall. They were too tired and morose to begin questioning either Edward Wickenham or his fiancée, who were still held in the cells at Richmond. Langton knew he had only few hours left to question them, so he gave instructions to apply for an extension.

★

The officers in the Incident Room had been updated with all the details from Mayerling Hall. They had been as depressed as the team there when nothing had been discovered and then as jubilant when the cellar was located. Then they received the news that their suspect had done a disappearing act.

Bridget stood in front of the photographs of the Black Dahlia, whose haunted eyes seemed to look at her accusingly. She whispered to herself, 'Dear God, don't let it happen again. Don't let him get away with it.'

The murder of Elizabeth Short had become so intertwined with the Red Dahlia case, it was almost as though if they captured her killer, the Black Dahlia could rest in peace.

DAY THIRTY

Langton was in the Incident Room by seven the following morning. There had been no report of any sightings of Charles Wickenham. He sat in his office, depressed and angry, arranging for a new team to relieve those who had been at the Hall all night.

Mrs Hedges was allowed to leave her room to make herself some breakfast; she was asked that she limit her movements to her room and the kitchen. She sat in her rocking chair, eating scrambled eggs and bacon. She had no real conception of what was happening: just that her employer Charles Wickenham had escaped arrest. After her breakfast, she got out all her papers and began to calculate how much savings she had and what she should do if he never returned. She was astonished to find that with all the cash she had hoarded, she had over seventy thousand pounds. Rocking back and forth, she looked around the sparse room at the single bed she'd had for twenty years and the old, wing-backed easy chair. She did like her large colour TV, but apart from that, she'd had nothing new for fifteen years. They might have redeveloped the barn, but nothing had ever been done to her quarters; it was becoming more and more difficult for her to get in and out of the bath in her ensuite bathroom and for her to yank the old pull chain on her wooden-seated toilet. She had some early photographs of Emily, and these were the ones that pained her. She had been such a pretty child, white blonde hair, and wide blue china doll eyes. It was Emily she had wet-nursed and it was Emily she loved most of all. She sat looking through her cheap Woolworth's album: Justine winning rosettes at her equestrian competitions, Edward as a boy, smiling with a cowboy hat on, and then there was one of his wedding to that nice girl. There were none of Dominique Wickenham.

Mrs Hedges closed the book; she had been on the periphery of the Wickenhams' lives for so many years. She had no life of her own, but she had never really minded that. The family had become her life. She thought of what Anna had said to her: hear no evil, see no evil; well, she was not the evil one. Nevertheless, guilt swept over her.

It was about twelve o'clock when she took her break-fast tray back to the kitchen. She brewed a pot of tea for the officers and handed around the biscuits. She was on her way back up the stairs when she heard a faint scratching sound. It seemed to be coming from beneath the servants' staircase. She listened, sure she had heard something, but there was silence. She continued to her room and closed the door.

Mrs Hedges sat back in her chair, put on her glasses and read Charles Wickenham's newspaper, rocking gently back and forth.

As the forensic team arrived at the Hall to continue their search for further evidence in the cellar, work back at the lab was at full speed. Wickenham's computer had been removed; his waste disposal unit had been dismantled; even his paper-shredding machine was taken. The collection of fibres and bloodstains also needed to be analysed. It would be weeks of work.

At the station, the officers gathered for Langton to give out his instructions to the duty manager. Still held in their cells were Edward Wickenham and Gail Harrington. They had both been allowed to make one phone call and they awaited the arrival of their solicitors. The loss of their suspect was a very big deal and they all knew it, most of all Langton. They had had no reported sightings. The hunt continued.

Langton would conduct the interview with Edward Wickenham himself; Anna and Barolli would concentrate on Gail Harrington. There was no let-up for him: he had to go to the magistrates' court to find out whether his application to keep Gail and Edward in custody had been granted. It had: he had three extra days. That was the good news.

At two o'clock, Gail Harrington was brought into the interview room. As she and Edward had asked for

413

the same solicitor, there had been a delay while they agreed who should be represented by whom.

Gail was obviously in a distressed state and cried as Anna read her her rights. She was arrested for attempting to pervert the course of justice and obstructing the police. She kept on saying that it wasn't anything to do with her, she hadn't done anything wrong. She had been shown photographs of Louise and Sharon and denied knowing either; now she was shown the mortuary photographs and given details of the horrific murders. She was so shocked, she could hardly speak.

Just over one hour later, Anna returned to the Incident Room. Langton was still questioning Edward Wickenham. She asked that Langton be called out so she could update him on what they had gleaned from Gail Harrington. Langton was not too pleased, but he and Anna went into his office.

Anna said that it had taken only one hour and fifteen minutes before Gail had made a statement. When shown the jewellery taken from the cottage, she admitted it was hers, and when shown a photograph of the brooch, sent to the station from the American dealer in Chicago, she said it was part of a set that had included the necklace and earrings, given to her by Charles Wickenham. To specify the exact time and date that the jewellery had been in her possession was hard, as she couldn't recall exactly, but she did know that it was after she had returned from the health farm.

Under pressure from Anna, she also admitted that she had known Sharon Bilkin. She recalled that Charles Wickenham had taken her to choose her diamond engagement ring; her fiancé, his son, was not even with them. She had arranged to meet up with Charles after she had been to have her hair done; it was at the salon that she had met up with Sharon. Anna was able to pinpoint that this appointment was after the murder of Louise Pennel. Sharon had been having some fresh hair extensions done; she had recognised Gail and had come over and talked while Gail was waiting for her tint to take. Gail had told her that she was in London to choose her engagement ring. They exchanged phone numbers, although Gail said she had no intention of seeing Sharon again. That was the end of their conversation, as Gail was taken over to the basins to have her tint washed out.

Shortly before she was ready to leave, Charles Wickenham had walked into the salon, motioned to her that he was waiting and then walked out. As she paid the bill, Sharon was also ready to leave. She asked if that was who she was going to marry and Gail had said that he was her finance's father. Sharon had followed her out of the salon and seen her getting into Charles Wickenham's Jaguar.

Anna surmised that it must have been quite a shock for him, not only to see Louise Pennel's flatmate, but for her then to have come over to the car and say she was looking forward to seeing Gail again.

However, Gail had told Anna she had never seen or heard from Sharon again. Charles Wickenham had shown her the diamond-and-emerald jewellery as a taster of what she could be expecting when she married into the family, but when she was given the large white satin box, there was no brooch.

Langton closed his eyes. 'So what do you think happened?'

Anna hesitated. 'Well, I think Sharon smelt big money, for one; for two, she had to have recognised Charles Wickenham, and he must have known it.'

'But she was not seen at the Hall?'

'Gail denies she ever saw her again. She also denied ever seeing Louise Pennel at the house. I can have another go at her – up to you.'

'Mmm, okay.'

'We've not got a lot to hold her on. She says she had no idea where Charles Wickenham could have gone, perhaps Milan to his wife. She is very distressed and crying.'

'Let her cool off for a while; keep her until I've finished with Edward Wickenham.'

'How's that going?'

'So far fuck all, but let me get back in there.'

Anna nodded. She collected her notes and followed him out to the Incident Room. There was still no news on the whereabouts of Charles Wickenham.

Lewis approached Anna and told her that Gail had asked to speak with her. They had actually had a doctor to see her as she had become hysterical, and he had prescribed a light sedative.

'Why does she want to see me?'

'I dunno, but if you want to go down there, you'd better ask the Gov if it's okay.'

Langton was wary about any conversation with Gail not being monitored at this stage, and without a solicitor present. Then again, if she did have anything that could give them a clue to Wickenham's whereabouts, Anna should perhaps agree to see her, on the condition that she was accompanied by either Lewis or Barolli.

Anna waited outside Gail's cell as the duty sergeant unlocked the door. Anna glanced towards Barolli to stand aside for a moment.

'You wanted to see me,' she said quietly, standing in the doorway. She was shocked by how haggard and sickly Gail appeared. She was sitting on the edge of her bunk bed, her body was trembling and her eyes were red-rimmed from weeping.

'Do you know where Charles Wickenham is?'

Gail shook her head; she was biting her lower lip as the tears welled up.

'Do you perhaps have any idea where he may . . . ?'

'No, no I don't know,' Gail interrupted, and wiped her face with the back of her hand as the tears trickled down her cheeks. 'If I knew I would tell you, but I don't know, I really don't. I have no idea where he would be; I mean, he could be anywhere but I don't know, I swear to you. I have said this over and over again; I don't know where he is!'

Gail glanced towards Anna, and then hunched her shoulders as she saw Barolli standing behind her.

'You asked to see me, but you must understand that without a solicitor present . . .'

Again she was interrupted as Gail clasped her knees and bent forwards. 'I am telling you the truth! It must be obvious why. Because if he found out it was me, that I called and gave you his name . . .' She suddenly straightened up and began brushing her skirt with the flat of her hand. 'That's why I wanted to talk to you, because I want to know if it will help me. I called the police, I gave you his name. If I hadn't, you might never have even questioned him.'

417

'Yes, that is correct; I know your solicitor is aware of the assistance you gave by calling the station with the information.'

'So it will help me, won't it? You will testify that I did speak to you. I mean, I know I tried to remain anonymous, but that was because I was afraid of what he would do to me if he found out.'

'We are obviously aware of how important that call was, and I am sure it will be made very clear to the court.'

'I can't go to prison, you have to help me. I can't, I'd rather kill myself.' Gail stood and took a step closer to Anna who immediately stepped back. She then felt guilty as Gail held out her arms as if she needed to be comforted. 'Please help me.'

Anna turned to Barolli who indicated they should leave.

'I have been so frightened for so long; Edward is almost as afraid of his father as I am. He's not a bad person; if we'd been able to leave and live our own lives, we'd have been happy. Charles wouldn't let him go; whatever you might say Edward has done is because he was dominated by his father and forced into helping him . . .'

Anna gave the signal for the cell door to be closed. Gail seemed not to notice. Whether or not it was due to the sedatives, she seemed unable to stop talking; her voice had dropped to a monotone. Anna turned away, walking beside Barolli; they could hear Gail continuing from behind the cell door. 'He had to work so hard on the estate and he was paid a pittance. He loved his sisters and tried to protect them, especially Emily. He really cared about Emily. He wanted to have children and it was such a lovely place for a child to grow up with the horses and the woods . . .'

Anna headed up the stone stairs towards the Incident Room, Barolli behind her. As Gail's voice faded, so did Anna's compassion for her. Barolli felt nothing; no amount of horror had made Edward Wickenham man enough to stop his depraved father from committing heinous crimes against young women, even his own daughters. The fact that Gail had made the call to the Incident Room, giving them Charles Wickenham's name, would be used by her defence, and might be enough to persuade a judge not to give her a prison sentence. As it was, they still had to find Charles Wickenham and until they did, neither his daughter-in-law nor his son would be released.

The forensic team were still taking samples and collecting evidence from the cellar. The stable boys had been allowed to exercise the horses, but there were police officers surrounding the house and estate. Charles Wickenham had not shown.

Edward Wickenham constantly conferred with his solicitor in whispers. He then became morose and wouldn't answer any questions. Like his fiancée, he paled visibly when shown the horrific photographs of the victims. Asked about the contents of the cellar, he denied knowing what went on down there, as he was never allowed access. Asked about his own sister's abortion, he denied that it had ever happened. He persisted in saying that Emily was mentally unstable and that no one could believe a word she said. He became agitated when shown the sexual photographs of himself with his own step-mother, but said that she was willing and there was nothing illegal about what happened.

He continued to say over and over again that he did not understand why he was being held or why they were asking him about the two girls that he had never met.

'Because these two girls, as you describe them, were brutally murdered, Mr Wickenham.'

'I don't understand. I have nothing whatsoever to do with either of them.'

Langton pressed on; all the while, he knew he was jumping the gun. He was desperate to get the forensic evidence to back up his accusations. After two hours, he decided to end the interview. He still refused to release either Edward or Gail because of their relation-ship with his prime suspect, much to the anger of their solicitors.

It was eight o'clock when Langton called a briefing. He was looking very tired, as they all were. He said to call it quits for the night, and reconvene first thing in the morning.

The team started to pack up. Anna could sense the depression and just wanted to get home. They had issued a press release and photographs of Charles Wickenham, asking for the public to be on the alert. The Red Dahlia yet again featured in all the papers.

Anna let herself into her flat. They should have some forensic evidence by the morning; she knew they all had pinned their hopes on it confirming that they had the right man. That in itself was a farce: they might have named him, but they did not have him. Her phone rang just as she was heading into the bathroom.

'Anna, it's me, it's Dick Reynolds.'

She said nothing.

'Are you still there?'

Anna took a deep breath. 'I have nothing to say to you.'

'Come on, let's just forget the coffee in the face and have a talk. I mean, these new press releases!'

'Piss off!' she said and hung up.

The phone rang again. She picked it up and dropped it straight back onto the cradle – so much for his cheek, she thought.

Anna had a shower, did some clearing up and was putting some laundry on when her front door went. She physically jumped, and was glad of her double locks and safety chain.

She picked up the intercom. 'Hello?'

If it was Justine Wickenham, no way would she let her in. Then she thought it could be Dick Reynolds.

'Hi, it's me; it's James.'

She was surprised, but eager to talk to him, sure he must have some new evidence. She buzzed him in.

Anna unlocked the door and swung it open. He headed up the stairs; his feet sounded leaden. He appeared at the top of the stairs and she knew he was drunk.

'You'd better come in.'

'Thank you,' he said and walked slowly towards her. She could smell the alcohol; he looked as if he was about to crash out. He was unshaven and his eyes were red-

421

rimmed. As he passed her, he rested an arm heavily on her shoulder.

'Well, I fucked up, didn't I?'

She shut the door and almost keeled over as his dead weight leaning on her made her stumble. 'Come on through, I'll make some coffee.'

He staggered down her small hall into her bedroom. She followed and watched as he flopped down on her bed. She helped him off with his coat; he was like a child, holding one arm out, then the other.

'How could he fucking walk out; how could he just disappear? It's fucking madness!'

She folded his coat and placed it on a chair.

'I'm going to have to release his son, and that stupid bitch of a fiancée, you know that, don't you?'

'Yes, but we've not had the results in yet.'

'I know, I know, but if they come in, and we get to know what the fucker did, we are going to look like prize fucking idiots, because he walked out right under our noses. How in Christ's name did he do it? And you know who's gonna get the bollocking – me! Me: because I should have put more officers on the bastard, but I reckoned with his handcuffs on he wasn't going to try anything. Shit! Why didn't I bang him up and take him in when we knew it was him? I'll tell you why: because I wanted to prolong his agony. I wanted him to know we'd got him cornered. My vanity, my stupid fucking ego!'

'He had every right to remain at the house while we searched: be it a good or bad decision, everyone went along with it.'

Langton gave a lopsided grin, and then lifted his

hands in a helpless gesture of defeat. 'I've lost my way, Travis.'

'You mean lost your way home or in life?'

'Come here.'

'No, we've been there once already, and this is not the right time to go there again.'

'Jesus Christ, I just wanted to hold you.'

'I'm going to put some coffee on.'

'I really care about you, Travis; why don't you get into bed with me?'

'Let me get you some coffee.'

'Fuck the coffee. Come here; let me hold you.'

'No, let me get you some coffee.' She went into the kitchen. This was exactly what she had wanted: for him to want to hold her and make love to her, but not drunk and certainly not in the mood he was in. So she brewed up a pot of fresh coffee; by the time she carried it into the bedroom, he was out cold. She pulled off his shoes and left him to sleep it off. She would sleep on the sofa. It had been yet another long day, and the frustration of losing Wickenham had got to them all. She could only think that, just like the suspect in the original Black Dahlia case, their killer had escaped justice. It would be something that they would all have to face unless he was caught, and the more time that elapsed, the less likely it was they would find him.

Chapter Nineteen

DAY THIRTY-ONE

Anna woke; her neck was stiff from sleeping crunched up on the sofa. She could hear her shower running and smell bacon frying.

She went into the kitchen and turned down the grill as the bacon was getting charred.

'Morning,' he said as he wandered into the kitchen, a bath towel slung around his hips.

'Morning; how's your head?'

'Swollen, but I'm starving hungry.'

'Me too; let me take a shower.'

'Sure, I'll get the eggs on. Coffee?'

She could hardly believe it. He wasn't embarrassed in the slightest; seeing his clothes strewn all over her bedroom made her even more amazed at his cheek.

By the time she went into the kitchen, his eggs and bacon had been wolfed down and her plate was under the grill, about to crack any second.

'You eat while I get dressed.'

'Fine, thank you.'

He smiled, and then put his arms out; she went into them and held him tight. He smelt of her shampoo.

'Thank you for last night, Travis.'

'It was nothing.'

'Yes it was; I didn't know who else I could go to.'

'I'm glad you came to me.'

'Are you?'

'Yes.'

'Good.'

He cupped her face in his hands and kissed her, a light sweet kiss, and then he was gone.

'Oh Christ,' she muttered. She wasn't sure how to handle it and could hardly eat a thing. He came back in, dressed, all smiles.

'Right, get dressed. Let's get out of here.'

She gave a mute nod; it was as if it was his apartment. He even started washing up the dirty dishes.

She drove them to the station. His good mood had already started to evaporate.

'I'm sorry about last night,' he said, gruffly.

'That's okay; it's over and done with.'

'Yeah, but I have to start watching it, you know.'

'What?'

'Boozing; you know you're in trouble when you blank out. It's a sign.'

'Well, if you know you drink too much, then you know what to do.'

'Yeah, yeah; did I do anything I shouldn't have?'

She laughed.

'I'm serious; I don't even remember getting to your place.'

She kept on driving, not looking at him.

'Did we screw?'

'No, we did not!'

'Ah! Just wondered.'

'You passed out.'

'So I didn't manhandle you?'

'No, you were the perfect drunk.'

He gave her a sidelong glance, then rested his arm along the back of her seat, his hand on her neck. 'I love you, Travis.'

She smiled, wishing that he meant it.

He fell silent, his hand still touching the nape of her neck. 'What if we've lost him? It'll be a repeat performance of the Black Dahlia case, and my career will be in the shit.'

She shook her head, and he took it that she didn't like him touching her. 'Sorry,' he said quietly, and moved his hand.

'We'll find him,' she said.

In the Incident Room, things were moving fast. Forensics had worked their butts off and information was coming in at a rate of knots. The scientists were still at work and even more damning evidence was being found. Masked and rubber-suited scientists with breathing apparatus were wading through the filth. Charles Wickenham had tried to wash the evidence away, but by removing the drainage pipes and going down into the sewer system, they discovered even more clogged blood.

He must have thought he had destroyed everything that could implicate him, but scientific developments had him trapped. They were also beginning to piece together how he had made the notes sent to the journalists and Langton at the Richmond station. They discovered in his shredding machine old newspapers that he had cut the pasted letters from. They also discovered charred sections of a receipt made out by *The Times* for running an advert; a box number scrawled on the back of an envelope and thrown into a wastepaper basket was possibly the one he had used to advertise for a personal assistant. Meanwhile, the labs had begun testing Wickenham's computer and hard drive. They were able to ascertain that Wickenham logged onto the Black Dahlia website two hundred and fifty times.

They found many pictures cut from the Black Dahlia books, sickeningly placed in an innocent-looking family album. The entire quest by the author of *The Black Dahlia* to expose his father as the killer had derived from the discovery of two hitherto unknown photographs of Elizabeth Short at his house. One photograph showed Elizabeth Short with her eyes closed and her head tilted back like a death mask. In the other, she rested her cheek against her hand with a soft sweet smile to camera. Photographs of Louise and Sharon, identically posed, were placed alongside copies of those pictures, between the innocent photographs of his own children. As the evidence mounted, the fact their prime suspect was on the loose fuelled an undercurrent of panic.

Press releases continued to be issued and news bulletins showing Charles Wickenham's photograph were being pumped out. The public were asked for any information and warned that they should not confront Wickenham, but report directly to the police. No sightings of Wickenham had been confirmed at any airport, train station or bus depot. He still remained at large: it was Langton's nightmare.

Edward Wickenham's solicitor was demanding that

Langton either charge his client or release him. Gail Harrington's solicitor was on firmer ground, yet Langton insisted both remained in custody, as he was certain that if Wickenham was hiding out, he would contact his son for help. Justine was informed of the situation, though it was unnecessary: every newspaper headlined that the Red Dahlia killer was being hunted.

It was early afternoon when Langton had Edward Wickenham brought up from the cells to be questioned again. One night holed up at the station in a cold, stinking cell had made him tense with pent-up anger. His solicitor tried to placate him, but Edward was implying that if he didn't do something about the situation, he would replace him. Langton sat with Lewis, ignoring the tirade from the sweating young man, and read him his rights again. Yet again he displayed the sickening photographs of Louise Pennel and Sharon Bilkin.

Edward screeched that he had nothing to do with the victims' deaths; he had never met either of them. He was so agitated, spittle formed at the corners of his mouth as he repeated over and over again that he was innocent.

Langton leaned forward, keeping his voice low, forcing Edward to shut up and listen to him. He described the cellar and then went on to list the evidence they had now discovered: the clogged drains, blocked by coagulated blood that had been drained from Louise Pennel's body; the sickening array of saws and knives; the video pornography that also featured the prime suspect's son. His monologue began to take effect.

'We have two hundred tapes of sexual perversion; your own sisters feature, so I am certain we will get to you, Mr Wickenham. So why don't you try and help yourself?'

'I swear before God, I did not have anything to do with those girls, I did not!' He was starting to blubber, twisting his body as he attempted to extricate himself from any connection to the murders.

Edward Wickenham was returned to the cells a little later. He was to be charged with obstructing the police enquiries and with aiding and abetting the depositing of Louise Pennel's body and Sharon Bilkin's body. He would be taken before the magistrate.

Langton stood before the team to give them a brief rundown of the contents of the interview. Lewis had been shaken by what had taken place and was sitting quietly, checking over the interview tape.

Langton touched Louise Pennel's photograph. She had, as Anna had thought, answered an advert for the position of personal assistant to Charles Wickenham. According to his son, Charles had interviewed a number of young girls, and had shown him some of their photographs and CVs. Louise Pennel was the girl he chose. He had subsequently acted like some kind of Svengali, buying her expensive clothes and giving her gifts, mostly cash. She was a very willing partner to his sexual advances, but when he became more perverse he had encouraged her to take drugs, or he had slipped them into her drinks. His son said she was not seen at the Hall itself but would be driven direct to the barn. He swore that he had not had any kind of sexual relationship with her, as his father appeared to be very enamoured of her. It had confused him because, although she was very pretty, 'she was rather a common girl'. He had never heard of the Black Dahlia; his father had never mentioned the case. He was aware that at times his father would have sex sessions in the cellar, but this area was always off limits to him. Often his father, fuelled by drugs, would remain closeted down there for days and nights on end. It was always locked; only a few of his father's friends were ever allowed inside.

Edward Wickenham listed his father's friends. These were men that had the same perversions; they were all into sadomasochistic sex acts. His father had attempted to draw his son into his sadistic sexual activities but he wimped out, deliberately becoming too drunk to perform. Charles had been a brutal and sadistic father, laughing when discovered by his son screwing his young wife. She had been given Rohypnol and had not known what she was doing; she had found out when Charles Wickenham arranged for a family viewing of the tapes. She had been forced to watch herself having sex with her father-in-law and four of his friends. She committed suicide three weeks later.

Even when he talked about his own debauchery and the rape of his wife, Edward was not emotional; if anything, he had become very calm. He never looked at Langton or Lewis; he kept his head bowed, speaking softly. He had occasionally sipped water and a couple of times he had coughed, as if he needed to clear his throat, but it was as if he was talking about someone else.

Langton described to the team how Charles Wickenham had called his son and told him to come round to the house. It was after eleven at night. He said he needed some help in moving some equipment. Edward had helped put the body of Louise Pennel into the back of the Range Rover. He said he did not know what it was, but when he lifted one of the black plastic bags, he could feel beneath the plastic what appeared to be a human hand. They had both driven to his sister's flat in Richmond. Edward was told to wait and make some coffee. His sister was in Milan visiting her mother, but they had a key. He recalled it was about two in the morning when his father left in the Range Rover; he returned about half an hour later. That was all the time it took to dump the two halves of Louise Pennel's dismembered body.

The body bags, which his father had still had from when he worked in the army as a surgeon, were tossed into a skip as they returned home.

Langton broke for a coffee and sent out for some sandwiches, then continued. Sharon Bilkin had called Edward from the local railway station, asking to be picked up. She had met his fiancée, Gail, at a hairdressing salon. She had the audacity to tell him that she had come to see not him, but his father. He saw her knocking on the front door as he returned to the cottage. He was then called about two hours later to drop her back at the railway station. After his return, his father was standing on the drive, waiting to speak to him in a fury. He said that Gail was a stupid bitch because she had brought that trash into their lives and he was going to have to deal with it. Edward swore he had not seen Sharon again, but just under three weeks later, at two o'clock in the morning, his father turned up outside his cottage.

Sharon's body was already zipped into a bag and already in the Range Rover. His father said he had hurt his back and needed him to help. Edward had tried to refuse and Charles had slapped his face. Charles had threatened that if he did not do exactly as he was told, then he and his fiancée could get the hell out.

Edward said they had driven around until they came upon a field that they could drive into, via a slip road. He had helped carry her body across a dirt track and through a double-fenced gate. His father then instructed Edward to return to the Range Rover. Edward again swore that he did not see his father tipping the dead woman out of the body bag but he did recall that he was bending over her for a long time. Charles returned to the Range Rover and then started swearing when he found a reddish coat on the back seat. He returned to the field but was back after only a few minutes. They went home and, as if nothing had happened, Edward was told to get an early ride set up for the morning.

The room was quiet as Langton finished. He gave a long sigh. 'They rode out at seven and passed close to the field where her body was dumped because he, Edward Wickenham, recalled seeing the dark maroon coat!' He gave a shrug. 'That's it, ladies and gentlemen. I am going before the magistrates and I want bail refused. I'd say we'll get it.'

The headline of the final edition of the *Evening Standard* screamed out RED DAHLIA KILLER SOUGHT.

Anna was at her desk when her mobile rang: it was Richard Reynolds.

'Hi, how's things?'

Anna couldn't believe his audacity. He asked if there was any chance of an 'exclusive' interview with Justine Wickenham.

'Why are you asking me?'

'Well, considering you've lost your man, it looks to me as if you need all the help you can get in tracing him. If you could put me in touch with her, you never know what . . .'

'Piss off,' she snapped.

'That's the second time you've said that to me. It's not very nice.'

'It wasn't intended to be.'

'It's almost like the original case, isn't it?'

'I'm sorry?'

'The killer of the Black Dahlia was never caught, right?'

She suddenly had a gut feeling he might be taping her so she hung up. She was so concerned that she went to see Langton. His door was ajar. He was on the phone and gestured for her to come in.

'He's being taken to the magistrates' court. I suggest if you want to speak to him, you should contact his solicitor. Pardon?' He listened and then covered the phone with his hand. 'Justine Wickenham.' He returned to the call. 'I'll give you five minutes, but I will have to have someone present.' He listened again and then said that he'd wait. He put the phone down. 'She wants a short conversation with her brother! Something to do with her sister. It's a bit unorthodox but . . .'

Anna nodded and repeated the conversation she had just had with Reynolds.

'Listen, those two-faced bastards are like hornets outside the station. He was just trying it on, don't worry about it.'

He reached for his jacket. 'He's bloody right though, isn't he? And the longer Wickenham's at large, the less likely we are to track him down. We don't know if he had fake passports; we know he has money. I've contacted Special Branch to get flight manifests, so they're checking on potential foreign travel. We've also checked with his ex-wife in Milan, and he's not there. Christ only knows where he is.'

As Justine only lived a short distance from the station, she made an appearance five minutes later. Anna was with Langton in the station reception. Justine gave a brief nod to Anna and then showed them a document.

'I want to get my brother's signature; it's giving me the right to see if I can get Emily home. I need to be there to look after the horses. Old Mrs Hedges is in a bit of a state.'

Anna was surprised at her calmness; she made no mention of the hunt for her father.

'Don't you think under the circumstances that taking Emily there wouldn't be that good an idea?'

Justine gave a sardonic smile. 'Well, our father's not going to be there, is he? So she won't have to worry.'

Langton checked his watch, and then stared at Justine. 'Do you know where he is?'

'No.'

'Do you have any idea where he might be?'

'No, but I told her.' She looked at Anna. 'I told you, didn't I? I said you'd never get him and I was right.'

Both Langton and Anna were present when Justine confronted her brother. Langton did not want there to be any opportunity for another Wickenham to escape. He was hardly able to look at her, his face was shiny with sweat, and he stank of body odour.

'Sign in two places.' Justine pointed calmly, and he dutifully signed.

'Gail was released from custody. Did she return to the house?'

Justine checked over his signature and folded the papers. 'Mrs Hedges said her aunt or someone came to collect her from the cottage. She took a load of suitcases; it didn't look as if she was intending to come back.'

'Did she leave a forwarding address?' Langton asked quickly. 'We'll need it when we go to trial.'

'Yes, yes,' snapped Justine impatiently.

Justine stood up and slipped the strap of her handbag over her shoulder. She thanked Langton, then walked out without a backward glance to her dejected brother as he broke down sobbing. Fifteen minutes later, with a blanket over his head, he was led out of the station and into the wagon for his appearance at court. There were, as Langton had said, numerous reporters and cameras waiting outside the station. The cameras flashed as they drove out.

Edward Wickenham was charged with perverting the course of justice and being an accessory to murder. He said only his name and address and that he would plead not guilty. Langton asked that no bail be granted, as his father was being hunted and he felt that Wickenham could be cajoled into helping him. Bail was refused and Edward Wickenham, again covered in a blanket, was taken to Brixton prison.

It was late when Langton was informed that forensics would require still more time at the Hall. The police still had no sighting of Charles Wickenham. Langton had to give yet another press statement, asking the public for every assistance: the fact Wickenham had escaped was still headlined on all the TV news bulletins.

Anna returned home and went to bed early, feeling depressed and tired out. She was well aware that, despite all their hard work, losing Wickenham would have severe repercussions. She had also half hoped that Langton would maybe say something about wanting to see her.

DAY THIRTY-TWO

The following morning, forensic tests identified blood, hair and skin samples from the Hall as belonging to Louise Pennel. Hair and semen stains had been tested from the plastic-covered operating table which also gave a DNA match for Sharon Bilkin. There were five other blood samples of unknown origin.

Langton stood with his hands stuffed into his pockets as Lewis gave him the update.

'Jesus Christ, how many women did that bastard kill down there?'

Anna watched him taking in all the new evidence. If Charles Wickenham had not escaped, it would have been a very jubilant morning; as it was, depression hung in the air. Langton tried to make a joke of it, saying that they now had enough to arrest him ten times over. He held up a cartoon from the *Daily Mail*, showing loads of uniformed police officers and a pair of empty hand-cuffs, the suspect crawling through their legs.

Langton had arranged for Anna and Lewis to accompany him back to the Hall, as the forensics chief was ready to pack up: he needed to make out the official report and have it signed off by Langton. The three drove in silence; it was pointless making light conversation as there was nothing light about what they would have to face. The press had surrounded their car as they drove out from the station car park. Langton had wound down his window and told them that the police were not looking for any other suspect. He then wound his window back up and muttered, 'We just can't fucking find him.'

All three tensed as they drove past the field where Sharon's body had been discovered. The flapping police cordons were now even more tattered. Langton pointed to a small hill beyond the field, ringed with elm trees.

'Bastard rode out with his son. He must have got a kick out of seeing her lying there, with Louise Pennel's coat draped over her naked body!'

The atmosphere remained strained as they drove into the long winding lane that led to Mayerling Hall's pathway; there were now hundreds of markers where the teams had searched and signalled clearance.

Langton got out of the car and winced, his long legs had cramped up. More yellow crime scene markers were all over the driveway; two white forensic vans being loaded up with equipment. Arc lamps were being carried out from the barn to be dismantled and packed up. Walking out of the front door was a tall, grizzle-haired scientist, John McDonald. He wore a tweed suit with a striped shirt and bright red braces. He carried his jacket in one hand and a large clipboard in the other.

Anna watched as Langton shook his hand; they conferred for a few moments before Langton introduced Anna and Lewis. McDonald had been coordinating the forensic teams and listing their findings as they were sent to the lab; he was eager to walk Langton through the crime scene results. He said that, although they wouldn't be ready to leave the premises for some considerable time, they had designated 'signed off' areas that had been cleared. This meant that the officers could go through some parts of the house and grounds without protective suits. He had been there almost day and night for three consecutive days; some of his team had been staying at a local hotel.

They all stood in the drawing room as McDonald listed the work that was still being carried out at the lab. 'We have your suspect's Range Rover being dismantled for evidence and his Jaguar; both are with a team in London.' In a rather tired voice, he ran through the items that had been taken and the evidence to date. 'Eight saws of various sizes, two electric; ten surgical knives; eight scalpels; one operating table; handcuffs; leg irons; various chains; rubber suits; six black body bags, army issue; two bottles of morphine; six large containers of acid; two acid baths; gynaecological equipment; stirrups . . .'

Anna sat down. The list was endless. McDonald, in his clipped, bored tone, continued to elaborate on the amount of drugs, from cocaine to heroin via speed and two hundred tabs of ecstasy; he even joked about the large quantity of Viagra.

Langton was the next one to take a seat, as McDonald said they had positive results from only half the blood samples taken. He continued checking off his list. 'White gowns, masks, and white rubber Wellington boots, three pairs!' Blood samples had been traced on the heel and sole of two pairs.

It had been a very unpleasant task for his officers, he said. Blood had blocked the drainage system from the cellar to the main sewer pipe, so they had been squelching around in human faeces and coagulated blood.

Lewis parked himself on the arm of the wing-backed chair that Charles Wickenham had sat in to smoke his cigar.

One arm of the sofa had a bloodstain where Ed Harris, the officer guarding Wickenham, had fallen. He had been struck with a solid silver candlestick; the edge of the base had left a deep laceration to the right side of his skull and he had required eight stitches. He had, however, been released from hospital. When he was questioned about what exactly had happened, he could hardly recall how he had been attacked. Wickenham had asked for a drink of water; when Harris turned to pick up the jug, he was knocked unconscious. Harris swore that he had only turned away from Wickenham for a few seconds. How many was immaterial: he had allowed their killer to walk out and escape.

McDonald continued, listing the clothes they had removed to test for fibre matches: shoes, slippers, sweaters, suits, riding habits, riding boots. Every item had to be checked and signed out in the event it would be used as evidence at a trial.

Finally, McDonald turned over his last sheet, and then tapped his board with his pen. 'Well, I'd say you've got enough to put your man away for a very long time. We'll be working at the lab for weeks to come. Maybe in that time, you'll have picked him up!'

McDonald checked his watch, then walked over to

the fireplace. He gestured expansively to the brick overlay and the massive slab of wood that acted as a mantel. 'The SOCO teams were busy; we had, as you know, the plans of the house, barn, stables, outhouses and the thatched cottage. They checked over the two listed hiding holes and they found a third one, behind some panelling in the dining room: quite a find, and historically very interesting. The families would hold secret masses; if it was discovered their priests were holding services, they would be hung, drawn and quartered for an act of treason, not to mention losing their property. These hiding places were very well disguised and, I have to say, very intriguing.'

For the first time since they had arrived, McDonald was energised. The discovery of the extra hidden chamber had created a lot of interest; it would be examined by the local historical society.

'You think that Wickenham could have hidden out in one of these chambers?' Langton asked.

'To be honest, we considered it, but they are not in this section of the house; this wing is part of an extension built a couple of hundred years after the original house.' McDonald checked his watch, then suggested they follow him down to the cellar. 'Just to clarify what I think this monster got up to.'

They went from the lounge into the hallway; passing the suit of armour, Lewis flicked up its visor and grinned. 'Just checking!'

It clanged back into place.

'That's a fake,' McDonald said, rather disgustedly.

They went into the laundry room. All the machines had been removed and were stacked outside the small room. The partition was open, and as they moved down the steps, McDonald pointed out how well soundproofed the chamber would have been. 'We reckon these walls must be about a foot and a half in width, with hard-board casing which was covered in two inches of thick cement.'

The stripped cellar smelt of disinfectant. Some of the stone flags had been raised, others removed. There were empty hooks where the various equipment had been hung up. 'Down here he could do his dirty tricks; he was even filming himself: there was a very good camera and video equipment. We've literally hundreds of videos; you need a very strong stomach to watch them.'

They were shown the dismantled sink and drainpipes, and McDonald described how they forensic team had unclogged the drains. 'Poor chaps were masked up for hours; it was obviously where he had drained your victims' body fluids. We know now from the DNA results that much of the blood was Louise Pennel's.'

They stood silently as McDonald lifted a grid to show them the ventilation shaft. It felt like they had been down there for a very long time; as they returned into the hallway, Anna checked her watch. It had only been twenty minutes, but it was such a sickening mono-logue, that they were all desperate to get out into the fresh air.

McDonald spent some time with Langton checking over the lists as Anna and Lewis walked round to the front of the house. She looked up at the gables and the latticed windows, and stepped back onto the grass verge. The disgusting nature of what had been carried out inside this elegant Tudor house made Anna shudder.

Lewis was standing on one of the steps, staring at the manicured lawns and flowerbeds, the clipped hedges and statues. 'How the hell did he do it? I mean, for Christ's sake, the place was swarming with SOCO teams, forensics teams and he just fucking walks out and disappears? How could they not have noticed?'

'I suppose with what was going on, you never know, he could have picked up one of their white paper suits, pulled a hood up and he was just one of them.'

'Yeah, I guess so; they did leave a big box of them at the front door.'

Langton came out to join them and they went over to the barn and the stables, McDonald giving yet another lengthy monologue on what they had removed. The sewer pipes had been dug up and were visible in some areas. It would take a lot of work to make sure everything was returned to how it had been found.

It was after five when McDonald left them to return to London. He had become enthusiastic again when he had shown them the priest holes; they were, as he said, only in the oldest section of the house. One was behind a large chimney; it must have been hideous, as it was such a small airless space. The second was at one end of what was now used as an extra dining room. The panelling slid back to reveal the hidden room: it had been filled with old boxes and broken picture frames. The third one that had not been listed was at the opposite end, close to the gabled windows.

Langton spent some considerable time making sure he had all the details and then he thanked McDonald who took off in an old Range Rover that was caked in mud.

Anna was standing by their patrol car when Justine rounded the driveway from the stables. She was wearing jodhpurs and carrying a riding hat. She glanced towards Anna, raising her crop in acknowledgement. 'Do you know how long it will be before they all clear out and get the place back into order?'

'No, I don't.'

'It's dangerous, you know, leaving those pipes and trenches. If we get a heavy rain, it'll be a bloody river of mud and sewage.'

'Have you moved back in?'

'Yes, I'm taking over the stables. We may go and live in the cottage: we've been told that has been cleared, but there's a whole load of areas we are not allowed to go into.'

'We?'

'Yes, my sister's here.'

'How is she?'

'Well, still very dodgy upstairs, but she'll be okay; she's started to eat, thank God!'

Justine went into the house after scraping her boots on the iron grid. Anna waited a few moments and then followed.

As she walked down the hall, she heard gales of laughter. She paused, listening, then continued into the kitchen.

Mrs Hedges was at the Aga with a pan of soup; the long pine table was set for three people. Above the Aga there was an old pulley with rope attached to wooden slats, where some clothes were drying. Emily was trying to haul them up and fasten the rope to a hook on the wall; she laughed as she tried to disentangle herself from a pillowcase that had fallen from the slats onto her head. Mrs Hedges made a grab at the rope to help Emily, who was fooling around as one item after another dropped from the rails.

'I said let me do it, but you wouldn't listen. Now look, we've got a pair of knickers in the soup!'

Justine tickled Emily, who collapsed into a chair as Mrs Hedges hauled up the pulley and tied the rope.

They all froze as Anna appeared in the doorway. 'Just to say we're about to leave.'

Mrs Hedges returned to her soup, and Emily curled up in a big old motheaten easy chair close to the fireplace.

'How are you, Emily?'

'Fine, thank you.'

Justine washed her hands at the sink and then turned, drying them on an old tea towel. She gave a sly glance to Emily, and then tossed the towel aside. 'Well, I was right, wasn't I? You never did get him. I told you, didn't I?'

Emily lowered her head and put one hand over her mouth. Anna thought she was about to cry.

'Goodbye then,' Anna said. As she turned, she caught Justine giving an admonishing look to her sister.

'Not funny, Em. It's not funny at all!'

Langton was sitting in the front seat of the car, impatient to leave. Lewis was in the back, the passenger door open for Anna to get in beside him.

'I've just been in the kitchen. Emily's there.'

Langton grunted as she slammed the door shut. They drove round the horseshoe drive and headed down the path towards the overhanging trees.

'They were laughing and joking; well, Emily was laughing.'

They fell silent as they continued the drive. Suddenly Langton hit the dashboard. 'Stop the car!' He turned back to Anna. 'Say that again?'

'Say what?'

'You said they were laughing and joking, right?'

'Yes.'

'What else?'

'Well, Justine said that she had told me we would never catch him, and Emily started to giggle.'

Langton took out a cigarette and tapped it on the dashboard. 'Now, I may be nuts, but that bastard scared the hell out of those girls, right?'

'Yes; well, Emily more so than Justine.'

'And Justine brings Emily back knowing that their father has escaped, right?'

'Yes.'

'Brings her back to the place it all happened.'

'Well, it's her home.'

'No: she hadn't been living there; she said she would never live there, that she hated him, yes? Yes?'

'Yes!'

'Okay: one, they don't know where he is, right? I mean, he could walk back in.'

'Yes, but the consensus is he's long gone.'

'But they found his passport, so that means he could still be in the UK; that he intends to use the girls to help get him abroad, whatever, yes?'

Anna shrugged. 'I suppose so, but he also could have had other passports, and we know he's rich as Croesus.'

Langton swivelled round to face them both. 'You said

they were laughing. Emily, a child he molested, tortured and Christ knows what else when he operated on her?'

Lewis was staring out of the car window.

'It doesn't make sense to me; does it make sense to you?'

'What exactly?' Lewis said, yawning.

'That they are sitting in that house, cooking up dinner, laughing and joking!'

Anna glanced at the bemused Lewis and back to Langton. 'They have to fucking know something we don't!'

'Like where he is?' Lewis asked.

'Exactly; he has to have made contact.'

'You think he might have done a deal with Justine? She's taken over the place, and she's running the stables. I mean, she told me that was what she had always wanted, to run her own stables.' Anna was picking up on Langton's energy. 'She was also asking me about when all the clearing-up would be done. Do we still have the place under surveillance?'

'No, we pulled it off. Christ, we had how many SOCO officers, not to mention the bloody Territorial Support Group, but we'll start it up again.'

Anna was still not one hundred per cent sure. She looked to see if Lewis was agreeing with Langton.

'And he's somewhere that they feel safe enough about moving back into the house? Is that what you think?' Lewis asked.

Langton took a deep breath. 'Exactly; now, we can go back in and put the frighteners on them, or we wait for him to make contact. If I was in his position, with the amount of press circulating . . . He's not going to hang around or make himself obvious, is he?' Langton patted their driver's shoulder. 'Let's go back; this time, I'll talk to them.'

The patrol car pulled a U-turn round the gravelled horseshoe drive.

Langton opened his car door. 'In the meantime, get onto the Incident Room; I want the surveillance team back in place round the clock. I want their phone tapped; book us into the hotel the forensic guys were staying at.'

'For tonight?' Lewis asked.

'For as long as this is going to take.' He slammed the door hard and headed towards the front door of the house. They saw him pull the old bell rope and also ring the doorbell.

'You think he's right, Anna?' Lewis asked

'I don't know, but anything is worth a try.'

Justine opened the front door.

'Hi, just to say we're out of here.' Langton smiled.

'I thought you'd already gone.'

'Nope, we just finished up in the barn.'

'Really?'

'I'll be getting people back to make sure any damage done to the property is repaired. Could be a couple of days. I'm sorry for any inconvenience; the equipment left in the barn will be collected sometime tomorrow.'

'Thank you.'

Langton stepped closer. 'If your father should make contact . . .'

'If he does, I'll make sure you know about it.'

'Has he tried to?'

'Tried to what?' Justine asked.

'If you know where he is, if you have any idea where he is, then you can call me on this number.' He handed her his card.

She took it and glanced down, then back to him. 'Thank you. Goodnight.'

Langton returned to the car. 'Well, now we wait.'

'It will take at least two hours for a surveillance team to get hooked up again,' said Lewis. 'We already had a phone tap, so that's organised. The hotel have two vacancies only: two double rooms.'

'I'm in with you, am I?' Langton shot a sly glance at Anna.

She was about to blush when Lewis laughed and did a mincing lisp. 'Yeah, just the two of us, Gov, but we've got an ensuite!'

The hotel was small but very accommodating, probably because they had not had so many customers in such quick succession for a long time. As they had no luggage, Langton suggested they have a quick wash and brush-up, then go and grab something to eat.

There was a communal bathroom on Anna's floor and she decided to have a shower. The door was rapped; Lewis said impatiently that they were across the road at the pub and for her to join them there.

By the time Anna had got dressed again, she didn't feel like going over to the pub. She asked the landlady if she could make her a sandwich and a pot of tea. She took out her laptop and began to write up her report. It had been three days and three nights since Wickenham had escaped. If he had, as they suspected, merely picked

up one of the white forensic suits and walked out undetected, that would have given him no time to make plans
for leaving the country. Had he simply disappeared, like
Lord Lucan, or had he been helped by one or more of
his close friends?

Anna brought up the plans of the Wickenham estate
on her laptop. She tried to place herself in his shoes.
She stared at the small screen: to walk from the drawing
room into the hall and take a left turn to the front door
meant that he would have had to pass a lot of people.
If he then walked outside and stopped to pick up a
paper suit, where did he put it on? Wouldn't someone
have seen him? If he had taken the other route, that
would mean taking a right turn at the suit of armour,
past the dining hall and then out into the corridor
leading to the kitchen. If Wickenham had gone that way,
he would have had to pass the narrow servants' staircase
that was next to the laundry room. This area would have
been heaving with officers. How could he have bypassed
them all to enter the kitchen and escape via the back
door? Anna was certain that this was impossible, so if
he walked out it would have had to be via the front
door.

She was interrupted by the landlady who had, as
requested, made some ham sandwiches and a pot of tea.
She placed the tray down, and Anna thanked her
profusely. The landlady was about to walk out when she
paused at the door.

'Everyone has been talking about what has been going
on. It's been hard not to, especially here with every room
taken by . . . forensic officers, I think they were.'

'Yes, they stayed here.'

'I don't usually serve meals, but a few times I made up a stew as they were working such late hours and the restaurants around here don't stay open after ten, well, not in the week. There's a chip shop but that closes early as well.'

Anna didn't respond; she wanted to get back to her work.

'I never knew him; he never came here, well, this wouldn't be a place for him, but everyone knew about that family. His daughters rode with my niece, she was quite friendly with them; she used to muck out and help groom their horses, but then something happened, and she said that Emily, the youngest, was sick. Course, they went off to boarding school and she went to the local comprehensive, so she hasn't seen them for years, She works in the local library.'

'Thank you very much for the tea.'

'Oh, that's all right. Their house is historically well known; the National Trust did some work there. It would have been very good for the locals if it had been opened to the public. The family who had owned it for generations before the Wickenhams lost their only son in the last war. They had a little daughter; she climbed into one of those priest holes and I think she died, but this was all before I even came here. They sold it to Charles Wickenham's father in the sixties, I think. In the old days, they would open up the gardens for a summer fête. When Wickenham took it over, he let it go badly. It was a shame, because it really was a very beautiful example of Tudor architecture; we all knew when his son inherited the place he was doing extensions and conversions that he shouldn't have been allowed to do; God forbid, if you put up a greenhouse without the council's permission here, but he used to get away with murder.'

Realising that what she had said was, at best, unfortunate, she left the room, rather embarrassed, to Anna's relief.

She had just poured herself a cup of tea when there was a light tap on her door. The landlady was back, this time with a folder with pictures of the Hall as it had been.

'Mr McDonald was very interested in these: they show the Hall before it had the extensions. You can see how over the centuries the house was rebuilt.'

'Thank you very much; I'd like to look over them.'

'My pleasure. It's one of the oldest houses in this area.'

This time, Anna got up to see the landlady to the door to make it obvious she wanted her to leave. She picked up a ham sandwich and stood flicking through the folder. Some of the photographs had a library stamp on them; from her niece, no doubt. Anna sat down and looked over them. After a while, she went online with her Bluetooth connection and tried to find more details.

It was after ten when she walked over to the pub; Langton and Lewis were obviously quite a few drinks the worse for wear. The table was littered with peanuts and empty crisp packets.

Langton made a show of looking at his watch. 'You took a long bloody bath.'

'I want to show you something.' She sat down. 'I've been logging onto some national heritage websites.' Anna told them about the over-helpful landlady, and then took a deep breath. 'Okay, there are four famous houses all built around the same period: Bucklebury Hall,

Thatchery Manor, but the one that really interested me is called Harrington Hall. It's famous because of the amount of priest holes that have been discovered there; two in the past couple of years! They've found seven in all and they believe there could be more.'

Langton said nothing, peering into the bottom of a crisp packet. He blew into it and burst the bag, sending crumbs flying everywhere. 'Can you get to the point of this historical tour, Travis?'

'The previous owners of Mayerling Hall were direct descendants of the original owners. The son died in the war – I need to find out a bit more – but they also had a daughter, she got inside one of these chambers and died. Anyway, the family sold up, and Wickenham's father bought it in the sixties.'

'Look, thanks for the history lesson, Travis, but is this leading us anywhere?' Langton picked up another packet of crisps.

'Yes; well, I think it is, if you just let me finish.'

'Do you want a drink?' It was Lewis.

'No, thank you.'

'I'll have another scotch,' Langton said.

Lewis got up and headed to the bar. It was a real olde worlde pub, with very few customers.

'Bloody chip shop was closed,' Langton said, as he finished his crisps and crumpled the packet. 'Chinese was closing and wouldn't serve us.'

Anna took a deep breath. 'I don't think he left the house.'

Langton looked at her; before he could say anything, Lewis returned with their drinks.

'Say that again, Travis.'

452

'I said, I do not think Wickenham ever left the house.'

Langton tilted his glass in his hand.

'I think it would be impossible for him to have walked out the front door, picked up a paper suit wearing handcuffs—'

'Yes, yes, get on with it; we've discussed all this.'

'I think there could be another hiding place, one we didn't find. I mean, they found one that had not been discovered before; maybe there could be another one. If they are still finding these priest holes in the Harrington Hall mansion, why not at Wickenham's?'

Lewis looked at Langton as he downed his scotch.

'If he did have a hiding place, it would have to be somewhere between the hall, the old servants' staircase and the kitchen.'

'So, let me get this right: are you saying he is still in the house?'

Anna shrugged. 'I don't know, maybe; he could have escaped while the work was going on.'

'You think his daughters know?'

'Well, this is where I come unstuck, because as you rightly said, they're not acting as if they're scared he's around.' She trailed off. 'It was just a thought.'

Lewis stood up and yawned. 'I'm knackered.'

'Sit down,' Langton snapped. 'Okay, Travis: what if you are right?'

'Well, we have only focused on his daughters, but there is someone else in the house as well: the old housekeeper. Her bedroom is above that old staircase. What if she is the one that knows where he is? Wickenham has money, but we have had no movement in any of his bank accounts; she told me she had savings, years of them. She has lived there for years, rent free, so she must have accrued a considerable amount of money. Maybe she helped him escape and gave him the money to do it?'

Anna kept talking as they crossed the road together. 'Justine said she got a call from Mrs Hedges. Remember, when she came over to the station to get her brother to sign documents to release Emily; could she have told her then?'

'Told her what exactly?'

'That it was safe, maybe? That their father would not be coming back? She keeps saying that we would never arrest him.'

Langton hooked his arm around her shoulders. 'Good on you, Travis; that little brain always ticking over.'

She shrugged away from him. 'What if I am right?'

'First thing tomorrow, we'll find out!'

'Why not start now?' Anna suggested. Langton gave her a lopsided smirk.

'Because after two packets of peanuts and Christ knows how many bloody crisps, I've had too much to drink to hardly walk straight!'

Chapter Twenty

Anna hated not having any toothpaste or cleanser, but washed her face and patted it dry. She would have no make-up for the morning either! Her clothes were crumpled, but she'd washed her knickers in the sink and left them over a radiator. She got into bed naked and pulled up the flannelette sheets; the pillowslip felt starched.

She could hear Lewis snoring in the room downstairs and Langton pacing up and down; everything Anna had said was going round and round in his head.

Anna couldn't sleep; the sheets made her itch. She got up and poured herself a glass of water from a decanter that resembled a specimen jar.

There was a light tap on her door.

After a moment, she heard Langton whisper, 'Are you awake? Anna? It's me.'

Anna hesitated, then wrapped the sheet around her and opened the door.

'I've just had a cold shower, they obviously turn off the hot water early.' He was wearing his shirt and a towel wrapped around his waist. 'Can I come in?'

She nodded and opened the door wider.

'Lewis sounds like a steam engine. I couldn't sleep.'

'Nor could I. I've got no drink; I can't offer you anything.'

'Can't you?'

'Oh, please.'

'Sorry, my attempt at a joke; obviously failed miserably.'

He sat on the edge of her bed; she sat in a chair by the window.

'So what do you want?' said Anna.

'Me?'

'Yes, you. Do you want to talk about the case?'

'I don't.'

'If you want me to go to bed with you, I don't think this is the right time or place.'

He patted the bedcover. 'Seems okay to me.'

'Well, not to me; for one, you've been drinking and for two, I just don't think . . .'

'Always thinking,' he interrupted. 'Do you ever do something without those brain cells working overtime?'

She turned away.

'Come here.' He held out his hand. 'For Chrissakes, Anna what do you want?'

'Listen, I am not someone who has a random one-night stand in a hotel.'

'But we've been to bed before.'

'You think I don't know that? I don't want to be just a convenient screw. Like you said, we've already been there.'

'Yeah I know; you didn't want it to go any further, so what's the big deal?'

'Maybe I want more.'

'Are you saying there is more?'

456

She shook her head. 'Why are you doing this to me?'

'Anna, what am I doing? I want to go to bed with you, hold you, make love to you.'

'Because Lewis is snoring and you can't sleep downstairs in his room?'

He got up and walked towards her. 'What if I was to tell you that for weeks, since we first started this case, I have wanted . . .'

She interrupted. 'You mean Professor Marshe didn't work out?'

'What?'

'Come on! You were all over her like a rash!'

'You mean you never sussed?'

'Sussed what?'

'She's gay. She's having a scene with the Commander.'

Anna was stunned; she said nothing.

'So, do we get into bed, or do I go back to Lewis and cuddle up next to him?'

Anna remained in her chair and he came closer.

'Anna, if you don't want to have sex, that's okay by me, I just want to hold you close.'

'Go back to your room. We both need to recharge our batteries and be ready for the morning.'

He turned and headed back to the door and had it half open when he turned to face her. 'If what you want is some kind of long-term commitment, then I can't give you that.'

'I know, but I can't just be a casual lay, because I really care about you. In fact, I think I might be in love with you, so you see this is far from easy.'

'In love with me?'

'Yes.'

'Well that kind of changes things, doesn't it? See you in the morning, Travis.'

She sat in the chair and wanted to cry. If he had touched her, kissed her, she would not have been able to say no. She could think of nothing that she wanted more than to have his body next to hers, flannelette sheets or not.

DAY THIRTY-THREE

Langton wolfed down his breakfast without so much as glancing at her. She wondered if he had been more drunk than she thought and he'd even forgotten coming to her room.

The local police had made contact, saying there had been no movement in or out of the Hall's main gates. They had positioned a car at the rear, and had done a drive round at intervals during the night. One car was still in position some distance down the lane; when the surveillance team arrived, they would take over.

'If, as Travis suspects, Wickenham was holed up at the Hall and then had time to get the hell out, this is just a waste of time. If, on the other hand, we grill all three of them — that's Emily, Justine and the old housekeeper — and put some pressure on them to cough up exactly what might or might not have happened, we might get a result. So far, there has still been no sighting of Wickenham. Barolli and the team have questioned everyone associated with him. No one's admitting to having seen him or having any contact with him and, let me tell you, we really put the pressure on them with those photographs. The whole bunch were shitting themselves that their part in his perverted parties would be released to the press.'

He spoke between mouthfuls of egg and bacon, buttering his toast and gulping down one cup of coffee after the next.

Lewis said nothing. He wasn't eating, but consuming a lot of coffee and paracetamol tablets.

Langton wiped his plate clean and then pushed it aside. 'I've also asked Barolli to comb through back issues of any newspapers that might give us more details about the family who previously owned the place. But it was a long time ago, so we may not get a result.' He checked his watch and phoned to see if their driver had returned to take them back to the Hall. 'Okay, he'll be out front in ten minutes, so I'll go and settle the bill and see you out there.' He pushed back his chair, wiped his face with his napkin and strode out.

'I don't bloody know how he does it,' said Lewis, disgruntled. 'He had a right skinful last night but you'd never know it this morning. He's been pacing up and down, making one call after another.'

Anna spread some marmalade over her toast; she had hardly touched her eggs and bacon. 'He's got me all nervous. I mean, it was just a thought.'

'Yeah, my thoughts exactly, but let's face it, we might as well have a go. I mean, we've bugger all else on tracing the son of a bitch.'

Langton reappeared. 'Car's here, let's go!'

Anna took a last sip of her coffee and picked up her toast.

They drove in silence towards Mayerling Hall. Midway down the lane, they saw a local squad car and stopped. Langton got out and had a conversation with the driver.

'Still no movement, nobody has been near the place or left it!'

They drew up outside the house. Langton checked his watch.

'Okay, this is how we work it: we each take one of them. Separated, we might get something. Let's go!'

They were about to head towards the front door when Langton gestured that they should go via the back way, and enter through the kitchen. They made as little noise as possible as they headed down the gravel path through the gate into the back kitchen garden.

Langton paused outside the door. They could hear someone singing; it sounded like Justine. Langton rapped sharply on the door and tried the handle: it opened.

Justine was carrying a packet of cornflakes to the table; Emily had a bottle of milk in her hand; Mrs Hedges was pouring boiling water into a teapot: they all turned in surprise. Emily dropped the milk bottle in shock. It smashed on the tiled floor.

'Morning, sorry if we surprised you.'

Justine banged down the packet of cornflakes and went to get a cloth from the sink. Emily looked at her fearfully.

'It's okay, don't worry; we've got another pint. Just pick up the bottle, will you? Mind you don't cut yourself. Put it on the draining board.'

Emily did so, and then Justine tossed down a wet cloth onto the floor.

'We would like to interview you.'

'What about now?' Justine said, rinsing out the milk-soaked cloth.

'Could you please accompany Detective Inspector Lewis, Mrs Hedges?'

'Me?'

'Yes, this shouldn't take long; if Emily would like to go with Detective Travis, I'll stay here and talk to you, Justine.'

Justine threw the cloth into the sink. 'No way. You want to talk to any of us, then we want a solicitor present. You can't just barge in here.'

''Fraid we can, Miss Wickenham, we still have the valid search warrants: so, we can do this quickly and be gone, up to you, or we can take you into the station and do it there. Mrs Hedges, would you mind?'

'Stay where you are! They are just trying it on. I know the law. I have to go and see to the horses.'

'You will have to wait.'

'No I won't.' Justine faced them, hands on her hips.

'Yes you will. Now, if you want to call someone out to be with you, then go ahead, we can wait.' Langton knew they had only search warrants for one visit, so he was bluffing. It paid off.

'What do you want to know?' Justine said.

'We just need to ask some questions; it shouldn't take long.'

'Questions about what? We've been interviewed over and over again, and there is nothing else we can tell you. We don't know where he is: he has not made contact with any of us. Is that what it's about?'

'Why don't you call your solicitor, if that is what you want?' Langton said and pulled out a chair to sit down.

'It's only bloody nine o'clock!' Justine said furiously.

Langton turned to Anna and Lewis and shrugged. 'We'll just sit here and wait.'

Justine glared at them and sat down. 'We are not going anywhere. Go ahead: ask what you want to know and then leave us in peace.'

'Who contacted you before you came into the police station to get your brother to sign?'

'Mrs Hedges: she called to say that there was a ruddy army traipsing all over the house looking for Dad.'

'So you called Justine, Mrs Hedges, to say what?'

'Just what Justine said. I thought she should know about what was happening.'

'And that was enough for you to arrange to bring Emily home?'

Justine took over again. 'Yes, Mrs Hedges said Father was under arrest, and that Edward had been taken into custody. I mean, is this necessary? You met me there. You were with me when I spoke to Edward. We've been over all this!'

'Yes I know that, but why did you think that it would be safe to bring Emily back home?'

'It's bloody obvious, isn't it? You had arrested Daddy!'

'But what if we had not found enough evidence to charge him?'

'It was fucking obvious that you had!'

'Please don't swear, Miss Wickenham. If you knew there was evidence here that would warrant the arrest of your father, your pleading ignorance of what happened here was a lie.'

'I did not fucking lie!'

'But you have just stated that you knew your father

would be arrested, so you had to have known he was guilty. So you are guilty of perverting the course of justice, which could implicate you as a party to murder.'

'That is not true; this is bloody ridiculous!'

Langton was at it again, bluffing her to scare her. But, as before, it was working. 'So, Mrs Hedges, what exactly did you tell Miss Wickenham when you called?'

Mrs Hedges was shaking, wringing her hands. Justine spoke for her. 'What she just said: that all the police were here and Father had been arrested. Do you want me to repeat it again?'

'But surely he was still at the house, and for you, Justine, to immediately begin to arrange to bring your sister home . . .'

'He'd gone by then.' Mrs Hedges had to clear her throat she was so nervous.

'Gone?'

'Yes, he'd already left. That's why I called Justine.'

'What exact time was that?'

She was now really agitated. She looked to Justine and back to Langton. 'I don't know, some time in the morning.'

'What exact time?'

'I don't know, I can't remember.'

'Leave her alone, she's done nothing wrong,' Justine said angrily and put her arm around the elderly woman.

'I would very much like to, but you see it's very important at what exact time you were informed that your father had left the house, so that it was now safe for you to bring back Emily.'

'Well, it would have been before I came to the station, just before twelve.'

'I see.'

'So this would coincide with your father disappearing?'

'Escaped I think is the word you're looking for; all this is just you lot trying to cover your tracks, because he escaped and you can't find him, so you want to interrogate us. Well, we don't know where he went, we have not been contacted by him, we do not know where the fuck he is and we don't bloody care!'

'But you must have had a pretty good idea that he wasn't coming back, otherwise why bring Emily home?'

'Because the less time she spent in that shithole of a mental institution the better.'

'Why didn't you take her to your flat?'

'Because, I have said this over and over, I had to come back here to look after the horses, so it just makes sense that Emily is here with me.'

'Even though your father could return?'

'He's not likely to is he, for Chrissakes? You've got patrol cars up and down the lane, the place has been swarming with police. Of course he's not coming back; it would be crazy if he even considered it. He is an intelligent man!'

'So you know where he is?'

'No I do not, we haven't a clue, all right? But it makes sense to anyone with half a brain that he is not coming back because he would be picked up, right?'

'So he did contact you?'

'No! Jesus Christ, how many more times. He has not called, he has not tried to speak to any one of us.'

'So where is he?'

'We don't know!'

'He has no passport, he has not cashed any money. Where do you think someone on the run could hide out for this length of time?'

'Ask some of his sicko friends; they'd hide him, just like that crowd helped Lord Lucan.'

'We have already questioned his known associates.'

'Well they would all lie through their teeth! They wouldn't want to be involved with that bastard, but he could blackmail them into helping him. Go and do your job: question them and leave us alone.'

'As I said, we already have and we are certain none helped your father escape. They are all scattered quite a distance from here, so how would he have got to them?'

'You tell me.' Justine stood with her hands on her hips.

Langton paused. He glanced to Travis and sighed. 'You see, Miss Wickenham, we have come to the conclusion that your father never left this house.'

There was a pause and then Justine laughed and shook her head. 'Well, you bloody searched long enough! If he was here, they couldn't find him, so this is all a bit of a farce isn't it? Surely wasting your time here isn't going to help you find him? I told her; I said you'd never catch him and it's true.' Justine pointed to Anna; she then took a look at Emily who was sitting, head bowed, chewing at her nails. She went over and put her arm around her. 'It's okay, Em; don't get upset, it's all right.'

'Mrs Hedges,' Langton turned towards her. 'You were, I believe, in your bedroom throughout the search. Is that correct?'

'Yes sir, I never left; well, just to make myself a sandwich and a cup of tea. I was told to remain in my room,

I never left it but for that; there were police officers here in the kitchen the whole time.'

'What did you think she did, hid him under her skirt? This is farcical!' Justine was at it again.

'Could you please take DI Travis to your room, Mrs Hedges?'

'Why?'

'We would just like to check something.'

Mrs Hedges looked at Justine who gave a shrug, smiling. 'Sure, that's okay, you take her up there. I'll carry on with breakfast.'

Anna followed Mrs Hedges out of the kitchen and up the narrow staircase, sidestepping piles of neatly folded sheets and towels. Mrs Hedges opened the door into her bedroom. 'They searched in here, twice,' she said.

'Yes I know, but I just needed to see for myself, thank you.'

Anna looked around the sparse, neat room. A low footstool stood beside her rocking chair. The single bed had an iron railing and a handmade quilt. There was an old-fashioned wardrobe and chest of drawers, plus two small cupboards either side of the bed. If anyone had tried to hide beneath it, they could very easily have been seen.

'This is the oldest part of the house, isn't it?' Anna said, with a friendly smile.

'Yes, yes it is; it looks out to the back, so it's very quiet.'

'Yes, I remember you told me how you would stay up here when the weekend parties were going on.'

'Yes.'

Mrs Hedges saw Anna looking at two sections of the wall which had been partly eased back.

'They did that, the police; it's a false wall: the panel was put up so I could hang pictures. It's thick stone behind the partitions.' Mrs Hedges pointed to an ironing board. 'I've been doing the ironing up here as the laundry room has been taken apart; it was really something for me to do.'

'Did you have much cash up here?'

'Pardon?'

'Any savings? Did you keep them up here?'

'Some, yes; never been too fond of banks. My sister was with a company that took all her savings, so I used to keep mine here.'

Anna pointed to a drawer. 'Do you still have them?'

'My money?'

'Yes, is it still safe?'

She opened the drawer and took out a biscuit tin. 'Yes, it's all here.'

'So you didn't give any money to Mr Wickenham?'

'No, no; he didn't know I had it, in any case. It was my secret, really; my wages were paid into a bank account at the local bank. This money's tips and extras the house guests would give me.'

'How much money do you have in your savings account, Mrs Hedges?'

'Oh, well, a lot.'

'Like how much?'

'I've at least seventy-two thousand pounds.'

'And you have not withdrawn any of it recently?'

'No, no, I've not been out of the house.'

'I see, thank you.'

As Anna turned to leave, Mrs Hedges caught her arm. 'Leave them be. They are blameless. Maybe now

467

they can have some kind of life without their father.'

Anna hesitated. 'But he could walk back in here, Mrs Hedges; maybe not right now, but sometime. If he did come back, you know they would be too afraid of him not to comply with anything he wanted them to do.'

'I'm here for them and he won't come back.'

'How can you be so sure?'

Mrs Hedges wouldn't meet Anna's eyes, she looked to the floor. 'Because I'll protect them.'

'You?'

'Yes me, I've taken care of them.'

'What do you mean?'

There was a pause, as Mrs Hedges chewed at her lip. 'I meant like I always tried to do when they were children.'

'But you failed; you know what he did to Emily.'

She made no answer.

'Mrs Hedges, two young girls – perhaps even more – not much older than Wickenham's daughters were murdered in the most brutal way.'

'I know; I know that now.'

'If he did come back, you know he would have them in his power to do anything he wanted.'

Before she could answer, Langton called for Anna. She hesitated, then thanked Mrs Hedges. Together they went down the narrow staircase and into the hall. Langton was standing with Lewis.

'This is a waste of time. If the sisters know anything, they are not about to tell us. If they want to get a solicitor, we can either wait or call it quits.'

They called it quits; the three returned to their patrol car. Anna had wanted to stay, but Langton's patience had worn thin. He leaned against the bonnet of the car.

'Listen, if they do know where he is, they are refusing to say. We've already run up massive costs for this waste of time, and I'm gonna have to go back and answer to the Commander: she just hit the proverbial.'

Anna folded her arms.

'What? We tried, didn't we, Lewis?'

'Yeah, that Justine is something else.'

'I'm not satisfied!'

Langton laughed.

Anna glared back at him. 'I'm not. Just come with me, the pair of you, please, it'll take a few minutes.'

Disgruntled, they returned to the house. Justine was standing in the hallway. 'You thinking of moving in, or what?'

Anna looked at her, and wasn't giving anything away. 'You can stay with us if you want, I just want to . . .'

'Do what the hell you like. I'm going to have my breakfast!' Justine slammed into the kitchen.

Anna looked around the hall. 'Right, we have forensic officers around the hall, we have others examining the dining room, and outside we have God knows how many officers.'

'Get on with it!' Langton snapped.

Anna walked into the drawing room. 'I am Wickenham. I get the opportunity to knock out the officer, so where do I go from here? Up the chimney? No, there's no access, so I'm desperate to get to the door where you are standing.'

'Jesus Christ, we've done all this, Anna!'

She pushed past them into the hall. 'To the right is

the kitchen full of officers, to the left the front door, with even more police outside. The cellar's crawling with forensics, so, the only route he could have taken is the stairs. If he makes it to the stairs, he could maybe get to Mrs Hedges's room; it'd take no more than a couple of seconds.'

'But she was in there, and she swears . . .'

'Whatever she swore could be a lie. What if he did make it there and she was able to hide him?'

Langton sighed. 'Her room was searched minutes later, she was alone. This has all been checked out, Travis.'

'I know, but it's the only route he could have taken.'

'He wasn't in her bedroom: it was searched within seconds.'

'So that leaves this area.'

Anna walked to the narrow servants' stairwell. They all stood looking at the narrow staircase.

'This is also the oldest part of the original house.'

Langton looked at Lewis.

'Have these stair rods been moved?'

'I don't fucking know.'

'The carpet looks as if it has been.'

Anna went down on her hands and knees, she crawled up four stairs and then hurled aside a mound of sheets and towels. She sat back on her heels and pulled at the stair rod; it came away in her hand. Bending closer, she could see an opening no more than an inch in width.

'I need some kind of jemmy to pull this open. Can you see the gap?'

'Yeah I can see it, but it's a sixteenth-century bloody staircase! Of course there's gonna be gaps!'

'This isn't just a gap. Get the entire carpet pulled back.'

Lewis and Langton peeled back the old stair carpet. Anna worked her fingers inside the gap, and the stair board opened a fraction.

'Jesus Christ, what is it?'

Anna reeled back as the stench hit her. Langton stepped in to help. The wooden slat slid sideways. She could see downward into a space no bigger than a coffin. 'It's possibly another priest hole that's been covered by the stair carpet.' Anna took out a handkerchief and covered her face.

Langton peered into the dark recess but could see nothing. He slipped his hand into the opening and recoiled. 'Get a torch: there's something wedged down there.'

Anna and Langton sat side by side on the lower stair as Lewis ran out to the car and returned with a torch.

Langton shone it into the recess. The beam of light lit up the face of Charles Wickenham, his mouth drawn back in a silent scream. His body was wedged inside the small space; his hands, still cuffed, had clawed at the stair to try and open it. The space was so small that his body pressed against the sides. Rigor mortis had made his body stiff, his fingers like claws.

Langton sat back in shock. Anna looked at the stack of sheet and towels. 'These covered the air vent.'

In the kitchen, Justine moved away from the door. 'They've found him,' she whispered.

Neither Mrs Hedges nor Emily could say a word. Justine gave a soft laugh. 'Saved us burying him. We didn't know he was there, did we?' She looked pointedly at Mrs Hedges. 'No we didn't! So just carry on as if we don't know what is happening, nobody can prove anything. We just look out for each other.'

'What if they find out what I did?'

'They won't, believe me; you didn't know about it, full stop!'

Mrs Hedges started to cry. 'But I did, I did; I knew.'

Justine gripped her tightly. 'No you did not; you just put the things there because the laundry room couldn't be used, right?'

Mrs Hedges wiped her eyes, and Justine gripped her tightly. 'We're here and nobody can do anything about it, just do as I told you, and you, Em. Emily!'

Emily was pouring milk onto her cornflakes, but the bowl was already full and the milk spilled over, dripping onto the table and onto the floor.

'Emily! Look what you are doing!'

Justine snatched the bottle away from her sister and placed it back in the fridge. 'Get a cloth and clear the mess up! Do it now!'

Emily just sat with her head bowed. 'You said he was gone.'

Justine was finding it hard to contend with the weeping Mrs Hedges and now the anxious Emily. She took a deep breath and put her arms around her sister. 'Shush and look at me, Em. He is never coming back, I give you my word. I cross my heart.'

The wailing of an ambulance siren made even Justine physically jump.

Emily sprang up and ran to the door. 'They're coming for me!'

'No, no! Just stay here with Mrs Hedges. For God's

sake, Mrs H, pull yourself together and look after Em. Let me go and see what's going on.'

Justine went out of the kitchen and into the hall.

Langton intercepted her. 'Please stay in the kitchen, Miss Wickenham.'

'What's going on?'

'You'll know soon enough; just go back into the kitchen.'

He signalled for Anna to take Justine back into the kitchen. Mrs Hedges was scrambling some eggs, allowing Emily to help her. They both turned as Justine gestured to Anna.

'She's going to sit here with us. Do you want some scrambled eggs? We like them runny with a lot of butter.'

'No thank you, maybe a coffee.'

'I'll get it, black or white?'

'White, no sugar.'

Anna sat at the big table; milk still dripped over one end. Justine busied herself wiping down the table. 'What's going on out there?'

'We're just checking something out.'

'Was that an ambulance we just heard?'

Anna didn't answer; voices were audible in the hallway. Justine banged down a cup of coffee and went to the door. Anna asked that she remain in the kitchen.

'Why?'

'Because I am asking you to.'

'I've got to go and see to the horses; they need feeding and exercise.'

'They can wait. I'll let you know when you can go to them.'

'You don't understand, they don't wait. They get their

473

nosebags on, they have a morning walk, then they go back into the stables; after we've mucked out, we take them out for some exercise.'

'There're still two stable boys working there, aren't there?'

'Yes, but I have to oversee what they are doing.'

'I'm sure they will do whatever is necessary.'

The two paramedics were kneeling down, trying to fathom out how they could lift the body out. Charles Wickenham's head was tilted back, his mouth gaped open. In a few hours the rigor would slacken, which might make it easier to lift the body out. They had ropes to loop beneath his armpits, but the sides of the chamber were too tight.

Langton suggested they grab him by the head and pull him up. He said if the body got in, it had to be able to come out. The stench of decomposition was overpowering. Lewis stood well back. They had tried loosening the steps above and below, but they were made of concrete.

Lewis went into the kitchen to relieve Anna, who was sitting watching Emily and Mrs Hedges finish their eggs. He took Anna aside and they whispered. After a moment, she nodded and went to Justine.

'Can I talk to you a second, in private?'

Justine shrugged. They stepped through the kitchen door and into the garden.

'We think we may possibly have discovered the body of your father.'

'No!'

'Yes, I'm afraid so. Would you be prepared to iden-tify him?'

'Christ, why me?'

'Well, surely it would be better to ask you than your sister.'

'Well, where is he?'

'If you agree?'

'Yes, yes I'll do it, but for Chrissakes, don't let my sister know, or Mrs Hedges; she's taking care of her. She's still not right in the head, you know; she poured milk all over the table this morning.'

Anna suggested that they walk round the house and go back in via the front door to avoid questions from the kitchen.

By the time Anna and Justine entered the hall, the paramedics had managed to draw the body halfway out of the chamber. It had been quite a procedure: they had gripped hold of his hair and eased his head up, then slid a noose beneath his arms. They had managed only to get his body out up to his waist: his legs were stuck firmly. For decency's sake, a sheet had been draped over him. As Justine entered the hall with Anna, she shrieked.

Langton held out his hand and drew her closer. 'Can you please look at his face and identify him? I'm sorry to ask you to do this.'

Justine held onto Langton's hand as he slowly removed the sheet. Justine stared for what seemed a very long time. 'Why is his mouth open like that?'

'We believe he suffocated; he was probably gasping for air.'

'What was he doing down there?'

'Hiding.'

'Gosh, I didn't even know this place was there. Is it another priest's hidey-hole, do you think?'

475

'Possibly. Is this Charles Wickenham?'

Justine stood up and cocked her head to the right and then to the left. It was so fast and so unexpected: she tried to kick her father's head. 'Yes, yes that's him. The bastard.'

Anna and Langton had to drag her back into the kitchen while the paramedics hauled the body out and put it in a body bag.

Anna stood beside Justine as she said she had something to tell them.

'They've just found Father; he was stuck in this hole by the stairs.'

Emily started to scream. Justine held her tightly. 'He's dead, Em, he's dead; he can't hurt you. It's over, it's all over now.'

Anna and Langton examined the chamber. It was hideously small, no larger than a stone coffin. The air vent, a wide strip at the top of the chamber where the wooded stair board covered it, was the exact place where all the sheets had been stacked.

'Do you think it was just an accident someone covered the air vent, or was it done on purpose?' she asked Langton.

'I don't know. If they knew it was there, maybe, but why didn't he call out?'

'If he knew the place was teeming with officers, he would have had to keep silent, then by the time we'd left, he maybe couldn't. There's hardly enough room in there even to move, and with no food or water . . .'

Langton shone his torch down into the chamber.

They could see the scratches like claw marks on the wooded slat. 'He tried to get out; maybe the mechanism had blocked. It slides back on a spring, and it's pretty rusted.'

Anna shook her head. 'I just can't believe they didn't even hear him scratching to get out. Especially Mrs Hedges: her room is directly above the stairs.'

'Right now I don't give a shit: we've got him and it's a bloody relief to me, I don't know about you.'

Mrs Hedges swore she had no idea there was anything beneath the stairs. She was very distressed, and when asked if she had heard any sound as the staircase was directly below her bedroom, she shook her head. 'Even if I had, I wouldn't have done anything about it. All the men working here were knocking and moving things. I didn't hear anything. I had my TV on.'

She broke down in sobs. Langton went into her bedroom.

'He was almost directly below this area,' he said and moved the old rocking chair aside and tapped the floor with his foot. 'If she did know that place existed, then if she had heard anything, she'd have surely gone to check it out. But if she didn't, and no one else knew about it, not even the historical mob . . .'

Anna nodded and wondered if the girls knew about it.

'They weren't even here; they didn't move in until days after he was missing. By that time, he'd have suffocated.'

Anna kept on looking around the room: she knew something was different, but couldn't quite put her finger on it. 'Yeah, you're right; let's go and leave the forensic guys to do their job.'

Langton had already called McDonald. At first, he was irritated that he had been contacted and then very interested.

'Shit, you mean they found another priest hole?'

'Yeah, and our suspect was rammed into it!'

McDonald agreed he would come straight away with a couple of his team. In the meantime, they cordoned off the area as a crime scene.

The news spread like wildfire round the Incident Room. It lifted everyone's spirits. Langton issued a press release saying they were not looking for any other suspects in the Red Dahlia case or for the murder of Sharon Bilkin: Charles Wickenham's body had been discovered and foul play was not at this time being considered.

Should any evidence be discovered that more bodies had been mutilated and perhaps buried at Mayerling Hall, further enquiries would be launched. As it was, they now had enough evidence to announce that Charles Wickenham was their killer.

Closing the case was complicated and would take days: the thousands of statements and files were all to be boxed and listed. The trial of Edward Wickenham was still to come, but that would be many months down the line. He was still in custody at Brixton prison; his solicitors had applied for bail since the discovery of his father's body.

Anna returned home at eight that evening. They had the next day off, the first for weeks on end it seemed. She showered and changed into clean clothes; she wanted to get her hair cut and styled; she wanted to feel cleansed. The Red Dahlia case had clung to her, but it was at long last over.

Chapter Twenty-One

DAY THIRTY-FOUR

Anna had an early appointment with her hairdresser, followed by a pedicure and manicure. She then hit Oxford Street; she bought four new outfits and two pairs of shoes. At home she had laid them all out on her bed, trying to choose which one she would wear to work.

It was strange, having a whole weekend off. She kept herself busy, washing, ironing and vacuuming; she even bought some fresh flowers for her flat. As she carried the vase into the lounge, she hovered, wondering where would be the best place; she decided to move an armchair and place them on a side table. She was moving the chair when she stopped in her tracks: that was what had been different about the bedroom. Mrs Hedges's rocking chair had been moved so that it was directly above the chamber.

Anna sat for a while, piecing the jigsaw together. If Mrs Hedges, contrary to what she had said, did hear scratches, did perhaps even hear Wickenham calling out, had she then made sure he would die in there? Had she blocked the air vent, and then moved her heavy old rocking chair over a possible second exit or air vent? Could she have sat there rocking back and forth, all the while knowing what was beneath?

Anna went to her local library and checked over the books about the houses where priest holes were still being uncovered. She then went to the Colindale Library to use the microfiche to try and locate any details pertaining to the previous occupants of Mayerling Hall. Sifting through births and deaths, she came across an article about the only son of Lord and Lady Hansworth. Arthur John Hansworth had been a pilot, his body never discovered after a bombing flight over Berlin in 1941. He was eighteen years old. It took another fifteen minutes of searching local newspaper files before she read SECOND TRAGEDY FOR THE HANSWORTH FAMILY. Their five-year-old daughter, Flora Hansworth, had disappeared and it was feared that she had possibly fallen into the lake. Her body was discovered eight weeks later trapped in a chamber connected to the old cellar via a narrow staircase. The family subsequently sold the estate.

Anna made her usual neat and copious notes, ready to discuss the article with Langton. She was certain that after the hotel experience, he would not propose another 'just want to hold you' scenario. She had decided that, no matter how much she really did care about him, he was not good news. Putting it, him, out of her mind was not that simple, but she was determined to do so. New hair, new outfit, even down to the shoes, she was ready for the next case and she doubted they would be assigned to work together so soon after the Red Dahlia.

DAY THIRTY-FIVE

The next morning she spent reading the papers, which headlined the fact that the most hunted man in the country had been caught. She made a mug of fresh coffee and was relaxing with her feet up when the door-bell rang. She wondered if it was the guy from upstairs who was trying to get them all together for a residents' meeting; the outside of the block of flats needed painting.

'Hi, it's me.' It was Langton. She was taken aback but buzzed him in. He was, unusually, wearing a pale blue sweater and jeans. 'I was going to call, but I thought you might put the phone down on me.'

She smiled and went into the kitchen to get him a coffee. 'I was just reading the papers.'

'Yeah, I've not had time. I've just come back from the Hall.'

She passed him his coffee, and he wandered into the lounge and sat down. He sat in silence for a moment and then took a sip.

'The only access to the chamber is via that concealed, sliding step; there is quite a substantial air vent, which could even have been used to pass food down to the hiding priest. It's actually not, as McDonald disappoint-edly told me, a real priest hole; part of it may have been, but the family that previously lived there were having extensions done and digging out the cellar. Their little girl climbed in.' He sipped his coffee.

'I know, I was checking it out.'

'Ah well, I should have known my little supersleuth would want to cover all the bases. When did you find all this out?'

481

'Yesterday, in the library.'

She sat opposite him and when he produced a cigarette and lit it, she nodded it was okay for him to smoke.

'Wanted to talk about a couple of things with you now.'

'Right.'

He inhaled and let the smoke drift from his mouth. 'She knew,' he said softly.

'I'm sorry?'

'The old housekeeper knew. There is a mark in her room where the carpet used to be: she moved it over the vent in that room and then placed her rocking chair over it. She then, I think, stacked the sheets and linen over the other air vent.' He paused and drank his coffee. 'Course, we can't prove it.'

Anna hesitated. 'Maybe not, but you realise that Mrs Hedges called Justine? It was Mrs Hedges who told her she could come home.'

'Yeah yeah, I know. I think some things are best left unspoken; I guarantee that you and I are the only ones that have the final piece of the jigsaw.'

'So what are you trying to say?'

Langton took a long pull on his cigarette and she pursed her lips in anger. 'Christ, you won't leave that alone, will you? What do you think I'm going to do, call up that piece of garbage from the newspaper?'

'Never even entered my head.'

He had wrongfooted her yet again; she felt bad for flying off the handle. 'I'm sorry; if this is the way you want it, then . . .'

'It is, Anna, it is. The less said about it, the better;

well, not for you but for me, as I'm running the enquiry.'

There was a pause. She really did wonder if she should keep silent about her suspicions, as he was suggesting. She changed the subject.

'You said there were a couple of things you wanted to discuss so, what else?'

'Well, you'll probably sound off at me again, so maybe I should leave that alone.'

'What?'

He stood up and ran his hands through his hair. 'Never mind.'

'No, now you've started go on. What is it?'

'You want to have dinner with me?'

She was so taken aback she said nothing.

He grinned. 'See, I should have kept my mouth shut.'

'No, no you shouldn't.'

'So is that a yes?'

She flushed. He held out his arms; after a beat, she went over and let him hold her. It was such a gentle, caring embrace.

'Say I pick you up at about eight?'

She was still in his arms. 'Yes, yes that will be fine.'

He tilted up her chin and looked down at her upturned face. 'Till eight then, and maybe think about what we discussed. If you are unhappy with it, then we need to decide what should be done, but you know where I am coming from. Up to you.'

He kissed her lightly on the lips and broke away. Then he was gone.

She couldn't stop smiling. It was crazy, she knew that, but she'd blown it once before and had regretted it. Maybe if it did evolve into something, she might still regret it, but for now, she could think of nothing she would like better than to be with him.

Justine led Emily out into the paddock. It had been such a long time since she had ridden. Justine was encouraging and gentle.

'You see, Em, it's just like riding a bike. We'll walk around the paddock, then you can try going round on your own. Okay, now let's just trot. Remember, let your body relax; hold tight with your knees. That's good, Em, yes that's it.'

Mrs Hedges watched from the fence as Emily slowly regained confidence, and the next moment was riding without the training rein, Justine shouting out encouragement. Emily tilted back her head and laughed, a little girl again, undamaged.

Mrs Hedges knew that what she had done would haunt her for the rest of her life: the sounds, the whimpering pleas, the scratching, that even the rocking of her chair back and forth could not hide.

Soaking in a bath filled with perfumed oils and lazily trying to decide what to wear, Anna thought about what she had agreed. She was still undecided whether it was right. Ethically, it was not. If Mrs Hedges had known Wickenham was hiding, and known about the hidden chamber, she could perhaps have saved him; but she had known the terrible crimes, not just to his own flesh and blood, but to Louise Pennel and Sharon Bilkin. In the end, Anna knew, the old lady had protected the girls who she had been helpless to protect when their father had been at large. He had died a long slow death, but it was nothing compared to the horrors he had committed and the pain he had inflicted for his own sickening sexual gratification.

Anna wrapped herself in a large white towel and sat on the edge of her bath. It was over. She could understand why the Black Dahlia case still held such fascination; no one was ever brought to justice for her murder. In a way, Wickenham's victims had had their justice. She wondered if, trapped and unable to breathe, he had given any single one of them a moment's thought. She doubted it.

He arrived on the dot of eight, wearing a smart suit. She had been dressed, ready and waiting like a teenager, since seven.

'You look good,' he said.

'Thank you.'

'Clean slate?'

'Yes.'

'Right, let's go. You know a restaurant called Fernandez?'

'No.' She shut the front door.

He took her hand and tucked it under his arm. She hadn't felt so happy for so long, and as they headed down the stairs she stopped.

'Can I just do something?'

He was on the step below her and looked up. She cupped his face between her hands and kissed him.